STILL
She
Speaks

SARAH DEPLEDGE

ISBN 978-1-68197-877-2 (Paperback)
ISBN 978-1-68197-878-9 (Digital)

Christian Faith Publishing, Inc.
296 Chestnut Street
Meadville, PA 16335
www.christianfaithpublishing.com

Printed in the United States of America

Dedications and Acknowledgements

To Mark: My best friend and biggest supporter. Your love has been the sweetest of all earthly gifts. Thank you for your patience and always making me laugh. If I go first...

To each of our precious kids: Hannah, Abby, Lydia, Andrew and Noah: If God puts a dream in your heart, follow it, no matter how long it takes. I love each of you beyond measure, and am grateful for you and excited to see God at work in your lives in marvelous ways!

To Mom and Dad: Thank you for laying a strong foundation under my feet. I love you, and am grateful to God for you both.

To Leah and Naomi: Could anyone ask for better sisters than you two? I don't believe so – Much love!

To Amy K., and Andrea J.: Thank you for sloughing through the earliest renditions – not an easy task, and I'm grateful.

To Lynne T., Susan A. and Amanda J.: Thank you for reading, and offering such kind endorsements-- your thoughtful words were just the encouragement I needed to keep moving forward.

To Amy T.: Thank you for your sharp eye and helpful pen of correction.

To Jim P.: You steered me soundly...Thank you.

To Deb L.: You helped form my understanding of what I was embarking on...Thank you.

To all the folks at CFP: – Thank you for investing in me. Your help was immeasurable, and your belief in this project gave me such confidence. Thank you for guiding me through every aspect of this wonderful journey!

To many dear friends, who have been my "Rene", "Susan", "Charlene", "Dawn" and "Loni" ~ Thank you for walking this journey of life with me…you are each precious to me and I thank God for you.

To the 'Titus women' in my life…I wrote "Linda" with broad strokes and each of you in mind…thank you for investing in me the way you have…you know who you are, and I love you.

And mostly, to my Savior, Jesus Christ, who adopted me into His family when He paid the price for my sins and I accepted that free gift. There are no possible words, just a thankful heart that sings His praise…

April 1977

Nine-year-old Sondra lay comfortably sprawled on the large woolen rug, the only warm spot in the basement, while her mother worked nearby. In the relative quiet, she could hear the ticking of the clock on the wall. Every fifteen minutes the little cuckoo bird hiding within would emerge from behind its tiny door and alert them of the passing moments with its perky tweets. Sondra had heard three such chirps in the time she'd spent lollygagging.

With no space upstairs, her mother had chosen this section to locate her writing desk with its cubbyholes for papers, pencils, and a myriad of office supplies, mostly for the strong lighting. Several overhead lights and her desk lamp showered the space with bright light and cast the shadows farther away. Sondra had learned to only look toward those far, dark corners when down here with her mother; otherwise, her imagination brought too many terrible ideas to life. Her feet couldn't carry her upstairs fast enough when that happened.

"Humph." Her mom's snort broke the silence.

"Is everything okay, Mama?" Sondra knew she might not answer. When she was in her writing world, her awareness of anything going on around her fell away. Sondra could understand since that's how she became when she wrote or read too.

"Yep." The clacking sound that had dominated the last hour resumed.

Sondra's feet swirled the air above her as she doodled on a pad of paper and listened to her mom typing on Grandpa's old typewriter. She loved the sound it made as her mother's fingers flew across the keys, pressing down firmly, making a loud *thwack* onto the paper. It reminded her of popcorn seeds popping in her grandma's old metal popcorn basket that she would fill and shake over the stove top till they popped into fluffiness. Sondra started to salivate and suddenly wished she had some of the buttery, salty treat to munch on.

To distract herself from her growing hunger, she glanced around. This section of the basement housed out-of-season decorations and boxes filled with odds and ends. Sondra imagined what treasures might be buried in the sturdy cardboard boxes that were stacked neatly against the walls. Multiple jottings from old magic markers scribbled on the sides tried their best to identify the contents, but really, it was anyone's guess. Sondra's dad annually threatened to pitch all the boxes without even opening them.

"We've made it for years without any of that junk, Julia," he would point out. "I'm fairly certain there's nothing we need from any of them."

Her mother would protest, "But, James . . ." She would give him a look that would make him sigh and relent and bought another year of life for the entire stack.

The top cinder blocks nearest the tiny window looked to be home to a spider, whose small nest had been bravely woven. For a moment Sondra entertained the idea of relocating the harmless creature to a safer spot outside. Little did he know that Sondra's mother did not tolerate spiders for very long: his webby home would be gone soon with their weekly cleaning. The idea of the little bug getting sucked up into the merciless vacuum hose made Sondra a bit sad. That thought brought to mind a new one: *Will Mom let me get out of cleaning on my birthday?*

Dreams of the celebration for her tenth year of life, still a few weeks away, filled Sondra's mind. She smiled with anticipation, imagining the whole family—including her grandma and grandpa and aunts, uncles and cousins—filling their small house, eating cake, and playing games. She thought of her grandma, who had funny sayings that Sondra didn't always understand, like, "Use your minutes well, and the rest of the day will order itself." Sondra would smile shyly, and her grandma's eyes would twinkle knowingly at her, like they shared a great secret.

Her grandpa would rush in, smelling of pipe tobacco and planting whiskery kisses on her soft cheeks and sharing jokes that would make everyone laugh.

I bet Grandpa could even make Felicia laugh.

Felicia was a new girl who had come to her school last week. Sondra, content to sit on the sidelines, had listened as the sad-faced girl explained how she had come to join their classroom so close to the end of the school year.

"I'm a foster child."

"What does that mean?" Benjamin had asked.

Felicia had fiddled with her pencil case a moment and then answered, "It means I don't have my own family, so I have to live with different families."

The children gathered around her desk had been respectfully silent at such a thought. Only Bobby had challenged her, "That's stupid. Everyone has a family."

The girl had turned her sober gaze on him, replying sadly, "Not everyone."

Their teacher, Ms. Miller, had hurried over then, so there was no time for more questions though many churned in Sondra's mind. At lunchtime, Rene had invited Felicia to join her and Sondra at their table. Felicia had gratefully accepted, confiding that she was with her second foster family since her parents' death two years earlier.

"I liked the first family I was placed with. But my foster mom got sick, and they couldn't keep me. That's why I'm here now. My new family lives in this school district." She had taken a small bite of her sandwich before stating, "I'm lucky. At least I don't have to go to the orphanage."

Rene had asked, "What's an orphanage?"

Felicia had drawn a deep breath before answering, "It's where you live with other kids, and there are no parents around."

Sondra had been horrified and meekly asked, "Will you get to stay with this family?"

A hopeful look entered Felicia's eyes for a second, then flickered away. "I don't know."

Sondra learned something important that day. *A family is the best of all. A family means you belong . . . Poor Felicia!*

"Drat. Ah, well, it is what it is," her mom muttered, breaking into Sondra's meandering thoughts.

"What's wrong?" Sondra asked.

"Oh, nothing really. I made another mistake, and since it has to be perfect for the copy editor, I'll have to retype the whole sheet. It can't have liquid eraser on it." Exasperated, her mom turned the carriage feed of the old machine, removed the sheet, and fed a fresh piece of paper into the metal clamp, turning the feeder bar that brought the paper to the right starting height.

"Mama, what do you write about?"

Her mother smiled and, with a glance at her daughter, replied, "Well, right now, I'm working on a book about trials." Seeing that her answer didn't fully satisfy her, she added, "About living a life of victory even when you're dealing with hard things."

"Oh," said Sondra. "I see." She frowned, picking at a small thread of the worn rug. "Are you dealing with hard things?"

Her mom laughed. "Well, not this very minute, honey. I mean, everyone has troubles in their lives, right?" Seeing Sondra nod, she went on. "What I'm hoping to share is that even when we face hard situations, we can still honor God with how we live. In fact, if we recognize the purpose of a trial, we can actually have gratefulness for it because we see His very hand involved in our lives through it. There are a lot of people who don't look at hardship in their lives that way. Lord willing, I'd like to offer a new perspective on it." She began typing again, leaving Sondra to ponder.

"Mom, can I write a book when I'm older?"

Somewhat distractedly, her mom answered, "If you want to. But first, you have to live life a little bit until you've learned something that's worth sharing."

She threw another quick glance at her daughter. "Darling, you know I would love to sit and chat with you more, but right now, I have got to get this done. The deadline for this draft is looming, and I'm running behind. Can we talk later?" Without waiting to see the nod she knew Sondra would give, she turned back once again to the machine in front of her, concentration on her face.

Sondra doodled on her paper.

Something worth sharing, hmm?

She tried to imagine what her life might be like in ten to fifteen years when she figured she would be really old. She looked at her beautiful mother, bent over the typewriter, squinting at the sheet rolled into the machine.

What could I write about someday?

Sondra pushed aside her pad of paper and reached for her notebook. Inside were stories she was working on and poems she'd written, anything she felt moved to write. Sometimes, she would come across a really great word, one she hadn't heard before. When that happened, she would add it, plus its definition to one of the columns in the front of her notebook. She had several pages full already. Her last word had been a real find: *perceive*. She had asked her dad what it meant. "Well, honey, it means 'to understand the truth about something—or someone.' As in, 'I perceive you are an obedient and kindhearted daughter.'" He'd winked at her, his eyes twinkling.

Sondra had hugged him and added it to her list. She'd already put it to use in her latest poem, which she'd only shown to Rene.

"I like when you write, Sondra. You write what I feel." Hearing that made Sondra happy. "What are you going to call this one?" Rene had asked.

Sondra shrugged. "I don't know yet. Maybe just 'Secretly.'" She glanced sideways at her friend. It seemed they'd always known each other, but of course, that wasn't true. They'd met on their first year of school. Sondra had spent that whole summer dreading the first day of kindergarten, where her brother also attended school. "Don't worry," Stephen had assured her. "Kindergarten is a breeze. Wait till you get to fourth grade, like me." His words had not helped.

Desperately wishing she could stay home with her younger sister and their mom, Sondra had reluctantly obeyed. The perky redheaded girl who had taken a seat next to her had alarmed her with her boldness. "What's your name?" she had demanded of the timid blond-haired girl. Sondra had ducked her head and whispered, "Sondra." The redhead had nodded. "Well, you don't have to be afraid. My sister told me that kindergarten is fun. I'm Rene Simpson, and we're going to be friends." She had smiled brightly at the shy girl, and they'd been best friends since.

Now in fifth grade, Sondra couldn't imagine what life would look like without Rene by her side. They spent every moment they could together, riding bikes and exploring the nearby woods and streams. Rene was fearless and spunky. With her, Sondra felt brave too.

At first she had felt a little embarrassed at sharing something so close to her heart as her poems and writings but knew if she could trust anyone in the whole wide world with those thoughts, it was Rene—*well, Mom and Dad too*—but not many other people in this world and certainly not her older brother, Stephen. They used to be closer, but since entering high school, he'd gotten mean.

Sondra's thoughts roamed back to a few days earlier when he had grabbed her special notebook and wouldn't give it back. He had torn a couple of sheets out, mocking her and dancing around the room, keeping the notebook out of her reach.

"Sondra is a nerd-turd, a nerd-turd, a nerd-turd. Sondra is a nerd-turd, a turdy, nerdy nerd-turd."

Sondra had gathered the ripped pages, trying to reach her book, but he laughed and dangled it over her head, repeating his song.

His little ditty had caught the attention of their mother. "Stephen Michael Spencer, what do you think you are doing?" She had stood in the doorway of the family room, hands on hips, demanding an answer from her fourteen-year-old.

Ah, sweet justice, Sondra had thought. *Here it comes.*

Stephen had shoved the notebook back into her waiting hands, pushing past her. "Nothing."

She won't let him get away with that.

Sondra had held her breath, anticipating the moment of judgment.

Her mother eyed Stephen up for a moment. "And what would you like to say to Sondra?"

He glanced her way. "Sorry."

Astonishingly, her mom had nodded and began to move from the doorway.

"But, Mom," Sondra had protested, "that can't count! He didn't even mean it!"

She watched her mom swipe her hand across her eyes in a weary way. "Sondra, please. He was wrong. He's apologized. You need to forgive him." She threw Stephen another warning look and walked away. He had smirked at her. Upset, Sondra had tucked her notebook under her arm protectively and went to her room, plotting revenge.

While he was out playing basketball with his friends that afternoon, she had snuck into his bedroom. In his dresser, she found what she needed: a crumpled and well-hidden note written to her brother from a girl in his class, Wanda Wilkinson. Sondra knew Stephen liked Wanda. *But what she sees in him is a mystery to me.* The paper smelled faintly of Love's Baby Soft. *What a waste of perfectly nice perfume.*

Sondra had quickly read the note, full of loopy letters spelling out words of fondness from Wanda, complete with pink bubble hearts cascading down the margin. *Oh yes. This will do nicely.*

A plan began to form in her mind as she had tucked the folded paper into her pocket and left his room, carefully putting things back the way they were.

He'll regret that he messed with me.

But now, she'd had a couple of days to think. As she lay on the floor of the basement, Sondra wrestled over what to do. *He can't keep getting away with stuff. Someone's got to teach him a lesson.*

She mulled over the changes that seemed to be happening. Lately, her mom was letting Stephen get off the hook for everything. Sondra didn't understand why and felt a little abandoned. She knew her mother carried a full load in caring for their home and family.

A lot of other people thought she was special too. Sondra knew because a few months earlier while in the church bathroom, a stranger asked if she was Julia Spencer's daughter. Hearing Sondra's reply, the woman's eyes had opened widely. "What must it be like to live with Julia Spencer right there in your home, always ready to dish out some wonderful scripture or timely advice?" Her frank admiration confused Sondra.

She had escaped the fawning woman, but not without being wakened to an entirely new view of her mom.

Upon hearing the story, Julia set her down and sternly warned her, "Sondra, I don't want you thinking that I am some superstar. I'm just a woman whom God chose to use to teach in a Bible study and speak to women. People look on the outside and get giddy about a gifted leader or an engaging speaker, but God deserves the praise for those traits because He's the one who gave them. I don't want you getting confused with the difference between praising God for giving gifts that let us bless others and becoming prideful over them."

Sondra's Sunday schoolteacher, Mrs. Harrison, had also addressed the issue of pride one week. "Don't think you're something special because you're not. God doesn't need any one of us, and if you think He does, that's pride talking."

On the drive home, Sondra had asked her parents about Mrs. Harrison's words.

Her dad cautiously said, "Since I wasn't there, I'm not sure exactly what she meant. But I can say this: sin is sneaky, and only God can see into hearts. We need to guard against craving recognition from people. It can breed pride in a heart very quickly. There's nothing wrong with acknowledging it if God has used us to be a blessing to someone. But He alone should be worshipped."

Sondra felt like her dad was looking right into her heart. Hearing his words, she wanted to crawl under the seat. Newly aware that her parents were held in high regard in their church, it was hard for Sondra *not* to get a sense of pride about it. They talked with lots of people on the phone. Sometimes people came to talk privately in her mom's study. Some of them seemed very upset. Her parents prayed with them and shared from their Bibles. It must have helped because the line of people wanting to talk with them seemed to grow longer as time passed.

I love Mom and Dad very much, but I wish some of those people could come see how, once in a while, my parents are unfair. They'll help all those people, but they won't stop Stephen from bullying me.

Sondra opened her notebook to her newest poem and read it again.

But how can I write that but not forgive Stephen? I bet Felicia would forgive him. She'd probably be grateful for the chance to have a big brother to fight with.

She sighed, pushing her notebook away. Wanda Wilkinson's note was still hidden away in her room; she had time to decide if she would carry out her plan against her brother or not. Sondra heard the perky chirp of the little cuckoo bird again as she stretched out on the rug and dreamed of doing big things someday too, like her mother.

Hopefully, something brilliant, like writing a book that helps a lot of people.

She turned back to her doodling pad, looping letters and figures across the paper, practicing her signature, and pondered what might be something worth sharing . . .

Secretly
"Secretly, you're just like me, and I am just like you.
We may have different thoughts and dreams,
But we're more alike
Than not.

If you could look into my heart and see my hopes and fears,
You might be surprised to find
You feel
Right at home.

Will I be liked? Ridiculed? Perceived as who I am?
Accepting or rejecting those
Who wonder
The same thing?

If we could only glimpse into each other's hearts and minds,
I'm certain we'd more likely be
More patient and
More kind.

'Cause secretly, you're just like me and I am just like you.
Together, we could go far, you and I,
If that became our
Starting point."

Ten Years Later

May 1987

Sondra clutched the stack of books closely to her chest with one hand, trying to balance while riding along the dirt path on her bicycle. Her tires kicked up a slight trail of dust behind her. Despite the sunny day, she had spent the past hour holed up in the town library, her favorite hangout.

Later this afternoon she would be meeting Rene. The girls were planning on shopping together for a dress Rene needed for a relative's upcoming wedding.

Afterward they were going to go to the movies together with Patrick, whom Rene had been dating, and his friend. Rene had arranged everything. All she would say about John was, "Trust me, you will like him."

Sondra didn't have much experience around boys and found her brother's friends dull. She hadn't left a lot of room in her life for socializing but was perfectly content. She had watched Stephen marry and liked his new wife, Grace, very much. But something in Sondra shrunk back a bit at the thought of upsetting the comfort of the way things had always been.

Upon high school graduation, she had lamented to her mother, "I don't ever want to leave you and Dad—I'd miss you both too much."

The alarming idea of change was a powerful weapon in her fight to keep everything familiar intact.

Her mom had smiled and assured her daughter, "You can stay here for as long as you'd like. This is your home."

Relief had flooded Sondra's heart, and she hugged her mother.

My home—were there ever more comforting words than those?

Her job as secretary for a small printing company in the nearby village allowed her plenty of time for her interests.

Sondra had finally agreed to Rene's suggestion of a double date.

"But only if we can go see *Three Men and a Baby*. I've been waiting to see it."

"Fine. That's a small price to get you to come."

Her coworkers had raved about the comedy. Bess, a chain-smoker who was on her third marriage, had declared Tom Selleck to be the hottest man on the planet.

Carol had disagreed. "I went just to see Ted Danson." She had sighed with a dreamy look. "He is so good-looking."

Pamela, closest to Sondra's age, asked her, "Have you seen it yet?"

"No. But I'm really looking forward to it. Rene and I are going tomorrow night."

"Oh, you're going to love it."

Sondra carefully veered right on the wide path around an oncoming walker and his little dog. The echo of a bark hung in the air as she peddled steadily toward home. Her mind played with the story line of the book she'd already begun reading.

If I hurry, maybe I can read more before Rene comes.

Reaching home, she pushed her bike against the brick wall of the garage in the worn space between the hydrangea bushes and raced into the house. She set her stack of books on the countertop, noting her mother's wide-brimmed straw hat hanging on its peg near the back door.

Oh, good—no gardening today.

Sondra's mother loved to tend to her vegetable garden and often asked her daughters to help. Sondra hated it. She tiptoed into her mom's study, peeking in the doorway.

Finger to lips, her mom waved. She was on another one of her calls. Sondra nodded and quietly went back to the kitchen to scour the fridge for red apples. Finding one, she crunched it happily, feeling the sweet juice stream down her chin. Grabbing a napkin and her book, she headed to her room and curled up in her favorite chair, captivated by the story.

Far too soon, the back screen door gave its distinctive slam, jerking Sondra back from the world her mind had traveled to over the past hour. Sondra heard her mom greet her friend, "You can go on in, honey. She's in her room."

"Of course, she is. Thanks, Mrs. Spencer."

The clucking sound coming from Rene's tongue conveyed her disapproval as she stood in the doorway and surveyed the scene.

Sondra looked at her friend. "What?"

Rene shook her head in disbelief, coming farther into the bright room.

Sondra's dad had built shelving on two of the walls, which housed dozens of books. The backboard of her bed held several more. Stacks of books occupied floor corners and tabletops. A stash of colorful bookmarkers graced her bed table. Sondra surrounded herself with books. When she needed comfort, she reached for old favorites. When she felt adventurous, she sampled new ones. Books were her dearest friends outside of Rene.

"I cannot believe you are sitting inside on this beautiful day, reading. And what are you so hooked on?" She saw the title and sighed. "*The Tsar and Tsarist of Russia*? I mean, come on, Sondra. You act like a little old lady curled up with a cat in your lap, spending your whole day, reading about snooty, dead people. Wouldn't you rather get out and live an adventure instead of living life through other people's eyes?"

This last part was said with Rene's arms swirling the air as if to indicate that, perhaps, Sondra might, with very little effort, even fly if she would only get her nose out of her books and at least try.

Sondra sniffed and stood from her cozy spot, pushing Mr. Biggs, her gray tabby, onto the floor.

"I know you don't appreciate a good story, Rene. But I do. I like reading about the extraordinary lives some people live." She looked away, then back at her friend with a bit of defiance in her snapping green eyes. "It's fascinating."

"Fascinating?" Rene said scornfully.

"Yes. I'd rather read about other people's lives than live my own." That wasn't exactly true, but she couldn't back down now.

"Oh, Sondra. That's so sad." Rene looked truly worried about her friend.

Sondra laughed. "Oh, come on, Rene. It's not like reading is the only thing I do."

Rene eyed her skeptically. "Name three other things you do that don't involve paper!"

"Easy. I like movies and games and . . ." She stopped, stumped.

Rene nodded. "Yeah, I thought so. You would read and write and do those stupid puzzles all day if it weren't for your job and me not letting you."

"Well, what's so bad about that? I don't require anything else to stimulate me. I'm perfectly happy," she said with a little flounce.

"You can say that all you want. But I don't believe you."

"What do you mean?"

Rene eyed her friend. "Well, I think you are scared. Life is meant to be lived, Sondra. There are adventures just waiting to be discovered." Rene glanced at the book in Sondra's hands. "But it's safer reading than doing." Rene's chin thrust out a bit.

Sondra ducked her head. *That hit dangerously close to the truth.*

Rene's voice softened. "That's why I'm so happy you're finally willing to meet John. Oh, Sondra, you're going to like him. He's super nice and cute to boot. Though, of course, not as good-looking as Patrick."

Sondra met her friend's teasing gaze and sighed. "Well, I will meet him. But I can't promise I will talk with him."

She carefully marked the spot where she'd left off and placed the book neatly on the table. The jittery feeling in her stomach started up again at the thought of having to converse for a whole evening with a perfect stranger.

A boy at that.

"It's going to be wonderful," Rene insisted, "if you'll just put down your book long enough to have a conversation with him."

She pulled on Sondra's arm to hurry. The two girls entered the kitchen, where something bubbled on the stove and homemade bread sat steaming on the countertop.

"That smells delicious, Mrs. Spencer! What are you making?"

Julia smiled at Rene's exuberance. "Soup. Are you girls heading out now?"

"Yes, Patrick and John will pick us up at my house around six. We'll go to dinner and a movie. I promised my mom that I'd be back by eleven o'clock, so we'll bring Sondra home by ten forty-five at the latest."

"That sounds good. Have a wonderful time, girls." She hugged her daughter. "I hope you find the perfect dress, Rene."

"Thanks, Mrs. Spencer."

"Bye, Mom," Sondra called out as the friends dashed outside.

With someone he knew in the used-car business, Rene's dad had bought her a blue convertible for her high school graduation gift. It was her pride. She drove everywhere she could with the top down, weather permitting. Though May and sunny, it was afternoon, and a bit of chill hung in the air of the small Illinois town that sat just outside of Chicago.

Their long hair whipped in the wind as they raced to the nearby mall. They parked and closed the top, noting that the skies had turned a shade of gray that could signal rain soon.

The second shop they stopped at elicited the perfect dress for Rene. Sondra's stomach began to knot again with anticipation of their evening out.

Back at Rene's house, the girls put on makeup and curled their hair, teasing it to make it as puffy as possible. Rene then sprayed both their heads with so much hair spray the locks took on the sheen and durability of aluminum.

"There. It might not be touch-ably soft, but it sure looks great," she said with satisfaction, setting the half-empty can aside.

They carefully eased their sweaters over their heads and draped colorful jewelry around their necks, finishing just as the doorbell rang. Opening the door, Rene threw herself into the arms of the dark-haired boy standing on the dim porch. "Patrick!"

Patrick embraced the striking girl until the boy by his side gave a small cough.

"Oh. Sorry. John, you know Rene. And this is Sondra."

Sondra was unprepared for the sensation she felt at seeing John standing on the porch.

Rene said he was cute. But wow.

She was not ready for the radiance of his smile or the deep blue of his eyes. She gulped and flushed, turning her gaze to the ground.

Rene came to the rescue. "I thought we could have dinner at Francesco's then go to the movies. Does that sound good?"

Patrick rubbed his jaw. "Sure. But do you girls mind if we go see the newest release that came out today? It's a sequel we were hoping to see—*Jaws: The Revenge.*"

Rene turned brightly to Sondra, knowing full well the problem this might present. Even she was surprised by Sondra's loud and sudden assertion: "Oh, that sounds wonderful!" Sondra blushed.

John and Patrick looked pleased. "Great. Let's go." He waved to Rene's dad, who had come to the door. "Hi, Mr. Simpson. I'll have her back by eleven."

Rene's dad nodded. "Okay, Patrick. Drive carefully, kids. And have a good time."

The loud Italian restaurant they went to was a popular place for families with kids and young people with limited funds, seeking good food and plenty of it. The owners, shunning the expected red-and-green tablecloths, opted instead for a palette of blue hues mixed with white. The jukebox in the corner could blare out a variety of songs if the requisite amount of quarters were plunked in. There was also a small cleared section of wooden floor for the braver souls to dance.

Quieter midweek, the crowd could be boisterous on Friday and Saturday nights; it was a fun place to bring a date.

Sitting in the booth, Sondra didn't notice much around her other than how charming her companion was.

He's so easy to talk to.

She got lost in the twinkle of his eyes and the brilliance of his smile. He was witty and smiled a lot. Sondra let her guard down, trying to get used to the new feelings of attraction that were invading her heart.

What was I so afraid of? He's fascinating.

"I'll finish college after my next semester. I fell a year behind." He shrugged, explaining, "I had to take time off to work full-time and save up more money first."

He's so sure of himself and what he wants to accomplish in life. And he's such a hard worker.

John took a sip of his drink and asked, "So what do you do for fun?"

"Oh, um, well, my job takes up most of my time. But I like to read whenever I can." She looked away, embarrassed at the sound of her paltry life.

Just admit it. You are a big snooze, Sondra.

"And actually, I . . . I love writing. Someday, I hope to get published." She bit her lower lip and looked back at him.

John seemed interested. In fact, he was leaning in, listening as if he found her hobbies as enjoyable as she did. The sound of the crowd around them grew distant as they focused on each other's words, and time zipped along.

When their food arrived, John and Sondra both reached for a napkin from the holder. Their hands barely touched, yet they each pulled back with the shock of the electricity that flowed between them.

The rest of the evening, Sondra couldn't get that moment out of her mind.

None of Stephan's friends are even an ounce as dazzling as John is.

She wanted to know everything he had ever done or said. She couldn't explain it, but there was a sizzle between them, and having tasted of it, she wouldn't ever again be content with her mundane existence.

It's almost like I've just now come alive!

As for John, the lovely girl with the electric spark bewitched him. Her voice was gentle, and he loved her laugh. It wasn't his nature to be so open so fast with a girl—or anyone else, really. But she was easy to talk with. She appeared to be enjoying herself. He sure hoped so. It was definitely worth the extra shift he was going to have to pull to take her out to dinner and a movie. If he knew no one was watching, he might have jumped into the air and given a shout for how light his spirit felt.

Having talked so easily during dinner, Sondra felt more comfortable as they drove to the theater. New sensations coursed through her as she took in John's close presence.

At the end as they poured out of the theater doors with the other moviegoers, the cool night air caused Sondra to shiver. John asked, "Would you like to wear my coat?" He held it out invitingly.

Sondra flushed. "Oh, thank you."

His hands draped the garment over her shoulders, and Sondra was once again shocked by the energy he seemed to generate whenever they connected.

The two couples got in Patrick's car and headed for Sondra's house. Sondra carefully hid her true feelings behind outwardly polite behavior. But she didn't try fooling herself: something big had happened, and life wouldn't ever be quite the same again.

Standing on her driveway, Sondra smiled shyly at John, handing him his coat. She wasn't good at small talk. A light went on in the house. "Thank you, John. I had a really good time."

John wanted to say something that would impress her but couldn't think of a single thing. It seemed his mind had gone completely blank. "It was great meeting you, Sondra. Can I call you sometime?"

She nodded and quickly looked down, unable to keep her feelings hidden from his gaze.

John shifted his feet. He didn't want her to go in but could see her mom peeking from the front window.

Sondra caught his glance and followed it, blushing at the sight of her mother watching them. "Well, I've got to go," she said, moving away.

"Sure. Me too. Well, good night, Sondra."

"Good night." She quickly ran to the front door and inside.

On the ride to his apartment, John was barely aware of Rene and Patrick's conversation. His mind was preoccupied with Sondra. He had to see her again.

* * *

Tucked away in bed, Sondra busily wrote in her journal. She poured out her thoughts about the entire evening, wanting to relive every moment. She finished with a quote from Dante that she once read: "Remember tonight…for it is the beginning of always." It captured her heart perfectly. She sighed happily, turned off her light, and dreamed of the man who had made sparks come from his fingertips.

* * *

Patrick was taking the long way to get to Rene's house while she held his hand.

"Well, what do you think? Do you think he liked her?" Her voice carried a note of anxiety.

Patrick grunted. "He was in the car two minutes ago. Why didn't you ask him?"

"Oh, Patrick. I couldn't do that. I don't know him well enough to ask him that." She paused. "He's your friend. You've got to find out."

Another grunt accompanied his look of exasperation. "Rene, if he likes her, he will ask for her phone number. Don't push it." He shook his head. "You girls sometimes like to push too much."

"Well, if we didn't, you boys wouldn't make a move." She released his hand, pouting.

"Aw, come on, Rene. Don't be like that. I will ask him, all right?"

She took his hand in hers again. "Well, it won't matter if he does or doesn't if Sondra didn't like him anyway." She hadn't noticed any overt sign of what Sondra's thoughts had been. Rene sighed, knowing she would have to wait till they could talk tomorrow. Patrick pulled Rene closer to him. He kissed the tips of her fingers, breaking into her thoughts.

"Honey, we only have a few minutes alone. I don't want to spend any more time talking about John and Sondra's possible future." He kissed her fingers again. "I'd rather talk about ours."

* * *

Nearly a year had flown by. John and Sondra's courtship had been filled with excitement. He devoted every spare moment he could with Sondra. He also spent time with her family, who adored him as well. He brought her flowers and sweets and left little notes declaring his love in creative places that she would find with great delight.

She told Rene, "He's the most wonderful guy I've ever met."

Her friend grunted, "That's not saying a whole lot. He's practically the *only* guy you've ever met."

Sondra laughed. "I only need one."

One day she confided to her mother, "I can't imagine life without John, nor do I want to." Julia smiled as she listened to her daughter. "How could we have walked the same streets, entered the same stores, seen the same sights in town, and not have known of each other's existence?"

What had I ever found worth getting up for in the morning before he entered my life?

Her mother hugged Sondra. "I'm glad your heart has been so fully captured, honey. It is good to see you so happy. But remember, even as marvelous as he is, John has feet of clay as we all do. One day, when you two have let each other down in some way, you need to remember that and allow him his faults without losing your love for him."

Sondra shook her head. "I can't imagine him ever letting me down, Mother. I know he isn't perfect. But he knows me and loves me, and I love him." Tears came to her eyes as she thought of the richness John had brought to her life. "Our love is so strong it will withstand anything, I'm sure of it."

Her mother gave a small laugh. "I know it is, my dear. Dad and I, well, we are both so grateful God brought John into your life. He is a good man, and I don't doubt that you two have a wonderful future ahead of you. But you need to be ready because somewhere down the road, you will disappoint one another. You need to decide now that when that day comes, you won't give up on each other." She saw the impatient look in Sondra's eye and held up her hand. "I'm not saying that your love isn't strong. But the trials life can bring have a way of making us forget our blessings. I just want you to be ready and choose now the path you will take when that day comes."

Sondra leaned in, giving her mom a kiss on the cheek. "I will, Mom. I know you mean well, and I know John isn't perfect. I'm not either, but we love each other. I can't imagine either of us hurting the other. But I know it might happen even without meaning to. Don't worry. If, I mean, *when* that day comes, we will be ready."

The starry look in her eyes made her mother smile again and shake her head. "I can see there's no talking to you about this when you are floating somewhere up in the clouds."

"They're called the wings of love," she teased.

"Yes, well, when you've landed back on earth, perhaps you'll be more ready to listen to reason." Julia hugged her again, whispering into her ear, "Such a love is a gift from God and needs to be protected. Make sure you protect it, Sondra."

Sondra squeezed her mom. "I know it is, Mom, and I will protect it."

* * *

A few weeks later while lingering at the table after dinner with the family, John turned to her and held her hand. "Sondra, these last thirteen months have been absolutely amazing. I am so grateful to have found you, and I never want to let you go." He slipped out of his chair and got down on one knee next to Sondra, whose eyes opened wide at what was happening. She gulped, her eyes filling with tears.

John pulled a small box from his pocket, opening it to reveal a small bright diamond ring nestled inside. He smiled up at her. "I love you, Sondra. You are the only woman for me. Please make me the happiest man in the world and marry me."

"Oh, John! Of course, I will marry you!" He slipped the ring onto her finger, and they both stood. Sondra flung her arms around his neck, and they kissed.

Delighted laughter and clapping filled the small room as everyone rejoiced in witnessing the momentous occasion.

"What a wonderful surprise!" Julia said.

"Oh, my dear, you aren't really that surprised now, are you?" her husband asked with a twinkle in his eye.

Julia laughed. "No, I guess you're right. I expected that it would happen one of these days." She rose from her chair and hugged John. "Honey, thank you for letting us be a part of this special day." She wiped at a tear. "That was precious, and we are excited for you both." Next she hugged her daughter tightly.

"Can I see your ring, Sondra?" Sophia asked.

Sondra gently broke from her mother's grasp, extending her hand for everyone to see.

Oohs and aahs filled the room as everyone admired the sparkling ring.

"I believe this calls for a celebration," James said. "Honey, do you want to pop open that bottle of wine we've been saving?"

"May I have a little bit too, Daddy, please?" Sophia pleaded.

Her father smiled. "A tiny bit. It is a special day, after all."

Julia went to the kitchen, found the bottle and glasses, and came back to the table. James uncorked it and poured out a small amount into each of the glistening crystal glasses and passed them around. As he lifted his glass, the others followed suit.

"To John and Sondra. May your love deepen over the years and fill your lives with joy. May God's grace rain down on you both, and may you keep Him at the center of your home."

"Hear, hear," everyone agreed, toasting the young couple and sipping the drink.

"I have one too," said Julia. Everyone lifted his or her goblet again, listening.

"To our new son-in-law-to-be and our precious daughter," Julia gulped, tears threatening. She pushed on, "May you grow closer to God as well as each other. And may you find when you've reached the end of your days that you would do it all again and that the richest of love that covers all offenses would be yours."

"Amen, my dear. Hear, hear," James nodded. They each lifted their glass and took another sip, enjoying the event that had turned into a time of blessing the young couple.

John turned to Sondra. "I'd like to say one too." Sondra bit her lip, not sure her heart could take much more of the tender expressions without bursting into tears.

John lifted his glass and looked into Sondra's eyes. "I want you to know right now and always, Sondra, that you have my devotion, my protection, and my undying love. My life has changed for the better because of knowing you, and—well, I'm just the happiest man alive right now for sure!"

They all laughed and lifted their glasses, sipping again. They took their time, lingering around the table, enjoying the time together, and rejoicing in the promising union to come.

* * *

Wedding preparations took time. After standing up as bridesmaid and best man in Patrick and Rene's wedding, Sondra and John had asked them to return the favor. Rene would be her matron of honor, and Patrick, John's best man. Sondra was relieved, for it would allow her to have her sister, Sophia, as her maid of honor still. Working out all the details was exhausting. There were times she wanted to chuck it all and elope with John.

But her heart pitter-pattered with excitement over the day in the not-too-far future. In less than two months, she would be Mrs. John Martin. Sondra Louise Martin. Mrs. Sondra Martin. She wrote it out on notepaper, in her diary, on a frosted window—anywhere she could. She loved the look of it, the sound of it, and the meaning of it.

Rene, newly married and feeling very experienced in all things about love, shared her excitement at what lay ahead. She took tremendous pleasure in the fact that her instinct had brought the couple together.

"Oh, Sondra. To think that you were content with studying the life of that Russian prince or whatever he was the day you felt the earth move."

Sondra laughed. "The Tsar of Russia, Rene. And yes, I have thought of that several times. I'm not sure how many more ways I might be able to express my never-ending thanks to you. Would naming our firstborn after you possibly put an end to your continual reminder that I owe you my very happiness?"

Rene laughed. "Oh yes, that would absolutely shut me up."

Regan Rene Martin was born precisely one year later.

* * *

In her naïveté while pregnant, Sondra dreamed of sweet snuggles with a powder-scented baby and imagined yawning chasms of time to indulge in various interests. The idea of such a charming life beckoned her as she envisioned a cream-puff existence. She pictured weekly gatherings with other moms, all their children participating in mellow playgroups in a circle of love on her continually clean floor, while the ladies sipped hot tea and talked over the latest baby trends that only parents were privy to.

Her eagerness grew along with her belly as other women shared their rapturous nostalgia of first-time parenting. Wherever she went, everyone instructed her to "enjoy those early years once your little one is here . . . it goes so fast."

Pensively, she leafed through baby magazines and parenting books that promised tranquility with a toddler in three easy steps or offered advice on how to maximize your baby's nap time by making cute do-it-yourself projects for the nursery. She and John prepared for their baby's arrival with tremendous anticipation, excited for the new horizon of parenthood.

All that was quickly dispelled by reality upon their daughter's birth. Middle-of-the-night feedings added to her constantly exhausted state, and dirty laundry piled up quicker than she could keep up with.

Where on earth did I get the idea that this would be easy?

She could barely drag herself out of bed each morning, let alone keep the floor perpetually clean. Laundry baskets did a seemingly endless rotation carting dirty clothes to the cramped room where the machines went into overdrive with a baby in the house.

I've gone from grand expectations to basic survival.

Nap time was revered and properly used to try to improve her own constantly exhausted state. Calls and visits with Rene became sporadic, timed around naps and nursing and keeping up with all the demands. She and John assured each other that things would balance out soon. It couldn't always be this exhausting, could it?

But when Regan turned out to be colicky, it pushed their fledgling marriage to the limits. Sondra felt guilt over her inability to comfort Regan through her struggle and fatigue from the amount of work that the addition of one little person could generate.

One day, she discovered that by putting Regan in a carrier on top of the clothes dryer, the vibrating motion helped comfort the miserable infant.

When he got home, John was impressed that she had found a way to soothe their baby until he discovered that the dryer was tumbling empty. "It's not like there isn't anything to be washed and dried." John looked pointedly at the giant pile of dirty clothes in the corner, waiting to be sorted. "How could you just throw cash out the window like that, Sondra?" he scolded her angrily. "You have no idea of the value of money. Everything has come easily for you. You didn't have to work two jobs at a time, growing up, like I did. But could you, at least, appreciate the fact that I work hard and not simply so you can have some peace and quiet?"

Any remorse she had disappeared with that last statement. She stamped her foot, green eyes flashing. "I am not that selfish, John. It wasn't just so I could have some peace and quiet. It was so Regan could have, maybe, a whole hour without suffering and crying." Tears filled her eyes. "At least give me the benefit of the doubt about my motives, if not my method."

John looked at his wife. He ran his hand through his light-brown hair, letting out a deep breath.

"You're right. I'm sorry. That wasn't fair."

The argument that had quickly flared also quickly ended. The young couple was still very much in love, just struggling with some of the normal pressures that parenting brought.

After the time of colic passed, things got easier. Sondra learned how to hear and address Regan's cries. The days passed quickly as things started to fall into a manageable routine.

She found she loved the tasks of mothering even as tiring as they were.

"Even laundry seems pleasant when it's baby clothes I get to fold." She laughed one day with Rene.

"You're so unselfish, Sondra. I want some more time with Patrick alone before we have children." She grabbed a baby blanket, folding it gently and adding it to the stack. "Do you think that is terrible of me?"

"Of course, it isn't." She added a pink cotton sleeper to the folded pile. "To be honest, we weren't even trying. Maybe I should have taken some birth control for a year or so, but it didn't even occur to me." She looked over at Regan sleeping peacefully in her little carrier. "Now I can't imagine not having her in our lives."

"Do you think you'll have more?" Rene asked.

"Oh, gosh, I don't know. Probably. Not right away, though. It was a big adjustment, having Regan." She spoke confidently, "But I'm nursing her, and I read somewhere that that's a pretty good form of birth control." She finished folding the last of the clothes. "I would like to take some time to do some of my old interests again too, like writing. It's enough for me being just Mommy to one right now." She went over, scooping the tiny infant, who was starting to fuss, into her arms and nestling her close. Rene looked on while Sondra pulled her baby in close, settling in to nurse her while the two friends visited a while longer.

* * *

As Sondra had shared with Rene, she loved being a mom. But even she was shocked when she found out a few weeks after their conversation that she was pregnant again.

John too was stunned. "You don't understand, Sondra. I'm under a lot of pressure every day." His hand swept through his hair, a nervous habit. "I can barely find the time I want to spend with you and Regan. How am I going to provide for another baby?"

She hid her disappointment at his response. "John, every baby is a blessing. It will all work out, you'll see." She looked up into his eyes, pleading. "This should be happy news. I want you to be happy with me."

He nodded. "I am happy. You're right. Somehow it will be okay."

"It will be more than okay. It's going to be marvelous."

He pulled her close, and she snuggled into him.

* * *

Cecilia Marie Martin entered the world with a howl and didn't stop for what seemed like months.

"And we thought Regan's colic was bad," Sondra lamented to Rene one day as she was over, visiting. "CiCi's is ten times worse."

Rene looked down at the little bundle in her arms. "Oh, she is precious, Sondra." She nuzzled the baby's tiny face. "I can't imagine her being anything but sweet."

Sondra raised her eyebrows. "Well, trust me. If you want proof, I will gladly send her your way during her next bout." The poor baby struggled with a bad case of colic that was taxing the exhausted parents. Their one consolation was that it wouldn't last forever.

It surprised her when after the birth of Cecilia, a younger mom stopped her in the church hallway one Sunday, asking her some questions about her own newborn baby.

With a second child, Sondra realized she had passed the threshold of new motherhood and was already considered a veteran. She encouraged the younger mom to give the idea of nursing a little more time and answered some basic questions that she herself had struggled with those first few months. Tucked away somewhere in Regan's baby book was a short chronicle she had composed during one of her many middle-of-the-night nursing sessions:

I started my new job this week. It seems to be going pretty good, really, except I don't get any sick days, and the hours aren't so great . . . I work from quarter to tired till half past exhausted, but I'm told that these may change a little as I put my time in. What do I do? Well, mostly, it's somewhat like being in the restaurant business. Except I'm the only cook, there's only one item on the menu, and I have just one customer. But boy, does she ever get the royal treatment. I stay open twenty-four hours a day to meet her every need. Still, it's been worth it. The only *steady* pay I've received so far are these deposits wrapped in plastic that don't smell so great, but I have a feeling that the benefits here are going to be fantastic. I've hopped between a few jobs in the past, but I'm in this one for the long haul. My heart is just really here. I've fallen so deeply in love with my customer that despite the trials, this is the one job commitment I know I'll never regret. And who knows, in a year or two, maybe I'll open a franchise. Well, back to work, my customer's dinner bell just rang.

But there was no time to spend on Sondra's other interests anymore. Every moment was taken up with caring for her two babies. Most days were exhausting, and at times her life seemed like an out-of-control whirlwind.

I love John and our girls. But have I given up all my other hopes and dreams? Is this all I will ever be now? A wife. A mom. What about becoming a writer?

One day she was at her parents' house, visiting with the girls. Her dad took Regan to see the birds in the backyard while Cecilia slept in her car seat, giving Sondra a few minutes alone with her mom. She sighed, enjoying the calm and familiar surroundings.

"Your new dishes are pretty, Mom."

"Thank you. And actually, they're not new. I've been going through all those boxes downstairs." Julia smiled. "Your poor dad's been badgering me for years to do it. I'm glad I have. I'd forgotten most of what was down there."

Sondra nodded and toyed with the cup sitting on the table, lost in thought.

Julia watched her quietly for a moment and then asked, "How are you doing, dear?"

Sondra said unconvincingly, "Oh, fine."

"Is everything okay with John?"

Sondra nodded. "Mm-hmm."

"Are *you* doing okay?" Her mother's brow tilted down in consternation.

"Yes. I'm fine."

Julia waited. "Are you sure?"

Sondra sighed. "Well, I mean, I feel tired all the time, but I'm okay." She looked her mom in the eye. "I guess that sometimes I do feel buried under the stress of running our home and taking care of the girls." Tears of self-pity formed in her eyes, and she wiped them away.

Her mom touched her hand. "I know it's hard, honey. No one ever said it would be easy. But things worth doing are often hard. You need to remember, God wants to stretch us and teach us even through the difficulties we face."

Sondra nodded, but in her heart she was discouraged.

She doesn't get it. If I told her my real thoughts, she would probably be shocked.

She sniffled. "Well, John sure doesn't seem to understand how hard it can be. He gets to go to work and be with adults while I'm the one dealing with everything at home. I feel very alone in my parenting sometimes."

Julia gave her daughter a stern look. "Now, Sondra, you know that isn't true. John is providing all he can. His job lets you stay home with your babies. He's the one who has the pressure to figure out ways to find time with you while providing the money for your home and food and all the bills. You need to appreciate him, dear. Don't let your self-pity get in the way of seeing the facts as they are."

Sondra bit her lower lip to keep from venting her frustration.

I should have known she wouldn't understand. Why did I even bother?

The sound of her dad returning with Regan prevented her from further voicing her thoughts, and she stood, stretching. She said frostily, "Well, thanks for the tea and the visit. We should get home."

Julia stood too, hugging her daughter. "Oh, honey, we loved seeing you and the girls, and I'm praying for you. I love you, Sondra."

"I love you too." She was stinging from her mom's words of gentle scolding.

She gathered the girls and their things. In the car, she popped Regan's favorite tape into the cassette player and sat back, listening to her sweet singing while they headed home. Some of her bitterness started to melt under the warmth of gratefulness for her daughters.

What's not to love about my sweet babies? How could I ever feel empty when I have them to love and care for?

She thought determinedly, *I am happy* but couldn't stop the thought from entering her mind, *if not exactly fulfilled.*

* * *

The weeks passed in tedious repetition. John was busy working, and money was tight. His job was more demanding, and his hours increased right at the time when Sondra could have used his help. Worn-out when he got home, he had no time to talk to his young wife about anything, let alone her lonesome days, caring for their children. Even if she simply wanted to share, it almost always came out as a complaint. They were talking less and arguing more.

She voiced her frustrations to Rene one day when she was over, visiting. They sat in the living room, which was sparsely furnished with a couch and a chair and a large basket of toys and books.

"What happened to me?" Sondra lamented. "I used to have fun. Now all I do is clean and work and eat and barely sleep. I don't have any 'me' time anymore. I feel like a big frump, and John couldn't care less." She turned her green eyes to her friend. "We've only been married just under three years, but it feels like twenty sometimes."

"You are not a frump, Sondra." Rene tried to encourage her. "You're as pretty as ever. You just need to take a few minutes for yourself each day. John still adores you. He's probably buried under work pressures. It's the same thing with Patrick. That's what happens once the honeymoon wears off." She continued. "If you could do anything, what would you want to do for fun?"

Sondra hung her head in her hands, wailing, "That's what's so pathetic. I can't even think of anything. What's wrong with me, Rene? Why am I always so tired? I'm too young to feel this way, like my life is already half over." She glanced at Regan playing quietly on the floor nearby and CiCi sleeping in her swing.

"Do you think you're depressed?"

She pondered that. "I don't know. I love being a mom, but sometimes I'm so lonely, and there are days the work is monotonous." She continued. "John doesn't appreciate the dreariness that raising children can be."

Rene grunted. "Try waitressing." She laughed. "Believe me, I'm grateful to have a job, and the tips can be terrific, but you want to talk about long days and hard work, well, look no further."

Sondra grinned. "Yeah, I know you work hard"—she grew serious again—"but at least you get paid."

Rene's eyebrows rose. "Now there's where you are not thinking right. I get a paycheck, yes. But you are wrong when you say you aren't paid for your work here because you are. Not in dollars, maybe, but in ways more valuable than that." She looked wistful. "You get to be a mom, Sondra. I'm sure it's hard, but you are blessed in lots of ways I might never get to know."

"Of course, you will, Rene. Why would you think that? Patrick only wants you to work for a few years first. He wants kids too, doesn't he?"

"He says he does. He thinks we will be better off financially if I can wait a little longer." She laughed. "Listening to you, maybe waiting isn't so terrible."

Sondra protested, "I love being home with Regan and CiCi. Sometimes I wish I could do other things too, that's all."

"You've got your whole life stretched out in front of you, Sondra. Be a mom, raise your girls, and then you can try other things. But stop thinking it's always so rosy on the other side of the fence." She stood, preparing to leave for work.

"I'll see you in a few days." The two friends hugged good-bye, and Sondra added their plates to the kitchen sink that was piled high with dishes and got busy with the day's chores.

* * *

That night's quarrel with John ran along the same lines as usual.

"You're unsympathetic," she accused him.

He turned to her wearily. "Well, you're a drama queen." They stood sparring distance apart, with angry words as their weapons to unleash on each other.

His accusation frosted her, and she was quick to defend herself. "I am not being a drama queen. I get no appreciation from you for anything I do around here!" She ticked off grievances on her fingers like a checklist, stepping angrily toward him, her voice getting louder as the list grew. "I take care of the girls, do the laundry, make the meals, run all the errands, and clean the house while you're gone all day with interesting people. You earn a paycheck and get out and do something. Other people tell you what a wonderful job you've done. How hard is that to take?" she demanded.

He shook his head and retorted sarcastically, "Oh, sure, I love the pressure and demands of my job. It's so wonderful being told you aren't doing this right and need to improve that. I'm under constant scrutiny and the stress of knowing that if I mess up, it could mean my job." His scornful look spoke volumes. "Give me a break, Sondra. You've got it made. You stay home all day, your time is your own. I only ask that you take care of the girls, make dinner, and keep the house reasonably clean. What's so hard about that?"

Tears streamed down her face. "Why can't you understand? It's not always that easy."

"What isn't easy about it?" he demanded. "I'd love to switch places with you for a couple of days. I could use the break." He shook his head with disgust at her complaints and turned away.

She seethed at his inability to grasp how she felt.

I'm not doing anything important with my life. What if I'm just wasting my time?

When Rene came again a few days later, she consoled her. "You've got to remember, Sondra, that John is simply not going to be able to understand how you feel. From his perspective, he's given you everything you've wanted. I mean you do love your girls, right?"

"Don't be silly, Rene. You know I do."

"Well, then think about it. You wanted babies. You have babies. You always said you wanted to stay home to raise your children. You get to do that. Why would John feel any empathy for how empty that task can sometimes feel when, at least, you're getting to do everything with your life you ever dreamed of?"

Sondra snorted. *Everything I ever dreamed of. Right.*

And yet, Rene was right about one thing. How could John understand? In his eyes, she should be perfectly fulfilled, and if she wasn't, what more could he do?

Rene rose from the couch. "I've got to get going." She gave Sondra a hug and let herself out.

Sondra sighed and pulled the basket of laundry close to fold. As she shook the scratchy towels, snapping out the wrinkles, her mind drifted to Rene's words.

Maybe I am searching for some impossible dream. What did I use to do that was fulfilling? She had to think through her few various interests. Reading always topped the list—and writing. "Hmm," she mused out loud, "when was the last time I had time for such luxuries like sitting alone for an hour or two to read or write?" She hadn't read a book that wasn't for children since she was pregnant with Regan. And the only things she wrote regularly were entries in the girls' baby books as she tracked their progress through life.

"Mommy, will you read to me?" Regan held out a stack of her favorite books.

Sondra pushed the laundry basket aside, reaching out to her sweet girl.

"Of course, I will, Ms. Magoo."

Regan giggled and climbed into her mother's lap. Together, they read through the whole stack. The two sat for a long time, snuggling and reading, till CiCi woke up and needed to nurse.

Regan went to play again while Sondra was left to her own thoughts. The inner voice that always led her astray was extra loud today.

John gets to do almost anything he wants while you're stuck at home all day. Haven't you given up enough?

Sondra was aware of her propensity to feel badly for herself, given half a chance. But why couldn't John acknowledge that she coped with some challenges in her day too? Maybe her trials weren't dealing with difficult people or meeting deadlines, but they were still hard.

I'm lonely and unfulfilled. I need some stimulation to feel like I'm contributing.

She finished feeding CiCi and put the infant down on her heavy blanket.

I just have to find something that makes me feel alive again.

She finished folding the laundry and went to clean the kitchen and start dinner.

* * *

A couple of weeks later, her sister came to watch the babies for the morning to give her a break. Sondra hadn't been out of the house in several days, and Sophia enjoyed spending time with her nieces.

Feeling desperately underappreciated, Sondra swished some color across her cheeks and lips. *Why not at least try to look pretty for my own sake even if John never notices anymore?*

With a kiss for each of the girls and another word of thanks to her sister, she dashed out the door with her list.

Stopping at the fresh foods market, she was in the produce section when she saw a strikingly handsome man glancing her way. He looked very distinguished and a few years older than her, but he had charisma that she could sense even from across the box of ripe melons that separated them.

It feels nice to be noticed, especially by someone so debonair.

The next time they locked eyes, she smiled gently back.

Maybe I haven't grown completely frumpy.

Pushing her cart through the store aisles, Sondra tried to dismiss her feelings of guilt from the road she had turned onto. *What harm can there be in a smile or two over the produce bin? I've been cooped up far too long. It's time I start living a little again.*

In the next aisle, she saw the man again and allowed herself another small smile when he looked her way. This time, he gazed at her, a light smile playing at the corner of his mouth. The way his dark eyes drank her in made her feel pretty. She hadn't felt that way in a long time. She grew warm knowing he was watching her.

I know I'm flirting, but it's harmless, isn't it?

As she worked her way through the store, she selected her products, lingering till she caught sight of him. Again, he sent a smile her way, and her heart jumped a little.

Is he waiting for me to catch up to him?

She turned the corner, easing around a display of dessert cups, searching for him, and nearly hit the cart of another shopper. The offended patron was annoyed. "Hey, watch out."

"Oh! Pardon me. I'm so sorry," Sondra said, flustered. She glanced up to see the dark-haired stranger nearby, carefully watching her with a relaxed smile and compelling brown-eyed stare. Sondra flushed.

What am I doing? I need to finish up and go.

She zipped through the last few aisles, then made her way to the front of the store.

At the checkout, she noticed the man was in the next lane over.

Oh, gosh, he's right there. Flirting is one thing, speaking is completely off-limits.

She set her items on the conveyor belt and searched her purse for the grocery envelope. Handing the money to the cashier, she looked around and was startled to see him a few feet away, looking at his receipt.

Oh, this is awkward! I hope he doesn't talk to me. Oh please, God, don't let him talk to me. I won't do this ever again if You help me escape his notice.

The cashier handed her the receipt, thanked her for coming, and greeted the next customer in line. Sondra gathered her few bags and began walking. She had to pass him to leave.

Don't look up.

The man looked directly at her and smiled again. Sondra grew warm under his fixed gaze.

"Hello." His voice sounded foreign, and the one simple word was packed with feeling.

Sondra gulped and replied breathlessly, "Hello" before marching out the door and to her car. Tossing the bags in the seat, she drove away, not waiting to see if he followed her or not.

Blocks from the market, she laughed nervously. "Sondra, you fool." She berated herself out loud. "He was only being friendly." She was glad to be away from the gaze of the stranger, who probably had put no more thought into their meeting.

Finishing her few errands, she treated herself to a short stop at the library, selected a few books, and headed home.

"Perfect timing," her sister said when she walked in the door. "I think CiCi is hungry."

Sondra put her bags and books down and reached for her to nurse her. "Sophia, thank you so much. It was wonderful to get some time out alone."

Sophia smiled. "It was no trouble at all." She snuggled Regan, who sat next to her on the small couch. "I had fun. Your girls are so sweet." Regan smiled at her aunt, and Sophia gave her a quick kiss. "I've got to run though. I'm meeting Adam for lunch."

Sondra teased her younger sister, "Oh? Are things getting serious?" Adam was a young man Sophia had met a few months earlier.

Sophia blushed. "I guess so. We've been spending more time together. I really do like him, but we'll have to see how things go."

She grabbed her bag and gave a gentle pull on Regan's blond braid. "Bye-bye, sugar pie. Bye, Sondra."

"Bye, Soph. Have a good time. And thanks again."

After the door shut, she sat alone with her thoughts.

I remember feeling that way about being with John. What's happened to us?

"Mommy?"

"Yes, honey?"

"Can I hold CiCi? Auntie Sophia said I could, but she forgot to let me."

Sondra smiled. "Of course, you can, honey, after I'm done feeding her. Come sit by me. I need a snuggle from my little Ms. Magoo."

Regan cuddled up to her mother's side and nestled under her open arm. They sat like that for a while, talking and snuggling together.

* * *

The following Saturday, John asked her to run to the village hardware store to have an extra key made of the front-door lock. Sondra was glad to get a few minutes to herself.

A clerk helped her at the lock-and-key desk. She paid the small fee, and he took her key to copy. "It will just be a couple of minutes."

Sondra wandered down a nearby aisle, looking at the shelves of products. Turning into the next aisle, she was startled by the appearance of the handsome man from the fresh foods market. He was sizing up some European cabinet handles and glanced up, surprised at the sight of her. He quickly regained his composure, greeting her.

"Well, hello again."

He sounds so cultured. He's definitely European.

"Hello," she answered shyly, smiling and feeling a blush warm her cheeks.

They both laughed.

My god, his smile is incredible. He's so handsome. What would he possibly see in me?

Sondra noticed he wore no ring.

He looked at her with a frankly admiring smile that made her feel guilty.

Sondra. You are married to John. You have two daughters. What are you doing?

He glanced down and then up at her. "I'm actually very glad that we meet again." He gazed at her, and she couldn't move. "May I compliment you and say that . . ."—he smiled with boyish charm—"you are a very memorable woman."

Sondra flushed.

The stranger continued. "Actually, I've been thinking a lot about you and wondering—"

Suddenly, as if from nowhere, the key clerk was at her side, interrupting the stranger's admission. The clerk handed her a small bag. "Here you go, miss. You're all finished." His words unintentionally broke the spell that had bound her to the spot, unable to break away from the stranger's captivating gaze.

Sondra took the bag and watched the clerk walk away. Though undeniably drawn to the handsome man, the guilt pushing on her heart suddenly left her with little wish to know what he had been wondering. "Oh," she stammered, "it looks like I'm all finished here. It was very nice bumping into you again, but I . . . I've got to go. Good-bye."

Turning quickly, she hurried toward the front doors and outside, breathing deeply of the fresh air and trying to clear her head.

He didn't have a ring. He isn't married. He was thinking about me! What was he wondering?

As she drove home, she thought about their meeting.

"It's not like I'm going out of my way to meet him. John sent me," she argued out loud.

There is nothing going on between us. I will probably never see him again. I don't even know his name.

* * *

The next couple of nights were calm. She and John were civil to each other, if not exactly friendly. But the next night, after the girls were tucked in, a whole lot of ugly came spilling out.

The day's mail had brought the bill from a shopping spree Sondra had taken when she'd been angry with him a few weeks earlier.

"How do you expect me to pay for this?" he demanded, his face flushed. He held the offensive paper crumpled in his hands, shaking it in front of her.

Defensively she replied, "I needed a few things for me and the girls." She drew a deep breath and rubbed her brow. "Besides, we have the money."

"No, Sondra, no we do not." He bit his upper lip. "When my car broke down, that took our margin away. That, plus the extra you insisted we spend to get pictures done for the girls, took all we had in reserve." He shook his head. "I just wish you would ask me first before spending lavishly."

She snorted. "It can hardly be called lavish, John."

His voice dropped a pitch. "Sondra, listen to me. I told you we have to be careful. I do not like spending money that I don't have. That's how people get in huge trouble." He ran his hand through his hair. "You may not count $165 as lavish. I call it extravagant when we don't have it." Frustrated, he turned and left the room.

I guess I should have asked him first. But really, to get so upset . . .

John walked back in, keys in his hand.

"Where are you going?"

"Out." He glared at her. "I'm going to go drive for a while and think about things."

She glared right back at him. "Fine. I'm not waiting up for you."

He grunted lightly. "I sure didn't expect you would."

He walked out into the night, and Sondra was alone with her thoughts.

* * *

The following week, she stopped at the post office. Her brother, Stephen, and sister-in-law, Grace, along with their young sons, Christopher and Brady, had recently moved. Sondra had picked out a small housewarming gift to send them. Her neighbor Paula was keeping an eye on the girls while she ran her quick errand.

Sondra was standing in line, listening to the two women behind her complain about the slow service, when she felt something gently brush her arm. Turning, she was shocked to see the dark-haired man. As before, he was dressed with an understated sophistication.

He grinned delightedly. "I thought it was you. Again we meet." He saw her astonished look and waved toward the rows of numbered metal boxes on the wall at the back. "I rent a post office box here and stopped by to collect my mail."

This is unbelievable.

Thoughts of him had crossed her mind quite a few times lately. Now, here he was, standing close enough for her to smell his cologne, which was wonderful and heady. Sondra felt herself flush as she was again drawn into his handsome smile.

"Oh!" Sondra stammered. "Oh, hello."

Seeing she was caught off guard, he spoke gently to her. "Forgive me. I did not mean to surprise you. I still have not had the opportunity to properly introduce myself. My name—"

The loud, obnoxious prompting of the post office clerk interrupted his words. "Next!" she barked out.

Sondra was ruffled when the customer behind her gave her a nudge. "That's you." It hadn't been enough of a push to lose her balance, but suddenly, she felt light-headed and wobbly. She almost dropped her package and started tipping forward. The mysterious stranger reached out, his hands firmly grasping her arms. She felt a thrill go through her as he helped steady her.

"Ah, *la bella*. I got you." His strong hands were gentle. "I won't let you fall." He looked down at her with tender concern on his face. His cologne wasn't the only thing intoxicating: so was his manner toward her.

Oh my god. What is happening to me?

"Are you all right?" His voice was deep and soothing. She could get lost in those dark eyes. Her breath quickened, and she felt a jolt of illicit attraction: the way he held her coupled with his gallantry made a powerful duo. Sondra felt the sudden, irrational desire to close the few inches that separated them and kiss him in wild abandon. If they'd been alone, she wasn't sure she would have resisted the temptation.

What's wrong with me? What is it about this man that I can't help myself?

She looked into his eyes, and her heart skipped a beat when she saw raw desire reflected there. Shocked with the response of her own carnal longing, she watched awareness come alive in his face as he saw the truth that she was willing to be wooed.

She flushed, aware that she had crossed an invisible line: she was open to his pursuit.

"Next in line!"

The woman behind her urged her again with growing annoyance, "What are you waiting for? An engraved invitation? You're next. I don't have all day."

Sondra turned to the handsome stranger, whose arms still encircled her, feeling flustered. "Oh dear. Thank you for your help. I'm all right now, but I'm sorry—I have to go." She reluctantly broke free of his grasp.

He courteously stepped aside, allowing her to pass. "By all means. You must go." He gave her a look of smooth self-assurance. "I'm fairly certain we shall meet again." With a short nod, smiling confidently at her, he turned and walked away.

Sondra stepped forward, putting her package on the counter and giving the clerk the instructions for service. "No, overnight won't be necessary. Insurance? Um, yes, please." She looked around but couldn't see where he had gone.

How does he know we'll meet again? Has he been following me?

She finished and left, not catching sight of him again. As she drove home, she thought about their encounters.

Is it possible that I have a secret admirer?

The thought sent a delicious thrill through her. "Get ahold of yourself, Sondra. No one is admiring you." She scolded herself in the silence of her car, "You're just an ordinary girl."

"A *married* ordinary girl," she reminded herself grimly.

* * *

The next few weeks were busy with their normal routine. She and John barely saw each other. When they did, things were frosty. She nursed hurt at his comments from days earlier. It had been their usual exchange. He criticized something around the house while she tried to defend herself, bringing up past battles to add to the mix. It hadn't ended well, with John sleeping on the living room couch.

He doesn't value me. All the work I do around here doesn't matter to him.

Lately, after she and John argued, she allowed her mind to meander along the tantalizing possibilities of how a meeting alone with the handsome stranger would finally look. It was a sweet way to pass time while blocking out the reality of her and John's crumbling relationship.

Open to the lure of feeling desirable and appreciated even if it meant seeking it from outside her marriage, she let her thoughts drift often to the mysterious stranger, who had been so gallant.

He is such a gentleman. He was about to tell me his name. I wonder if I'll see him again?

She sighed, remembering the way he'd held her. And the look she had seen in his eyes.

He called me memorable. It's been so long since I've felt attractive to anyone . . . I wonder if he's thinking about me?

In the deepest privacy of her mind, she entertained what crossing the next line would look like.

He wanted to kiss me too. What would that have been like? I know I shouldn't, but I hope I see him again soon. He's so handsome and strong! What would it be like to be with him, I wonder? I bet he would appreciate me . . .

* * *

One sunny day Rene had off work. The two women made plans to spend the day together, taking the girls along. In the small village, they popped into various shops, trying on fun hats and smelling expensive perfumes. Finally, they decided to stop for an early lunch.

"There's a great little sandwich-and-coffee shop I used to eat at when I worked at the printing company. Do you want to go there?"

Rene agreed, "That sounds wonderful."

Lunching on the outdoor veranda of the little café, Sondra was enjoying the warmth and light breeze and the time spent with her best friend when she saw him: the dark-haired man stepped out onto the sun-dappled patio.

No! Not here! Not now!

Sondra ducked her head, squirmed sidewise, and tried to avoid his eyes. To her horror, he spotted her, his face lighting up as he walked over with an easy grace to greet her. As usual, he was dressed with a subdued elegance, like he had just stepped off the pages of an advertisement for a European airline.

"Good afternoon." His delight was unmistakable. "What a wonderful surprise to see you here. Somehow, I knew our paths would cross again." His effortless ease was appealing. "I have to confess, I have wondered if you've been following me." His charming smile completely disarmed her, and Sondra blushed.

He held out his hand. "I am kidding, of course. I think it's about time we actually met. I am Nicholas Bianchi." Sondra grasped his hand and shook it. His skin was so soft, but his grip was strong. Feeling a thrill again at his touch, Sondra self-consciously pulled her hand back and smiled.

"I'm Sondra. Sondra Martin," she replied shyly.

Next to her, Rene cleared her throat slightly.

"Oh, and this is my friend—Rene."

"It's truly a pleasure to meet you both."

Nicholas turned to Rene, confiding with a twinkle in his eyes, "Your friend has good taste. I have seen her in only the finest shops in our village."

Sondra thought of the hardware store and post office and gave a small smile, blushing madly.

He eyed up Sondra with his mesmerizing gaze. "It seems every time I'm popping in, she's popping out, so we've only had the merest of time to become acquainted."

Rene said, "I see" though clearly, she did not see at all. Rather, the look on her face evidenced her outright confusion. Hoping to stop Rene from asking any embarrassing questions, Sondra quickly asked, "You must work around here?"

Nicholas nodded. "A few months ago I opened a shop of Italian goods that lies around the corner from here."

That accounted for how often Sondra bumped into him when she was in the area. She pushed a coloring book toward Regan, hoping the little girl wouldn't overhear anything that could be shared with her daddy.

"How . . . how very nice." Sondra couldn't come up with any of the witty responses she had prepared in her mind when she had day-dreamed of this moment since their last encounter at the post office.

He looked at her intently. "I like to think I provide people an introduction to some of the finer things in life." He grinned. "I am rather like a self-proclaimed goodwill ambassador, if you will."

Sondra smiled. "Well, I hope your store does well." She was very aware of Rene's presence as well as Regan's little ears and didn't want to say anything that could give away the thoughts her heart had been dallying with lately.

Nicholas's eyes twinkled. "Thank you. I have great hopes for our success. I think it might be just a matter of time." He paused as if choosing his words carefully. "Sometimes, people aren't exactly sure what it is that they want. That's part of the service I offer: helping people discover what it is that will give them tremendous satisfaction and happiness."

Rene interjected, "You must be terribly busy, being newly opened and all."

"Oh, indeed. But one of the arts of life is knowing when to work hard and when to pause and smell the roses as I believe your American phrase goes?" Nicholas indicated the frosty cup of iced cappuccino in his hand. "I worked hard all morning, so I decided to stop over for a cool drink. I must confess it is one of my many weaknesses." His smile dazzling, he looked at Sondra meaningfully.

She had the grace to blush. "Ah. I see. Well, that sounds lovely."

Oh, this isn't going at all how I imagined it would! Certainly, Rene and the girls were never in the picture. Nor was I stammering all over the place with the tongue-tied incompetence of a schoolgirl.

Of course, in her dreams, neither was she already married. She made some inane comment about the café, lamely explaining, "We were just finishing our lunch and enjoying the sunshine."

Nicholas raised his hand, indicating the beautiful garden surrounding the little patio. "I can certainly understand why. It is a delightful spot for some lovely ladies to refresh themselves."

He glanced at his expensive-looking watch, noticing the time, and said, "As tempting as it is to remain in such beautiful company, I must get back to my shop. A break, after all, by its very definition, ought to be just that . . . I hope you'll excuse my interruption and enjoy the rest of your luncheon."

He turned first to Rene. "It was a delight to meet you." He gave Sondra his pointed attention. "I am very glad to finally make your acquaintance, Sondra. It is a long-awaited pleasure." Even her name sounded exotic on his tongue. "I would love for you to stop in my little shop someday soon, so we can have more time to become . . . better acquainted."

Oh, dear God, what must Rene think?

"Arrivederci, ladies." Nicholas lifted his cup in a small toast to them, giving Sondra a lingering look, before walking away. She breathed a sigh of relief when he was gone.

Rene turned to her. "Okay, spill it. I know everyone you know, and I certainly would have remembered him. Who, on earth, was that?"

Sondra took a sip of her tea, avoiding her friend's challenging gaze for a moment. Finally, she explained how she had first bumped into the charming Italian, downplaying the interactions.

"It was completely innocent, Rene. I would never allow it to go further than the store aisles."

Rene searched her friend's face in disbelief. "And yet, here we are, at a sandwich shop, and even I can tell he is clearly interested in getting to know you better. He seems under the impression that you are available."

"That's not my fault. I never had a chance to tell him that I am married. Seriously, Rene, it is absolutely nothing."

"Sondra, may I remind you, you are betraying John's trust even if this never went anywhere at all? And if it did, it would be ruinous to your entire marriage."

Sondra squirmed. She hadn't anticipated her and Nicholas's harmless interactions would ever have left the safe confines she had allowed them to bloom in when she had first engaged with him at the fresh foods market.

The way I melted in his arms last time certainly didn't discourage him any.

Rene squeezed her arm, looking at her with concern. "I love you, Sondra. You are my best friend. I know marriage isn't always easy, but John loves you. And you love him. You both just need to put some time and attention back into your relationship." Rene's eyes looked at her imploringly.

"But you don't understand, Rene. John isn't the same man I married. He doesn't seem to care about me or even value what I do in our home." She shook her head. "He's so busy with work, I don't think I matter to him anymore."

Rene touched her arm. "Of course, you do. I get that the excitement has worn off. That's normal. But *that*"—she tilted her head toward the gate Nicholas had exited through—"would be a huge mistake and one that you would greatly regret. Sure, it's exciting to think of starting a fresh relationship. After all, you don't know the person's faults yet, and they don't know yours." Sondra nodded slowly, and Rene continued. "But stop and think of all you and John have been through together." She gestured to the girls. "And look at these two precious babies you created together. Think about what you would be throwing away. If not for your own sake, then for theirs."

Sondra looked at Regan quietly coloring her book and glanced at CiCi sleeping in her carrier. Nicholas had probably thought the two little girls were Rene's daughters.

He didn't do anything wrong. I did. Rene is right. What have I been thinking?

Sondra hung her head in shame.

If John knew, it would break his heart to think I was even enter-taining the idea of heading toward the playground of unfaithfulness.

Sondra looked her friend squarely in the face and nodded soberly. "You're right, Rene. You're absolutely right. John isn't perfect, but neither am I." She faltered, then admitted, "I knew better. It was just so hard to resist feeling admired and appreciated for a change."

Rene squeezed her hand. "I know. But better to keep your self-respect than to cave in and lose everything in the end."

Back at home, she put the girls down for an afternoon nap and then went to the kitchen to work on making dinner. Her mind replayed the events from earlier, and again she felt the shame of her behavior.

I'm going to have to avoid the village.

But she realized the real issue was deeper than avoiding the temptation of seeing Nicholas again. There could always be another Nicholas Bianchi waiting around the corner.

No, I need a better plan than simple avoidance.

She needed to change her whole way of thinking. Her faith, strong as a younger girl, had weakened as she had neglected her own spiritual growth.

"I'm sorry, God." She hadn't prayed in a long time, and her words hung in the air, sounding empty.

Outwardly, she'd still attended church each week with John and their girls, but she had spent no real time in God's word, so she had become vulnerable to the attack on her heart.

She tried again, haltingly. "Thank You for Your protection of having Rene with me today. I'm sorry that I ever let thoughts of Nicholas creep up in my marriage." A tear formed in her eye, and she wiped it away.

"I know John isn't perfect, but neither am I. He is a good man and an excellent father. He loves our girls so much. I've spent far too much time dwelling on the things about him that I don't like instead of being grateful for the things about him that are good." She covered the pot on the stove, setting it to simmer, and sat down on a chair at the kitchen table, playing with the saltshaker while praying aloud. "If I'm going to be honest, I know I haven't been easy to get along with lately either." More tears came into her eyes, and she leaned toward the counter, grabbing a tissue from a box nearby. "O God, please help me. I *do* want a good marriage. I can't just change overnight though. Help me be the kind of wife that I can be with Your help."

She remembered her mother's words of warning from years earlier.

The trials came, and I didn't protect our love.

It was alarming how effortless it had been to have her heart so quickly drawn away, and she found herself at a crossroad. Remorse filled her heart, and she knew there was only one answer to the problem she faced.

"Sondra," she spoke sternly to herself, "you need to choose: are you going to keep playing games with God or get serious and start following Him wholeheartedly?"

She stood up and found her Bible on a shelf in the living room, where it sat untouched all week long except for a few moments on Sunday mornings. She thought of her parents' Bibles, the pages worn with use, heavily lined and marked up as they studied God's Word and tried to apply it to their lives.

"Oh, Sondra," she spoke out loud again, "how did you get so far off the path God wants for you?"

She sat in the living-room chair, opened her Bible, turning the crisp white pages, and began reading.

* * *

That night when John came home, he saw the mess of toys all over the place. It had been a long week, and he was exhausted. He ran his hand through his hair, wanting to control his frustration.

"What does she do all day?" he muttered. Sondra seemed constantly unhappy, but he couldn't figure out what she wanted from him. Lately, he sensed that her mind was elsewhere whenever they were together. He wasn't certain what the distraction might be. Entering the kitchen, he smelled food cooking. "Well, at least she made dinner tonight," he muttered. Steam rose as he lifted the lid. "Mm-hmm. One of my favorites too." He set the lid back down on the steaming pot and went in search of his family. Regan was playing quietly with her stuffed animals.

"Daddy!" she squealed and toddled over to him.

"Hi, sweetheart. Where is Mommy?"

"I will show you." She took her father by the finger and led him into the next room, where Sondra sat, rocking Cecilia.

John looked at his wife. He forgot about the messes around the house and really looked at her.

Her hair was a mess, and she had a smudge of something on her cheek, but he caught his breath and slowly exhaled.

Things haven't been good at all between us lately, but she can still make my heart leap.

He watched as she got up and tenderly placed CiCi in her bassinet. Sondra walked to him and stopped. Tears shimmered in her eyes, but not like the tears of late, full of self-pity and frustration. No, now there was a definite softness on her face that wasn't there when he left this morning. He wasn't sure what was going on, but he sensed something had changed. Yes, something was undeniably different.

"John, I need to tell you something." He saw a tear stream down her cheek, and she brushed it away.

Panic rose in his heart. *Is she leaving me?*

"What's going on, Sondra?"

"We've been fighting so much these past months. Today, I came to realize that maybe I haven't really appreciated the things about you that I should have." She halted, gulping, as she shared her admission. "I've been frustrated by the kind of husband I've felt you have been, without being willing to look at the kind of wife *I've* been." She shook her head as a few more tears spilled out of her eyes.

Down by their legs, Regan looked up at them with concern. "Why are you so sad, Mommy?"

"Oh, honey, I'm okay." Sondra lifted Regan up, holding her and brushing her hair back with her free hand. "I just had to tell Daddy some things that I have been thinking about and that made me cry. Don't worry, sweet girl. It's all going to be okay."

She nuzzled Regan's cheek and looked back at John, who was watching her with a tenderness that she hadn't seen from him in a very long time. "Sondra, I love you. I don't know what you need me to do to show you that, but I know I can do better too. I hate how much we've been fighting."

She nodded and through fresh tears, she leaned into her husband's arms, holding Regan, the three of them hugging. "There are things that I know we still need to talk through, but I don't want to keep fighting with you either."

Cecilia stirred in her bassinet and started to fuss, breaking up their embrace. John took Regan, and Sondra went to pick up the baby.

"Mommy, can we eat now? I'm hungry," the little girl declared, throwing her arms around her daddy's neck.

They laughed. "Yes, we can eat now, sweetheart." The family walked into the kitchen, where dinner simmered on the stove. Sondra settled the baby in her swing, cranking the handle to start the soothing motion she loved. They pulled out their chairs and sat down together, dishing their plates full of food. For the first time in months, John tentatively reached for Sondra's hand as he gave a word of thanks over their meal. She extended her hand to him and then reached for Regan's soft little one, and the three of them sat in a little circle, thanking God for the gift of His many blessings.

* * *

At church that weekend, the young family occupied the same pew together as usual. Sondra had been sober-minded the past couple of days as she felt the Holy Spirit doing His work in her heart. For the first time, she felt the overwhelming desire to go to church, not out of duty, but because there was a desperate need in her spirit to do so.

During the worship time, Sondra listened to the soloist onstage sing the words:

> For Your blood poured out and paid the price for
> all my sin and pride
> I am ready, Lord, to embrace the grace that You
> alone provide.

Tears stung her eyes as she realized how God was working in her heart, convicting her of all her ugly sin. It wasn't only her willingness to have taken up with Nicholas that she had to confess, and it wasn't only her frustrations with John. It was everything she had become and was still holding on to. It was the ugliness of her pride, her heart, and her sin.

She suddenly realized: God was ready to set her free if she would only accept it.

As the young woman onstage sang the refrain again, Sondra stood up, with tears streaming down her face. She didn't care who was watching. She needed God to see she was serious about seeking Him in her life.

Oh, me too, God, I am ready too. I can't do this alone—I don't want to try anymore. I'm weary of trying to make this life work on my own. Please help me. I want to follow You with my whole being. I don't want to just stop sinning. I want my life to honor You.

Next to her, John rose to his feet too. A cry caught in her throat as he grabbed hold of her hand, and they stood there, side by side, recommitting their lives to God and to each other.

Five Years Later

February 1995

The words moved from Sondra's mind, through her fingertips tapping the keyboard, and onto the screen in front of her:

"Startled, Colette tried to shake off the feeling that she was being watched. *Just some kids,* she tried to assure herself. A knot of fear welled up in her. *Get ahold of yourself.* Suddenly, she heard a soft rattling sound. *This can't be happening.* Someone was testing the door, which she foolishly hadn't locked. As the knob slowly turned, she watched in horrified fascination, unable to move . . ."

"*Ffwwwhooot!*"

Tommy's horn blasting into her right ear grabbed Sondra's full attention.

"Whoa there! Why'd you do that?" Sondra covered her ears, wishing she'd taken better advantage of his nap time. Scrambling away from her chair, Tommy, three-and-a-half and full of exuberance, ran to jump on the jumping couch with his older sister Cecilia, narrowly skirting around the ExerSaucer on the floor, containing Mylah.

"Look at me! I'm Peter Pan!" shouted Tommy, dropping his horn and brandishing his orange plastic golf club at his sister. Cecilia fluttered her arms, pretending to be Tinker Bell, as they jumped and played together. The floor was littered with stray books and plastic figurines and a variety of small toys.

"CiCi, do it like me," Tommy urged his sister and playmate to copy his moves. She did, nearly stepping on the sharp pieces that were scattered every which way.

"Kids, stop and pick up some of those toys before someone gets hurt," their mother directed.

The two of them stopped jumping and running long enough to crouch to the ground, pushing the mixture of toys into a big pile, clearing a spot on the carpeting to jump and run without danger of piercing their tender bare feet. Then they were back at it.

Sondra sighed and turned back to the computer screen, trying to ignore the clamor and focus on the words in front of her.

Ten more minutes. Please, just ten more minutes.

The words floated in space. She sighed again, clicked the Save button, popped out the 3.25-inch floppy disk, and shut down the system. Writing would have to wait.

Sondra glanced at her watch.

I'd better get started on dinner, or we won't be eating tonight.

Grabbing the baby, she called over her shoulder, "CiCi, Tommy, play nice together while I go make dinner." She bounded up the stairs from their basement into the bright kitchen.

Late afternoon sun poured in through the windows and cast an amber glow into the room. Even with the snow on the ground outside, their home was snug and warm. Sondra loved how cheery their kitchen was although piles of books and toys were everywhere. It opened to a small family room that boasted a cozy fireplace and deep windows where light poured in. It was the kind of room that people could relax in: comfortable and slightly shabby, unpretentious and inviting. Sondra's favorite chair graced the corner, a sturdy basket of blankets within reach. The light-brown leather couch was worn yet inviting; thick rugs adorned the wooden floors and guarded against the cold.

Sondra tucked the baby into her swing and called for Regan to come help as she cranked the handle to begin the soothing movement Mylah loved.

"Reeegaaaan! I need you!"

Fairly tripping, Regan came running into the room, long hair flying loosely.

"What do you need, Mama?"

"Please help me move those piles into the living room."

She flew around, pulling food from the fridge and pantry. Concentrating on the recipe card in front of her, Sondra barely heard Regan's whisper.

"What did you say, dear?"

"Nothing, Mom. I know you're busy."

She looked at Regan and saw the sadness in her face. Suddenly, she remembered.

"Oh, sweetheart, did you talk with Kayla today?"

Kayla was Regan's best friend, but recently, the two girls had squabbled. Sondra knew it was weighing heavy on Regan's heart. She pulled her daughter into her arms, wrapping her up and wishing she could erase all pain from her life.

"Well, not exactly. I went over to her at lunchtime and tried to sit next to her like you said I should. I thought she would be ready to make up." Regan pulled back, looking at her mother hurtfully. "Instead, she made fun of my Cinderella hair clips. I told you Cinderella was for babies. And I'm not a baby anymore, Mom."

Tears started to spill out of the green eyes that looked so much like her own, and Sondra was struck with the realization that her little girl wasn't little anymore. Rather, in the scale of childhood, Regan was standing in the doorway of middle age, and Sondra could feel a cold wind blowing in. Gone were the days when she would stray out of the lines while coloring, imagine her doll was really alive, or prefer the twenty-five-piece puzzle to the one-hundred-piece one.

Hugging her daughter close while praying for words to offer her that would ease her pain, Sondra brushed Regan's long blond hair with her hands, noting the gleam of gold spun through her thick head of hair. Pulling back, she saw her daughter's sweet face, which was dotted with a light sprinkling of freckles, almost as if God, upon His completion of creating her, had held His artist's brush and, with a final flick of His wrist, had whimsically scattered them gently across her nose and cheeks.

Sondra smiled at Regan, wanting to see her beautiful smile back, loving how the green specks in her eyes sparkled when she was delighted. But now, they were clouded with the pent-up emotion of a weighed-down heart. Sondra stifled the urge to sigh again.

"Maybe I should call Kayla's mom." She wanted Regan to learn to handle her own childhood battles, but sometimes it *was* part of a mom's job to help her kids cross through some of the tougher parts of the war zone.

Regan pulled away, pleading, "No, please don't! If you do, I won't ever tell you anything ever again. If you tell Mrs. Carpenter, she might get upset at Kayla, and that will make her madder at me."

Sondra gently traced Regan's eyebrows with her finger, wanting to soothe the angst her daughter was feeling, but knowing she needed to teach her daughter how to handle conflict. There would be plenty more episodes like this for her in life; shielding her wasn't the answer either.

"Fine, I won't call—yet. But if you girls can't work this out soon, I may have to jump in to help out."

The sounds of Tommy and Cecilia pounding up the stairs signaled the end of their chance to talk privately about the matter. Sondra turned back to making the meal, praying God would work in the hearts of both girls so their friendship could be mended.

As she arranged the whole chicken into the countertop rotisserie, she chuckled at Tommy's questions. "Mommy, does it hurt the chicken to go around in there?"

"No, honey, it's dead, so it doesn't feel anything."

He persisted, "Well, does it hurt when we bite the chicken?"

She laughed and said, "No, Tommy, it doesn't feel anything because it's dead."

"How did you dead the chicken, Mom?"

Sondra patiently explained, laughing when he called to his favorite companion, "Hey, CiCi, come see the dead chicken Mom's got in this box!"

He watched it revolve through the little glass window while Sondra made the rest of their meal. He began counting the rotations and tapping the door of the rotisserie with his horn. "Okay,

Tommy, enough watching the chicken. Go help your sisters clean up the mess."

He obediently hopped off the bench he had dragged over, then right behind her, he blasted on his horn again. Startled, she spun around in exasperation.

"Thomas James Martin, you put that down this minute and help your sisters clean this kitchen before your daddy gets home."

"Too late for that," came a booming voice from the front entry.

"Daddy!" Squeals of joy filled the small kitchen as the kids ran to greet the handsome tall man taking up the whole doorway. A blast of cold air raced in. He shut the door firmly, stomping snow onto the entry mat.

"John." His wife came along after the pack of kids, who were laughing and stumbling to get all the hugs in. He held her close as their children watched, giggling.

TJ offered a blast on his horn that he still held and, like a herald, announced, "Daddy's kithing Mommy—on the lipth!"

"Shh!" said Regan, watching her parents. A little smile played around her mouth as she saw her daddy lift her mom off the floor.

Sondra protested, "John, put me down! What will the kids think?"

He laughed and lowered her down. "They'll think I love their beautiful mom—and they'd be right, I do." Blushing as he nuzzled her neck, she heard Mylah start to fuss and ran back to the kitchen.

"Kids, come help me get the table set. Dinner's almost ready."

The family came in the room, chairs scraping, laughter mixed with the talking, and commotion filled the cozy house.

"Your foot is touching my chair. Get it off," Regan demanded of CiCi.

"Is not. Mama, tell Regan it's not her chair. It's Daddy's."

"All right, you two. That's enough."

"It's not me. It's her. I asked her nicely."

John jumped in. "Girls, that's enough. Cecilia, turn so you face the table instead of your sister's chair. There. Regan, stop making faces at your sister, and eat your dinner."

A few moments of peace descended as everyone ate.

"This chicken is delicious, honey," John said appreciatively. Sondra smiled. She knew it was one of his favorite dishes.

"I finished my ABC book at school today," Cecilia announced.

"That's wonderful, sweetie," John replied.

"Daddy, did you know Mommy deaded the chicken on your plate?" Glad he could share this important information, Tommy nodded knowingly.

"Did she now?" John kept a barely straight face as he winked at Regan, who was giggling into her napkin.

CiCi said scornfully, "Tommy, they die chickens at the store. Mommy just made it crunchy in her big box."

Her parents burst into laughter at this pronouncement, which caused all the kids to melt into giggles.

Despite the minor bickering from the children, Sondra cherished this time when all those she loved most in the world were gathered together under one roof. Looking around at her family, she felt gratefulness well up inside her.

Even my frustration with that half-done project downstairs can't ruin what I've got going on here.

Later, after the dishes were done, stories read, prayers said, and the kids were tucked in to bed for the night, she and John sat in the family room, talking.

"Jonathon wants to have us over for that dinner since they ended up cancelling the Christmas gathering."

Jonathon Waters was one of John's coworkers at Trinity Bank. While John worked in Risk Management Services, Jonathon worked in the wealth management division. He and his wife, Gisele, held an annual Christmas bash for selected guests from both their workplaces—the bank where Jonathon worked and the advertising agency where Gisele's career had skyrocketed.

Sondra felt way out of her league with Jonathon's wife. Gisele was everything Sondra felt she wasn't: sophisticated, gorgeous, accomplished, and confident.

John knew Sondra felt awkward in social settings of people who occupied a much higher social sphere than her. The Waters fell into that category as they came from money, had no children, and brought in a dual income. They traveled frequently to Europe, and their primary interests were skiing and collecting wine and expensive art, none of which Sondra had any knowledge.

She looked so glum that John laughed.

"Honey, it's going to be fine. You told me that you liked Gisele."

"Oh, I do. She can be nice, certainly."

"But . . . ?"

"Oh, John. You should already know. I mean I spend my days answering questions like, 'Why do they call it stuffing if I can't stuff it up my nose?' or 'Can I write on the wall with my new crayons?' Women like Gisele live in a world apart from mine." Her brow was furrowed as she tried explaining. "I feel like such a simpleton around people like her," she finished lamely.

"But you're not. Stop being so hard on yourself."

"Have you forgotten last year's party?"

"Apparently, I have. What happened last year that was so bad?"

Sondra hated reminding him. It was embarrassing.

John prompted, "I'm waiting to hear what awful thing you had to endure."

Sondra cleared her throat. "Well, you remember when the women separated from the men, and you left me by myself?"

He shook his head and grunted. "Honey, I could hardly hang out with the women while all the men went to the other room."

"I know, John, but you don't understand. Most of Gisele's friends are single and dress fashionably. They carry handbags that cost more than my weekly grocery budget and get their hair done at expensive salons. I don't fit in," she whined.

John folded his hands under his chin. "So what happened?"

"Well, Gisele always has all those funny sayings. You know how much she travels. She finished telling an amusing story—because you know, all *her* stories are amusing—and then she said, 'C'est la vie.' So I did."

John looked confused. "You did what?"

Feeling sheepish, Sondra blushed.

Great, I can feel humiliated all over again.

"I said, 'lavi.' I didn't know what she meant. So when she said, 'Say lavi,' I thought we were supposed to say 'lavi,' and something would happen."

She couldn't bring herself to tell him the most painful part: that Gisele had mocked her when she thought she was out of earshot. Sondra overheard her laughing with one of her coworkers. "Have you ever seen such a rube? Anyone quite so naive?"

John broke out laughing, startling Sondra from her thoughts.

"Oh, honey. I can't believe you have spent a whole year, hanging on to this sort of silly thing. So you didn't understand her stupid French phrase. Who cares? You are a smart, beautiful, accomplished, caring woman. I love you, and you need to start seeing yourself in a healthier way."

She sighed. "All right, fine. We can go to their dinner party. What else is going on at work?"

Sondra settled back with the warm cup of tea in her hands, ready to listen.

"I had to intervene today when Hal was harassing Matt, who is, as you know, one of our hardest-working employees." John ran his hand through his hair. "I really don't know how Hal has made it as far as he has in his career. He's poisoning our work environment. I've tried persuading him to be more professional. He said, 'Real leaders show their strength in how firmly they are able to address those around them.' Then he turned on me with a few choice words."

Sondra shook her head. Hal was a new addition to the office, but not a positive one. His presence was causing trouble as massive as his ego.

She struggled with the unfairness of the situation, expressing crossly, "Does Tom know what's going on? He'd better do something soon, or they'll lose everyone worth anything."

"Calm down, honey. It's not easy, but God's in control, right?"

"Yeah. But I wish God would bring out His justice more quickly."

John laughed. "Let's not pull out the rocks to stone him just yet, okay? How about we pray that God softens his heart instead?"

Sondra felt chastened. "I love you and hate seeing you mistreated."

"I love you too, honey. And I appreciate your wanting to defend me. But something will change. It has to."

The conversation drifted other directions. They discussed Regan and what the next steps should be in helping heal her friendship with Kayla.

"I can't imagine their fight will last long, but what if it does?" Sondra mused aloud. "Kayla's birthday is coming up, and it would be nice if this were settled before then."

"I'm sure it's a normal spat kids sometimes have. These things have a way of working themselves out." He ran a hand through his hair, yawning. "I bet the girls are friendly again before the end of the week."

"I hope you're right."

"Did you get a chance to write today?"

She caught herself in the middle of another sigh and stopped. "Well, a little, I guess. It's hard to get it all done, you know? This morning after Regan went off to school, I watched Susan's daughter while she had a doctor's appointment and did laundry. I made lunch and got Cecilia off to school, put TJ and Mylah down for a nap, replied to some e-mails, and talked with Sophia and Mom for a while. Before I knew it, CiCi and Regan came home, and the other two were awake. They actually played nicely downstairs, but I still didn't get in more than thirty minutes before it was time to start dinner."

She sipped some tea. "I don't know, John. I really want this more than almost anything—except being a mom, of course," she hastily added. "But sometimes it feels selfish working on my book while I'm trying to live an actual life here and now. The kids are only this age once. I don't want their memories of these years to be ones that I sat hunched over my computer screen while they entertained themselves. And yet . . ."

A couple of tears slipped out of her eyes. *Why can't I just be content with what I have? I love my family, so why does there seem to be this continual tension at work in my life?*

"Come here." He patted the couch next to him.

She moved from her chair, sinking into the warm leather, and John reached for Sondra's cup, putting it on the nearby table. He took her hand and began stroking the delicate skin of her fingers. She leaned against him, listening. "Honey, I know you struggle with this, but I don't know exactly what the answer is. Do you think . . ." he hesitated, and she picked up on it.

"What? You want to say something. Go ahead."

"Okay. Well, don't get mad, but do you think"—he shifted on the couch, wrapping her in his arms—"that it's possible that you want this thing more than God wants you to have it? I think you are amazing. But maybe this goal that you have chased all these years, well, maybe now isn't the time to follow this exact dream. It hurts to see you hurting. Maybe it's time for you to put it aside. Not forever, but for a while."

Tears sprang to her eyes. "Why would you say that? Don't you think I am capable?"

"That's not fair, Sondra. You know I think you are a great writer."

She tried to push back at the temptation to feel betrayed. John had been nothing but supportive.

He took her hand. "Listen, maybe instead of tackling such an enormous goal when you have so little free time, you could write something simpler—like children's stories."

She nodded slowly. "Hmm. That could be a good idea." She sat forward, with growing excitement. "Maybe you're right. It would still give me an outlet, and maybe I could build up my name in the writing industry. Then when all the kids are in school, I'll have more time to spend on my book."

"Exactly," John said. "Our kids love your stories. I'm sure other kids would too."

Musing over the possibilities, she fell back against his chest, ready to start exploring this new venture. The dream that she had chased since she was a young girl might elude her for a bit longer, but maybe her approach had been wrong. Creative thoughts were already flooding her mind.

"That's actually a great idea, honey. I have a couple already written, with some ideas for more. I'll start working on them tomorrow."

She snuggled closer to her husband, grateful for his sensibility. They talked a bit more before heading to bed, and Sondra slept deeply, better than she had in a while.

Submission   Title: *Mommy, I Think I Hear*

Page 1   "Mommy, I think I hear"
Page 2   "A big, scary lion roaring!"

Page 3   "That's not a lion roaring, that's just your daddy snoring
           Now good night, I love you ~ Go to sleep."

Page 4   "Mommy, I think I hear"
Page 5   "A huge, gigantic, enormous bear"
Page 6   "Counting rabbits in my chair!"

Page 7   "You don't hear a bear at all. That's the clock ticking on your
           wall.
           Now good night, I love you ~ Go to sleep."

Page 8   "Mommy, I think I hear"
Page 9   "A purple, flying monkey screeching nursery rhymes at
           me!"

Page 10   "A train whistle is what you hear,
           Blowing far away my dear.
           Now good night, I love you ~ Go to sleep."

Page 11   "Mommy, I think I hear"
Page 12   "A wild blue horse with a big stripe of red,
           Running in circles around my bed!"

Page 13   "The noise that you hear is not near your bed.
           It's an airplane outside,
           Way up overhead
           Now good night, I love you ~ Go to sleep."

Page 14   "Mommy! Come see what is under my bed!
           It makes all sorts of noise and has more than one head!
           It's five different colors, it snores and it flies

It has long rabbit ears and big brown bear eyes!
It roars like a lion and counts up to eight—
Oh please come and see!
Before it's too late!"

Page 15   "Darling, there's not a thing under your bed
You're dreaming of things that are all in your head;
See? Nothing's there—but your white, stuffed toy sheep
Now good night, I love you - Go to sleep!"

The next morning, soon after Regan had run out the door for the bus, the phone rang.

"Hello?"

"Sondra? Hi, it's Carolyn."

Maternal indignation filled Sondra's heart. Carolyn was Kayla's mom, as well as one of Sondra's friends though they hadn't really connected in a couple of months. They'd seen each other at school and, occasionally, at church, but Carolyn hadn't been to their small group in weeks. Sondra could guess what prompted her early morning call.

She tried unsuccessfully to infuse some warmth into her voice. "Hey, Carolyn. How have you been?"

"Good, well, pretty good anyway. I guess you probably know why I'm calling?"

"Yeah, I know the girls haven't been getting along lately. It's really tearing Regan apart."

"Same with Kayla. That's why I thought maybe you and I could talk and see if we can get to the bottom of it."

Sondra bit her lower lip. She had wanted to do that very thing but had told Regan she wouldn't.

Sondra, this isn't a contest to see who is a better mom. It doesn't matter who started the conversation, just be glad it has begun.

Still, Sondra wondered if Carolyn even knew about Kayla's actions that had first caused the rift. She was very distant lately, like her mind was in another world.

I wouldn't be surprised if she's not even fully aware of the situation.

"Well, do you want to come over, and we can have coffee and talk about it? We haven't had a visit ourselves in quite a while." The question hung in the air between them. Sondra sensed Carolyn weighing her answer and waited.

"You know, I appreciate that, I really do. But I've got some things I need to get done this morning. I hoped we could just clear the air over the phone about what Regan did to Kayla, and maybe we can get past this whole mess."

What Regan has done to Kayla? Surely, Carolyn knows that most of the blame is Kayla's?

"What do you mean?" She hadn't meant to answer back quite so sharply, but there her response sat with all its prickles, too late to pull back and soften.

"When Regan told her she couldn't be friends with the new girl at school, it really upset Kayla. I told her she didn't need to always listen to Regan, especially when she was giving her bad advice."

Sondra tried to ignore her self-righteous tone. She felt her face flush as she took in what Carolyn was telling her.

That does not sound like Regan. Something sounds wrong, but how do I word it so it doesn't come out as blindly defending my daughter?

"To be honest, Carolyn, that's not quite the same story I heard. Regan told me that she asked Kayla if they could invite Zoe to join them last weekend when they were going roller-skating but that Kayla said no. According to Regan, *Kayla* didn't want Zoe along. Since the two of them had been planning the outing for a couple of weeks, Regan said okay. She felt bad for Zoe but didn't want Kayla to think she was—I don't know—maybe *replacing* her would be the right word."

Sondra took a breath and went on. "In fact, Regan said that Kayla was mad at her for even bringing up the idea, but this past Monday at school she saw Kayla sitting with Zoe. When she tried to join them, Kayla said there wasn't room at their table even though a chair was open. I'm not sure why Kayla told you this other version, but clearly, one of them isn't being totally truthful."

Sondra said this last part in a rush as she could hear Carolyn's impatient intake of breath as she prepared to interrupt her.

"Listen, Sondra, naturally, you believe Regan. You're her mom, so of course, it is hard to admit when our kids do wrong things. But Regan has lied to you, and you need to know the truth." Carolyn's voice had a tough edge to it, something Sondra hadn't heard before.

I wonder if Regan's been completely honest with me?

The women coolly agreed to each talk with their respective daughters again to try to get the facts of the matter. Their good-byes were tense and left a pang in Sondra's stomach. Now, Regan's problem with her friend really had become hers as well as she considered how much her relationship with Carolyn was going to be affected till this thing either blew over or was resolved.

This time, she didn't even try to stop the sigh from escaping her lips.

* * *

Rene stopped over for a quick visit. She and Patrick had been struggling lately. One of her biggest complaints about him was how close-mouthed he could be after nine years of marriage.

"I think he might be having an affair, Sondra."

"No, Rene. You must be wrong. Patrick loves you. He's just quiet. He's always been quiet."

Her best friend shook her head. "There's something more going on. I can tell."

Sondra knew Rene was lonely. She and Patrick had waited to have kids. When they finally decided to try, they found it wasn't going to be quite as simple as that. Several expensive tests drained what little money they had put aside and left them with a lot of unanswered questions. The whole thing had put a strain on their marriage.

"He never listens to me when we are together. He watches TV or goes to hang with the guys at the gym. I don't mind him taking time with his friends, but I feel like he's lost interest in me. In us."

Sondra prayed, wanting the right words. "Rene, why don't you surprise Patrick with a little trip, something that would be spontaneous and fun? Stephan and Grace went to a bed-and-breakfast in Wisconsin. She said it was wonderful and not very expensive either. I could get the name of it if you'd like?"

A firm look came into Rene's eyes. She wasn't a redhead for nothing. "You're right, Sondra. We just need to reignite the passion a little. Get me the name of that place. Patrick isn't going to know what hit him."

Sondra laughed at her friend's determination. "I will get it for you."

"What about you? What have you been up to lately?"

"Oh, this and that. You know—mostly stuff with the kids."

"Yeah. Anything new in your writing?"

Sondra nodded. "Actually, yes. I've decided to start writing children's stories. I'm hoping to submit several to a children's publisher. Who knows? Maybe I can, at least, get my foot in the door with some writing, then later when I've got more time, I can keep working on my novel."

Rene smiled. "I'm so proud of you, Sondra."

Sondra snorted. "Why on earth? I haven't done anything."

"That isn't true. You have so." Her friend was adamant. "You're actually moving forward, doing something. At least you're trying. Lots of people sit and dream, but you're working toward a goal." She looked down. "I think it's great."

"Thanks, Rene. That means a lot to me." She smiled. "Do you want a bite of something? I made banana bread this morning."

"Thanks, but no. I've got to get going. Thanks for letting me stop over."

"Of course. You know I love seeing you anytime."

They hugged, and Rene left. Sondra tidied the room and then headed to the kitchen to make a snack for the kids and clean up.

* * *

Sondra set the family room up with the special pillow for CiCi to sit against while they would go through her baby book. It was a tradition on each child's birthday.

CiCi was hopping up and down with excitement. Tommy was grinning from ear to ear, ready to hear the stories, since he knew his name was mentioned in her big book nearly as often as hers. Little Mylah sat in her favorite seat in the house: her baby swing, happily gnawing the edges of her rubber teething toy.

Gathered together on the cozy couch, Sondra opened to the first page, showing the picture of a tree with various names written on the branches.

"This is Julia and James Spencer—that's your grandma and grandpa, my mom and dad. Tommy, your middle name is after my dad."

Tommy pointed excitedly to the next picture. "Hey, there's Papa and Grammy!"

Sondra smiled. "Yep, those are Daddy's mom and dad." She paused. "In fact, Grammy Margaret and Papa Timothy are taking you three older kids somewhere fun next week."

Tommy gave a whoop. "To the zoo again? Maybe we'll ride one of those camels, CiCi!" Sondra laughed. They loved all their grandparents, but Papa Timothy was extra special with the fun places he took them and his candy and quarter treats.

"No, honey. Not the zoo this time, it's too cold out. It's somewhere fun, but I told Grammy I would keep it a secret. You'll just have to wait and see. Now, do you know who this is?"

Sondra worked at making sure their kids understood that they came from a line of people who had gone before them. They spent some time looking at more of the pictures of family near and far.

Tucked into each child's baby book was a copy of a song, sung with an Irish lilt, that she remembered her own grandmother singing when she was young. She had taught the simple words and tune to her own little ones, wanting the legacy to continue. They sang it together; Tommy pushed at CiCi to squeeze closer to see though he couldn't read yet.

> God says of Jesus, "I am pleased with You.
> On You my fullest favor rests.
> You obey everything I ask of You,
> My Son, my Son, my Son."
>
> Jesus looks tenderly at me, His child,
> And says, "Through Me you can do all things.
> Will you step out in faith and follow Me?
> My child, my child, my child."
>
> Will you come join me in this race for Him?
> Following Jesus all the way.
> Wholehearted devotion will reap the words:
> "Well done, my son, well done.
> Well done, my daughter, well done.
> Well done, my child, well done."

They leaned in closer as she flipped to some pages with pictures, laughing at funny ones, like recent ones of Tommy and CiCi together in a laundry basket in the living room, hats on their heads, pretending to be voyagers in the ocean, using TJ's plastic golf club and a wooden yardstick as their oars.

Pictures of CiCi as a baby brought nostalgia to Sondra. She glanced over at Mylah chortling in her swing, glad that the season of having a baby around wasn't over yet.

She sighed and turned back to the book. "Do you remember this day?" She pointed to a picture of CiCi covered in chocolate and whipped cream. "You were almost two years old. I baked the cakes and left them to cool on the counter while I went to change Tommy's diaper. I told you I'd be right back, and then we would decorate them together. Somehow, you dragged your bench over to the counter. By the time I came back into the kitchen, this was how you looked."

Sondra chuckled at the memory.

I sure wasn't pleased at the time, but looking back, it's funny now.

She was glad she'd thought to take a picture before cleaning up the huge mess. The younger CiCi's winsome smile gazed back at them through the chocolate-and-cream covering. Sondra snuggled her girl close.

There were many other pictures: Daddy leading the kids in singing the birthday song at last year's party, her cousin James busting open the piñata with candy raining down on everyone—everyday activities like splashing in the pool, playing at the park, several at the local pumpkin patch with friends, she and Regan sitting on a little pony at the fair, ordinary yet unique moments of her young life captured through colorful pictures.

Sondra read some of the entries out loud. "CiCi continues to delight everyone who meets her. She has a beautiful smile ready for all. I love what Aunt Sophia said about her—it cracks me up: 'CiCi reminds me of a Japanese tourist—always smiling so hugely like they're so happy to be in America!'

"CiCi loves to sing songs, kiss Mylah, play house and dollies. She says the funniest things like, 'I'm CiCi, nice ta meetcha!' and 'I a poleeseman!'"

Sondra turned to a page where she had recorded CiCi's first words and random phrases she had said the first several years of her life.

"At eight months old, she started saying, 'Dadadada.'"

"Hey, that's as old as Mylah!" Tommy noted.

They all looked over at Mylah, with some hopeful expectation that she might suddenly produce the sound herself. She giggled and started kicking her legs. Sondra cranked the crank to make the swing start up again.

Noticing the time, Sondra gave her darling daughter a kiss and a hug. "Oh, Cecilia. You are our precious girl and a gift to us from the very hand of God."

CiCi beamed and asked, "When do I get to open my presents?"

TJ piped up, "And what about the cake and ice cream?"

Sondra smiled. "We'll have all those things tonight. After Regan and Daddy are home."

The two kids ran to the kitchen to help make a quick lunch before CiCi took the bus to afternoon kindergarten. Tommy watched his mom slicing apples and said, "I know how God makes apples, Mama."

Curious about his answer, she smiled at him and asked, "Really? Tell me."

"Well, the garderner puts seeds in the dirt, then God gives the sunshine and the rain and the love to grow it!"

She laughed delightedly and wrote down his explanation, including his mispronunciation of the word *gardener* on a nearby slip of paper to tuck into his book later.

The kids gobbled their lunch. CiCi put her coat on, grabbed her book bag, gave her mom a kiss, and ran to the bus waiting at the foot of the driveway. A rush of cold air burst in through the open door when she left.

Sondra called out, "Good-bye, Cecilia. I love you," while Tommy waved and turned from the window sadly. He already missed his older sister.

Sondra cleaned up the kitchen while Tommy ran to the bathroom. She pulled out some Play-Doh and the box of tools and put them on the table.

Tommy walked back into the kitchen, hiccupping loudly, and his mother laughed. "Thomas James, where on earth did you pick up those hiccups?"

He looked forlornly at her as another big hiccup escaped his mouth. "While I was sitting on my potty-chair."

A bolt of creativity hit Sondra as she dashed for the pad of paper on the counter and started scribbling down lines as they cascaded into her brain, unbidden.

Tommy stood watching her, asking her repeatedly, "Whatcha doing, Mommy?" till she finally responded.

"I got another idea for a children's story, Tommy—and you were my inspiration!"

He giggled in between the loud hiccups as she tickled his tummy and snuggled him close, ruffling his blond hair. She gave him a spoonful of peanut butter to stop his hiccups.

"Will you play with my Play-Doh with me, Mommy?"

"Of course, I will, Mr. Martin."

He laughed again. "I'm not Mr. Martin. That's Daddy!"

Sondra smiled, enjoying his sweet innocence and cheerful heart. She sat down with him to squish the Play-Doh between their fingers, rolling it out, making pretend food and dinosaurs and whales. TJ peppered her with questions: "Mommy, how does blue stick to Play-Doh?" and "What sound do whales make?"

Sondra enjoyed her curious little boy, but there were times she couldn't help tuning his constant chatter out. Her mind drifted.

As he reached for more of the Play-Doh, Tommy knocked over his cup of milk that was sitting too close to the edge. Milk dripped everywhere, mixing with Play-Doh that had fallen. Because he wanted to be like the big kids, he had balked at her putting a spill-proof lid on the cup. Panic struck his face, and he looked worriedly at his mom.

"Tommy," she scolded, "you weren't being careful. Now do you see why I have asked you to keep a lid on your cup?" Frustrated, she surveyed the mess. As she reprimanded him, she saw tears well up in his eyes.

She sighed and said more softly, "Tommy, I'm sorry for yelling. We all make mistakes. It's not the end of the world. Help me clean it up lickety-split, okay?"

He nodded, relieved, and ran for the kitchen cloth, bringing it back to help her sop up the mess.

She prayed in her heart, *Thank you, Lord, for helping me handle that in a way that is more honoring to You and less frightening for my son. I'm learning.*

She had become keenly aware of her tendency to snap at her kids when Mylah was still a newborn. After one long exhausting day, Regan had slammed the door when she got home, waking the infant and starting her crying.

Sondra, at the end of her rope with the demands of a new baby and the seemingly endless care of her growing family, had lashed out at her daughter with an intensity that had frightened the children and shamed her. Even as she vented, she knew it was wrong. But she had persisted anyway, only stopping when she saw the big tears streaming down her daughter's cheeks.

Thoroughly disgusted with herself, she had run into her bedroom and threw herself down on her bed, sobbing. The kids tiptoed in one at a time, whispering, "What's wrong with Mommy? Doesn't she like us anymore?" Hearing their discussion, she had sat up on her bed and beckoned her children to come to her.

Regan had crept over to her, crawling into her mom's waiting arms, CiCi and TJ following.

"Kids, I'm so sorry. Please, won't you forgive me? I never should have yelled at you like that, Regan. Mommy was absolutely wrong for getting so angry at you."

Her children each wrapped their little arms around her and hugged her. "I love you, Mama. I'm sorry I slammed the door. I should have been more careful."

"Sweetheart, it's all right. I need to learn to control my temper. See? Mommies have things to learn too."

Sondra had looked into her sweet daughter's eyes and seen total forgiveness and love.

Hugging them close, Sondra had cried, praying out loud, "Lord, please help me. I get so tired. I just can't do this on my own. I don't want to yell at my children. God, help me."

Little Tommy didn't know exactly what all the crying was about, but he totally wanted to be in on the hugging and making up.

It had taught Sondra a valuable lesson. She really was working on becoming more patient. Over the past months, with God's help, she was learning self-control and seeing some success as she kept cultivating a heart of reading her Bible and praying about the areas she struggled in.

As they played with the Play-Doh, they talked and sang songs, enjoying the time together before Tommy's nap. He fought back a yawn, and Sondra chuckled, noticing the lengths he went to, trying to hide his weariness from her.

"Come on, buddy. We have time to sneak in one book before your nap if you help me clean up this mess quickly."

Together they stuffed the Play-Doh back into the containers, tossed the tools back in the bucket, and wiped down the table. He ran for the whale book, tucking it under his arm, and marched down the hall to his room, with Sondra following.

His mom tucked him under his blanket and opened the book, reading it the way he liked, with all kinds of sounds and special effects. He yawned again, his eyes drifting shut despite his best efforts. Sondra gave him a kiss, and he was fast asleep, dreaming of whales and birthday presents waiting to be opened.

Then while nursing Mylah, she browsed through their baby books further on her own, alternately chuckling and tearing up as she meandered through the pages and pictures, so thankful for each of the precious kids God had given her and John.

* * *

"Regan? Honey, we need to talk."

Tommy and the baby were still napping, and CiCi was playing quietly in her room after her busy afternoon at school. Regan put her book bag down and sat next to her mom on the couch. The same sad look was on her face; clearly, she and Kayla hadn't worked things out yet.

"Mrs. Carpenter called me today. She wanted to talk about the situation between you two girls, only her version was a little different from yours." Sondra scrutinized her daughter's face as she shared the next part. "She said it was Kayla's idea to become friendly with Zoe and that you'd tried to stop her."

This news was greeted with a cry of indignation. "Mom, that's not true! I was the one who wanted to invite Zoe to join us. Kayla was mad and said that if I was really her friend, I wouldn't try to look for other friends."

The hurt in her daughter's voice rang true to Sondra's ears, but how would she be able to convince Carolyn of that?

She hugged Regan. "I believe you."

The little girl's face crumpled under the weight of the false accusation and broken friendship.

Lord, please give me words to encourage her.

Sondra turned her daughter's face to look into her eyes. "You know, this week I was reading in the Bible about Joseph. Do you remember what happened to him?"

Regan nodded. "Yes. His older brothers sold him into slavery."

"That's right. But you know, I noticed something when I read it again." She grabbed her Bible lying on the table nearby and flipped open to Genesis and read, "As Joseph's brothers sat down to eat their meal, they looked up and saw a caravan of Ishmaelites coming from Gilead. Their camels were loaded with spices, balm, and myrrh, and they were on their way to take them down to Egypt. Judah said to his brothers, 'What will we gain if we kill our brother and cover up his blood? Come, let's sell him to the Ishmaelites and not lay our hands on him. After all, he is our brother, our own flesh and blood.' His brothers agreed."

Sondra stopped, and Regan looked searchingly at her. "Okay, so what? I don't understand what you are telling me."

"So the Bible tells us he spent almost twenty years away from his family and all he had known. He had been wronged over and over again, and it had all started with his own brothers' betrayal. In our minds, that could amount to a fairly legitimate reason for some revenge, right?"

Regan nodded. "Yeah, that would be really terrible."

Her mother nodded. "I agree. But this is what popped out at me this week when I read it. Flip over to chapter 43, and read right here."

She handed Regan her Bible and pointed to verse 11. Regan read out loud, "Then their father, Israel, said to them, 'If it must be, then do this: Put some of the best products of the land in your bags, and take them down to the man as a gift—a little balm and a little honey, some spices and myrrh.'"

Regan stopped reading.

Sondra asked, "Do you know which is the strongest of our five senses?"

Regan shook her head.

Sondra said, "Our sense of smell. It is so powerful that when we smell something, it can take us right back to whatever memory we associate with that smell in an instant. Now remember, what were the traders who bought Joseph from his brothers, carrying to Egypt all those years earlier?"

Regan slowly replied, "Spices, balm, and myrrh."

"Exactly. Now, here come the brothers all these years later, searching for food in Egypt, not knowing that the man in charge of the supply is their own brother Joseph, but trying to get on his good side by bringing those exact gifts: spices and balm and myrrh—very fragrant items."

She closed her Bible. "I would imagine that on his whole long trek to Egypt, Joseph smelled those smells the entire way. Now, his brothers bring him the very things that remind him of their cruelty: being sold, the frightening journey as a young man, not knowing what would happen to him, day after day smelling the spicy, aromatic smells of those items the traders were bringing to Egypt—it would all come rushing back in one gigantic wave to him. It makes what he says later all the more incredible. The enormous way he not only forgives them but also invites them to come share in the blessing of his new prominence and position."

She tilted Regan's head back to look into her eyes. "Whatever is happening with Kayla, we need to forgive her and pray for her. She has done some hurtful things. But let's trust God to work out the details even if right now it looks scary and we're not sure what's going on, okay?"

Regan nodded, and Sondra prayed, "We don't know what to do, Lord, but we wait on You to show us how we should handle this. And please help Regan as she is sad with the hurt of this broken friendship. Help us forgive Kayla, Lord, like Joseph did his brothers. In Jesus's name, we pray. Amen."

Sondra opened her eyes and saw the tears escape Regan's eyes.

Hoping to distract her with some happier news, she brightly offered, "Hey, you know what? Daddy and I are looking for a vacation spot to go with your aunts and uncles and cousins for spring break. You only have a few more weeks left of school, and then break is here. That will be a lot of fun, won't it?"

Her imploring look brought a little smile to the corner of Regan's mouth.

"Yes, that will be fun."

The kids always enjoyed spending time with their cousins, and the distraction would be good for her hurting girl.

Sondra relaxed a bit, knowing it would all work out okay given a little time. "That's my girl." She gave her a gentle squeeze. "Now let's go get dinner started before your brother and the baby wake up from their naps.

While dinner simmered on the stove, Regan helped her hang some colorful balloons and streamers to celebrate CiCi's birthday. Sondra was grateful for the time they had together, enjoying the simple shared activity, glad for the comfort of family.

* * *

"Where on Earth did you pick up those Hiccups?
From a shell in the sand?
From an old soup can?

From inside this shoe?
From a lion at the zoo?

On a walk in the park?
From a bright singing lark?

Did you get them from a hairy bear?
Or while sitting on the potty-chair?

Did you find them while digging for buried treasure?
Or while walking in soft fields of heather?

Hmmm . . . How to get rid of them now?
Can you pass them off to a slow-moving cow?

Could you climb a mountain and throw them down?
Or give them to a circus clown?

What if you hide them under a rock?
Or shove them into an old dirty sock?

Hiccups like to sneak up and getcha
So I am pretty willing to betcha

The only way to lose them is to
Have someone sneak up and say:
BOO!!!!

Did it work?"

The next day Susan Cleveland came for a visit. Sondra hoped to get some ideas from her as they settled in with their steaming cups.

"We are trying to find a fun place to take the kids over spring break, and I can't come up with anything."

"How about camping? We love it."

Sondra eyed her up skeptically. "Seriously? You camp?"

"Sure, why not?"

Sondra persisted, "Outdoors?"

Susan snickered. "Of course, outdoors. Why is it so hard to believe I go camping?"

"Well, I'm just trying to picture it. You don't strike me as the camping type, that's all."

Susan laughed at her mystified look. "It's not so bad, Sondra."

"Well, help me out here because I really do want to understand. Why would anyone give up comfortable living quarters to drive far from home with a porta-potty and a tent? Was your electricity turned off? Did your basement flood? Your roof cave in? Because aside from those sorts of calamities, I don't understand why anyone would want to leave their nice house and go sit under a tree. The reasoning escapes me."

Susan laughed. "Well, I didn't say camping is for everyone, but David and I enjoy hiking and canoeing and making our meals over a campfire. We haven't camped in a few years, but when we did, we always loved it. We used to use tents but had a few fiascos with them blowing down in heavy winds and rain. I fully admit *that* was not fun." She sipped her coffee. "Then we rented campers. That's totally the way to go. All the amenities of home, but out in the woods with nature."

She grinned over the rim of her cup at the skeptical look on Sondra's face. "It doesn't look like I've persuaded you."

"Well, no, it's not that. It could be fun, I guess, if you knew what you were doing. But I don't. And neither does John. Besides, we're going with Stephen and Sophia's families too, so I have to pick something that everyone would like to do."

"What about going to one of those indoor water parks?"

Sondra sat up excitedly. "Of course! Why didn't I think of that? That's a wonderful idea. Thanks, Susan."

"No problem." She took another sip of coffee. "So how have things been going?"

"Oh, pretty good. I decided to put aside my book for now and focus instead on writing some children's stories and poems. I'm actually feeling pretty hopeful. I mean, my own kids like my stories. Maybe someone else will too." She took a bite of cookie.

"That's great, Sondra. Something will pop for you. You just have to keep trying. And remember, no one can do it all."

Sondra grimaced. "But I don't even want to do it all. I just want to be able to do this one thing. Is being good at one thing asking too much? I mean after all, you have your volunteer work at the adoption clinic, counseling women." She went on. "You've said how satisfying that work has been for you."

Susan nodded. "Yes, that's true. But you aren't good at only one thing. You're a great wife and mom—and friend too," she added.

Sondra hated that it sounded like she was fishing for compliments whenever they went down this path, but she persisted, trying to make Susan understand.

"I don't think I do anything special. So many people are making huge differences in the world. All I seem to do is cook and clean and try to keep the kids from destroying the place."

Susan shook her head. "That's not true. You're involved in shaping the lives of your children. That's huge, Sondra."

Sondra nodded. "I am grateful I get to stay home with my kids, I really am." She hesitated. "I just would like to have one skill, though, that is outside of being a mom and wife. I love writing, but I don't seem to be able to make any headway with it."

Susan took a deep breath. "Well, you never know what's around the corner, right? I mean God could have this great opportunity waiting out there for you. Don't give up. But meanwhile, don't think that what you're doing isn't important. For sure, it's more important in the long run than getting published." She took a big gulp of her coffee then asked, "How are things going with Regan and Kayla?"

Sondra sighed. "Not great. I don't understand it. Carolyn has been so distant lately. And Regan really misses Kayla. They did everything together, and now Kayla and Zoe have become best friends and are leaving Regan out. I hate not being able to do anything about it, but John says I shouldn't interfere, it will all work itself out." She shook her head doubtfully. "I don't know. Something doesn't feel right."

Tommy came running into the room. "Mommy, CiCi took my golf club and won't give it back." The little boy was in tears.

Sondra looked at Susan, shaking her head. "I'll be right back."

In the playroom, CiCi sat with TJ's club. When she saw their mom, she said, "I knew you would tattle. Tommy, you are a big tattletale. I bet you didn't tell Mommy that you hit me with your golf club, did you?"

"That was an attsadent, CiCi. I dint mean to. And I said I was sorry."

"Okay, kids, that's enough. CiCi, please give him back his golf club. And Tommy, no more swinging it so you hit other people, understand me?" TJ nodded.

CiCi grudgingly handed the club back to her brother. Sometimes the two of them were best buds, but other times, they were like oil and water.

She made her way back into the kitchen, where Susan waited. Mylah started to fuss, and Sondra picked her up, swaying to soothe her.

She confided, "Boy, there sure are days when I feel overworked and underpaid."

Susan wryly asked, "You get paid?"

Sondra snorted. "You know what I mean. I'm serious. There are days when I feel like I didn't know what I was getting myself into, having four children. Of course, I love them all very much. And it's not like I would trade any one of them for anything. I just wish it wasn't so hard sometimes. Putting up with the spats and dealing with the petty little things kids fight over. I sometimes wonder what it would be like to have a nanny or, maybe, only one child. That would be easier, I bet." She glanced at her friend's face. "Oh, Susan. I'm sorry. That was stupid of me. I wasn't thinking. Please forgive me."

Susan gave a little laugh. "It's okay, Sondra. Don't worry about it. You're right. Having one is a lot easier, I'm sure."

Sondra moved uncomfortably, feeling badly.

Sondra, you idiot . . . how could you say something so insensitive?

"Well, while we're on it, how have you been doing?"

Susan took a deep breath, letting it out slowly. "It's gotten a lot better." She hesitated a moment. "You know, though, that wasn't the first baby David and I have lost."

Her friend had suffered a tragic miscarriage seven months earlier, but Sondra hadn't been aware of any others. She shook her head. "No, I didn't know."

"Before we had Meghan, I had three miscarriages."

Sondra sucked in her breath. *Three?*

"The doctors told us we would never have a viable pregnancy. David and I had given up all hope." Her voice softened with remembering. "I told God, 'All right, God. I'm done fighting and begging. If You don't want me to have a baby, somehow help me learn to be content.'"

Sondra sat down, quietly listening. "Oh, Susan, I'm so sorry. I never knew that. We've been friends for what? Like four years? And I never knew that about you."

Susan gave a little shrug. "Not many people know. I guess I didn't want their pity. I'm grateful, Sondra. God didn't have to give me a cotton-pickin' thing. But He chose to give us Meghan. When I carried her to term, I remember telling Him, 'Lord, if You let me have this baby, You won't hear a word of complaint come from my lips about her.'" She smiled. "I can't say I've always kept that promise, but I've tried. Whatever trials come along with the blessing of having her are fine with me. I'm just so grateful she is in my life."

Knowing the unreasonable expectations she sometimes put on her children, Sondra felt guilty.

They're not even bad kids. Sure, they have their moments. But who doesn't?

After Susan had gone, Sondra tidied up the kitchen, washed the dishes, and thought again about the gift that children truly were. Tears began falling into the sink as she confessed her shortcomings to God. "Please help me, Lord. My kids are developing and learning and need my guidance, not my angry impatience. I know there'll still be times when I fail at this, Lord. Please help me do better."

Tommy and CiCi came in the kitchen for their lunches, and Sondra gave them extra long hugs and big kisses as she served up their plates. "I love you so much, my darlings. I am so grateful to be your mommy, do you know that?" She snuggled each of them as they giggled.

"Mommy, not so tight," TJ protested. "You're squishing me."

She laughed and gave her boy a quick last squeeze. After their lunch, she jumped up to help CiCi put her coat on and gave her a kiss good-bye.

Cecilia called over her shoulder, "I love you too, Mommy. Bye, Tommy!" And she was gone, swallowed up through the door of the big yellow bus.

Sondra rocked Mylah, enjoying her sweet baby smell. She carefully placed her in her crib, then read some books with Tommy. After he was napping, she stole away to her computer for a while to work on some of her stories, writing till Regan and CiCi got home.

* * *

That weekend at church, Pastor Paul's message was a calling for his flock to boldly share the truth of Christ's salvation with those around them. "We don't know how much time we have to make an impact on this world. Let's be working while it's light and sharing the Good News with those who need to hear it."

The worship team led them in a new song, and Sondra sang the words:

> Give me boldness to share Your truth
> Courage to walk where You're leading
> Wisdom to know Your heart
> And a love that comes from You.

Give me strength for endurance to run
Hope for the moments of heartache
Mercy to forgive offense
And a love that comes from You.

Give me valleys to build up my trust
Mountains for faith to grow deeper
And at the end of this journey we're on
May we enter our heavenly home.

Sondra prayed, "Lord, please help me be better at this. I want to share my faith with others. Please help me be bolder for You." She wasn't sure how God might answer it, but she wanted to be praying bigger prayers to be used by God for His glory.

* * *

Over the next several weeks, Sondra noticed that she never seemed to encounter Carolyn. She didn't know what to say to her anyway, so for now, it was probably best to let things lie.

Besides, any extra moments she had lately were spent writing children's stories. Carefully worded cover letters had accompanied her submissions as she sent them to a few different publishing houses. Now she waited with barely controlled excitement.

Saturday, the night of Jonathon and Gisele Waters' dinner party, arrived. Timothy and Margaret came to stay with the children. They would use the guest room and spend the night. Driving to the Waters' palatial home, Sondra reminded John not to leave her side needlessly.

"Honey, I wish you felt less intimidated."

"Trust me, I do too."

Arriving, they entered the spectacular hall. "It's all so lovely," Sondra marveled.

"Thank you." Gisele confided, "I shop every chance I get. Jonathon knows it keeps me occupied so I don't start asking for children."

Behind his wife, Jonathon rolled his eyes, giving Sondra a tolerant smile while shaking his head.

Sondra smiled uncertainly at them both, unsure how to respond.

They entered the lavishly designed living room, where other guests sat or stood in clusters. The heady scent of sandalwood and strains of Mozart hung in the air. Introductions and greetings were made with those standing nearest the door. She and John looked for familiar faces to greet, here and there, stopping to say hello. These moments afforded Sondra the chance to take in her surroundings.

Everything is so lovely, just magnificent.

As they strolled around, passing by clusters of people, they caught parts of conversations: "My favorite is the one that says, 'Real people, not actors'—my first husband was an actor, trust me, he was real enough, the jerk . . ." John led Sondra by the elbow, farther into the living room, overhearing more snippets of animated discussions: "Don't you know that Chicago boasts the best theater houses in the country—better than New York or LA?"

Weaving past strikingly dressed women, Sondra looked down at her own dress, wishing she had invested in something more stylish. John led her past a final cluster of people: "Imported—but here's the crucial thing to remember . . ."

On the other side of the crowds, they made their way toward a large table filled with tall stacks of small white plates and appetizers of every imaginable sort. Behind her, Sondra heard a loud burst of laughter, followed by the sounds of tinkling glass as a group of people clinked their glasses merrily in a drinking game.

Sondra barely recognized most of the exotic foods. Trained waitstaff circulated, offering trays of hors d'oeuvres and heaping platters of fresh shrimp. A huge selection of wines and specialty drinks graced an entire corner of one room. No matter where Sondra walked, she saw amazing arrangements of foods and beverages placed all around. One extravagant display was a tiered collection of slate boards that held imported crackers and specialty cheeses like Brie and Gouda and Camembert, mingled with succulent clusters of red-and-green grapes on the vine and other fruits that she didn't recognize.

Sondra helped herself, remarking to John, "Wow. Can you believe this? My cheese platters are like a can of Cheez Whiz and a block of Velveeta on a plastic tray."

He grinned. "You should try looping some clusters of grapes around the can of cheese next time." He popped a crisp grape into his mouth and started crunching. "Seriously, it could make the difference."

She snorted with laughter.

Gisele floated over to them, her gorgeous gown hugging her tiny frame beautifully. "I hope you are finding everything you'd like?"

"Oh yes. It's all so lovely, Gisele. Thank you."

"Good. Have you tried the crudités?"

Instantly Sondra's insides clenched. *Oh, good heavens, what might that be?*

"Um, I'm not sure. Where would I find those?"

Gisele's smile turned slightly mocking as she indicated the fresh vegetables on Sondra's plate. "Right here."

"Oh. Well, yes, they're delicious, thank you."

Sondra was relieved to hear the formal announcement given from the dining-room doors: "Dinner is served." Their hostess produced a bright smile and led the way into the dining hall.

Seated at the massive table, they were served the courses by uniformed butlers, hired for the occasion. Kobe steaks—paired with scrumptious twice-baked, loaded potatoes—followed the first course of lobster bisque.

Sondra sat back, admiring her surroundings in slight awe.

John leaned over to her, whispering, "This sure beats the macaroni and cheese the kids ate tonight, hey?"

She knew he was teasing, but protested in an injured tone, "Hey—I made applesauce and steamed carrots too."

He lifted his hands in mock surrender. "Oh well, *that* changes things. You're right—how can this paltry feast compare to that?" She jabbed him in the ribs.

From the far end of the long table, Gisele asked, "So, Sondra, tell us what you do. Do you work outside your home?"

Sondra flushed. She hated that question—especially since Gisele already knew the answer.

She cleared her throat, wishing that for this moment, she did something more universally admired. "Um, no. I stay home with our children."

To her left, John's coworker Denise Carter said, "You have three kids, right?"

Sondra smiled at her. "Four. Our youngest, Mylah, is nine months old."

Penelope Mason, three seats down on her right, leaned back in her chair with a loud sigh. "Bless your heart. I'd have lost my mind if I'd had to stay home with our two children."

Her husband, Derek, murmured loudly, "And the children would have probably lost theirs as well, my dear."

Penelope chuckled good-naturedly. "No doubt, Derek, no doubt." She dabbed at her mouth with the expensive linen cloth and reached for her wineglass, lifting it in a mock toast. "To nannies everywhere. God's best invention yet." Most at the table laughed appreciatively.

Sondra squirmed, hoping the inquisition was done. John leaned forward, mentioning proudly, "It's a tough job. I'm grateful Sondra invests in our kids the way she does." She was pleased to hear her husband's praise, but horrified at what came out of his mouth next as he continued. "But she doesn't just take care of the kids. She's also been working on her writing and has submitted some stories to a publisher."

Sondra could have belted him right where she sat.

How could he do this to me? All eyes turned to her.

"Why, that's wonderful, Sondra. You must tell us about it." Her hostess's lovely face held an expectant smile as she waited for Sondra to expand upon John's announcement.

Sondra felt stymied.

What am I supposed to say? That I wrote a bunch of silly children's stories?

"Oh. Well, John shouldn't have said anything yet. I mean, I submitted a few short manuscripts. I don't even know if they'll get published or anything like that."

Her hasty reply, meant to push attention away from her and onto anyone else, failed to do so as Gisele gushed, "I think that is marvelous. Let me know if you want the name of a good publishing house. My mother is good friends with a wonderful publisher based in New York City. I would be happy to connect you with him. They publish all genres of writing—fiction and nonfiction."

Sondra knew it was time to come clean. "Well, I appreciate that very much, Gisele. I really do. But these are children's books. I don't think your mom's friend probably accepts children's manuscripts."

Sondra thought she could almost see the other woman's admiration plummet.

"Oh, how charming. I'm afraid you're right. I don't believe he accepts children's manuscripts. But I'm sure your little stories will be accepted wherever you've submitted them." With raised eyebrows, she tilted her wineglass toward her, offering the words, "Best of luck with that."

They were served steaming hot coffees with a selection of liqueurs and crème brûlée for dessert.

Gisele's husband, Jonathon, turned to one of the other guests. "Ben, I understand you've made an extraordinary acquisition of a bottle of Château Cheval Blanc?"

Ben's wife, Liz, who worked with Gisele, laughed. "You could say that his wine collection is more demanding than a mistress." She patted her husband's arm good-naturedly. "Ben has spent more on the showcasing of that one bottle than he did acquiring all the rest of them combined."

The table of guests laughed, and Sondra slumped slightly in her chair.

John knows these interactions are already excruciating for me. Why would he purposely expose something so close to my heart for others to dissect and ridicule?

Later on the car ride home, her dismay spilled out. "I can't believe you shared something like that, John. It was embarrassing.

Did you see how unimpressed she was once she found out that I'm only writing some children's stories?"

He protested, "That's not true, Sondra. She didn't say anything to make you think that."

"Well, she didn't say anything *not* to make me think that either."

John shook his head. "That's ridiculous. What more did you want her to say? She wished you luck with getting them published."

Sondra sighed.

He doesn't get it, she thought as she looked out the window. *Why do I feel inadequate around people like Gisele?*

Suddenly, the thought occurred to her. What would Gisele feel like in Sondra's little world? Would she feel insecure, unable to handle the demands of children, and uncertain how to care for their needs? This hadn't crossed her mind before, and she mulled it over a few minutes.

Finally, she turned to John. "Honey, you're right. I shouldn't feel so insecure around Gisele. But can I ask that you, please, not tell people that I'm trying to get anything published? I'd rather share that I've succeeded than feel like you're bragging about me when I haven't done anything worthy yet."

John took her hand. "Sondra, you have to get over this idea that you haven't done anything worthy. I love your creativity. I think you are too hard on yourself. But if it makes you feel better, then fine, I won't say anything to anyone else about it."

Sondra looked at him gratefully.

I've got to work harder to come up with something truly magnificent. Then I can feel proud of myself, and John can tell anyone he wants about it.

She yawned. When they got home, everything was dark and quiet. Sondra gratefully crawled into her own bed, falling fast asleep.

* * *

After church the next morning, she told Rene about the embarrassment of the night before.

"I am surprised that John didn't know better." Rene understood the importance of timing.

"Oh well, maybe by next year's party, I will have something published," Sondra said hopefully. "How are things going with you and Patrick?"

The couple had gone on the surprise trip that Rene had arranged.

"Well, at first, I thought things had turned around. Patrick seemed to love the fact that I had worked out all the details behind his back, and the bed-and-breakfast was really fabulous." She hesitated. "But I am sensing that something is going on that he doesn't know how to tell me. Whenever I push him, he clams up. But it's starting to drive me crazy. I just want to know."

"Would it help if John talked to him?"

"I don't know," Rene said slowly. "On the one hand, Patrick might open up to John and share something with him that he can't with me for some reason."

Sondra saw Rene musing. "But wouldn't that be a good thing?"

"Well, yes, of course. But I'm also worried, Sondra." Her blue eyes clouded. "When I've asked him outright what's wrong, he gets—I don't know, not exactly angry with me, but something weird. That's what makes me think he's hiding something. If John asks him, and he gets mad at him . . ." She broke off.

"John doesn't have to let him know we've asked him to talk with him. I mean they *are* old friends. Can't they get together without Patrick becoming suspicious? Besides, John could actually use an evening out with him. He's been pulling such long days at work, and I know he would enjoy some time with him. Though I can't promise it will be this week. Remember, we're taking the kids to the water park in a few days. But after that he should have time to call him."

"Okay, maybe it would help. Thanks, Sondra."

The two women hugged, agreeing to talk again in a few days.

* * *

The next morning, Gisele Waters called her at home. "Hello, Sondra. My housekeeper found a stray scarf in the foyer closet, and I'm wondering if it might be yours from Saturday night?"

"Oh, um, no, I didn't wear one."

The other woman hesitated. Sondra wondered if the scarf had been a cover for the real reason she called. She ventured kindly, "I hope you can find out whom it belongs to."

Gisele said, "Yes, I'm sure I will." She paused and then asked, "Sondra, may I ask you a question?"

What could beautiful, accomplished Gisele want to ask me?

She pushed back at the self-doubt, replying, "Of course."

Gisele let out a slow breath on the other end of the line. "Do you know all the women in John's department at the bank? I'm trying to find out if there's someone who works in the Risk Management Department named Tamara." She paused and then said in an uncustomary moment of confidence, "I found a note from her to Jonathon that I don't think I was meant to see."

Sondra wanted to handle this with tact. She could imagine the pain of a discovered betrayal.

"I'm sorry, Gisele. I don't know anyone by that name. I can ask John when he gets home, if you'd like me to?"

Gisele was quick to shoot that idea down. "No, that's fine. I don't want to start a rumor at the bank or anything." She gave a light laugh. "I'm sure it's nothing. I probably am reading into it."

Sondra wasn't sure what to say. She thought about the message Pastor Paul had given the week before on boldness with her faith but didn't know how to do it without sounding awkward. She was surprised at what she blurted out: "I don't know if you would ever want to come with me, but our church has a women's Bible study that meets on Wednesday nights, if you'd like to join me?"

Gisele gave a small laugh. "Thanks, Sondra, but I've tried the whole God thing. It's not for me. I couldn't get past all the ruthlessness."

"What do you mean?"

"Well, right after college I took a sabbatical. I spent my whole summer reading the Bible. I had a grandmother I really loved." Softness crept into her voice as she shared, "Before she died, I promised her that I would at least try to read it from cover to cover before making any judgments. You might be surprised, but I read the entire thing, both the Old and New Testaments, well, almost all of it, and the thing that struck me the most was how harsh the God of the Bible was. I remember one story where King David was bringing the Ark of the Covenant back, and the animals that were pulling the cart stumbled. One of the men assigned to safeguard the Ark reached out to keep it from falling, and God killed him right there. I mean, if God can see into hearts, couldn't He see that the guy was just trying to stop the Ark from falling? I don't want to serve such a mean God."

Sondra knew the account Gisele referred to. She answered carefully, "I know it can be hard for us to understand sometimes. But the Bible makes it clear that we cannot even grasp how perfectly holy and righteous God is. To our ears, it sounds unfair and extreme. But those people had been given explicit instructions on how to handle the Ark. So God wasn't being unfair in punishing them when they knowingly ignored His commands."

Gisele answered, "Well, when you say it like that, I guess it makes sense. But that wasn't the only thing. There were other inconsistencies and contradictions I found that made me decide Christianity wasn't for me."

Sondra didn't want to keep pressing her, but couldn't let such a statement go unchallenged. "If you have time, I sure would love to hear them. I would hate for something that could be simple confusion about cultural differences in Bible times be a barrier to your understanding how much God loves you."

She could sense Gisele's hesitation, then heard her say, "Well, I don't get how the Bible says God hardens someone's heart, like that Egyptian pharaoh, but then punishes him for having a hard heart. That sure doesn't seem fair. And I didn't like how God had the earth swallow up all the innocent little children along with their parents when He judged the man who challenged the guy in charge—I think it was Moses. I mean, why not just punish the bad guy? There were other examples like that too, but I can't think of them all right now. Anyway, I couldn't get past all the hate. I mean, why was God so angry all the time?"

Sondra was overwhelmed with the rush of examples Gisele gave.

"Wow, Gisele, I really appreciate your questions. Like I said, it can be so hard for us living now to understand what it was like in that time, but I guess that is where we have to trust that God is loving and knows the truth even when we, in our human weakness, don't understand. I guess the biggest thing I would say is that our sin is exactly why Jesus came. We are all sinners and do things we shouldn't. God demands that sin must be paid for, but we couldn't possibly pay. That's why He sent His own Son, Jesus, into the world—to pay the price we couldn't."

Gisele laughed. "You sound just like my grandma. That's exactly what she would always say to me too."

"Well, she was right. Clearly, she loved you and wanted you to know the truth that Jesus loves you and died for you."

Gisele drew in her breath. "I don't want to sound rude, Sondra, really. But I've heard it all before. I made a deal with my grandma that I would read the Bible, and I did. I mean, I think that there were definitely parts that made more sense than others and parts that, I admit, really made me think. I've got time though. I don't want to rush into anything. I appreciate your invitation. If I change my mind, I'll let you know."

Sondra didn't want to push her away by pressuring her further. "Okay, that's fair enough. John and I enjoyed our evening Saturday night. Thank you again for having us."

"You're welcome. Jonathon and I were glad you could both make it."

Gisele's cool reserve was back in place, and they hung up with polite parting words, but Sondra's spirit was unsettled.

* * *

Rene called her excitedly the next day. "Hey! I was flipping through my *Women's Digest* and came across a writing contest. They're looking for poems about kids. Listen: 'All submissions should capture the essence of children, whether in a whimsical, funny, or tender way. Limit one per contestant.' You totally should do this, Sondra."

"I don't know, Rene. I guess I could maybe try."

"Of course, you should. You've got all kinds of poems you could use." Rene's confidence bolstered Sondra's own.

"All right. Can you send me the details? Thanks, Rene. I appreciate your encouragement."

She hung up the phone, wondering what piece she should submit. She kept folders of starter ideas and lines that popped into her mind periodically that she recorded, hoping to use them later. Inside she found a snippet of paper in her handwriting: "Piano keys. Don't forget."

She sighed. "Not only have I forgotten, I can't even imagine what I was referring to."

She looked up as Regan came in her room, dragging her book bag behind her. "Hi, sweetheart, I didn't hear you come in." She noticed Regan's face. "What's wrong?"

Regan's eyes spilled out tears. Sondra put her papers down and hurried over to her side, pulling her close. "Regan? Tell me what happened."

The little girl gulped. "Kayla had her birthday party. And she didn't invite me."

"No—oh, honey, are you sure? How do you know?"

Regan sniffled. "Because Tina Schneider told me so." She looked sad. "Tina said that all the girls from our class were there. Except me." She leaned into her mother's arms, sobbing.

Sondra was devastated for her daughter and furious with Kayla. "Oh, my darling girl, I'm so sorry. I cannot believe she did this to you." She tilted Regan's head back, cupping her chin, and looked in her eyes. "Do you want me to call Mrs. Carpenter? You girls have been best friends for years, it doesn't make sense why she's acting so mean all of a sudden."

Regan shook her head. "No, Mama. Please don't. I don't know either. But I don't want her to make fun of me for tattling about it." She plucked a tissue from the box on her mom's bed table and wiped her eyes and blew her nose. "She seems—I don't know, different somehow." Regan's expression looked confused. "It's almost like she never was my friend."

Regan wasn't the only one baffled by the behavior of Kayla and her mother.

But to hurt a poor little girl like this, what kind of person does that?

Sondra couldn't help the sudden feeling of anger that welled up in her heart.

God, please help me know what to do. I know I'm not supposed to hate anyone, but this is really painful, Lord.

She sighed, giving her daughter a long snuggle and saying a silent prayer over her head as she stroked her daughter's hair.

Regan looked at the bed, which was covered in papers. "What are you doing?"

"Oh, I'm going through my writings, looking for something to submit to a contest. You want to help me?"

Sondra let her look in her folder. Regan read one of Sondra's poems titled "Use Me" that she had written a few years earlier, before TJ and Mylah were born. Sondra cringed, hearing it read out loud, embarrassed at its simplicity.

But her daughter tilted her head and commented, "I like that one."

Sondra smiled at her. "Thanks, sweetie." She held a sheet, scanning the words. "What about this one for the contest?"

Regan read the title out loud, "Mommy, Tell Me Again." She read it and nodded. "I like this one the best."

"Great. Then this is the one." Sondra set the paper aside.

Regan watched her mom, head bent, leafing through the piles of papers, pulling some sheets out and discarding others. "Mom?"

"Yes, honey?"

"What do you think I'll be when I grow up?"

Sondra looked up, pausing in her work. She smiled at her daughter and sat next to her on the bed. "Oh, sweetheart, I can imagine you'll be anything you have a dream to be. God has given you so many wonderful gifts, Regan. I think the harder part won't be deciding what to be, but what not to be. Sometimes making those choices means turning our backs on lesser things so we can do the better things. And that's not always easy to discern. Does that make sense?"

"Yes, I think so . . . but how will I know what *not* to do compared to what I *should* do?"

Sondra laughed. "Well, for starters, God has given you two parents who love you and will help you make some of those decisions when the time comes. Second, as you continue to grow, God will make some of your interests become stronger and some, less important to you. And lastly, you don't have to worry about the future. God's already there, and He just wants you to live in the moment today."

She patted her daughter's arm, pulled her in for a hug, and nestled her cheek in her hair, loving the smell of her and being able to hold her.

"I love you, Mom."

"Oh, Regan, I love you too, my girl."

"Mommy, tell me again—
How does blue stick to paint?
Why can't I say, "ain't?"
And how do birds fly?
And how high is the sky?

Tell me again—
Why do clowns dress so funny?
How does "sticky" stick to honey?
Why does twirling make me dizzy?
How do slippers become frizzy?

Where does the moon go during the day?
How does the wind chase the clouds away?
How fast can I run from there to here and
Why won't this penny fit in my ear?

Tell me again—
Why do mice like cheese?
Can lions sneeze?
Who planted trees?
How does water freeze?

How do our faces make frowns and smiles?
Why do trucks push dirt up in big piles?
And Mommy, Why do you look so tired?
And what does it mean when you say that I'm "wired?"

Mommy, tell me again—why must I nap?
Instead, can't I just climb up in your lap?
I love to snuggle ~ I'll just close my eyes
While you think of the answers to all of my, "Why's."

That night, after cleaning up the dinner dishes, Sondra and John sat down in the family room. The kids, not far behind, were soon clamoring for a story. Sondra asked, "How about the brownie one?"

"Yes!" they all chorused and jumped onto the couches to cozy up with their parents, pulling soft blankets from the basket.

"Well, one time my grandma stayed with us overnight while our parents were gone. Our mother had left the instructions that we were to eat the pan of breakfast bars she had made for our breakfast the next morning. They were full of whole grains and very dry. Our grandma didn't know what the breakfast bars looked like. She also didn't know that before she had left, our mom had made a pan of thick moist chocolate brownies with gooey chocolate frosting for a gathering she was having the next day when she would come home. Those were tightly covered and tucked into the back of the fridge."

The kids started giggling, anticipating the moment of their mother's disobedience.

"When morning came, your uncle Stephan secretly switched the pans around, and he and I convinced our grandma that the brownies Mom had made were the breakfast bars."

Regan leaned against her dad, smiling, while CiCi and TJ were giggling.

Sondra's eyes twinkled with the memory. "It was a pretty fabulous breakfast, for sure. But when our mother got home later that day and went to find the brownies to serve to her friends, she could only find the tray of the dry breakfast bars that we had buried in the refrigerator. She had to serve them to her guests since we had polished off the delectable brownies, and she didn't have time to make more. Boy, did we get in trouble after her friends had gone."

Everyone laughed, enjoying the retelling of a favorite.

CiCi turned to John. "Daddy, you tell us a story now." They all agreed, begging.

John protested, "Sondra, you're the storyteller."

"Come on, John. You've got some terrific stories to share."

He looked at the kids' hopeful faces, thinking furiously. "Well, did I ever tell you about the time that one of my friends and I pulled a trick on the meanest man in our neighborhood?"

Eyes round as plates, the kids shook their heads.

"He was a grumpy old man whom we used to call Mr. Pickle because he was so sour all the time. One day, my friend Rudy and I were playing in the neighborhood ditches. When it would rain, the ditches would fill with water and made a wonderful place to throw rocks and stir in acorns and leaves and things—somewhat like making a soup out of outdoor ingredients."

"That sounds yucky. Did you eat it?" CiCi asked.

"No. It was just for fun, not eating. Anyway, Mr. Pickle came outside and started yelling at us even though we hadn't done anything wrong. We left, but decided that we would show him. We made a package out of dog poop and newspaper, carefully rolling it. Then we snuck back to Mr. Pickle's house and put the package right in front of his door."

The kids were captivated, and even Sondra waited with interest to hear what they had done next.

John looked at their faces, paused dramatically, and said, "We took some matches and set the paper on fire, rang the doorbell, and ran, hiding behind nearby bushes to watch. Mr. Pickle came to the door and began stomping out the small fire, getting his shoes covered in the mushy mess. He was so mad he started yelling and cursing." He chuckled with the memory.

Tommy let out a little breath of wonder at his father doing such a naughty thing.

John smiled. "Well, don't think it was worth it. It wasn't. Rudy and I both got a whooping for it. And even if he hadn't ever found out who had done it, God knew."

"Like God knew when CiCi hit me today, right, Daddy?"

"I did not, TJ," Cecilia protested.

Sondra sighed. "Tommy, that is over. Remember? When we forgive someone, we move on."

The little boy sat in his daddy's strong arms and curled in toward his chest, hiding his face in the protective shelter of his arms.

CiCi took the opportunity to remind her brother, "Yeah, TJ, you're s'posed to move on and not keep telling me about it."

Sondra said in a weary voice, "And, Cecilia, do not lie. You know you hit Tommy. Yes, I know you already told him you were sorry. It's over and done. But you shouldn't tell a lie either, honey."

John said, "All right, everyone. It's time for bed. Your mom and I are tired, and it's past time for you all to hit the hay."

Sondra carried Mylah into her nursery. It was a welcoming room made up in colors of gentle pink tones mixed with creamy white. Tan stuffed teddy bears sat on a high shelf overlooking the white crib below. A soft pink throw was draped over the arm of the beige rocker. Beneath that sat a white woven rug. The whole room was dreamy and soft.

Sondra settled her baby into the crib with a short prayer over her and moved into Tommy's room. Stuffed animals were piled on his bed, and his orange golf club, a reachable distance away.

He lay on his bed, outlining the cars printed on his blue comforter with his finger. Sondra picked up a stray model car from the floor, placing it back on one of the white shelves that were attached low on the wall, where Tommy could reach them. Large blue block letters above his bed announced that this boyish room belonged to TJ. He leaned over to turn on his night-light, giving the corner a soft glow, as his mom came over and sat on his bed. She tucked the blanket under his chin, making him giggle, and leaned in to give him a kiss and a hug. He clutched his favorite stuffed animal, a gray whale he'd named Murray. "Mommy, can I tell you something?"

She nodded, wondering what was on his mind.

His wide eyes looked up at her, and she stroked his eyebrow with her finger. "Of course, honey, what's up?"

"Well, I have a secret to tell you."

"Okay, what?"

His lip turned down in a frown. "You 'member how you said you want to wash my golf club?"

She nodded. "Yes, it is filthy with gunk from you dragging it all over. I have to scrub it up."

He smiled proudly at her. "I did by my own self."

"You did?" She was surprised. "What did you use to clean it with, sweetheart?"

"Soap."

"Really?" She was impressed that he actually thought to use soap. "Well, Tommy, that's great. But why is that a secret? Wouldn't you want me to know that you did such a good thing all on your own?"

The little boy licked his bottom lip before answering, "Well, I used soap, but I also used something 'cause I didn't know what else to use."

Suddenly, Sondra stiffened. "Tommy, what did you use?"

He made some funny movements with his mouth and craned his neck to look at his beloved golf club.

"Tommy. I am waiting to hear."

"It's okay, Mommy. It's made to clean things." He beamed at her. "I used a toothbrush."

"Eww, Tommy, are you telling me you used your toothbrush to clean the gunk out of your golf club? Yuck!"

He shook his head and put his hands up to assure her. "No, no, I didn't."

She nodded thankfully. "Oh, good. Because that would be really gross."

"Yes." The little boy nodded his agreement. "So I used CiCi's."

* * *

"Did you brush your teeth, sweetheart?"

Cecilia hesitated then guiltily confessed, "No."

Sondra hid her relief. "Hop up, little girl, and take this. It's time for a new toothbrush for you."

CiCi jumped out of bed, took it, and ran to the hallway bathroom.

Sondra called into the hall, "And toss your old one into the cleaning bucket under the sink."

"Okay," CiCi answered back.

Sondra looked around the room at the bold purple wall, remembering back to the day they'd decorated it. Sondra had tried to persuade her daughter toward a softer shade of lavender, but the little girl was adamant.

"You said I could pick any color I want, and I want that." Her finger had pointed decidedly at the third block from the bottom on the color strip, and Sondra had stifled a sigh. They had compromised, putting the deep color on only one of the walls and painting the other walls a delicate gray. Loads of creamy white accents in the quilts and shelving, lamps, and decorations kept the room from looking like a dark cave.

Running back into her room and leaping onto her bed, Cecilia crawled under her blanket and confided to her mom while she tucked her in, "I love hearing stories from you and Daddy."

Sondra smiled at her little girl and stroked her soft cheek. "I know, honey. I always liked hearing stories from my parents too. But one of the best things about stories is that you can learn lessons from them without getting into trouble yourself. Remember that little saying I taught you kids?" She recited it, "Today is tomorrow's yesterday. Let's live it in such a way that we won't regret the choices we made when tomorrow becomes today." She smiled at her little girl, stroking her arm. "No one is perfect, and we all sin. But we should do our best to follow and obey Jesus, right?"

CiCi nodded sleepily, her eyes heavy. Her mom tucked the blankets warmly under her chin and gave her one last kiss, and she was fast asleep.

* * *

Regan was reading in bed, waiting for her mom to come in. For her colors, Regan had chosen a cheerful buttercup yellow with accents of spring green and white. John hung white picket fencing against the walls right above the white baseboards, then Regan and her mom had tucked bunches of colorful silk flowers above and around the pickets. The feel was that of an English garden—a fresh, floral delight. In the corner, a colorful butterfly wind chime hung from the ceiling. When the window was opened, the breeze caused them to flutter their wings, making a lovely chiming sound. The finishing touch was the ceiling, painted a gentle sky blue, with some puffy white clouds painted on.

Sondra gave a little knock on the door, walking in. "Hey, honey. Did you get your teeth brushed?"

Regan nodded and put her book on her bed table.

Sondra sat on her bed, smoothing the soft yellow-and-white cover. "Is there anything special you'd like us to pray about?"

Regan sat quietly for a minute before saying, "Well, I don't know if we should pray for Kayla to become my friend anymore, Mom. I think God has forgotten about me."

"Oh, sweetheart, no. That isn't true. God doesn't forget about anyone. He loves you, Regan. Just because Kayla isn't being the kind of friend she should be, it does not mean God doesn't love you. You need to keep trusting Him." She stroked her daughter's hair. "I know it's not always easy. People in life will disappoint and fail us, but God never does."

"Okay, Mom. We can keep praying that she wants to be my friend again."

Sondra bowed her head. "O dear heavenly Father, how grateful we are we can come to You with big things and little things. Please help Regan as she misses her friend, and help Kayla want to do right. We don't understand why this has happened, Lord. But we want to trust You through it. Please help us. In Jesus's name, we pray. Amen."

The sad, sober look on her daughter's face brought a pang of hurt to Sondra's heart as she realized again the depth of loneliness she was feeling. She hugged and kissed Regan tenderly, wishing there were something she could do to ease her pain.

Standing outside of Regan's room, she prayed again, more urgently.

"O God, please, won't You heal her hurt? I don't know what to do. Why does she have to suffer through this? She's just a little girl. Please help us, Lord."

* * *

"John?"

"Mm-hmm?"

"Is there someone named Tamara who works at the bank?"

Distractedly, he answered, "No, I don't think so."

She snuggled closer and mulled over Gisele's quandary, eventually drifting to sleep.

* * *

The next day Sondra was racing around, trying to get the house tidied and their bags all packed for their spring-break trip with the family. It seemed every time she would place something in one of the canvas bags, someone else would take it out. Finally, she turned to John, exasperated.

"John, help me!"

"Okay, well, for starters, stop cleaning the house. It will all be here when we get back," he supplied matter-of-factly.

Sondra bit back a nasty retort, instead explaining, "I realize that. But I like coming home to a clean house and not having to face a huge mess on our return. It's not like I'm repainting the woodwork or something—I'm zipping the vacuum around and trying to empty the sink of dirty dishes."

He didn't look convinced.

She wailed, "They'll stink by the time we get home. Can't you please help me?"

He tilted his head in resignation. "Fine. What do you want me to do?"

"Oh, honey," she moaned, "anything. I'm beat. I still have my own things to pack, and I keep remembering stuff for the kids—swim diapers and splash toys from the bathtub for Mylah. The girls need their suits and extra underclothing. Oh—and don't forget their pajamas. And their dolls for the car ride and a stack of books—especially Tommy's whale book. Oh—and he's probably already got it, but let's not forget his orange golf club."

He ran his hand through his hair. "Good grief. Anything else?"

"No, that should do it. No, wait. I also need to bring the directions to the park. I wrote them down and left them near the phone in the kitchen. Oh—and the snacks—don't forget the snacks. The whole bag is packed and ready to go on the counter."

He was halfway out the door when she called, "And, John,"—he turned back toward her—"I love you."

He smiled tiredly at her. "I love you too, honey."

She tried to encourage him. "This will be a great vacation. Just wait. The getting ready is harder than I thought it would be, but it will all be worth it."

He called the kids to come help and went to gather the various things to help her finish her frantic packing.

* * *

After about an hour drive for each family, they arrived. The water park boasted a labyrinth of slides and tunnels, surrounded by a lazy river, complete with water basketball courts and hot tubs and topped off with a massive wooden structure of buckets to dump water on victims below. Built-in water pistols and spray hoses on every tier could soak everyone within range in seconds. It was a water lover's indoor paradise, and the kids were bouncing with excitement.

The ladies were to be off duty the first day while the men herded the children around the myriad of waterways. The second day would be the moms' turns to jump into gear while their husbands took it easy.

The three women luxuriated in their time off. They swapped stories of their children's lives and commiserated about various challenges they faced, enjoying the chance to relax and do nothing.

Occasionally, one of their sopping wet children would shout, "Watch me!" The moms would all dutifully stare toward the hole that the child would pop out from, like the cork from a bottle of champagne, and the delighted child would scamper off to find a new adventure.

In one such show, CiCi emerged and landed in the pool. She stood up, yanked on the seat of her swimsuit from last year that she had outgrown, and wandered off, looking for another tunnel. Sondra groaned inwardly. *Of course, you forgot to buy her a new swimming suit. What kind of a mom are you?*

Then she berated herself for her self-criticism. *Enough. It's not the end of the world. She is enjoying herself. Let it go.*

Sondra's mind whisked back a couple of years, and she sighed. "I need to stop turning around. Every time I do, the kids all seem to grow older."

"No kidding, isn't that the truth?" They agreed.

Seven-year-old Brady came running over to his mom. "Mom, it's not fair. Christopher is cheating." Christopher was the oldest of the kids. At age nine, it seemed he jollied in finding ways to torment his younger siblings.

"How is he cheating?" Grace wanted to know.

Full of indignation, Brady related his brother's offense, "He said to me, 'Supercalifragilisticexpialidocious—spell it.' But every time I start to say, 'S-u-p,' he cuts me off and says, 'Nope. Spell it,' and it's not fair!"

Grace sighed. "Go play, Brady. Hang out with your cousins, and ignore your brother."

"But, Mom . . ." he protested, vexed by his mother's tolerating the clear wrong being done to him by his bully brother.

"Brady, I mean it. I'm visiting with your aunts. Now either go and play, or you can sit on a chair here with us."

Brady looked at his mom with dissatisfaction. As he turned to head back to the pool, he saw his aunt Sondra give him a wink. "Hey, Brady, come here a second first."

He trotted to Sondra's side and leaned in when she indicated she wanted to whisper something in his ear. He straightened, a gigantic smile on his face, and ran off.

Grace looked at her. "What did you tell him?"

Sondra grinned. "I told him to find Christopher and say, 'I-t.'"

Sophia laughed, and Grace shook her head with a smile.

Sondra remembered well what it was like to have an older sibling who teased; she had a soft spot in her heart for the plight of all middle children.

Sondra settled back in her lounger, a cold drink at her fingertips, soaking in the fact that she could close her eyes without being found negligent for these few passing hours.

I could totally get used to this. This must be what it feels like to have a nanny.

Grace turned to them. "So remember how I told you guys about Candace?"

The sisters nodded.

"Well, things got worse." Grace shook her head sadly.

Sondra asked, "What happened this time?"

"A couple of weekends ago I was working in the church kitchen with a woman named Kristy. We were part of the team making meals for shut-ins. Kristy and I had been talking when Candace barged in and made her cry right there."

Sympathy welled up in Sondra. "How?"

"Candace asked us both if we were going to attend the next service. She was going to be on some panel that she felt was important for everyone to hear. I said yes, and Kristy said no. But before she could explain why not, Candace said, 'There's no excuse for not being in church. I don't care what you have going on, you should cancel it.' Then she flounced out of the room."

Grace rearranged herself in her chair to better see both her sisters-in-law.

"Before Candace came in, Kristy had shared with me that the man who had been like a father to her had died a few days earlier. The funeral was that afternoon. Kristy and her husband had come in to serve in the meal ministry since they had made the commitment, but then they had to leave. I had been in the middle of telling Kristy how sorry I was when Candace came blustering in with her usual know-it-all attitude."

Sondra sat up in her chair. "Did you tell anyone? Did Kristy do anything?"

"Sondra, who were we supposed to tell? Sometimes it just is what it is. You can't go around, fixing everybody. It doesn't work that way."

"Well, what is someone supposed to do? Just sit and take it?"

Sophia pointed out, "That is somewhat the idea behind turning the other cheek."

Sondra didn't like the idea of not fighting injustice and retorted to her sister, "Kristy can turn the other cheek. Grace, however, could say something on her behalf since she was there."

Grace shook her head. "Stephan is right. We're still pretty new ourselves. I don't know anybody to talk to about it. If Kristy is hurt enough, she and her husband can go to someone in charge. Or they can always leave the church and find a better one." She paused. "In fact, they already may have." Grace knit her eyebrows, trying to remember. "Now that I'm thinking about it, I haven't seen her since."

That upset Sondra even more. *Why do the innocent ones have to leave? Why can't the guilty be dealt with?*

She was about to say just that when Sophia jumped in. "Well, if she really wants to handle it the right way, Kristy needs to go talk with Candace. I'm not saying that's easy, but that's the right thing to do."

Grace shook her head. "You don't know Candace. She isn't what I would call approachable." Grace raised her eyebrow, amending. "On the other hand, I have seen her be kind to people too, but she's very opinionated and controlling, so she scares most people, including me," she admitted sheepishly.

Sophia interjected, telling Sondra, "She sounds like Mrs. Harrison from our old church, growing up. Remember her? She used to act like *she* owned the church and was letting the rest of us come be a part of it. No one did anything about her either."

Sondra nodded slowly. "I sure do remember Mrs. Harrison and not with fondness." The woman had been famous for making acidic remarks to people—mostly, the kids under her care.

Sophia said, "Like anywhere else, I bet every church has at least one person who is more aggressive than most people. I know our church does." She plucked at her towel. "Adam and I have talked about this. He thinks that assertive people who can get things done should be given more latitude. I'm not saying that I necessarily agree with that," she added hastily, seeing the indignant look on her sister's face. "But sometimes pushy people *are* super effective, you have to admit. The man I'm thinking of does have lots of great ideas, and since people are intimidated by him, he gets his way most of the time."

So that's an okay excuse for lack of gentleness or kindness? Where is effectiveness on the list of fruits of the Holy Spirit?

Sondra spoke up, "This is a real problem, you guys. How has it become so accepted that people who claim to be Christians are looking less like Christ and more like the world? Isn't it our job to point out the difference to them—or, at least, to the leaders?"

"Not necessarily," Sophia said. "In fact, unless you were the one who was offended, you really shouldn't be saying much anything about it."

"That's crazy, Sophia," Sondra disagreed. "Some people have a really hard time speaking up—especially against strong-willed people. What you're saying is for everyone to step aside and let bullies do whatever they want—even make others cry, like Candace did to Kristy?"

"No, that's not what I meant. I'm saying that, how is it any better for us to be talking about these women who aren't here—isn't that gossiping? How is that any better than what Candace did?"

Grace spoke up, "I don't think that's gossip."

Sophia said, "I think it's gossip to talk about someone if you're saying things you wouldn't say to their face."

"Well, I would have no trouble telling Candace what I think of how she treated Kristy, if she were here, trust me," Sondra stated firmly.

Grace shook her head. "I don't think so. She is pretty formidable. Besides, from the stories I've heard, Sondra, you are all bark and no bite."

Sophia laughed. "Yeah, I remember when you got all upset about that girl who bullied you for months. You cried, telling Mom and Dad how mean she was. They finally told you to go ahead and stick up for yourself, but the next time she challenged you, you still didn't stand up to her." Seeing her sister's face, Sophia held up her hand. "Trust me, I understand. She was a brute. I wouldn't do it either. But it's a lot easier to *say* you will stand up to nasty people than it is to actually *do* it."

That's true. My track record at fighting back is pretty abysmal.

"Besides," Sophia said, "I think that there are plenty of bigger issues to cope with than dealing with bullies. My friend Brenda's son has Down's syndrome. Her struggle is huge, but she never complains. It's really remarkable when you think of it."

Sondra replied, "Well, sure, there are bigger issues, Sophia." She paused. "But that doesn't take away from the fact that pain comes in all shapes and sizes. Maybe in light of what your friend Brenda deals with every day, Kristy's problem with Candace may seem small, but that doesn't mean it didn't hurt."

"Well, fine, I will give you that. I'm just saying that people have got to develop stronger backbones. There is a lot of junk in this world to face, and you've got to keep it in perspective."

Sondra lay back in her chair and rubbed her forehead, feeling a headache coming on. She yawned. Lolling in the humid warmth of the heated room, she dozed off for a short nap, waking to hear Sophia talking. Sondra stretched.

"Ah, you're finally up. You can thank me for stopping two of your kids from waking you," Grace informed her.

"Is everyone okay?"

"Oh, sure. It wasn't anything John couldn't handle. If you could fall asleep with all the screaming and splashing, I figured you must really need it."

Sondra yawned. She still felt tired. Or maybe this was her normal state, and she rarely got to indulge in doing anything like napping in the daytime.

"What's the plan for dinner?"

"The guys said we should order pizzas for everyone. They'll come eat and maybe swim for another hour before we head upstairs."

The pizzas hit the spot, everyone gobbling up the cheesy slices. The women cleaned the mess and gathered the scattered belongings while the men finished swimming with the kids.

Agreeing that they'd had their fill of water activities, they all went up to the three adjoined rooms. While the kids munched popcorn and watched a Disney movie in Stephan and Grace's room on one end, the adults gathered to visit in the middle room with the door open between them while the two babies, Mylah and Sadie, slept in Sophia and Adam's room with their door slightly ajar as well. It was the perfect arrangement to keep the noise from the youngest ones.

Hailey came in once to tattle, "Auntie Sondra, CiCi won't give me a turn in the spinning chair."

Grace scolded her youngest with a push back toward the other room, eliciting from her mouth the protest, "But she's not sharing, and that's not being a good example to me." The spoiled little girl pouted her lower lip; she was used to getting her way and would wait till she did.

Sondra got up and poked her head into the next room, telling Cecilia to give her cousin a turn.

Her daughter reluctantly vacated the coveted desk chair, and little Hailey climbed in, spinning contentedly.

Sighing, Sondra turned back to the adults, joining in their conversation.

After a couple of hours, she yawned. It was hard to keep her eyes open. John said, "I think it's time for us to hit the hay. You ladies are on duty tomorrow, and I can see that Sondra is pretty exhausted from her rough day, lying by the pool."

His eyes twinkled, and Sondra chuckled. She didn't know why she felt so tired all the time. In fact, she couldn't remember the last time she had felt deeply rested.

Adam stood, stretching. "You women are in for a real treat. Although I would say we took the worse shift of the two. At least the kids are sort of worn-out now."

"Aw, that was good of you, honey." Sophia stood and gave him a hug. Grace and Stephan stood and started cleaning up the empty cups and pushing chairs back into place.

All the kids were asleep, but not necessarily in the right places. Their parents voted to leave them all where they were and headed to their own beds.

* * *

The next morning, after breakfast, they hit the park for round two. Sondra didn't mind being on kid duty. Zipping down the tunnels of water, screaming at the turns and twists, was exhilarating.

At the end of the long day, she joined the older kids on the wildest ride, swirling and spinning, shrieking all the way down. When they tumbled into the massive pool at the bottom, they were all out of breath and waterlogged.

Once again, poolside pizzas were ordered and consumed by the hungry crowd. This time, the kids had had enough and asked to go to their rooms early, exhausted from two days in a row of water play. The younger kids fell asleep, and the older ones played some board games together while their parents all gathered in one of the rooms again to visit.

In the quickly passing hours, the couples discussed a wide variety of topics. The state of the nation was remarked on and analyzed. Their children's activities were discussed, and they shared how their extended families and aging parents were faring.

Sondra yawned, weary and content.

They finally broke up the party, carrying sleeping children to the various beds and retiring to their own rooms.

The next morning, after a delicious breakfast, they all prepared to go their own ways. The three women hugged, glad they could take the time for special moments together.

* * *

Within the stack of mail collected while they were gone was a special gold envelope addressed to Sondra. She ripped it open, noting the heavy paper the letter was typed on. She scanned the contents with growing excitement and called John at work, leaving a message in his voice mailbox.

He called her twenty minutes later. "Hey, what's up?"

"Do you have time to talk?"

"Sure. You sound chipper. What's going on?" he asked again.

"Well, honey, I have a question. I guess I could have waited till you got home, but I was so excited about this that I thought you wouldn't mind."

"Sure. Let's hear what's got you so excited. I love it already." He laughed.

"I was going through the mail, and something came from a publisher, directly mailed to me. I read it a few times, and I really would love to do this, John."

"Why don't you tell me about it?" He sounded curious.

"Okay. But please listen to the whole thing first, okay?" She unfolded the sheet of paper and read it out loud:

Dear Sondra Martin,

Congratulations. You have been specially selected to participate in a rare opportunity. Enclosed is an exclusive invitation for you to submit one of your written works to be included in a leather-bound, limited-edition collection. This honor is being extended only to writers who are serious about their craft, such as you. Act soon as the deadline is approaching for us to add your piece to the publication of this high-quality album. Imagine you and your loved one's delight at seeing your work in an heirloom collection that will bring you years of satisfaction and joy.

She stopped reading, listening to John's breathing on the other end of the line.

"Well?" she asked tentatively.

John laughed out loud. "Sondra, you've got to be kidding me. It's a vanity book."

She pouted a little. "How do you know? Only certain people received this. It's very exclusive."

John snorted. "Right, *exclusive* as in every house in the county, no doubt."

She protested, "I don't think so, John. You should see the high-quality paper this was printed on. It's truly an honor to be invited."

John snorted again. "Honey, I can't believe you're being taken in like this. How much is this so-called honor going to cost us?"

She paused then said quietly, "$59.95."

"What? You've got to be kidding? Sixty dollars to see your name printed in some book, alongside hundreds of other suckers? Oh, Sondra, I can't believe you can't see this for what it is. They probably got your name from that contest you entered and are sending letters out to everyone who submitted something."

Until he called her a sucker, she was ready to let it go, but now he was insulting her.

"That was mean, John. It's not some scam. It is a legitimate invitation to a legitimate book, but you wouldn't know because you're judging it before you can even see it."

He sighed, and she could picture him running his hand through his hair.

"Listen, honey. I love you. I know you've been disappointed about your writing. But I don't see how being included in something like this is going to make you feel like you've achieved anything. It's a huge publication with the work from lots of other striving writers crammed together in one big book."

She felt a tear form and said quietly, "I know, John. I guess I have been so desperate to get something done with my writing that I thought, maybe, if I had this one achievement, this one success, no matter how minor, it might jump-start my writing career, and someone out there could read what I wrote and find it worthy."

"That's what it comes to, isn't it, honey? For some reason that I can't understand, you don't feel worthy. You have struggled with this for years. I love you, Sondra. I think you are magnificent. You are a wonderful wife and a loving, fabulous mom. You have so many gifts and talents, but you can't seem to see them." He sighed again. "If this is going to finally give you some sense that your writing has gone somewhere, then fine. Sixty dollars is a small price to pay if this will finally put to rest this angst you've continually struggled with."

Sondra couldn't speak. His words had landed squarely on the truth. Tears clouded her eyes.

"Listen, I have to get back to work. But you can select one of your pieces and submit it to this, all right? In fact, I've changed my mind. I *want* to see you do this. I think this is important for you to do."

She felt terrible and wished she had never brought it up to him, never received the letter with all its promising glitz and glamour.

"Okay, Sondra?"

She sniffed. "Okay."

"Good. Do it today. When I get home, I want you to be able to tell me you got this done." He was about to ring off when he remembered something. "Oh, hey, and, Sondra?"

She put the phone back to her ear. "Yes?"

"You asked me the other night, and I don't know how you knew it, but there is a new woman working here at the bank. Her name is Tamara."

Her heart skipped a beat. "Oh? How old is she?"

John replied, "Maybe late twenties, early thirties. All the guys around here are talking about how pretty she is. But frankly, I don't see it. I only have eyes for you." He finished proudly.

She was touched, but troubled. "I love you, John."

"I love you too. I will see you tonight, honey."

They hung up, and Sondra bowed her head.

"Lord, please don't let there be anything going on between Jonathon and this woman Tamara. I pray You would draw Gisele and Jonathon to Yourself."

She sighed and fingered the letter she still held in her hand. Her initial joy at the idea of participating in the book had been sullied. Scrutiny by John's steadier heart had cast the whole thing in a less attractive light. Yet hope prevailed.

What if this is my big break? I need to at least try.

She sighed again and went to her file of writing to find the right piece to submit.

* * *

"I'm sorry I'm so late, honey. I had stuff to catch up on."

"It's okay, John. I understand." He'd missed dinner and the whole evening. She hoped it wasn't going to become a pattern.

"So did you send one of your writings to that publication?"

She nodded. "Yes. I decided to go with my Thanksgiving poem. It's a long one, so if I only get one shot at this, I thought, at least, it would make a noticeable presence."

"Good thinking."

"John, thank you for letting me do this."

He nodded and pulled her close, kissing her deeply. "I love you, Sondra. I want you to achieve your dreams too, you know. I wish you understood how valued you are even if nothing ever happens with your writing."

She leaned into his arms. "Just wait. You'll see. Maybe someone who is in publishing will see it and want to see other things I've written."

"Mm-hmm." He removed his tie and hung it in their closet.

Hating to add anything to his already overloaded schedule, she tentatively asked, "Honey, do you think you could talk with Patrick? You know, like, check in to see how things are going with him."

"Yeah, sure."

"No, I mean, like, soon."

John turned and looked suspiciously at her. "Why are you asking?"

"Well, honey, don't you want to see your old friend?" Sondra tried to act nonchalant.

"Sondra, don't play games with me. Just tell me what's going on. Did Rene ask you to ask me?"

"No, she didn't. Seriously. I was the one who said you wouldn't mind. I know you haven't had any time lately to get together with friends, and she shared that Patrick has seemed a bit distracted lately. So I thought the two of you could, you know, hang out and talk." She looked at him coaxingly.

He smiled, shaking his head. "That's fine. I can try to find out if something's going on. Not for a couple of weeks though. I've got so many late nights ahead."

"Thank you, darling." She put her arms around his neck, kissing him.

He hugged her back. "You and your feminine charms."

She laughed. "Let me show you a few of my other tricks."

"Hmm," he responded appreciatively.

John nuzzled her neck and closed their bedroom door.

True Thanks by Sondra Martin

Three old men were expounding on what it meant
to have a thankful heart.
They thundered and wrangled and quarreled as
each tried to express their part.

"No doubt my way is best," the first man did pomp-
ously say.
"I save it all up for one heaping, thanks-filled, glo-
rious day."
"I live my life throughout the year, remembering all
that I hold dear.
Then on that most important day I express my
thanks in a marvelous way.
I thank my Maker for my house and my cat, from
my old brown slippers to my Babe Ruth–signed bat,
I thank him for food, my car and my health, for
family and friends and all of my wealth.
For books and collections and ALL of my stuff."
Then the old man sat down in one breathless huff.

The second man vehemently shook his head. "That's
not good enough," he said.
"If you truly are thankful, there are things you must
DO.
There are rules to follow—let me tell them to you:
You must get down on a bended knee, fast for two
days and only drink tea,
Use a prayer blanket and a gilded-paged Bible, read
Old Testament verses—be humble and mild.
Keep silent and meditate, bask in your prayer—that
way they'll be sure to get there."
Knowingly, he nodded, pride on his face, gave a tri-
umphant smile and sat in his place.

Not to be outdone, the third man laughed, "You
didn't set the mood—you both are daft!
I dress my table with the finest linens and cloths,
delicately trimmed and freshly laundered, of course.
We use our Spode china, setting for eight, with a
freshly picked flower upon each plate.
Adorn each chair with bows of gold, and at each
plate an elegant napkin fold.
A calligraphy place card per setting is grand and is
always most fitting when done by hand.
Our goblets are gold rimmed and trimmed with a
bow, I use a stunning centerpiece arranged just so.
Amid such finery you can give your thanks best."
Finished, he proudly sat down with the rest.

Nearby a young woman was listening and the men
all turned to her,
"You've heard our thoughts—who do you think is
right?" They waited anxiously to hear.

"Before I answer that, if I can, I have a story," and
so she began.
"When I was little I dreamed of the life of being a
mother and a wife.
So, I grew up and met a wonderful man and all was
radiant as our marriage began.
He loved me and I loved him, and we had a baby
boy we named Tim.

I was abundantly happy, and I thanked God every day
For my precious husband and child, and each night
I'd pray:
'Your generous hand of blessing on my life has been
richly poured—
My heart is full—my faith is strong—my deepest
thanks to You, Oh Lord!'"

"Then one day while I was cleaning our lovely, happy home
My phone rang and in one instant, all that I had was gone.
A car wreck took my husband, and it took my baby's life
In one nightmare of a moment, I was no longer a mother or wife.

My heart cried in desperate sorrow, I grieved over my double loss,
My faith in God did waver, on waves of loneliness I did toss.
I cried out in despair to God to come take my life, too . . .
His reminder came to me, His child, 'I still have a plan for you.'

My grief finally ebbed, and His merciful comfort filled my life.
I learned that true thankfulness to God is not just for what is nice.
It's a moment-by-moment attitude that puts my trust in Him
And I know someday I'll be in Heaven with my husband and baby Tim."

She tenderly touched the locket hanging near her heart
And one by one, the old men stood, ready to depart.
The first man strode away worrying about his precious things.
He completely missed the point about what true faith in God brings.
The second man shuffled off muttering—"That poor girl has no clue—

God took everything—And she thanks Him! Well that's nothing I can do."
The third man asked, "How do you know you'll see them again? How can you be so sure?
God gave them to you once—then look—He took all that you held dear."

A tender smile lit her face and spread into her eyes.
She fingered the locket and said with a voice of one who has grown wise,
"I know Jesus died on the cross for me, He paid for my sin the penalty.
And by putting my whole trust in Him, one day I'll see my husband and Tim.
And here on Earth, where life has pain, I trust God's plan for me,
My story can touch others, and reach them for Christ, for eternity."
The old man nodded, he understood, and asked her to help him pray.
They knelt and in a halting voice, he asked Christ into his life that day.

As she heard his words, she prayed, and a thrill in her heart soared:
"Your generous hand of blessing on my life has been richly poured!
My heart is full, my faith is strong—my thanks to you, Oh Lord."

The days flew by, quickly turning the fun of their vacation into a distant memory. Sondra was still waiting to hear back about the children's stories she had submitted. Meanwhile, she worked on a new idea, writing greeting cards.

After the kids were in bed, she cranked out several to submit. She printed them off precisely in the manner she'd been instructed. She coded the entries with her initials and assigned them a number, then described the type of card and designated what words went on the outside and the inside:

SLM-001 (Congratulations on Baby's Birth)
O: Tomorrow . . .
      Another rose will bloom
      Another butterfly will break free and fly
      And the sun will set again in a brilliant brush of color.
      But for today, those things are especially breathtaking
      Because today, we celebrate the birth of your precious new baby!
I: Congratulations!

SLM-002 (Mom to Mom Humor)
O: If you've ever left your baby's car seat on top of the car and actually got behind the wheel—
      Welcome to Motherhood!

      If you carry a diaper bag as a purse, even when you're alone—
      Welcome to Motherhood!
      If you ever find food in the microwave that you heated the day before—

I: BONUS! Dinner's ready!

The next day, in the mail, a neat stack of envelopes sat in their mailbox, the names of publishing houses displayed neatly in the upper left-hand corners.

Replies for my children's stories! Sondra eagerly grabbed for them, ripping them open. She read each one, her heart falling a bit more with each sheet of paper passing under her eyes.

Different in their wording, each was similar in their ultimate message: "Thank you for your submissions for our Young Readers Department. However, at this time, we are unable to use your children's manuscripts for publishing. We are returning them and wish you success as you pursue other avenues to publish your work." Blah, blah, blah.

She knew it was the opinion of a few various publishers, but all the same, the rejection cut deeply.

I can't even cross the success line for stories geared to four-year-olds.

Heartsick about the dead end, she prayed, "Lord, please help me. I don't want to become bitter, but this hurts." She went into her and John's room. Carefully, she put the envelopes containing their messages, along with her manuscripts, into a dresser drawer, spotting the floppy disk containing her half-done story as well. She sighed. When she had first begun storing all her writings in it, she had laughingly called it her drawer of dreams.

It's more like my drawer of dismal failures.

At least, she still had hope that maybe some of her card submissions would be accepted. She slid the drawer shut and went to immerse herself in some mind-numbing activities with her children.

* * *

Susan and another friend, Charlene Jeffries, arrived at Sondra's house the next morning. The three were going to plan for the children's summer camp that they had run together the past few years. Sondra wasn't especially looking forward to their visit today. She loved her friends, but was certain that everyone remembered the fiasco from last summer.

It's so embarrassing. I wish I could go back and undo it. But I can't. Oh Lord, please give them both amnesia about what a fool I made of myself.

Susan helped herself to the tray of coffee and treats on the table and started the discussion, "Well, let me say, I, for one, hope we don't have a repeat of what happened last year."

Charlene nodded, giving a hearty "Amen" before taking a sip of her tea.

Sondra sighed. *So much for that prayer request.*

"Trust me, I am far more embarrassed than you were from it," Sondra assured them. "That is the last time I will take such a risk, for sure. But can we please move forward and try to forget it?"

Both Susan and Charlene looked at her with their eyebrows raised.

"Sondra, why would you be embarrassed?"

"Susan, how could I not be? You two even remember it being a fiasco. Of *course*, I'm embarrassed. I was the one who got up there and sang that song I wrote in front of all those moms and their kids on the last day—and started to cry in the middle and forgot half the words." She looked at them in confusion. "Isn't that what you're talking about?"

Susan started chuckling. Charlene joined in, and soon the two of them were laughing and leaning against each other for support.

Sondra watched her two friends. Self-pity welled up in her, and she felt tears threaten.

Susan noticed. "Oh, Sondra, we aren't laughing at you—honest. Well, maybe a little. But really, you have to admit it was kind of funny. Honestly, I had completely forgotten about that—and it wasn't as bad as you seem to think. If I remember right, Linda told me later that she talked with a couple of the moms, and they told her that they admired you for taking the risk."

Charlene nodded. "Oh, that's true, Sondra. I had a talk with Kelly Simpson afterward—you remember her? Something similar happened to her, and it really made her feel better to know that other people mess up once in a while too."

"That's terrific. I'm so glad I can encourage others through my failure and humiliation." She looked glum.

Susan laughed, reaching across the space, touching her arm. "Don't be upset, Sondra. As my mama used to say, 'If that's the worst thing that happens to you, you've led a pretty good life.' I guarantee you're the only one who still thinks about it."

Charlene chimed in, "So you tried something new, and it didn't work out exactly the way you wanted. So what? It wasn't the end of the world. Besides, I remember when I went out on a limb and signed up to play the part of Mary Magdalene in the church play two years ago. On the night of the grand opening, I forgot all my lines. I ended up reading them from a sheet, and I am pretty sure I recall you telling me then that it wasn't a big deal, that it made me more human, and people could relate. That was no different." She took a sip of her tea. "In fact, I remember backstage when I cried to you about what a disaster it was, you zinged me with, 'Well, I would agree with you, but then we would both be wrong.'" Charlene chuckled. "That line stuck with me." She set her empty cup on the table. "You were right when you said it to me then, and I'm right when I say it to you now."

Susan piped up, "And have you forgotten last Christmas when Pastor Paul asked me to participate in the service? It was supposed to be a solemn and reflective part of the ceremony, and I botched one of my lines."

Charlene started chuckling. "I remember. You got up in front of the entire church and read, "But for the geese of God, there go I." She threw her head back, laughing heartily.

Susan watched her for a moment then interrupted her glee. "Yeah, but who was it that typed up my sheet wrong?"

A secretary at the church, Charlene stopped laughing and cleared her throat. "I already apologized back then, and I'm not going to again. You should have known the word was *grace* and corrected it yourself."

Susan started laughing. "For weeks I had people honking like a goose at me."

Sondra laughed too; she was feeling better. *They are right. I need to swallow the pride that makes me feel like I have to do everything perfectly. It is an impossible standard.*

"Well then, what are you guys talking about? What else happened last summer that was so terrible?"

Susan responded, "Oh my gosh, don't you remember? Practically the entire three-year-old room came down with hand, foot, and mouth disease. It got traced back to that one little boy whose mother knew he had it, but didn't want him to miss camp."

Charlene added, "She wasn't very apologetic either. If I remember right, she made some comment like, 'It's going around anyway. Chances are, they'll get it from somewhere, if not from my son.' Even though we sent out an e-mail, it was too late. By that point, there was nothing we could do, and a lot of kids got sick."

Sondra did remember. It was the classroom ahead of Tommy's, and quite a few of her friends' kids came down with it, infecting whole families at their church.

I'd forgotten . . . I have to admit, that is worse than me making a public fool of myself . . . but not by much.

The rest of the morning flew by with the trio working on details to enhance the wonderful program where so many families in their community enrolled their kids. The reputation of a quality week for a reasonable fee was a hard one to keep improving, but they tweaked here and there, fine-tuning the schedule and all the components until they felt it was as good as they could make it.

As they readied to leave, Charlene asked, "Hey, what ever happened with you doing those greeting cards? Did you write any or send them out?"

Sondra nodded. "Yeah, I sent some just the other day, so I won't hear back for a while yet."

But when I do, it'll probably be another rejection because that's all I seem to ever get.

Even as the criticism popped into her mind, Sondra scolded herself. She needed to keep things in perspective. Okay, so she had gotten rejected about her children's stories. That didn't mean something wouldn't work out with one of her other submissions. Maybe someone down the road would like something that she wrote. She couldn't just stop trying.

Charlene said, "Well, I'll keep praying. My friend loves doing it, and it's been a great way for her to earn some extra money. You're a good writer, Sondra. Something will come up for you."

Susan added, "I love your poem *'How Can It Be?'* I framed it and put it in Meghan's room. Charlene is right. One of these days, you'll get something published, don't you worry."

Her friends gave her a quick hug good-bye. As she closed the door behind them, she thought about what they had said.

But what if I never get published? What does God think about the failure I am?

Sondra bowed her head. "Forgive me, God. I know that isn't what You think about me." Why was she yoked to this heavy burden of feeling like she was a failure? She knew God loved her. She needed to park in that truth because that was the only place she could find comfort.

She sighed and started cleaning up the mess. It was time to pick up the kids from her neighbor Paula's house, where they had been playing all morning. She relaxed in the silence of the house for a few minutes, drinking the last of her coffee that had gone cold, before heading out the door.

* * *

While speaking with her mom a couple of days later, Sondra began coughing.

"Honey, are you okay?" Concern laced her mother's voice. "Are you coming down with something?"

Sondra tried to bring her cough under control, finally speaking, "Oh, I'm fine. Well, I'm tired. But I'm always tired, it seems." She gave a little laugh.

"Yes, that seems to be part of the stage of life you're in. I remember falling into bed absolutely tuckered at the end of a day when I was a young mom with little ones around." Her mom reminisced. "Make sure you're eating well, dear. Are you taking vitamins?"

"Yes, yes, Mom."

At least, that is, when I remember to.

"Well," her mom continued, "if you're drinking plenty of water and eating well, what you're feeling is probably just normal weariness from all that you do all day with your kiddos."

"Yeah, I'm sure you're right." She hesitated. "Mom? I wanted to ask you something. Do you happen to have any connections from when you wrote your book? I mean, I wondered if maybe you could help me a little. I've been submitting some things to various publishing houses but can't catch a break." She finished quickly, hating this feeling of desperation.

"Oh, honey, I wish I could help you," Julia paused. "But everyone I knew over at Pfisher and Son Publishing is gone now. In fact, I heard their whole business closed. I'm sorry."

"Oh, that's okay. I just thought I'd ask."

Julia sensed Sondra's discouragement. "Sondra, are you getting enough sleep? Maybe this isn't the time to be working on writing, when life is so busy with your little ones. I worry about you."

"Mom, I'm fine," Sondra said firmly. "I can't just quit trying. I have to write, whether I want to or not, it's almost this compulsion that I can't resist." She saw Tommy come in, dancing around to get her attention. "Okay, well, thanks anyway. I've got to go now."

"Okay, sweetheart. I love you. Hug those grandkids for us, and we'll look forward to talking with you again in a week or two."

"Okay, I will. Bye, Mom."

"Bye, darling."

Tommy had been impatiently hopping around her feet while they said their good-byes.

Sondra hung up, asking, "What do you need, honey?"

"Mommy, I have two questions."

Sondra chuckled. *No surprise.*

"Okay, what are they?"

"Well, first, I want to know why your shoe won't flush down the toilet."

"What? Oh, Tommy, no! Tell me you didn't!" she cried out as she pushed him aside, running to the hall bathroom.

She went to the toilet, seeing her blue sneaker jammed down under the water. "Tommy, I can't believe you did this. We've talked about putting things in the toilet before, remember?"

"Yeth, I remember, Mommy."

She shook her head wonderingly. "Then why did you do this?"

He looked at her with surprise. "I thought I would show you that your shoe *can* flush down the toilet. You said it can't, so I thought I would try to see if you were wrong. I thought you'd like to know."

She reached down into the water, pulling the shoe out, water dripping from the laces, and sighed. "Tommy, when I said that it can't, what I meant is that it shouldn't." She saw his confusion, and she turned to face him, kneeling down at his level and speaking slowly.

"Listen to me. The only things we put in the toilet comes from our bodies when we sit on the potty. Nothing else. Do you understand me? Nothing else." She repeated it for emphasis. "It could ruin the toilet. Now you are lucky that this didn't go down partway and get stuck."

Tommy had listened attentively. "Get stuck on what, Mommy?"

Sondra said irritably, "I don't know. I'm not a plumber, honey. But I know that shoes and toilets don't go together. Got it?"

Tommy nodded. "Got it."

His mom fished around for a plastic bag under the sink, opened it, and dropped the shoe inside. She carried it to the laundry room while he padded behind her to watch.

She put the shoe in a bucket and added some cleaning liquids and hot water to let it soak. Standing there, she suddenly remembered something he had said when he first came in the kitchen. She turned to him warily. "Tommy, you said you had two questions."

Tommy nodded.

"What was your other question?"

He looked off to the side and scratched his cheek.

"Tommy? I'm waiting."

Tommy looked unhappily at her. "Well, my other question was . . ." He stopped.

"Yes?" His mother squinted at him. "What was your other question?"

He took a deep breath, looked at her, and said, "Well, I wondered why Mylah's shoe *did* flush down the toilet"—he looked accusingly at her—"since you said shoes can't."

Sondra smacked a palm to her forehead and cried out in dismay, "Oh, Tommy, no!"

* * *

The big package that arrived in the mail the next day bore Sondra's name on a gold-foil label. Ripping open the box, she removed the heavy leather-bound volume inside. Sondra feathered through the pages, noting how thick and heavy it was. In the index inside, she found her name listed: Martin, Sondra . . . page 267.

Well, it's a small satisfaction that if I have to be so far in the back, at least mine will take up a big chunk of space.

At $60 for one poem, it was expensive real estate.

She flipped to the page but saw only a small portion of words printed. She turned the page, expecting to see the remainder, but only found writings by other authors.

"What happened? Why isn't my whole poem included?" she wondered out loud, dismayed.

She opened the letter that accompanied the book. "Dear Madam: We were delighted to receive your submission. However, we found it necessary to edit your piece as it exceeded the allotted size restrictions."

"What size restrictions? There were no size restrictions," she argued and kept reading. "These restrictions might have been difficult to find as we mistakenly placed them in the area of fine print rather than prominently in the body of our invitation. Please accept our apologies for this unfortunate necessity. We trust you will still find tremendous satisfaction in seeing a portion of your work displayed in this high-quality book that should give you years of joy and delight."

Sondra moaned, "You've got to be kidding me. What did they do to my poem?"

She pulled the volume close and read it, her mouth dropping open in disbelief. Someone had chopped her piece mercilessly, leaving unrelated lines paired together. The patched-together stanzas reflected the skill level of a third grader. And there was her name, given full credit in bold lettering.

"It sounds utterly ridiculous now," she wailed. She groaned and put her head in her hands. "I can't believe I paid $60 for them to slaughter my poem." She shook her head, lamenting, "Oh, Sondra, look where your vanity has taken you." She wanted to hide the whole miserable thing away somewhere but knew John would be asking about it. "Let's get this over with." She sighed, reluctantly placing the book by his place at the table, and began making dinner.

When he walked in that night, Sondra could see weariness about him. She ran to greet him. He rubbed his forehead, giving her a tired smile.

Why does he push himself so hard?

She worried for his health, knowing that nothing she could say would change him.

"I'm so glad you're home, honey. I made one of your favorite meals." She grabbed a stack of napkins and buckled Mylah into her high chair. The rest of the kids were already around the table, waiting.

"Thank you." John smiled appreciatively and washed up at the sink, turned to see the large volume sitting by his place, and perked up. "Hey, what's that? Did your book arrive?"

She grimaced. "Yeah . . . yeah, it did."

"Honey, that's great. How does it feel to have your name in print?" He looked excitedly at her.

She stammered out, "Well, I have to say that it's not quite what I expected."

"This calls for a celebration, don't you think?"

"John . . ." Her voice wavered.

He looked at her, confused. "What's wrong?"

Tears shimmered in her eyes. "John, you were right. I was wrong. I . . . I . . ." She couldn't finish. All afternoon she had dreaded this moment, and here it was. He would see where her vanity had taken her. She felt so ashamed. "They botched my poem. You were right. It was just a ploy that I fell for." She choked up.

"Oh, Sondra, I'm sure it's fine. And now you have a legitimate piece of work in a beautifully bound book. I'm proud of you, honey."

She shook her head. "You don't understand. They changed everything. It's not all there."

"What? Why not?" She handed him the letter, which he read. He flipped open to the index, found her name, and opened to page 267.

"All that money you spent. I'm so sorry, John. I wish I had never done it."

She watched him read the highly modified piece but wasn't prepared for his sudden laughter. Sondra and the children stared as he shook with pent-up emotion.

"John? What is so funny?"

He waved her away, unable to answer. He hung on to the counter for support, his head shaking and tears streaming from his eyes. Finally, his laughter subsided, and he wiped at his eyes, giving a big sigh. "Oh, Sondra, I'm sorry. I couldn't help it. That's been building up for a while, and I just needed to laugh." He saw her look and shook his head, smiling. "You have to admit, this is funny."

She allowed a small smile. "Yeah, I guess it is, a little."

"A little? Did you read this?" He pulled the book close again and read aloud:

A woman shared with some grumpy old men: "I've learned a lot since I was ten. When I was little, I dreamed of the life of being a mother and a wife. My parents instructed me from young to thank our Lord for all that He's done. I thank my Maker for my house and my bat, for my old brown slippers—and my gray house cat. When I got married, right from the start, I showed God I had a thankful heart: my goblets are gold rimmed—they're trimmed with a bow, and I use a centerpiece arranged just so. Sadly, one day I was cleaning our snappy, happy home; my phone rang, and I learned my whole family was gone. A car wreck took my husband, and it took my baby's life. Now I'm no longer a mom—or wife." The woman reached up near her heart to touch her golden locket. "But I'm thankful to the Lord—and I've got money in my pocket."

John started laughing again as did the three older children. Sondra couldn't help herself as the tension she'd carried all day burst from her like a balloon finally popping, releasing its pressure. She laughed, picturing the lunacy of the patched-together poem. The room was merry with the sound of hilarity.

John took a deep breath and pulled his wife close. "Listen to me." He tilted her head up to look her in the eye with a smile. "I love you. Nothing is going to change that, understand?" He gestured to the volume sitting open on the table. "This whole book could be filled with every word you've ever written, and I couldn't possibly love you more. I want to encourage you in your dream, honey, but don't let the pursuit of it define how you see yourself if it doesn't work out how you want. Okay?"

She nodded gratefully, and he kissed her.

"All right, family. Let's give thanks and eat." He sat down, rubbed his hands together, and smiled at the kids, who were smiling and intently watching their parents. They all joined hands, and John prayed. Sondra looked at the bowed heads and felt a rush of thankfulness for her husband and children.

O God, thank You for Your patience with me. Forgive me and help me, Lord. I don't want this to consume me—may You alone consume me.

* * *

John was busier than ever, coming home late several nights in a row. "I think Jonathon is interviewing for a new job. He's been missing a lot of time at work. Since Gisele makes good money too, he can afford to look around a little."

A stab of guilt hit her in the gut. If she had a job that helped with their finances . . .

He didn't mean it that way, Sondra. Don't go there.

Still, Sondra felt uneasy. Was Jonathon interviewing with other banks? Or was he involved in something more scandalous with the mysterious Tamara?

Am I obligated to tell Gisele that there is a woman named Tamara now working at the bank?

She told John her concerns, and he ran his hand through his hair. "Are you sure Gisele said, 'Tamara'? What was in the note she found?"

"I don't know. But I know it was from someone named Tamara. That's why I knew her name before you did. But Gisele didn't tell me what the note said."

"Well then, honey, I don't think we can assume the worst right away. Do you realize how many meetings we have during a day? Tamara could have written a perfectly innocent message to Jonathon that Gisele is taking way out of context. She should just ask him if she wants to find out the truth."

"Maybe you're right." She changed the subject. "How were things today at work?"

John stretched, groaning. "Same old stuff. Hal is really a piece of work, let me tell you. I didn't want to get involved, but I think upper management is starting to hear some complaints coming from our branch. I don't know how it's gone on as long as it has."

He stretched out on their bed and was sound asleep almost immediately. Sondra covered him up, turned off the lights, and crawled in next to him, praying for him. She tried to remain understanding when John missed a few dinners or came home way past the kids' bedtimes. She worried for her husband and found herself pleading with God, "He works so hard, Lord. Please do something about Hal. It's not fair that he is causing so much pain for so many people."

She lay in the dark, thinking about the troublemaker's treatment of others. John had asked her to be praying for Hal, for his heart to soften, and for God to be at work in his life.

But can a person like Hal ever change? Besides, it's his fault I've been running solo in the role of parenting these past many months.

She preferred to use him as an easy scapegoat, placing the blame for their extra stress on him since his actions were causing John the additional headaches to cope with, which trickled down to her own life. Then words John had challenged her with broke into her thoughts: *What if no one else in this world is praying for Hal?*

She sighed, knowing her husband was right: she needed to cultivate a heart that longed to see others come to know Jesus Christ too.

With a renewed commitment, she turned on her lamp and added Hal's name to her "prayers for salvation" sheet, asking that God would do what He alone could: bring a sinner's heart to repentance.

She had to trust that God would take them through this time. Meanwhile, she would have to adjust to the additional weight put on her shoulders by John's absences and pray for extra strength for her husband, who had to deal daily with the conflict. She turned off the light, cuddled up to her husband, and fell asleep.

* * *

For a stretch of a few weeks, Sondra was able to forget about the discouragement of her writing shortcomings. She decided to use some of her time instead to set up playdates for the kids and to focus on getting to know other women better.

When Sondra heard that Linda Peters, the leader of Women's Ministry at church, had asked Charlene to be on the welcoming team, she was surprised at the jolt of jealousy she felt.

"I would never be asked to join such a team," she noted to John that night.

"You do plenty as it is. Besides, Charlene is just outgoing. Anyone can choose to be outgoing. It doesn't take some special skill or something."

She mulled his words over, realizing he was right. "All my life I've struggled with being shy and insecure. I'm tired of that."

"Well, honey, some of it is a choice. You need to become more confident. Then you'll feel more able to talk with people. It's really not as hard as you seem to want to make it."

"I am going to try harder at this." She declared determinedly, "I want to become known for being friendly too."

He grinned at her devilishly. "I think you're wonderfully friendly."

She laughed, and he pulled her close, kissing her with gusto.

The next day, she invited Rene, Charlene, Susan, and Dawn Phillips, a woman whose family was new to their church, over for coffee. Rene had to work, but the others were able to come.

After the women had arrived and introductions had been made, they were all upstairs visiting when the phone rang. Sondra answered it. Tommy's voice came over the line.

"Mommy? This is TJ. This boy down here called me a poopy-head, and I told him that wasn't nice."

Sondra was baffled. "Tommy, how on earth did you call me from the basement?"

"On this phone you got down here," he replied matter-of-factly.

Excusing herself for a moment, she ran downstairs and found Tommy hanging on to the handset still. He hung up when he saw her.

I had no idea you could even do that. Leave it to the children to figure it out.

Tommy was standing next to a boy, pointing his finger. "This boy here called me that bad name, Mommy."

Dawn's little boy, Drew, looked like he was about to cry under the weight of the accusation.

"Well, now." Sondra got down to Drew's height and looked at him with a gentle smile. "Is that true, Drew? Did you call Tommy something that wasn't nice?"

The tears that plopped onto his plump red cheek spoke of his misery. His doleful defense came out in a whisper. "Yes. But he called me a bug in a rug."

Sondra almost laughed, but clearly, Drew's feelings had been hurt.

"Oh my goodness. Well, can I tell you a little secret about that, honey?"

The little boy gave a small nod.

Sondra spoke gently. "That's part of a little game we play at nighttime. I tell Tommy that I hope he sleeps well—like a bug in a rug—when I tuck him into bed at night. I don't think he meant to hurt your feelings when he said that to you, did you, Tommy?"

Drew's tears and the misunderstanding that had started the whole episode moved Tommy, who was listening nearby.

"I'm sorry, Drew." He wrapped his arms around his new friend. "I didn't mean to hurt your feelings. I like bugs. And I like when Mommy says that to me. I thought you would laugh and like it too."

"That's okay."

"Will you forgive me?" Tommy leaned in closer, whispering loudly in Drew's ear, "That's what we say in our house when we hurt someone's feelings."

Drew stood quiet, unsure what to say, but nodding his head slightly.

Susan's daughter, Meghan, and Charlene's daughter, Christina, had stopped playing to watch the exchange.

"I have some cookies upstairs. I will see if your mommies all say you can have some, okay?" Sondra went back upstairs.

Dawn, Susan, and Charlene were all laughing when she walked back in.

"What did I miss? What's so funny?" Sondra asked.

Susan said, "I was just telling them the story about when Regan brought your neighbor's ferret home to watch without asking you first."

Sondra laughed. "It might not have been so bad if someone had only told me before it popped up from between the couch cushions when I sat down. I'm sure my scream was heard in the next county."

The women laughed, and Susan remarked, "David thought that story was hilarious."

Sondra chuckled, wryly noting, "I'm glad you're getting so much mileage out of it."

Her friend laughed cheerfully.

Sondra asked, "Are you all okay with your kids having some cookies?"

She called TJ to come get the plateful to share, made a fresh pot of coffee, and rejoined the ladies.

Dawn shyly said, "We were surprised at how much more expensive homes are up here compared to the Carolina area. Taxes alone are so much higher here."

Charlene nodded. "My sister lives down in Tennessee and has said that too. It doesn't make sense, considering that we don't even have great weather going for us."

"What are you talking about, Charlene? You don't *like* the five feet of snow and blizzard conditions we can get for four months a year?" Susan's eyes twinkled over the rim of her cup at her friend.

Susan turned to Dawn. "Is the cost of living higher here in other ways too, or is it just housing?"

"Overall, it costs us more to live here, but costs are rising all over the country. At least, it seems that way." All the heads nodded.

Sondra took a sip of her coffee and stated, "Ah, well, as someone once said, 'In spite of the cost of living, it's still popular.'"

"You and your quotes, Sondra." Susan laughed. She turned to Charlene. "Do you remember when she would e-mail out a quote of the week to all of us?"

Charlene chuckled. "Yes, that's right, I'd forgotten."

"I remember one that said, 'In your moment of strength, get rid of your objects of weakness.' David read it and took it on himself to throw away my entire stash of chocolate."

"What?" Sondra laughed. "I didn't know that."

"He told me he didn't think I'd ever have a moment strong enough to do it myself."

She laughed good-naturedly, and the other women joined her.

"Hey, speaking of chocolate, have any of you met that new woman, Jennifer, yet?" Charlene asked. "She has two kids and looks to be about our age, maybe a little older."

"How does chocolate remind you of a new woman at church?" Susan asked.

"The color of her hair is like dark chocolate," Charlene replied matter-of-factly.

"I don't think I've met her," Sondra replied. "What's her last name?"

"I don't know. She seemed a little lost the first week I met her, and I wanted to know if anyone had reached out to her and her family. That was at least three weeks ago."

"You're so good at that, Charlene," Sondra said. "I want to get better at welcoming people. If you see her again, introduce me. Maybe she would like coming to Women's Ministry." She took another sip of her drink.

"I wrote down her number. Maybe I will give her a call. If I remember right, I think Carolyn and Keith Carpenter are the ones who first invited them to come to our church."

Susan glanced at Sondra, who masked her surprise well: only John, Susan, and Rene knew that things had not been going well between Sondra and Carolyn.

Sondra turned to Dawn, wanting to pull her into the conversation. "So, Dawn, tell us more about where you moved from. And what does your husband do?"

Dawn shared her story, and the morning sped by with the simple luxury of doing nothing but talking and laughing together for a couple of hours.

* * *

That night, John went out with Patrick, the two men meeting for dinner. It seemed to be taking forever for him to come home. Sondra was waiting anxiously for him to share the details of their visit. Finally, she saw the headlights of his car pull into the driveway. She met him at the door, impatient to hear.

"So? How did it go? Did you find out what's going on?"

She scoured John's face for clues, noting the ragged weariness there.

"Yes, I did."

A pit started in her stomach. His eyes seemed red, like he'd been crying. She was getting scared.

"John. Is it what we thought? Is he leaving her? Tell me."

John ran a hand through his hair and pulled Sondra over to the couch.

"Honey, sit down."

"Oh no. He's having an affair, isn't he?"

John shook his head. "No. He's not. It's actually worse than that."

"What's worse than an affair?"

She held her breath but wasn't prepared for her husband's next words.

"Sondra, Patrick is dying."

* * *

For the first time in their friendship, Sondra didn't know whether to call Rene or wait for her to call. Should she race over there? It was almost the middle of the night. What if Patrick hadn't told his wife yet? Sondra didn't know what to do and began pacing in the kitchen.

Dying? Patrick is dying? How can this be?

"From what?" she asked, horrified.

"He has brain cancer, actually. His doctor isn't sure how long he has. It has taken him a while to come to terms with it himself. Of course, he was going to tell Rene. I guess he thought he had done a better job, hiding it than he has."

Sondra was frantic for her friends.

Patrick is too young to die. How can this be?

John said soberly, "He wants Rene to be cared for. He asked me if we would keep an eye on her. She really doesn't have anyone, you know."

Rene's parents were living, but in poor health; she also had a sister, who lived in Texas, but they weren't very close.

Oh, poor Patrick! Poor Rene!

Sondra wept for her friends and the awful tragedy they were facing.

* * *

She ended up calling Rene the next morning. She needed her to know that she and John were there for both of them. When she answered the phone, it sounded like Rene hadn't slept all night.

She probably didn't. Would you have if John told you he was dying?

"Hey."

"Hey."

"I just wanted to check in on you. Would you like me to come over? I can ask Paula to watch the kids."

Rene sighed. "Thanks, but you know, I'm actually pretty exhausted. I think I'm going to rest. I didn't get much sleep last night.

Sondra wasn't sure just what to say.

O God, please give me the words for this. I don't know how to comfort her.

"I hope you know, Rene, that we are praying nonstop over here for you and Patrick. I don't know what to say to help you, but if there is anything, anything at all that we can do to help, please let us know." She trailed off, knowing there wasn't anything they could do.

"I know, Sondra. Trust me. I know you and John are here for us. And thank you for praying. I really do believe God can heal him if He wants to." She paused. "To be honest, I've been thinking all night about—well, so many things, really. But one thing that really struck me was that I don't want this to get us down." She gave a light laugh. "I know that sounds so weird, right? But I feel like God has been telling me, 'I got this.' I don't know how it's all going to turn out, but Patrick is still here, and I don't want him to start giving up hope before the end. Does that make sense?"

Sondra brushed back tears. "Yes, it absolutely makes sense."

Rene continued. "Anyway, his doctor isn't positive about anything. It looks bad, but miracles happen. And I'm praying for a miracle."

Sondra gulped back her urge to weep. Her friend needed her to be strong. "Oh, me too, Rene. Me too."

Rene cleared her throat. "I need to tell you something else. My other news got buried under this. But guess what? I'm pregnant."

Sondra was speechless.

Rene sniffled. "It must have happened on our trip to the bed-and-breakfast. This wasn't quite the way I had planned on telling you, but there it is."

"Oh my goodness. Wow, Rene. That's wonderful. I'm so happy for you." She bit her tongue.

Why would you tell a woman who just got news that her husband is dying that you're happy for her?

"I'm so sorry, Rene. I am happy and sad all at once for you. You know what I mean?"

Rene was quiet for a moment. "Yeah, I do. I was thinking last night of all these years that we've been waiting for a baby. Now, we are finally going to have one, but my husband is facing a terminal disease. Pretty ironic, isn't it?" A note of bitterness came through the phone.

Completely understandable, Sondra thought, *I would be bitter too.*

Rene continued. "I couldn't help but wonder and ask, 'Why now, God?' But the strange thing is that somehow I feel such a peace." Sondra heard the old verve come back into Rene's voice. "And I really think that now, Patrick has something to fight for—if sheer willpower can keep someone alive, then maybe the dream of having this baby now, when he is in the biggest battle of his life, is exactly what he needs to help him stay strong."

Sondra laughed gently. "It sounds good to hear your old badgering ways again, Rene. Maybe the hope of this baby can give Patrick a needed boost of strength to fight. I pray you're right."

Please, God, let her be right.

The two friends prayed, promising to talk again soon, and Sondra hung up, feeling the urge to pray right then and there again. "O Lord, please, won't You have mercy on Patrick? Give him strength, and heal him, Lord. I know You can. I ask that You would."

* * *

One day while at church, Linda Peters asked Sondra if she would consider speaking to the "moms of young children" group for a special ladies' evening gathering a few weeks away.

"But I'm not a public speaker, Linda. I know I would mess up. I don't think I am gifted that way."

Or any other way, for that matter.

The older woman smiled at her. "Sondra, I've seen God doing a work in you. I've watched you with your kids and can clearly see that you have learned some things that could bless and encourage other women. You don't have to be perfect. In fact, if perfection were required, *none* of us would qualify. God has gifted you with more than you think. Please at least pray about it."

Sondra didn't feel so gifted but agreed to pray about it.

That night she shared the truth of her biggest worry with John. "You know how easily I sweat. I would be so embarrassed."

John scratched his neck and yawned. "Listen, honey, why don't you do something about it if it bothers you so much? There are solutions out there, you know."

Sondra scrunched her nose. "You mean those Botox injections you told me about? No way. The last things I need are puffy armpits."

He laughed. "Sondra, the doctor knows how much to inject. You wouldn't get puffy armpits." He shook his head. "I don't understand why you spend so much time worrying about things, but won't do what you can to fix them."

"Forget it. I'd rather tell Linda I can't do it," she said stubbornly.

But over the week after praying daily, Sondra felt God stirring her to accept Linda's invitation. She offered a few words back in argument. "Really, Lord? You're sure about this? But You know my propensity to cry. And I sweat easily, Lord. What about that?"

She still felt the quiet conviction in her soul that God was asking her to do this. Resignedly, she called Linda while she was tender to obey the small voice inside.

Linda was elated. "Oh, I'm glad, Sondra. You don't know what an encouragement this will be to so many women."

I don't know about that.

"Is there anything specific you would like me to speak on?"

"Oh yes. We are doing a theme on patience."

You've got to be kidding. I don't hit the mark on that one myself, certainly not enough to get up and talk to others about.

She barely caught the rest of Linda's instructions. "You'll have about twenty-five to thirty minutes to share. Also, if you could weave the gospel in somewhere, that would be good. Many women bring unsaved friends to this event, so it's important we share it. Thanks so much, Sondra. I will be praying for you."

After hanging up, Sondra was horrified at what she had agreed to. "I'm not a public speaker. What was I thinking?" She groaned. "And the topic is patience? Great, just great."

Oh please, Lord, have mercy. How will I make it through this?

Another regretful sigh escaped her lips.

* * *

The dreaded evening arrived quickly. Sondra got ready, sweating through two shirts before she even left the house, nervously shaking the whole time. She changed again and, as a safety measure, taped thick underarm pads inside of her shirt, pressing them hard to keep them in place. John stopped her before she headed out. He tilted her head to look her in the eyes.

"Sondra, I know you are nervous. But if God calls us to do something, He will also equip us. Linda sees you have gifts to share, and I think you do too."

"But what if I forget what to say?" Her eyes held fear.

John hugged her, praying, "Lord, please help Sondra as she talks with these women. Help her be unafraid and use her words to bless someone as she shares some things You have taught her. In Jesus's name, we ask, amen."

Sondra gulped and kissed him and headed out the door. On the drive over, her stomach clenched up. Sondra knew God did not want her to walk in fear, but the worries persisted.

What if they hate me? What if my deodorant stops working, and I sweat all over the place?

Disgusted with her negative self-talk, a different thought broke through.

How about you think how Rene and Patrick are feeling right now and stop your complaining?

Upon arrival at the church, Sondra saw that the fellowship hall was packed with women finding chairs and visiting before the event began. She glanced down the front row, spotting Victoria Wilson, a woman known for being gossipy.

O Lord, if I make it through this, it's going to be all You! Please help me!

Fidgeting as Linda brought everyone to order, she felt like tossing up her dinner and shot one last prayer heavenward as she heard her name announced. Nervously, Sondra stepped up to the podium after being introduced by Linda, smiled, took a deep breath, and dove in.

"Um. Good evening, ladies. Let me tell you, this is a tough topic to speak on because it forever puts me under a microscope. When I saw my name written on the little sign in the bathroom this past weekend, I cringed. I wished they'd written, 'Speaker: Anonymous.' I can hear it now: '*Sondra Martin* is speaking on *patience*? Didn't I just see her yelling at her kid in the hallway?'"

The women laughed, and Sondra gratefully paused, praying again for God's strength.

"So please do not see me as up here lecturing to you on how I am perfectly patient all the time and how I have it all together, because I don't, and both God and I know it. And my husband and kids do too." She paused and added, "And probably most of the neighbors."

A smattering of laughter followed.

"But hopefully, um, through my own struggles in this area, God may use something that you hear tonight to help teach you the way He is teaching me. That is my prayer. Before I get too far, let me point out the Bible verses hung up behind me." She pointed to the two poster boards on which she'd written some verses in big lettering.

"If your attention wanders, I thought it would be good for you to have something worthwhile to look at."

When she moved her arm back down, she felt the right pad inside her shirt, shifting around as if the tape were loosening. Resisting the impulse to make any noticeable adjustments, Sondra swallowed hard and went on. "Whether we like it or not, we are models for our children. The question is, what are we modeling? If we teach and model righteousness, peace can follow in our homes. If we teach and model unrighteousness, chaos can reign in our homes. Wouldn't it be great if patience were something we could sign up for that showed up in a box on our doorstep?"

The room was silent. The smirk on Victoria's face confirmed that her little attempt at a joke had failed miserably. Sondra felt a trickle of sweat forming.

Oh please, no!

Her voice shaking a little, Sondra continued. "Sadly, that isn't how patience is acquired. Ultimately, there is one way. The only answer for growing in patience is growing in God's Word. We are told in Psalms 119:11, 'Thy word have I hid in my heart that I might not sin against Thee.' It is a sin to act impatiently. Everything else we can do if we ignore this most basic prevention of sin is our own works and isn't going to get to the core of the issue."

A few heads nodded.

"We can identify some of the things that can try our patience: weariness, lack of boundaries, poor planning, unsupportive spouse, trying circumstances, overwhelmed with duties, new babies, a move, et cetera, but you know, this verse in Philippians covers all of it." Sondra held a poster board up high with the verse written in big letters. "I can do all things through Christ who strengthens me," she read. "It takes spiritual maturity to respond with patience. That can only come through cultivating our hearts to be more like Christ by reading God's Word."

As she started to lower the sign, the pad under her right arm suddenly popped out from its hiding place and landed squarely on the floor at Sondra's feet. Horrified, she stared down at it, her cheeks flushing deep red.

Oh, dear God, why? This was her worst nightmare coming true right in front of her! She swallowed hard, certain she heard Victoria snicker. *Well, do something. You can hardly pretend it's not yours.*

She lowered the poster board and sighed. "Oh dear. Ladies, as those of you up closer probably saw, I seem to have lost one of my attachments. Forgive the interruption, please."

She stooped over, retrieving the rebellious pad, and shook her head, muttering loudly, "Pesky little bugger." Some of the women laughed sympathetically, and Sondra shoved the pad in her pocket.

Distracted, she looked at her notes, fanning her warm face with the stack of papers. "I'm sorry, where was I?"

A few ladies called out, "You were saying we need to be in God's Word."

"Wow. Thank you. Right. Would you like to come up and finish this for me? No? Are you sure?" She smiled good-naturedly. "Let me say that it's good to see you're listening." The women chuckled, and Sondra found her spot again.

Feeling a little more confident, she stated, "Okay. Of course, there are other things we need to do to grow in sanctification as well as helpful things we can do to alleviate situations that lead to becoming impatient. Those are definitely important and worth going over. I decided to go with words that start with *P*, so let's begin."

She went through her list of words, expounding on each of them in turn. The time zipped by. She realized about halfway through that she didn't feel as nervous anymore.

"So we can parent with a firm, but loving hand without giving in to the unreasonable demands of immature children, who don't have the capacity to know that loving discipline is actually a gift from God."

She'd grown more comfortable and was in a groove now. "I think we also need to be aware of our children's perspective. This little story I came across somewhere is a good example of how we often assume that they have a full understanding of what we are saying to them:

A father was at the beach with his children when the four-year-old son ran up to him, grabbed his hand, and led him to the shore where a seagull lay dead in the sand.

'Daddy, what happened to him?' the son asked.

'He died and went to heaven,' the dad replied.

The boy thought a moment and then said, 'Did God throw him back down?'"

The room filled with laughter.

Sondra smiled. "Children's minds are not like adult minds. Sometimes we need to fill in the blanks for them and give them the benefit of the doubt if we're not clear."

She saw some heads nodding, bent over their papers, writing down some of the points.

She looked back at her notes, continuing, "Personal time. Carve out some time each day for you to feel more refreshed. Most of us can't afford to spend a week at a spa, but we can do small things that refresh our souls and soothe our weary bodies. After I get our oldest daughter off to school most days, I try to get my younger ones busy playing, make myself a cup of tea, and spend some time reading my Bible. I have come to cherish this bit of time when I do, and it prepares me to parent in a loving way that is pleasing to God. If you can, find a small corner where you can retreat when you need a break."

Sondra chuckled, recalling a story to share. "Our home isn't very large, and I told my oldest daughter—who, at the time, was about four—that I needed to find a special place in my room to go when I needed a few minutes to myself. Regan suggested, 'How about under your bed, Mommy?'" The burst of laughter from the women gave her a moment. She paused and then said matter-of-factly, "If that's what it takes . . ." She drifted off, letting the laughter carry for a couple of seconds.

"Of course, I'm kidding. Hopefully, you can create for yourself a small corner somewhere in your home even if it means packing up all the essentials in a basket and bringing them out when you need them."

Sondra held up a small basket she had prepared that was filled with a small devotion book, a candle, wrapped chocolates, a lovely teacup, and a box of tea and asked, "Who here has two children under age five?" A bunch of hands went up. "Three children under five years old?" Quite a few hands dropped. "Four?" A haggard-looking pregnant woman called out, "I have two-year-old triplets and a baby due in two months!"

The whole room whooped in agreement that she took the prize.

"Clearly, you need this more than any of us!" Sondra passed the basket along; the woman smiled with delight at winning the reward.

Sondra went back to the podium and gathered her notes, looking at her final points.

"Have a plan. This point has two parts—first, plan *before* a situation arises how you'll deal with it. You've heard the suggestion to count to ten, and if that works for you, great. For me, I would count to ten and *then* blow up. I found it was better for me to grab those ten seconds to recite a verse in my head—*anything* that yanks me back to God's Word so I don't violate the sixth Commandment: Thou shalt not kill."

The ladies tittered, and Sondra went on. "The second part of having a plan is for when you do lose your patience. Are we teaching, by example, how to have a tender heart to ask forgiveness when we *do* blow it? I have often found myself on the side of having to apologize when I have yelled at my children or not treated them in a Christlike manner. I am so thankful that my children are forgiving. And it is a blessing to see that more often, when my children misbehave, they come to me and ask forgiveness. Remember that we are models for our children, and what they see is often what they do."

Sondra took a deep breath. Linda had asked her to weave an invitation for the gospel in, but she wasn't good at this sort of thing.

"So if you are here today and you have been listening to me talk about becoming more patient, you should realize that this is not some self-help method to improve your parenting skills. It's an act of obedience for believers who have put their faith and trust in Jesus Christ.

"If you have never made a decision to give your life to Christ, to accept His free gift of salvation, you can do so right where you are sitting. The Bible is clear that we are born into this world spiritually dead and on our way to hell. But God provided the only way to heaven, through the shed blood of His own Son. John 3:16 says, 'For God so loved the world that He gave His only Son that whosoever believes in Him should not perish, but have everlasting life.'"

Sondra forged ahead. "Ladies, this is such good news. There is nothing we can do to earn or work our way into heaven. Ephesians 2:8–9 says, 'For it is by grace you have been saved, through faith, and not of yourselves, it is the gift of God, not by works, so that no one can boast.'"

Linda smiled and nodded encouragingly at her.

Whew, I did it. That wasn't so bad. Wrap it up, and you're out of here.

She glanced down at her notes. "In finishing, I want to ask a couple of questions for us to ponder: When they think back to *home*, will our kids remember a haven, a place where they had freedom to make mistakes and learn from them, and know without a shadow of doubt they were loved no matter what? Or will they remember a hard, cold, impossible-to-please place where sins and mistakes were never forgotten, and anger was never far under the surface?"

She paused for a moment, letting that sink in. "I pulled this out of a magazine and thought it was appropriate for this talk. Just listen: After the baby dedication of his brother in church, Tyler sobbed all the way home in the backseat of the car. His father asked him several times what was wrong. Finally, the boy replied, 'That preacher said he wanted us brought up in a Christian home—but I want to stay with you guys!'"

A loud burst of laughter filled the room. Sondra smiled along and then stated, "As funny as this little story is, it is also sad. If we are going to proclaim ourselves to be Christians, we need to conduct ourselves in a manner worthy of His name."

She indicated the signs behind her. "Out of curiosity, did anyone read any of the verses up here?"

Most of the hands went up around the room.

"See—*our* attention wanders at times also. How much harder must it be for our little ones, who are still learning character traits like self-discipline and focus and obedience? My prayer is that we all be more like Christ as we dig into this *most wonderful job on earth*, patiently teaching and guiding the little ones whom God has entrusted to our care while cherishing the time we spend raising them to love God and to respond to Him in their own lives. Let's pray."

After she prayed, Sondra stepped out from behind the podium, relieved that other than the wardrobe mishap, she hadn't made any major gaffes and had lived through the harrowing experience.

She smiled when Linda gave her a hug and encouraged her with the words, "I knew you could do it!"

As the women were filing out at the end of the evening, Charlene walked over to her with another woman.

"Good job, Sondra," she said, giving her a hug.

Sondra grinned at her friend. "Thank you. I'm grateful it's over."

Charlene turned to the woman with her. "I'd like you to meet Jennifer. Jennifer, this is Sondra. Jennifer is the new gal I told you about."

Sondra smiled, greeting the new woman warmly.

Jennifer shook her hand. "You were marvelous. I appreciated all you spoke of tonight. You were so calm too. I would have been a nervous wreck up there."

Sondra laughed. "You must have been sitting in the very back not to have noticed that I *was* a nervous wreck up there. Good grief, the only reason I calmed down was that after that pad popped out on me, I figured that had to be about as bad as it could get."

Charlene chuckled. "What happened?"

"I don't know. The tape must have come loose. I nearly died, especially when I heard Victoria Wilson laughing. But since I didn't fall over dead, I realized it wasn't the end of the world and decided to be bold."

"Oh, forget Victoria. She never has anything nice to say about anyone, so take her with a grain of salt. And if you really wanted to show boldness, you should have shoved the pad back in."

Sondra laughed. "Charlene, couldn't you see that I was already melting?"

Charlene touched her arm. "Sondra, what I saw was a woman who was up there doing what most people won't do—speak in public in spite of her fears. In my book, my friend, you are brave."

"Well, I guess I've got another story to tell." She confided to Jennifer, "Charlene knows that without even trying, I seem to collect embarrassing stories like some women collect shoes."

Jennifer laughed along with Charlene.

"Charlene was so nice to invite me to come tonight. I'm glad I did. My family only started coming to this church a few weeks ago. We go to the early service so my husband can get to work on Sunday afternoons."

Sondra responded, "Well, it's so nice to meet you. My family and I usually go to the later service, so we just haven't crossed paths. We were planning on going to the early service next weekend, though, so maybe we will bump into you. How old are your children?"

"Our son, Brian, is twelve, and our daughter, Lily, is nine," Jennifer replied.

They chatted a few minutes longer before parting. Charlene and Jennifer praised Sondra's efforts again before she headed home, relieved and weary and ready to tell John all about the night.

* * *

It didn't take long for Sondra to have to put to practice what she had just finished preaching. Mylah, getting around more, found new activities to do in any moments of unsupervised glee. The very next day she scribbled on their dining room rug. Sondra suspected that Tommy had left the markers near her reach.

"I dint, Mommy. I promise." His earnest expression melted her heart, and she relented.

"All right, Tommy." She sighed. "Will you please help me clean this up?"

He eagerly ran for the cloth and cleaner that got regular use in their home.

She put the baby in her crib, breathing a weary prayer, "Please, God, keep her quiet for me—ten minutes, that's all I ask," and ran back to work on getting the stains out of the carpeting.

When she returned to the baby's room, greasy white streaks were all over the bedding, the crib rails, and the baby.

"What on earth? Mylah! How did you—" She broke off as she saw the open tub of diaper crème with her sweet dimple-faced baby digging into it and smearing it all over herself and her surroundings.

Sondra couldn't blame anyone else. She nearly cried at her stupidity in leaving the container where she had.

"Where is your brain, Sondra? You would think you would learn by your fourth child." She wrung her hands. "Oh my gosh. Where to begin?" she wailed. The cleanup took an hour.

A couple of days later, she and Tommy were sitting on the floor, playing with Mylah.

"Ew, there's a stink." Tommy held his nose.

Sondra took a sniff and recoiled. "You're right. It's a bad one." She flipped the baby down on the mat she kept on the floor and quickly changed her. Wrapping the offensive bundle in a plastic sack, she jumped to her feet.

"I'll be right back. Just watch her." He nodded, happy to be a big helper to his mommy. Sondra ran from the room to dump the smelly package in the trash can out on the back patio.

When she returned, the whole nursery looked like a winter scene from a Christmas movie.

"Tommy! What did you do?" she wailed.

TJ looked proudly around, holding the empty container of baby powder. "I helped you, Mommy. I shook it like you do."

They were in the middle of cleaning up the mess when John got home.

"We're in Mylah's room," she called out when she heard him calling her name.

He stepped unbelievingly into her chaotic world and said with slight amazement, "What happened here?" He shook his head. "You're bigger than they are. What goes on around here all day?"

It hadn't helped that he'd taken that afternoon off work to golf nine holes with Jonathon—a rare treat for him, Sondra knew. But seeing him standing there with a light tan from his time outdoors, questioning her pushed her over the edge. The entire concept of patience went out the window as Sondra lost it.

"You're kidding, right? Don't you realize I can't be everywhere at once? What am I supposed to do when I need to throw out trash or use the bathroom? Tie them up? Clearly, you don't realize how much chaos can happen in a few seconds!" She shouted this as she pushed past him, running to her room and flinging herself on their bed, crying. She sat up again, ranting further, "This is hard work, you know! Kids are messy and demanding. You go off and golf while I'm here cleaning endless messes. How about some *gratefulness* for what I do around here all day every day?" Sondra blew her nose, her anger spent. She sat in the silence of the bedroom, thinking.

She felt her spirit quieting after some minutes in her room away from the noise and commotion. John came in to their room and sat on the bed near her. "Sondra . . . you know I didn't mean that like it came out. I actually was trying to make a joke."

She looked at him skeptically. "Well, it failed."

"Yes, clearly. Look, I wasn't trying to say you aren't a good mom or that you . . ." His voice trailed off. "I mean can you at least understand where I'm coming from? I walk in and see white powder covering every surface and what appears to be sticky peanut butter on the door handle." He swept his hand to indicate the house. "I don't think it's fair for you to get upset when I simply question what's going on."

Sondra sniffled. "But you don't understand, John. I can't always stop the messes from happening. They happen, and I do my best to clean them up. I can't always know what the kids might spill or get into or think of." She blew her nose. "Besides, what you *don't* see are the things I *did* get cleaned up. What you don't know are the near misses I did stop from happening. You only see the ones that got away from me."

John snorted and raised his brow. "Well, that's probably true." He looked at her tearstained face. "Listen, honey, what I should have said was, I love you and am proud of all you do around here every single day to make our house into a home. These messes the kids make—they don't matter."

He sighed lightly and ran his hand through his hair. "In the light of all eternity, that stuff is nothing. I know you work hard and that sometimes it feels like the challenges of this season will never end. But they will. And I love you. You are my wife, and I couldn't be more proud of the kind of mom and woman you are."

She shifted on their bed, looking up at him, and gulped. "I'm sorry, John. I shouldn't have gotten so upset. You had every right to ask what had happened. I just—" She stopped.

He leaned in and kissed the tip of her nose. "Listen. Take a little time for yourself. I'll manage the kids and order in some pizza for dinner."

"Thank you. That would be so wonderful." Tears threatened again, this time from a heart that was overwhelmed with thanks. He kissed her again and headed out to the family room.

Sondra indulged in the rare opportunity of thirty minutes all to herself by taking a short bubble bath. Luxuriating in the scented warm water, she started to feel guilty for her overreaction.

If I came home and saw the same gargantuan mess, I might have asked the very same question of him.

She sighed and answered out loud, "In fact, I most certainly would have."

She was torn. She knew John worked hard too, but he got well paid, and at least once in a while, he was recognized and complimented.

"He runs a fairly low risk of being thrown up on or finding his car keys in the toilet at work," she argued, letting warm water and bubbles run through her fingers.

She, on the other hand, received no paycheck, no annual review with a detailed account of the strengths she brought and weaknesses she needed to work on.

I deal with Kool-Aid on cream-colored carpets, smashed crackers shoved into electrical outlets, and ketchup squirted onto curtains.

Every morning started in breathless anticipation of what antics she might encounter that day.

She drained the tub, watching the water swirl away, and wrapped herself in a terry-cloth towel.

When Sondra came out of their room, the kids were quietly coloring, the mess was cleaned to a reasonable level, and John looked tired. Even though he had been golfing that afternoon, Sondra knew it was a very small reprieve from the struggles he faced daily at work, and the guilt returned.

After the kids were tucked in to bed, Sondra brought up what she'd been thinking about.

"I know this sounds childish, but it means a lot to me when you tell me that what I'm doing matters." She bit her lip. "I'm not saying that you should notice every single thing, but so many of my days I feel like no one sees anything I do around here. I get to the end of my day and just have to start all over again the next day. It doesn't always feel like I'm making progress toward anything particular. You know?" She looked at him imploringly.

John nodded thoughtfully.

Sondra continued, wanting him to understand. "I love being a wife and mom. I do. But it's a role that doesn't come with any instructions. I don't always feel like I have a goal I'm shooting for, except to keep the messes at bay and everyone clean and fed and cared for. So many of my friends have gone back to work part-time. I don't want to do that. I love being here at home with our children. But it's hard when I hear from Charlene how fulfilling her part-time job at the church is, and all I got done that day is to degrease the stove and reattach the drapes Tommy and Drew swung from." She pushed away a tear.

He pulled her close. "I will try to do better. I guess I thought you knew how much I admire all you do. I didn't mean to stop telling you so." He kissed the top of her head. "And I, for one, am grateful you degreased the stove and reattached the drapes." He smiled, nuzzling her neck, and she hugged him tightly.

* * *

That Sunday, the family attended the early service. Sondra told John she wanted to get there early to see if she could find Jennifer to welcome her and meet the rest of her family.

"Please come with me, honey. They barely know anyone yet. It would be nice if you could talk with her husband."

"Sure. What's his name?"

"I don't know yet. I forgot to ask. Come on."

In the crowded lobby, clusters of people stood conversing and laughing; some prayed together. Sondra and John navigated around the groups, keeping an eye out for Jennifer and occasionally stopping to greet other acquaintances they saw along the way. Finally, she spotted Jennifer. Walking toward the lovely woman, she stopped as she caught sight of the man standing next to her. It had been a long time, but not so long to keep her from recognizing his dark eyes or mesmerizing gaze. She barely heard Jennifer's voice.

"Oh, Sondra, hello! I'd like you to meet my husband, Nicholas Bianchi."

* * *

His hand felt the same—same strong grip, same soft skin. The same tantalizing scent surrounded him. Sondra did her best to mask her shock at seeing him again after all these years. But she had been so unprepared for it; she was certain everyone around her could see her dazed expression.

Nicholas was as charming and gallant as ever. "Sondra. It is a pleasure to see you. And is this your husband? John, is it? How do you do? I'm Nicholas Bianchi. This is my wife, Jennifer."

John smiled and shook their hands. "Hi. John Martin. It's nice to meet you."

Jennifer smiled at Sondra. "You were so kind the other night. I told Nicholas all about your talk and what an encouragement it was to me."

Sondra's breath quickened, and she found herself struggling to put words together. "Oh, thank you. I, um, well, let's just say I was grateful when it was over."

Help me, God, not to throw up! I must be as white as a sheet.

She wanted desperately to excuse herself and run to the bathroom. *I can't do that though, can I?* She needed a moment alone to regain her composure. *How on earth is he so poised?*

Nicholas looked perfectly comfortable as if he were enjoying himself.

Doesn't he recognize me? It has to be—what—five, six years ago now?

Her mind raced to remember all the details of their encounters so long ago. Had she shared her last name with him? Did she look so different that he didn't realize who she was?

I need to sit down.

She felt like she was doing a verbal dance around a viper's nest, trying to avoid disturbing dangerous snakes with the wrong trigger of words. How could this be happening?

Get a grip, Sondra. Nothing actually happened, remember?

Well, that much was true. The most she could be accused of was entertaining impure thoughts at a time when she was not walking rightly with God. She was a different person now. She loved John and hadn't thought about that period in their marriage in a very long time.

Thankfully, the ushers were urging people to enter the auditorium and find their seats. Service was about to begin.

John gave the couple a smile. "It was so nice to meet you both. I hope we run into you again."

It was all Sondra could do to look Nicholas in the eye. She was afraid he might say something that would make her entire world explode.

I need to be bold—to let him know I'm not the same person I was when he first met me.

"Jennifer. Nicholas." She forced a smile and shook each of their hands. "I'm glad you came today. It's nice to see you again, and I hope you feel very welcome here."

Jennifer smiled at her. "Thank you, Sondra. I look forward to seeing you at Women's Ministry this week."

Nicholas looked at her appreciatively. "It was a pleasure, Sondra. Jennifer had wonderful things to say about you. I hope we can all spend more time together soon."

She blushed and left the couple and hurried to the nearest ladies' room. Grateful to find it empty, she closed herself in a stall and leaned against the door. She still wasn't certain if Nicholas even realized who she was. Another wave of panic hit her heart, and she nearly whimpered with dread.

What if he realizes who I am and reveals my sin in front of my family and friends? Oh God, please help me. My reputation could be ruined if word gets out about this. What about John and our children? Oh God, what have I done?

She took a few minutes, breathing slowly. As she stood there, the Holy Spirit calmed her heart. In the silence of the room, she whispered, "O Lord, I still want my life to honor You. I can't control what Nicholas may say or do, if he remembers me or not, but help me be the woman You want me to be. That sin is in the past. And You forgave it long ago. Help me trust that even if this comes out, You have a good plan. If being painfully transparent is what You're asking me to do, help me." She stood silent a moment, thinking. "But, Lord, since it doesn't hurt to ask, I sure would love for You to help him forget." Even as she put that last plea out there, she scolded herself.

It doesn't matter. Whether he does or doesn't, I am a different person.

If she had the opportunity to talk with Nicholas alone, she would tell him that what she had done those years ago was wrong. She shouldn't have flirted with him while she was married. God had grabbed hold of her heart, and she was committed to honoring Him with her life.

She left the bathroom and walked briskly into the auditorium, where sunlight poured in from the stained glass windows that were set high on the walls, casting prisms of colors on the congregants below. Sondra slid into the pew next to John and took his hand.

My life is with John. I hope he knows that. Oh please, God, help him know that.

Somehow, she hoped that the arrival of the Bianchi family wasn't going to reveal sins from her past. She barely heard the message as she spent most of the time praying quietly in desperation.

* * *

Over the next few weeks, in her off hours, Rene came over often to hang out during the day while Patrick was at work. The couple had gone through a period of near seclusion, grieving together over what appeared to be an unstoppable progression of a very aggressive disease.

Rene had dropped a lot of weight the past month as her appetite had vanished with the tragic news. The nausea wasn't helping, and tea was about the only thing she could eat or drink.

"I've been so weepy lately," she shared ruefully while sipping her tea. "I don't know if it's from the hormonal changes I'm going through or . . . well, you know." Tears pooled in the vivacious woman's eyes. Sondra grabbed the box of tissues, taking a couple for herself and handing the box to her dearest friend.

They spent a lot of time together, crying but also laughing about times past and what it would be like when the baby arrived.

More than once Rene shared her gratefulness that Sondra was in her life. "I don't know what I would do without you around. I really think I would go crazy. I mean, I can talk about my fears with you." She looked at Sondra. "I can't tell Patrick. Not everything. It would weigh on him and make him even more worried than he already is."

"I'm glad I can be here for you." She truly meant that.

Patrick had a strange form of brain cancer. He could still work, and he had some strength. He was able to get around reasonably well. Nonetheless, he was dying.

Rene had researched the disease and shared some of her discoveries with Sondra. "I mean, all those months when I couldn't understand why he seemed like he was growing distant and hard to reach—those sorts of behavioral changes are common with this type of tumor."

The two friends prayed together, sometimes just sitting in the stillness and pleading with God for His mercy. Thousands of tears had fallen, and even as they carried the weight of the trial together, more than once they reveled in their certainty of God's love, sharing verses that offered special hope.

The children were very sensitive to Auntie Rene's presence and need to spend time with their mother. Mostly, they played quietly nearby and watched the women as they bore this burden together.

Rene insisted that she not interrupt the entire schedule of their days, though. "For today, he is still alive. So I want to live with gratefulness and laughter and all the good things we can squeeze out of whatever time we have left together."

Sondra learned a lot about grace under pressure, watching her friend walk this journey. It made her more aware to cherish the moments God granted her as well and to enjoy the simple things in life.

They spoke about the amazing appearance of Nicholas and his wife.

"I could not believe it was him standing there."

Rene, as equally shocked to hear about it, was sympathetic to her friend. "You don't have to hide though, Sondra, because really, nothing happened. So you don't have to tiptoe around church."

"I know, but I still feel ashamed that he probably sees me as a hypocrite. I flirted with him, albeit years ago, and now he sees that I go to church. What message does that send to him?" She sipped her drink. "I just wish it had never happened. Even though nothing really happened."

Rene said, "Listen. Everyone has regrets in life. I know I do. You can't go around always looking in the past, wishing you'd done everything differently. That is no way to live. You confessed this to God long ago. You didn't really engage in anything that had lasting consequences, like an actual affair, and you have done a lot of growing in the years between. Besides, have you thought about the fact that he could be just as nervous about seeing you? He was married at the time too, you know. How old are his kids?"

"Wow. That didn't even occur to me. You know, you're right." She shook her head. "Isn't it amazing? If I had gone ahead and—well, you know, had an affair with him, Jennifer would have been the woman I would have hurt." She blushed with shame that the thought had even crossed her mind so long ago. "It's sobering thinking of it from her perspective. She seems so nice. I really think she and I could be friends. If only I didn't feel so guilty around her husband."

Rene shrugged. "You can still be friends. She doesn't need to know that you flirted with Nicholas years ago. How would knowing that help her?" She shook her head. "It wouldn't," she answered her own question firmly.

Sondra appreciated Rene's perspective. She was glad she could talk with her about it because this was one topic she sure couldn't talk about with her husband.

How am I going to explain to John why so soon after my newly proclaimed desire to reach out to new people, I'm dragging my feet, sending the Bianchi family an invitation to come for dinner?

* * *

In light of all Patrick and Rene were going through, it seemed effortless when Rene was around to remember the brevity of life and not get buried under the disappointments. When she wasn't there, however, Sondra found herself reverting back to her own struggles and sense of failure.

One day while cleaning up the kitchen, she was wrestling with the angst of wanting to use her time well. She didn't want to get to the end of her life and feel she had failed God or not done all He had asked of her.

Sondra, you still don't see yourself in the right way.

Where did that thought come from? What more could she want? John was being more purposeful in telling her how much he appreciated her efforts. That was making her feel a little better.

But something is still missing.

"What is it, Lord? Am I not doing something You are calling me to do? Am I ignoring something? Tell me what it is—I will do it. I don't know if I'm pleasing You with my life."

As she wiped down the table and counters, she thought about her struggle to identify some goal to shoot for that could provide her with a sense of accomplishment.

Washing dishes, she thought back to the talk she had given on the topic of patience, where she had exhorted the women to see what they did in their homes, raising their children and making a haven, as important tasks assigned them from God.

Somehow, I'm able to encourage other moms to see the investment they're making as worthwhile, but I lose sight of that truth for myself.

In her mind she knew that what she did mattered, but in her heart, some days it felt like it didn't. Knowing her propensity to feel bad for herself, Sondra prayed again where she stood, hands in the sudsy water.

"Lord, I know You are with me. I know You see what I do every day, and You know my heart. I don't want to complain about the very gifts I was delighted You gave us. I don't want my children feeling like they were a burden to me, especially since I really *am grateful* I get to stay home with them. But if I keep looking at every difficult and exasperating situation as a disappointment, that's exactly what they'll think they are—a disappointment, a mistake, a regret. I love my husband and kids, Lord. Please help me do a better job showing it."

* * *

One week brought a flurry of a dozen rejection notices that came for her greeting-card submissions. The same mail deliveries brought additional rejection letters from other publishing houses where she had tried to get her children's manuscripts accepted. Surrounded by torn envelopes all containing the same message, Sondra felt dejected. *All right already. I can take a hint.*

That night she shared with John, "I've decided to set my writing aside for a little while. Give myself some space from all the rejections I've been getting. Maybe come up with some new ideas."

John supported the idea. "That might be smart, honey. At least for a few weeks." Poking around for something to eat, he observed, "Besides, the fridge looks like it might grow legs and walk out of here on its own if it doesn't get cleaned soon."

She took his lighthearted hint and promised to begin the task of cleaning it out.

For a stretch of time Sondra enjoyed the freedom from the angst of feeling rejected every time she tried to do something with her writing besides tuck it into a drawer. She almost wished she could never write another word again. But she knew it was only a matter of time before she would feel the irresistible compulsion to write.

Until then, I am determined to enjoy this reprieve.

* * *

They were gathered at the kitchen table one Saturday morning a few weeks later. Sondra poured a coffee for herself and walked over to John, freshening his mug.

"Thank you, sweetheart."

"Hmm." She smiled at him.

"Oh, hey. I just remembered. I signed us up to serve communion tomorrow."

She put the pot down with a thump. "You did what? Why would you do that?" She was aghast.

He shrugged. "Charlie Peters called and asked me if we could help out. A couple who regularly does it is on vacation. I told him sure." He looked confused. "Sondra, it's not a big deal, what's wrong?"

"Are you afraid, Mommy?" Tommy piped up.

"Of course, she's not, honey. There's nothing to be afraid of." John looked at her pointedly.

She looked at TJ. "No, darling. Not exactly afraid, more like nervous."

John scoffed. "Nervous? About what?"

"John, I'm just not comfortable serving communion. It's a lot harder than it looks."

Her husband laughed. "Oh, Sondra, that isn't true." He took a sip of coffee. "It will be fine, you'll see."

She shook her head. "Oh, John, I wish you hadn't. What if I mess up?"

He shook his head, chuckling at her in amazement. "Sondra, seriously? You're that afraid of passing a little tray of juice and crackers up and down a few aisles? You've got to be kidding me."

Cecilia said, "You can practice with my kitchen set if you want, Mama."

John laughed. "There you go. That's a great idea. The kids can line up on the couch, and you can hand them each a tray. That's about as hard as it gets." He shook his head wonderingly.

Sondra good-naturedly laughed. "All right, fine. But I'm warning you. It's not as easy as you think."

They finished their breakfast and then went to strip their beds and do their weekly chores.

* * *

The next morning Sondra and John met Charlie at the back of the church sanctuary.

"Thanks for helping out, guys. I appreciate you jumping in like this."

"No problem at all," John assured him.

"Great. So I assigned you two the section in the back along the right wall." He showed them a map designating the area they would cover.

Sondra leaned in, looking carefully. *Maybe this won't be so bad. It's just eleven rows.*

"So take two silver trays each, and working together, pass one down each row, collecting the one coming back at you. Then return the trays to the table at the back. That's it."

"See. Easy-peasy." John grinned at her.

Sondra jabbed him lightly with her elbow, and he laughed.

"The only other thing you've got to make sure you do is make sure you serve anyone who may be sitting in the wheelchair section right in front there. We don't want to overlook them."

"Right. I'll handle anyone sitting over there," John offered, and they went back to their seats. Through the worship time, Sondra had an edgy feeling that she kept trying to push away.

Lord, please help me not to be nervous. Help me do this well and as unto You.

At the end of Pastor Paul's message, he gave the invitation for communion. "Would all our servers kindly prepare, please?" Sondra rose from her seat and nervously followed John to the back.

At the white cloth–covered table, they found two stacks of silver serving trays, each holding many servings of two small nested plastic cups. The bottom cup contained the small cracker representing Christ's body, and the cup sitting on top of the cracker contained the juice representing His blood. It was a solemn occasion, and Sondra didn't want to do anything that would dishonor it.

Shaking slightly, she carefully lifted two of the trays and made her way to their assigned section, where John already had started sending one of his trays down the first row. Thinking he would hit rows one and two, Sondra went to the third row and sent one of hers down, then moved to row four to send her second one down. John started frantically waving, and Sondra froze.

What? Did I do something wrong? Her eyes questioned him.

Then she saw the issue. John had alternated, sending his trays down the first and third rows, not the second. Helplessly, Sondra watched as the one she had sent got about eight people in when the two trays met in the middle of the third row while no one in the second row had yet been served.

"I'm so sorry," she whispered loudly, "can you please send that back to me?" Both trays came her way. The section of people looked amused, and she smiled embarrassedly. "Thank you." She quickly walked back to the second row. The man on the end of that row had his foot stuck out, and Sondra accidently stepped on it. He winced. "Oh, sir, I'm so sorry. Please forgive me." Her whisper carried to the ears of people nearby, and heads craned to see what had happened.

The man pulled his foot in and nodded his acceptance of her apology. She handed him one of the trays and ran to the fifth row to receive the other tray that John had sent down her way.

Uh-oh. I think I lost a tray.

Where was the fourth tray? Oh, good, there it was. She was concentrating so hard she didn't even notice whom she was serving. Suddenly, she was looking into the face of Nicholas Bianchi.

"Hello, Sondra," he whispered, giving her a brilliant smile. He took one of the trays from her, taking two nested cups and passing it to his wife. "Oh, hello," she whispered. Jennifer gave her a small wave, and she gulped and smiled back. They were the only two people sitting in that row, so rather than sending it down to John, Sondra took it back from Nicholas, who was gazing at her with a curious expression.

Don't get distracted now.

She turned her attention back to her task.

Darn it. I lost track again. Where did the two trays go that I'm supposed to collect?

A man on the end of a row held one of the trays into the aisle, and she hustled forward, seeing John gesturing madly at her from the other side.

What? What does he want me to do?

Suddenly, she realized she had all four trays on her side. People on the end of the rows were holding them, waiting for her to collect them, but she only had two hands. Drawing closer, she noticed that one of the people holding a tray was Victoria Wilson. The smirk on her face caused Sondra to redden.

Oh, good grief, how did this happen? I told John this was harder than it looked!

Panicked, she stacked two of the trays and grabbed the third from Victoria, noticing John wildly gesturing that the last row still hadn't been served. Grabbing the fourth tray from the man on the end who was holding it out for her, she ran to the last row and held it for the woman sitting on the end to serve herself before passing it down the aisle. The woman smiled at her as she took a set of nested cups. Completely by accident, Sondra bumped the woman's cups with the silver tray, causing the cracker that was in the bottom cup to jump out of its nestled space and land in the cup of juice that sat on top. It was a one-in-a-million shot, and Sondra nearly groaned.

The woman's mouth opened in surprise, and she looked at Sondra, dumbfounded, as her cracker floated on the top of her juice.

This is unbelievable. What are the odds?

Sondra looked up and saw John, who had seen the whole thing. He put his hand on his forehead, covering his eyes and shaking his head as people all around them snickered. They too had seen the crazy feat. Sondra sighed and held out the tray.

"I'm so sorry," she whispered loudly. "Please put that one back, and take another one." The woman did, and Sondra passed her the tray to send along that row. Balancing the two trays in one hand and the third tray in her other, she made her way back to the table. The servers of all the other sections were already seated. In the silence, Sondra felt all eyes of the church on her. Looking up front, she realized that Pastor Paul was waiting for her and John to finish serving their section. John hurried to the table with the fourth tray. They each grabbed a serving for themselves and hustled back to their chairs. As they sat down, Pastor Paul cleared his throat and addressed the congregation on the solemnity of what they were about to partake in. Sondra's face burned as she realized the comedy of errors she'd committed in passing out the elements.

At the end, after they were dismissed, John turned to her, his tongue tucked into his cheek to keep from laughing.

"Sondra Martin, you really are something else. I can't even imagine how you managed to do that." He started laughing. "You could hit that tray one hundred more times on purpose and not make the cracker jump from the bottom cup into the top cup. And did you step on that poor fellow's foot? How you do these things is beyond me."

She shook her head. "I told you. It's not as easy as it looks."

He chuckled. "Well, I have to say that I never dreamed it was as complicated as you've shown me it can be." He put his arm around her. They saw Charlie coming down the aisle toward them. The older man was wheezing slightly as he came closer.

"Hey, guys, thanks again for filling in. Just one thing though: I heard from a group of people in your wheelchair section that none of them got the elements?"

John smacked his head, groaning. "Oh no! I totally forgot!" Sondra shrugged, smirking and shaking her head.

"I told you!"

* * *

The following Tuesday Sondra was tidying the house in the late afternoon while Regan read books to Tommy, and Cecilia played with Mylah nearby.

She worked her way through the kitchen and headed for the family room. One look was all she needed. She called a blitz, and everyone came running for the cleanup game. She set the timer, and they all dashed to and fro, tidying, cleaning, and running to pick up as much as they could before the timer went off. They were all laughing and out of breath as the timer went off, the room cleaned and presentable again.

As they lay together on the couch, panting to get their breath, Sondra tried out one of her new riddles on them. "I am a tiny cave. I drip in colder weather. Sometimes a little finger comes and steals away a treasure. What am I?"

The kids called out all kinds of funny answers; CiCi finally landed on the right one, shouting, "A nose!" They hooted and laughed together. Pleased, their mom laughed along, amused that they could be so easily delighted.

The phone rang, and Sondra rose from the couch and answered it, still chuckling at her children's sweet laughter.

It was Linda Peters. "Sondra?" Her voice was sad.

Sondra shushed her kids, motioning with her hand for them to head downstairs where they could play. "Yes, it's me, Linda." She held her breath, suddenly wary. "What's wrong?"

"Sondra, I hate to be the one to have to tell you this terrible news, but Jennifer Bianchi's husband, Nicholas, died suddenly last night."

Sondra gasped in shock. "What?"

Nicholas dead?

Sondra sank weakly into a nearby chair and tried to listen, but she was having a hard time focusing on what Linda was saying.

How could he be here, living, breathing, walking with us one minute, and the next minute, just gone? I saw him Sunday, and he looked perfectly fine. What went so horribly wrong?

She realized with a start that Linda was still speaking into the phone, oblivious to Sondra's wandering mind.

"Of course, Jennifer is absolutely devastated. It's so frightening, really. He was only thirty-eight. That's a crazy young age to just die in your bed like that. I don't know how Jennifer had the courage to even call for help. If Charlie died like that in our bed, I can't imagine what I would do."

The older woman continued. "They're so new to our church, but I think she has made a couple of friends. Charlene is going to go spend some time with her after she gets off work." Linda paused. "If you think you could help out, I've started a sign-up for bringing them meals. Jennifer's mom is going to take the kids for a few days while she tries to get the funeral arrangements made. There are so many little details at a time like this. Are you able to help?"

"Oh my goodness, of course, I will, Linda. I'm just in shock. I . . . I'm so sorry. I am simply caught off guard. Do they know what caused his death?"

"I don't think they'll know until after an autopsy is performed. When Jennifer called me, she sounded so . . . dazed." She sighed and continued. "I went over there to help her keep the kids out of their bedroom while she called the police. Neither of us was sure whom should be called. She seemed remarkably calm by the time I arrived." Linda's voice lowered a bit. "But I'm waiting for reality to hit. In fact, I've got to go. I have a lot more calls to make, and I told Jennifer I would go back and be with her until Charlene can get over there."

Feeling like her head was in a fog, Sondra suddenly offered, "Well, let me help you. I can at least call all the women from my table. That will mean a few less for you to make."

"Thank you, Sondra. That would be a big help."

"Sure. If there's anything else I can do?" She offered.

"Really, just pray. That will be enough." The women hung up, and Sondra sat there, struggling to absorb the fact that Nicholas was dead.

She tried to stand, feeling her legs wobble underneath her, and sat back down. "Oh, dear God, please help Jennifer." Her heart filled with sorrow at the other woman's sudden and tragic loss. "And her children, Oh Lord, please help." She sat that way, her head in her hands for a few minutes, silent, praying. "What else can I do, Lord? I feel like I should do something more than bring a meal and make phone calls to my group."

As she spoke, a pang of regret pierced through her as she realized: though she'd been sporadic in her attendance for many months, Carolyn Carpenter was on that list.

* * *

With a weary sigh, Sondra hung up the phone and rubbed her aching eyes. On the list in front of her, she wrote the date that Susan Cleveland signed up to make a meal for the Bianchi family.

She had spent the evening calling nine of the other women in her group, answering their horrified questions as best she could, agreeing how terrible death was, and generally feeling overwhelmed and underequipped to have taken on such a task. She had spoken with or left messages for everyone on the list, with the exception of one: she'd put off the most difficult call for last.

Sondra looked at Carolyn's name at the bottom. Avoiding the task for a moment more, she began doodling on the edges of the paper. She let her mind wander to the suddenness of Nicholas's death and the inconsolable ache that poor Jennifer must be feeling. Tears began to spill from her eyes again as she was gripped by the finality of it all. The laughter coming from her kids' bedrooms hit her sharply.

How awful it would be to have to tell the children that John wasn't going to come home ever again.

Sympathetic grief overwhelmed her, and she began to cry.

Nicholas was alive and well just yesterday, never dreaming that it was the last day he would walk the earth. How is Jennifer coping with this?

"Oh God, please help them" was all she could get out. She decided she would put off calling Carolyn till morning. She felt an urgency to pray for Jennifer and her children. She tucked her own kids into bed with extra long hugs while her own husband dozed peacefully in their room after his long day at work. At the kitchen table, Sondra flipped open to a blank page of her prayer journal and began writing.

> Lord, this is so hard. I can't even imagine what Jennifer is going through right now. Please give her a peace that goes beyond human understanding. Let good come from it, somehow, and bring others to Yourself as they see the tender love You shower down on Jennifer and Brian and Lily.

As tears streamed down her face, Sondra kept writing, doggedly trying to pour her heart and prayer onto the page. She blew her nose and continued.

> Oh Lord, how can this bring You glory? He's not even my husband, and I'm questioning the why of this whole thing! Please build Jennifer's faith deeper that she would cling to You and trust You as You carry her through this awful journey . . . In the matchless name of Jesus, I pray. Amen.

That night, she slept restlessly, with the repeated cycle of waking and praying and crying and sleeping. The morning revealed a tearstained pillow, but she woke to a surprising feeling of peace and a quiet sense that heaven itself had heard her pleas.

* * *

"Carolyn?" She knew the weariness sounded in her voice, but she didn't care. This was too big a deal to let even the deep misunderstandings between them prevent her from carrying out.

Surprise was in the response. "Yes? Sondra?"

"Yes, it's me. I don't know if you heard the news yet . . . about Nicholas Bianchi?"

Bewilderment colored Carolyn's quick and sharp response. "N-No—what's going on?"

The tears threatened to bubble up again, and Sondra shoved them down with a strong swallow. "He died yesterday—well, the night before last, actually." She knew the inevitable line of questions that would follow and prepared to answer them as if from a prewritten script.

The gasp on the other end of the phone was audible, and Sondra was surprised and ashamed by the small sense of satisfaction she felt at the power of making the other woman feel something— anything—even if at such a cost.

Maybe she does still have feelings for the hurt of others.

Sondra hadn't been so sure these last many months as she had watched her daughter suffering from the loss of the friendship of Kayla, without any indication from Carolyn that either of them was capable of feeling any empathy.

"Oh my god, no!"

The jagged breathing on the other end of the line confused Sondra, and the enormity of her cry, like that of a wounded animal, made Sondra uncomfortable.

"Carolyn?"

"Oh, Sondra, you don't understand! I—oh my god, what am I going to do? I have to get the letters back! Sondra, I know we've been fighting, and you have every right to turn me down, but I need your help. Not only for my sake. Honestly, it's for Jennifer's sake, I need you to help me."

Every hair on her head tingled with an unnamed fear as she gripped the phone tighter.

"Carolyn, what is going on? What are you talking about?"

Another small moan came through the line as Carolyn struggled with the abrupt horror of Sondra's news. Then she shared her own terrible secret, and Sondra's heart plummeted.

* * *

John exhaled and ran his hand through his hair. The blow that Carolyn had carried on an adulterous affair with Nicholas Bianchi was hard enough to take. The fact that his widow had been unaware of the liaison and could, at any moment, discover the letters Carolyn had written to Nicholas was what they were now discussing.

"The only reason I thought getting the letters back could be justifiable was to spare Jennifer more heartache."

Her husband shook his head. "I don't think this can be kept a secret, Sondra. It wasn't some small matter." He clasped his hands together and tapped his fingers against his bottom lip, deep in thought.

I know Carolyn and Keith have had marital issues. Who doesn't, at some point? That doesn't mean you rush out and become involved with the first guy to show you some attention, does it? Sondra's anger was barely contained as she considered the costly ramifications of Carolyn and Nicholas's selfish actions. Then it struck her: that could have been her—ironically, with the same man even.

How can you be so angry with Carolyn and her selfish behavior when you were capable of the very same thing?

She looked at John as she wrestled with the voice inside.

Not exactly the same. Not anymore. That was years ago. I'm a new woman now.

But only by God's grace. And only because Rene had woken her up to the dangerous path she'd turned onto. The Holy Spirit reminded her of her own wretchedness apart from God at work in her life.

This was such delicate ground. She desperately wanted to handle this in a way that honored God yet didn't open new unnecessary pain to old sins that were dealt with long ago.

Sondra spoke hesitatingly. "John, I think I need to talk with Carolyn. After all, she is probably shocked and grieving as well."

John searched her face. "Honey, I appreciate that you want to be there for her, but what she did is so wrong. How can you have any sympathy for her?"

Sondra squirmed. She couldn't say aloud the thought in her mind.

Because I can relate to what the temptations were like.

She sighed again, wishing desperately that she hadn't been the one who made the call to Carolyn Carpenter. What would Carolyn have done if Linda had called her? Would she have divulged the terrible facts to her? Sondra didn't think so. Carolyn would know that Linda wouldn't have even considered hiding such an awful secret from Jennifer, so why was Sondra even entertaining the idea?

Why, oh, why did I have to be the one who found out this horrible truth? I don't want it.

She pushed at the thought of carrying the weight of this. It wasn't fair. Why would Carolyn, who hadn't even had the courtesy to pick up the phone once in any attempt to restore their friendship, feel she had the right to burden Sondra with this heavy news? She had nothing to do with it, and yet she certainly shied away from the idea of poor Jennifer having to shoulder any further heartache.

What am I supposed to do?

* * *

Her phone conversation with Carolyn was short.

"Please, Sondra. I need someone to help me through all this. You and I used to be so close. I don't know what happened. I think when Kayla and Regan had their falling out in February, I was so wrapped up in my own little secrets that I couldn't see that my daughter was starting to follow in my footsteps. Oh, Sondra, there's such regret in my heart! How I wish I could go back and undo all the pain I've caused. That's one thing I have really learned—there's no going back, no do overs, no second chances."

Sondra sensed desperation and even signs of remorse and appealed to John to let her have a talk with Carolyn. He relented, hoping it might lead to repentance.

In anticipation of their meeting, Sondra brought the kids over to Adam and Sophia's to spend the weekend with their cousins. Not knowing where the conversation might lead, she didn't want them around when she met with Carolyn.

Sondra set out a pot of coffee and waited nervously in the quiet house for her to arrive. Her thoughts turned to Carolyn's husband, Keith. "I wonder how he's taking all this?" she said aloud.

Sondra knew that he was a responsible, hardworking man. She realized he was a man of few words, and he wasn't exactly lavish in his praise, something Carolyn had confided early in their friendship that, in her words, drove her crazy. But that was a paltry excuse to cheat on him.

Again Sondra squirmed, remembering the excuses she herself would have used.

Really, the biggest thing now isn't to get the sordid details of why Carolyn cheated. It's to see if she'll repent and let God restore her marriage.

The doorbell rang, and Sondra jumped up to answer it. She was shocked at her old friend. Sondra had been expecting Carolyn's appearance to reflect anguish of the tragic news that her lover had died and that their tryst had been found out. But rather, her blond hair was arranged in a striking updo, her makeup was flawless, and she was wearing a bold printed top with her tight jeans and heels. Her nails looked freshly done too. She entered the house like she was arriving for a high time on the town. Sondra was miffed. *What happened to all the "regret in her heart" business? Doesn't she have any remorse for the pain she and Nicholas have caused Jennifer and Keith?*

Perching on the edge of the chair, Sondra eyed the other woman carefully.

I'm not going to make this easy on her.

She sat with her hands on her lap, waiting for Carolyn to speak.

Carolyn's blue eyes looked nervous for a moment, and then she opened up. "Thanks for letting me come over, Sondra. I know you are upset with me. Everyone is, I guess." She looked at her frankly. "I . . . I deserve everything I'm going through now."

She looked down into her coffee. "No matter what was happening with Keith, I knew it was wrong. It just felt so good to be noticed for a change." She paused. "You didn't know Nicholas. He had a way about him that was—I don't know—maybe *addicting* is the right word. He made me feel desirable and special." She sniffed. "To be called beautiful and to feel loved are some things I haven't had in a long time."

Sondra nodded slightly. *I remember well how captivating Nicholas could be.*

Carolyn pled with her, "You've got to believe me when I tell you I never meant to hurt anyone. Truly, I didn't. In fact, I was getting ready to tell Nicholas that I couldn't see him anymore unless we told Keith and Jennifer. Even though Keith had no clue, and I was pretty sure Jennifer didn't either, I couldn't keep up the pretense anymore. Then you called and told me the terrible news . . . I still can't believe it. I wish I hadn't asked you to get those letters back for me. I wasn't thinking straight. It was unfair for me to drag you into this whole mess, and I am sorry for that."

Carolyn rearranged herself on the couch, took a tiny sip of her coffee, and sniffed. "I don't know what is next for me now that the whole world seems to know about it. To be honest, Nicholas got off easy."

She caught the look of surprise on Sondra's face and reworded her statement.

"What I mean is, he isn't here to face the looks, the murmurs . . . the truth out in the open." She traced one of her arched eyebrows with the tip of her long nail. "I don't think Kayla or Benjamin really know about it unless people at school or church are talking about it." She sniffed again with some agitation at the thought of the gossip that certainly had to be circulating about her.

"Now Keith is talking about starting a new life without me . . ." She glanced at Sondra, then at the cup in her hands. "I'm not sure I'd want him to stay around anyway. I mean if things had been better between us, none of this would have happened to begin with, right?"

She sat, eyebrows raised, as if waiting for a reply from Sondra, who sat quietly, listening.

Carolyn continued. "Somehow along the path, I got buried under the pressures of life. I was lonely, bored. I know, I had friends—like you and the other women in our group, but it all seemed so . . . unfulfilling, I guess. I wanted to be like the women I watch in the soap operas: glamorous, leading exciting lives. Like the people I read about in the magazines—doing things, not just sitting on the sidelines, raising children."

She looked down into her cup again and then went on. "The kids' lives are going to be upended. I know the stats for kids of divorce." She sighed, plucking at a thread on her shirt, then continued with an injured tone, "There's nothing to be done now, I guess. We'll just have to take our chances."

Sondra shifted in her chair and cleared her throat, finally speaking. "Carolyn, it doesn't have to be that way. You could make the choice to start again with Keith and rebuild your marriage. I understand it wouldn't be easy, but if he could sense in you some amount of repentance for what you've done, maybe he would reconsider leaving."

The suddenly bitter look in Carolyn's eyes made Sondra shrink back as she replied bitingly, "I'm not sure I want him back. I've spent my whole life pouring into a lackluster husband and our ungrateful kids and letting my best years fly right past me." She softened her tone, saying cajolingly, "I mean, come on, Sondra, don't try to pretend with me. You must struggle with boredom too. Don't you ever dream of a more exciting life? I mean, what if the joke is on us? What if there isn't a reward for faithful living or hard work or a strict adherence to a set of rules? What if the fun *is* the reward and all those other people are right—that nothing is at the end of this road but a long cosmic laugh at our expense of being duped?"

Sondra carefully answered, "I can relate to sometimes having feelings of boredom or like some zest is needed in life. But there are plenty of healthy pursuits to keep us occupied—ministries at church, for example."

Carolyn shook her head. "That wasn't enough. I tried those things. Something was still missing."

Sondra gently asked, "Carolyn, I need to ask you: are you really a follower of Jesus Christ? I'm not the one who needs to hear the answer—you do. You will have to stand for your own decisions, and the biggest of them all is, what are you putting your trust in for your salvation?"

Carolyn sat very still for a few seconds before she replied quietly, "All my life I tried to do the right things. When Keith and I got married, I tried to be a good wife. When Kayla and Benjamin were born, I tried to be a good mom. I joined the church and the ladies' small group. I think God would be pretty pleased with my life. Well, most of it anyway . . . until recently." Small tears formed in her eyes.

Her words struck a tender spot in Sondra's heart: she understood all too well the enticements that were all around, ready to snare people with their lure of happiness or excitement.

Sondra prayed for boldness and shared what she firmly believed. "All God expects us to do is repent—to tell God we know we are sinners but that we are accepting the gift Jesus paid for us. There is no sin too big for God to forgive."

Carolyn sat listening quietly then nodded and said, "That's all right for you, Sondra. But it seems unfair that I'm stuck playing a part that I no longer wish to play, simply because some dead men in a dusty old book say so. The biggest reason I had the affair with Nicholas was—well, to be honest, it was exciting. Life had vitality, and I felt alive and free. Is that such a terrible thing?"

She wouldn't quite look Sondra in the eye as she continued. "Keith is a decent guy, but our best days are way past. I think I'm ready to see what else is out there for me. I am sorry other people were hurt, but I guess I can't help that."

She carefully set her nearly still full cup on the table nearby and stood, looping her bag over her shoulder. "Thanks for letting me come over today, Sondra. It was good to have someone listen to my needs for a change and help me sort through my feelings. I have to get going, but I'll see you around."

Helplessly, Sondra watched Carolyn go, knowing she was purposely walking away from the chance to put a stake in the ground and make a decision to follow Jesus.

* * *

That night John came home early from work, surprising her with a bouquet of beautiful flowers, which he bestowed on her while greeting her with a kiss. "Go get ready. Since the kids are at Sophia and Adam's, I'm taking you out to dinner."

"Oh, honey, what a wonderful surprise! Where are we going?"

"I'm not telling you. It's not fancy, but the food is great, and they have music, so wear your dancing shoes." He grinned at her like an excited teenager.

"Oh, John, how sweet of you." Her mind raced.

It's not our anniversary or my birthday. What is going on?

It was a bit of a drive, but she was touched when they pulled into the parking lot of Francesco's.

"Oh, John! Francesco's!" Tears welled up in her eyes.

John requested the same table they'd occupied when they were on their double date with Rene and Patrick years earlier, and the two of them slid in, observing that the decor hadn't changed a bit.

"What made you think of this, honey?"

John grinned. He reached across the blue tablecloth, pushing the napkin holder out of the way, and took her two hands in his own. "Can't I have a special night out with my sweetheart?"

Sondra grinned back at him, remembering the first time they'd touched hands and the electricity that had passed between them. "Oh, honey, this is so wonderful. I can't believe you went to all this trouble."

"It wasn't any trouble at all. I wanted to do this. I've been thinking a lot lately about how much I've had to work and all that you do at home every day." He brought her hand to his lips and gently kissed her fingertips. "With all that has gone on with Carolyn and Keith, I guess it made me realize I want to keep working to make sure our relationship is strong, you know?"

Sondra gulped and nodded. She appreciated her husband's attention to their marriage. She too wanted to keep it strong and alive.

They spent over two hours eating, dancing, and talking together, uninterrupted and thoroughly enjoying themselves. On the drive home, he reached out and held her hand.

"You know, from that first date, I was so entranced by you." John glanced at her.

Sondra blushed, and he continued. "I remember the way I felt watching you stand on your parents' driveway, the light of the moon glinting off your hair. I had never met anyone else like you, and I didn't want you to leave." He kissed her hand again, and she slid closer to him, laying her head on his shoulder as he drove them toward home. "As I watched you run into your parents' house, I felt so excited that we had met. In those months that followed, I remember telling God that if I ever was so lucky as to get to marry you, I wouldn't stop loving you for the rest of my life."

Sondra clutched her husband's free hand tightly. "Oh, John, I love you too. I wouldn't want to be married to anyone else. This has been such a wonderful night. I can't believe all the effort and planning you went to."

He pulled into their driveway, turned off the car, and came around to her side, opening her door and pulling her into the shelter of his arms. "The night isn't over yet, my darling."

They walked into their home, closing the door. She whooped in delighted surprise as John lifted her off her feet. Kissing her passionately, he carried her into their bedroom. Together, they made sparks fly.

* * *

With the kids gone, they were sleeping in late when the phone rang the next morning. It was Rene. "I need to talk with you. Can I come over?"

"Of course. What time is it?" Sondra squinted at the clock—almost ten o'clock. She remembered the night before and blushed, looking at her husband, who was still asleep. "Of course, you can," she repeated. "Is everything okay?"

"Yes, but I need to tell you something. I'll be right over."

Sondra quickly ran a brush over her teeth, dressed, and made a pot of coffee. Rene could be erratic at times but didn't usually sound panicked like she had on the phone.

A light knock on the door announced her arrival, and Sondra ran to unlock it.

Rene stood there, looking a bit disheveled, but radiant. She had been feeling much better than she had in her first trimester and was enjoying every minute of her pregnancy.

"What's wrong? You sounded almost out of breath. What's going on?"

Rene took her hand, led Sondra over to the couch, sat, and turned to her. "We're moving."

"What do you mean moving?" Sondra was not prepared for this news. "Where to?"

"Texas."

Sondra sat dumbly. "Texas? Why?"

Rene explained, "Listen, Sondra, there is a team of doctors down there at a world-famous hospital called MD Anderson that specializes in cancer—even glioblastomas like Patrick has. They really believe they can help him." She stared intently at Sondra as the news sunk in. "Oh, Sondra, I know this is coming as a shock to you. It is to me too. But we have to do this. If there's anything we can try at all . . ." Her voice trailed off as she looked down at her lap. Rene gulped and continued. "My sister says we can stay with them, even after the baby is born, until we find a place to rent." She looked excited and nervous all at once. "I will miss you so terribly, but we have to try this. For Patrick . . . for me . . . for our baby."

Sondra was shocked. "Oh, Rene, of course, you have to. I will miss you so much." A few tears escaped her eyes. She couldn't imagine what life without Rene would look like: the two had been best friends since they were five years old.

O God, please help me be strong for her.

She reached out, touching Rene's hand, wanting to encourage her friend. "But if there's even the slightest hope that they can help Patrick, of course, you've got to try it. When are you leaving?"

Rene quietly answered, "The end of next week."

Sondra protested, "But why so soon?"

Rene saw her stunned expression and gently explained, "There's no reason for us to stay here. Patrick is already on extended sick leave with work. The longer we wait, the more his disease progresses. Every day could make a difference."

Sondra nodded. She was trying to hold back a torrent of tears. She needed to be strong for her friend, but seeing Rene's sudden tears unleashed her own, and the two women wept together, hugging and holding each other for comfort and support. Sondra reached for nearby tissues, taking some and handing the box to Rene.

Rene wiped her eyes. "I'm going to miss you so much. You can't begin to know how hard this decision was. But it's a chance we can't pass up." She blew her nose.

Sondra nodded, wanting to reassure her friend that it would all be okay. "God will go with you. I know He has good plans for you." She thought about Rene's words from long ago. "You're getting out and living an adventure," she reminded her with a teary smile.

Rene nodded. "Yeah, I guess I am." She touched her belly, rounded with the precious baby inside. "I'm going to have so many questions." Worry covered her face. "I'm scared, Sondra. I was counting on you to help me."

Sondra reached out to squeeze her hand. "Oh, Rene, I'm not going anywhere. You can still call me anytime, day or night. You know that. I will still be here."

Rene nodded, and the two friends stood, hugging again.

Sondra choked up. "I will be praying for your move and, of course, for Patrick's treatment. If I can help in any way, please let me know. And please keep us posted on everything," she implored.

"I will." Rene looked around the comfortable room where they'd spent so many happy hours sharing life together. "I can't quite believe we are really leaving."

She turned to Sondra at the door. "Patrick wants to say good-bye to John too. We will plan on stopping by before we leave. And I promise I'll call you as soon as we get settled in with my sister. Good-bye, Sondra."

"Good-bye, Rene. I'm going to miss you so much. I love you."

"I love you too."

Sondra held the door, watching her friend walk back to her car. So many thoughts tumbled through her head—concern for their move and getting settled, prayer for Patrick's healing. But she was ashamed of herself for the one selfish thought that pressed most on her mind.

How will I make it without my best friend?

Ten Years Later

June 2006

Sondra studied her reflection critically in the full-length mirror in their bedroom and sighed. Hair that was determined to turn gray and a few more wrinkles around her green eyes revealed the march of time.

Maybe I am carrying a few extra pounds too.

At thirty-nine she was long past the day of striving for a nonexistent perfection. Nowadays, she was grateful to be mostly ache free and reasonably healthy.

It was hard to believe that so many years had come and gone. They had recently celebrated Regan's high school graduation. She was excitedly planning for college to start in the fall. It would be a tough season, watching their oldest embark on the next venture in life, but one that Sondra had known was coming and had been trying to prepare her heart for. She was thankful that Regan was going to a nearby college, only thirty minutes away, so she could still live at home and commute each day for classes.

She turned from the mirror, sighing, then prayed out loud, "Lord, help me be grateful for Your gift of life and not complain about the havoc that aging causes. I know there are plenty of people who would gladly switch places with me for the chance at a few more years with their loved ones."

It was a subject she thought of often as various friends and loved ones of friends faced severe illnesses and even death.

Knowing how Sondra felt about the fleetingness of time, Linda asked her to speak periodically to the young moms' group at church, like she was going to today.

Driving to the church, she prayed, Oh *Lord, please let my message be Yours.*

She stood before them, opened in prayer, and began. "I want to encourage you as a mom who has been where you are. I remember the weariness, the challenges, what it's like to feel short on temper and long on time. Trust me, I remember. At least, on my good days, when that part of my brain stays with me," she quipped, pausing as they tittered with polite laughter. "I remember the craziness of life with young energetic kids—the seemingly endless questions like, 'Why won't my shoe flush down the toilet?' or worse to hear—'Why won't *yours?*'"

The women laughed, and Sondra smiled. "So yes, I do know what you are facing. But more importantly, God knows, and He has some answers for us on how He wants us to use our time as moms. Please open your Bibles to Genesis 24. Most of you know the beautiful account of how Abraham instructed his servant to find a wife for his son, Isaac, from Abraham's own land, five hundred miles away. The servant humbly prayed for direction from God to supply exactly the girl he had in mind for Isaac. God miraculously allowed the servant to identify Rebekah, and she agreed to return with him and become Isaac's wife."

Sondra said, "Often when we read Bible stories, naturally, we focus on the key players. But when I read it recently, this very obscure character leaped off the page at me."

Sondra explained, "We have to remember, in that culture and time, most children would usually live in the same town as their family. Rebekah's mom probably would not have anticipated such an amazing thing as someone showing up from hundreds of miles away, ready to take her daughter off to be married to a man in a strange land, far from home, where her days of input were essentially over. There were no telephones, no computers, and no social media. Her precious daughter was moving five hundred miles away to live, and they would possibly never see each other again or, at least, not often. She was a real woman, who had feelings, just like us, and regrets and sorrows, just like we do. The Bible doesn't mention this, but is it possible she wished she had taken better advantage of the opportunities she had while they were within her grasp? Like her, we have no control over what God may bring into our lives tomorrow, but for today, we have the moments that are right in front of us. Let's use those carefully and in a way that we won't wish we had done it differently when the seasons of our lives change."

Sondra continued. "I stand before you today, a mom now with teenagers and one heading off to college soon. I knew these days were ahead of me, but somehow, it still caught me off guard."

She gulped hard, pushing back the tears that threatened, and moved on. "Through those younger years, I remember struggling at times, thinking that what I was doing at home with my kids in the daily minutia of raising them was not really that important," she paused, looking at them imploringly, "when it turns out, it was what mattered most of all."

Sondra leaned in. "You are in such a wonderful season to cultivate a love for learning about God in your child's heart, but weariness and apathy can be fearsome enemies. I've heard it said that 'the days move slow, but the years move fast.' That's so true, isn't it?"

A lot of heads nodded; one woman called out, "Amen."

Sondra continued. "In the daily grind, we can become distracted with the pressures of life and overwhelmed with the challenges and look for escape by whatever is around us that gives us reprieve. It's certainly good to take a break. But after we are refreshed, we need to get back to our first priority in training these precious young lives God has given us to raise. Are we building into them and instructing them? Spending regular time in God's Word? Actively modeling a vibrant prayer life, where they see us on our knees, pleading for God to be at work in our own hearts?"

She paused, looking around the room. "This season is just that: a season. It doesn't last forever. We need to use the time while we have it. Then as our children are growing and going and gone, we can sit back, knowing we gave our best to the building of something wonderful with God's help.

"The world will tell you, 'Parenting is so thankless and hard that you shouldn't bother trying,' or that it's 'drudgery and demeaning to spend your time at home.' What we need to remember is that none of these statements are what God tells us about the role of motherhood. Please, let me be clear, I'm *not* talking to the woman who needs to work outside the home here, because there are legitimate situations where a mom does *need* to work."

A few of the moms nodded, and Sondra continued. "I'm talking to the mom who, because she finds no personal fulfillment in being at home and doesn't see it as a calling from God, decides she'd rather pay a nanny and let someone else raise her kids while she takes on other interests. I'm talking to the mom who, day after day, turns on the television and tunes out the kids while she watches soap operas and dreams of a better, sexier life full of passion and drama. I'm talking to the mom who is with her kids begrudgingly and yells all the time, making everyone around her miserable, telling her kids in essence, 'You are unwanted.'

"But may I gently suggest that the very difficulty—no, the *impossibility*—to do it day after day on our own is exactly why we need to seek God's strength. We must ask that His grace be poured out on us to help us be engaged, patient, kind, loving, and filled with His insight and wisdom. We must remember Philippians 4:13, 'I can do all things through Christ who strengthens me.'"

She paused. "Trust me on this. As a mom who wishes I could go back and do plenty of things differently, I'm telling you, there will come a time, down the road, when you would take even one of the bad days for a chance to live the season you're in again for a moment. Hang in there!"

She leaned in. "Let's pray right now for God to help us stay engaged and that we would find the joy God wants us to have in partnering with Him to shape and raise these treasured gifts from His hand."

A young mom came up to her afterward. "Thank you, Sondra. Your message was exactly what I needed to hear. I always feel so tired. It's been hard to find much joy in my days at home with my kids."

Sondra gave the younger woman a hug. "God doesn't ask us to do this life alone. Call me anytime you need to be reminded. And if you need a break, I'd be happy to watch your kiddos for you to dash to the store or for you to get some time for yourself."

She thanked Sondra again before running off with a renewed spring in her step to get her children from the nursery.

* * *

John, busy with work, was gone for longer stretches these days. As he had climbed the corporate ladder, he had also spent more time in the corporate jet, flying to other branches, putting out fires, and handling tough situations that senior leadership left in his capable hands.

Since watching how John had handled Hal and his poisonous attitude, Tom Hillers, the company CEO, had finally fired Hal and handed the reins of running their branch office over to John the past seven years—a blessing, but with many additional responsibilities and challenges.

With the kids busy with their own activities, it would be a good day to work on her latest project. Sondra had heard about a contest open to the public to come up with a story line to market a local company, Ganda Beef. All submissions were due within two weeks. Sondra wanted to try her hand at coming up with a story to submit. She had been writing and tweaking and was almost ready to share it with her family for review before she would turn it in. The hours flew by in a rare day of quiet in the house.

"There, that ought to do it."

She tucked the notebook away and went to make dinner as one by one, her family returned home.

John dragged in last, washed his hands, and dropped wearily into a chair. "Honey, can you please pray over our meal?"

"Of course." They joined hands around the table; she prayed and then looked at her husband with concern. "Are you okay, John?" Everyone looked at him worriedly.

He rubbed his hand across his face and tried to stretch a kink in his neck. "Oh, sure. I'm fine. Just beat." He yawned and took a bite of his dinner. "How was everyone's day?"

Mylah piped up first, "Me and Trixie spent the day picking out what we are bringing for camp. She let me feed her pig too." She smiled.

Sondra corrected her, "Trixie and I."

"Oh, right." Mylah took a bite of food.

TJ offered, "Drew and I went to the movies."

His dad nodded. "That sounds fun. What did you see?"

"*Ice Age 2* and *Superman Returns.*"

Confused, his mom asked, "Wait, what? How did you see two movies? I only gave you enough money for one."

Tommy looked at her sheepishly. "We movie hopped."

"You did what?"

"They movie hopped," Cecilia interjected. "They watched one movie, and then when that one was done, they watched another. It's no big deal, Mom. Everyone does it."

Appalled, Sondra protested, "Well, it's a big deal to me! Don't you kids see that that's wrong?"

"Why? If you already paid for your ticket to get into the theater, it's fine. Besides, the way they stagger the start times, you don't get to see the whole second movie anyway."

Sondra shook her head. "I'm shocked that you kids don't see that this is wrong. We have taught you better than that."

John caught her look and chimed in, "Your mom is right, kids." He held up a hand to stop CiCi's coming argument. "I know you paid to get into the cinema. I get that. But they're trusting that you only go to the showing you paid for. It isn't right to cheat them out of their money by seeing a second movie." He sternly eyed up all the kids. "I don't want any of you doing that anymore, got it?"

They all nodded.

Silence descended as everyone ate, each busy with their own thoughts.

John stabbed a forkful of food. "Did you get any time to work on your Ganda project, honey?"

Sondra nodded. "Yes, I finished. In fact, I was hoping to run it past you all tonight." She jumped up and fetched her notebook, bringing it back to the table.

Suddenly, she panicked.

What if they hate it?

She argued with herself.

This is your family, Sondra. Knock it off. Even if they do hate it, they'll still love you.

She sat down. "First, I guess I should explain that my idea is for an animated man, the mayor of a small town named Fanda, to be the one talking. The backdrop is that an entire truckload of Ganda burgers has been delivered to Fanda by mistake. At first, the mayor is—well, here, I'll just read it to you." She cleared her throat nervously and read:

> "I'm fizzled and fuzzled
> Perplex-ed and puzzled
> There is no denying
> My insides are crying—
> Confused and confiding:
> My 'Oops' pressure's rising!
> I'm flummoxed and fit-foofed
> And wondering—Who goofed?
> How could this have happened?
> We're stuckered and trappened—
> No way to escape it
> We must now embrace it . . ."

Pausing, he takes a big bite of the juicy Ganda burger—then surprised he enthuses:

Derlicious! Sure Licious!
You say its nertricious?
It's simply outstanding!
My dismays disbanding!
I didn't expect it—
We must now protect it—
I proclaim from here forward
We'll push ever tor-ward
This scrumptious derlicious
Nertricious, ferficious
Pernicious pugnacious
Entirely gracious
Yummy Fo Fanda
Burger by Ganda!"

She stopped and looked at her family expectantly.

Awkward silence filled the room, and Sondra's heart dropped.

"I don't get it." Mylah's nose screwed up. "What do all those weird words mean?"

Regan said, "I think Mom made them up, Mylah."

John tapped his finger held on his lip as he thought about it. "Huh. Well, that was interesting, honey."

TJ laughed. "I think it was pretty funny. I mean, I'm not sure I would buy a Ganda burger from it, but your rhyme is sick, Mom."

Tears formed in Sondra's eyes. CiCi saw and disdainfully said, "Good grief. That means he likes it, Mom. You don't have to cry."

Sondra closed her notebook and pushed it away. "I was trying to think out of the box and come up with something unexpected."

"Well, I think you achieved that." John smiled.

Tommy declared, "Sometimes it's good to stay in the box. The box is good. The box is safe."

They all laughed; even Sondra had to smile.

John rubbed her hand. "Honey, I think we just expected something different. You shouldn't quit simply because we didn't understand. The main question is, what will Ganda Beef think about it? They may love it. And I'm proud of you for even trying."

She gulped, nodding.

They all cleared the table, putting food away and cleaning up the dishes. The four kids agreed to play a game together. "You want to play, Mom?"

She loved games and often joined in, but not tonight. "No, you kids go ahead. I think I'm going to read for a bit."

John looked at her, giving her a big bear hug and lifting her off the ground. She protested, "John, you'll hurt your back."

He stubbornly hung on. "I'm fine." He lowered her to the floor and gave her a kiss. "Once in a while I need to show you that I've still got it." He grinned at her, and she laughed. He gave her another hug. "I need to work on some things in my office. I'll be in later, okay?"

She nodded, grabbed her notebook, and went to their bedroom.

* * *

When he came to bed, John confided, "We've been dealing with some cyberbullies at work."

"What is that?" she asked, putting her notebook down.

John ran his hand through his thinning hair. "We don't know exactly how many, but some people at work have been visiting a certain Web site and writing some pretty horrible things about fellow employees and management, including yours truly." He ran his hand through his hair again. "These posts could ruin people's reputations and careers. Tom assigned me the task of tracking down who is doing it."

"Do you think Hal is behind any of it?"

Though he had been fired years earlier, the office was still feeling some of the effects of his disastrous leadership and the fallout from that period of time.

John raised his eyebrows. "No, at least, I don't think so. Whoever it is is writing some really nasty things, but they also seem to know enough current details to distort the truth." He glanced at her wonderingly. "At least I don't think Hal's involved."

"Well, this sounds like the type of thing he would have done."

John mused, "Now that you bring up his name, I do wonder where he is."

Sondra said matter-of-factly, "Probably dead of a heart attack."

John turned to her, shaking his head, lightly scolding, "Sondra."

"What?" she protested. "He fits the type, and you know it. It's not my fault he had such a terrible temper. I'm only saying that lots of people with bad tempers die suddenly of heart attacks."

He rolled his eyes. "Well, that's true, I suppose."

"You know it's true." She continued. "He was a terrible man, and I'm glad he's gone. You can't tell me you aren't relieved that he is no longer at the bank?"

Silent a moment, John replied, "No. I'm not saying that. But there are times I have wondered if I did all I could to show Christ's love to him."

Sondra looked down. She struggled to find sympathy for the man who had caused such pain in her husband's life for so long. "I don't want to hold a grudge. But I can't help being grateful that God removed Hal from our lives. Wherever he may be, if he's still alive, I hope God grabs hold of his heart. But I'm glad you're spared from having to cope with him any longer."

John sighed. "Well, this search is going to keep me pretty busy. I'm sorry, honey. I know I've been working a lot lately." He walked into his closet to hang up his clothes.

He came out, and Sondra assured him, "I understand, John. Don't worry. I will be praying God helps you find the people who are doing it."

He climbed into their bed. "Are you going to submit your Ganda burger proposal?"

She bit her lip. "I don't know. I think I am going to wait on it a while and see if I can think of some other ideas."

He nodded. "Okay. Well, you know I love you no matter what." He gave her a kiss, and she moved into the shelter of his arms.

* * *

Out of curiosity, a couple of days later Sondra visited the Web page John had mentioned, wanting to know what kinds of things were being discussed.

When she saw a thread containing her husband's name, she clicked it and instantly regretted it: the outright lies about her husband brought her immediate pain. Whoever was behind it clearly had lost all hold on reality.

What cowards! This is all untrue filth. How could anyone be so cruel to write such garbage?

She exercised great self-control, resisting the urge to type out angry replies to the vile lies, but quietly exited the site with disgust.

That night after dinner Sondra told John what she had done. He ran his hand through his hair and shook his head wearily. "Honey, listen, I don't want you going on there again, okay? There is nothing that will edify you. It's not worth sifting through. Promise me you won't? I have to because it's my job, but I don't want you to carry the weight of reading all that trash and being unable to do anything about it. It's a waste of your time and will only bring you pain."

Sondra said vengefully, "I hope you find them John, and I hope the company brings charges against whoever it is, and some good long jail time is involved. They deserve to suffer for the awful lies they've written, and I hope they do!"

John chuckled at his wife's fierce defense of him and hugged her. "I appreciate your loyalty, Sondra, but you, of all people, shouldn't be exposed to this junk. You take it way too personally." He gave her a kiss and went into his office.

Alone, Sondra wrestled with the truth.

I'm trying to become more forgiving, but when it comes to defending those I love, it's hard.

She knew the Bible was clear on this point: James said that judgment without mercy would be shown to anyone who himself had not been merciful. And Jesus warned that if anyone refused to forgive other men for their sins, God wouldn't forgive them for theirs.

Sondra sighed. "Lord, please help me. I don't want to hold grudges. Somehow give me Your love to spend on others."

* * *

She and John had agreed that the time she had to fill while he was so busy with work could be a good time for her to make another attempt at writing her book that had been long set aside. But when she revisited the project, she found she had outgrown it.

I'm almost embarrassed to have written this. Have I changed that much?

Glancing at her lowest bookshelf, she saw her old journals lined up neatly. On impulse, she pulled an early one. Thumbing through the pages, she stopped at an entry.

> I hate him. He's so mean to me, and Mom won't let me get out of his class. I wish Mr. Anders would just leave me alone. There are times I think about doing something to myself. That would make him feel bad. Maybe then he'd feel sorry for how he treats me. But I'm too chicken. And I don't want to hurt Dad and Mom. I guess I'll just have to live with it . . . till I can't anymore.

Sondra drew a quick breath and looked at the date—November 1978. Like a slap, clarity struck her. Mr. Anders, her sixth-grade teacher, had been a terrible teacher, and Sondra remembered feeling dark and helpless during that year. But she marveled that she had ever felt so utterly desolate to consider the thought of hurting herself.

How could I have forgotten this? Oh Lord, thank You for letting me get past that tough season.

She browsed through a few more entries before pushing the book back onto the shelf and pulling a folder of some writings to work on.

She was reading when Mylah bounded into her room and onto her bed.

"Mom, do you think you'll ever get new furniture? Trixie showed me her parents' bedroom, and their furniture looked really nice."

Sondra chuckled. The pieces had been passed down from John's grandparents. The style was out of fashion, and some of the drawers of her dresser stuck horribly, but she enjoyed the history associated with them. She was under no illusions that her children would be interested in the pieces when they had homes of their own, but she was content using the antiques that had seen better days.

"When the Pearsons come, can I get the door first? I want Trixie to see my new shoes!"

Her daughter excitedly ogled her new footwear.

Sondra laughed. *Oh, to be eleven again and have the simple pleasures of life mean so much.* "Sure, honey, that's fine. Are you sure you're all packed up?"

"Yep. I've got everything I need. I went over my list three times, and CiCi and Regan helped me put it all in my bag, so I am ready."

Summer camp had been a favorite of all the kids. Now, after hearing about it for years from her siblings, it was Mylah's turn, and she was excited for the adventure ahead.

"Me and Trixie are going to pick archery and horseback riding for our first choices and canoeing and beading for our second ones."

Sondra couldn't let the poor grammar go. "Trixie and I."

She looked at her daughter, grinning. Mylah smiled back. "Oh yeah, Trixie and I."

She jumped off the bed and looked in the full-length mirror, admiring her shoes again. The doorbell sounded. She squealed and ran to answer it.

Sondra followed quickly behind and greeted the statuesque, lovely woman at the door. "Hi, Loni. Hi, Trixie. Thanks again for driving Mylah. It's such a help."

Loni replied, "We are happy to do it, aren't we, Trixie?"

Her daughter nodded, helping Mylah with her bag and sleeping bag and pillow.

The two girls had hit it off quickly when the Pearson family moved into the area a few years earlier and started attending their church. Loni, a kindhearted African-American woman, fit easily into the women's group that Sondra was a part of while John had discovered several mutual interests with her husband, Denny. Their son,

Kyle, was a year younger than CiCi. From what Sondra had heard, he was someone who took his faith seriously, a rare thing to see in anyone these days, let alone teenagers.

Sondra gave Mylah a kiss and a long hug good-bye. "Have a wonderful week, my darling girl. I can't wait to hear all about it when you come home." She released her, and Loni let the girls pass to take Mylah's items to the waiting car.

She gently pulled her aside, asking, "Sondra, are you available in the next couple of days to talk with me about something?"

Only now, Sondra saw the tension written in Loni's expressive eyes. An inexplicable burst of worry went off in her mind. "Of course. Absolutely, we can."

Relief erased whatever had been on Loni's face only seconds ago. "Good, I will call you in a couple of days then."

"Better yet, why don't you stop by? Let's make it tomorrow or Wednesday and stay for coffee. That way we can visit a bit too, okay?"

The tall woman agreed the next day would work and hustled out to the car, where the girls were giggling with excitement over their weeklong adventure away from home.

Sondra waved good-bye as the car backed out of the driveway, closed the door, and stood there for a moment. "What could Loni want to talk about?" she wondered aloud.

She stifled a sigh, heading for the kitchen, where Tommy stood with one foot up on a chair for extra support, strumming on his guitar. He was a good player and had potential to make a career out of music if he stuck with it.

Regan came into the kitchen, playfully reached up, and tousled Tommy's hair, dodging his return swat. "So, Tommy, did you tell Mom about the girl who posted on your wall?"

"Be quiet, loser."

Sondra turned around, astonished.

"Thomas James! What did you call your sister?" She was shocked—and troubled—by the ease with which he said it.

"Oh, it's okay, Mom," said Regan, defending her brother, "everyone says that. It doesn't mean what you think. It's really a term of affection now, not like in the olden days."

Tommy grinned and nodded, looking sheepish. Almost fourteen, he already towered over the rest of his family.

"Well, it may be fine with you kids, but that doesn't make it right. You shouldn't casually throw around such awful words at one another, and I am telling you now, if I hear it again, I will wash that person's mouth out with soap. None of you are too old for that," she finished sternly. She turned back to the sink, grabbing the last of the vegetables to peel for steaming.

Cecilia walked in, grabbed a carrot, and began munching. "Not too old for what?" she asked, catching the last part.

"Too old for Mom to wash your mouth out with soap if she hears you calling me a loser again," replied Tommy unhappily.

"What's the big deal? Everyone says that," said CiCi, scorn written on her face.

"Not everyone, young lady, and certainly not in my family." Sondra wiped her hands on the towel and pulled the bag of marinated chicken out of the refrigerator.

CiCi replied, "I hear people at church say stuff like that all the time—and a whole lot worse."

Sondra said, "That doesn't make it okay. We all sometimes say and do things that look and sound more like the world than someone who claims to follow Christ with their life. That's the danger: that we become so much like the world people can't see a difference anymore. What kind of light will we be then?"

CiCi muttered under her breath, "It's not that big a deal."

Sondra thought a moment and said, "You know, I hadn't thought of it in a long time, and I don't think I ever told you kids, but back in grade school, I had a really awful teacher. He ridiculed me along with two other kids in my class. The three of us were shyer than the other kids." She cleared her throat. "Once I remember him telling me, 'Sondra, you don't have what it takes, and you're going nowhere in life.'" She gulped, the pain of the memory cutting freshly through her heart. "I didn't find out till later that his father was close friends with the superintendent of our school district, so he was untouchable, and he knew it."

Regan's voice cut into her thoughts. "Why didn't Grandma and Grandpa go in and talk to him?"

"Oh, trust me, I asked them to. I begged them to intervene or, at least, to get me into a different class. I can still hear my mom's words: 'Sondra, as you go through life, you are going to run into good authority and bad authority. You can't escape every hard situation that comes up, you must learn how to trust God to take you through it.'" She took a deep breath. "It was a very hard year for me. If Rene hadn't been around, I don't know what I would have done."

She couldn't bring herself to admit to them the forgotten confession in her journal—that she had considered the thought of taking her own life over it.

Sondra went on. "The other two kids' parents moved them, one out of the school entirely, the other to a different classroom, leaving me to bear the brunt of Mr. Anders's unkindness alone."

CiCi said, "Mom, people say stupid stuff to each other all the time. You can't go around crying at every last insult in life. Maybe Grandma was right. You needed to learn how to toughen up a little."

Sondra looked at her and sighed. "I admit I'm probably too sensitive. But I don't like people who use others as their comedic punching bag to hurt them." Sondra wiped her hands on the towel.

CiCi persisted, "Well, sure, but you tell us all the time that good things can come even through trials in our lives. So even though the guy was a jerk, there must have been something good that came out of it."

Sondra nodded. "I'm not saying that *nothing* good came from it. Actually, it taught me a mixture of things. Some good, some not so good." She remembered back. "One good thing was that I became more tuned to the hurting of others." She took a deep breath. "But one of the hardest things to overcome was a resentment I grew against my mom. I felt like she should have protected me better. It took me a long time to get to the place where I forgave her."

CiCi crunched her carrot. "Well, if you ask me, calling someone a loser isn't the same. No one minds being called that nowadays."

Sondra saw Tommy nod slightly.

Sondra challenged Cecilia, "How do you know? When you call someone something unkind like *loser* or *dirtbag* even though *you* may mean it to be funny, how do you know that they don't take that to heart?"

She stood quietly for a moment. "My grandma used to say, 'Among my most prized possessions are words I didn't say.' That unkind thing—once it's out there, you can't take it back. Can you kids just please think about that before you say things you might regret?"

CiCi bit her lower lip. Tommy turned to Regan. "I'm sorry for calling you a loser, Regan. You know I didn't mean it like that."

Regan gave a little laugh. "No problem, TJ. I forgive you."

Regan came over to her mom and gave her a hug and whispered in her ear, "I love you, Mom. You're right. I guess it could hurt someone, and I would feel bad about that . . . but no one calls anyone *dirtbag* anymore."

Sondra smiled ruefully as her daughter gave her a peck on her cheek and ran to answer the phone that was ringing.

Tommy picked up his guitar and began working on his song again. CiCi stood quietly while Sondra started to prepare the chicken for the Crock-Pot.

"Are you okay?" she asked her middle daughter.

"I—" She was interrupted by Regan standing in the doorway, holding out the phone.

"Mom? It's Mrs. Jeffries."

Sondra quickly washed and dried her hands and took the phone, vaguely noting the look on CiCi's face as she walked out of the room.

"Hey, Charlene."

"Sondra, hi. Do you have a minute?"

"Sure, what's up?"

"I know you're so busy already, but could you maybe meet with Theresa and me? I'm out of ideas to share. We only have Christina, and overall, she and I are really close. I haven't dealt with some of the problems Theresa is having with her daughter." Charlene hastily added, "Not that I'm saying you are. I didn't mean it that way."

Charlene knew about the periodic challenges she'd had with Cecilia.

Sondra hurried to assure her, "No, I understand, Charlene. Absolutely, I would be happy to meet with you guys. It might encourage her to know how often I've been praying for her."

"That would be great. Our next meeting isn't until late next week at my house. As I thought about it, with all that's going on at Tim's company, we could be transferred sooner than we thought. Theresa really needs someone who is likely to stay around for a while to counsel with."

"When do you think you'll be moving?"

"It's hard to say. It could be a couple of months or six." The other woman sighed. "Either way, I'm going to miss you all so much."

"Oh, Charlene, we will miss you and your family so much too. I still can't believe you're going." She sighed. "But wherever you end up, I know you will be a blessing. Any idea of where yet?"

Charlene replied, "If it all goes well, Tim should have his pick of either Switzerland or France. I am hoping for France."

"Wow. What an exciting opportunity."

"Yeah, it is, but—oh, hey—Susan is beeping in, so I need to let you go. Thanks, Sondra."

"Okay, bye."

She went back to the kitchen and wrote the upcoming meeting on her calendar.

Sondra went in search of CiCi and found her in her room, listening to her iPod.

"Cecilia? Is everything okay?"

CiCi barely took the earbud out of her ear. "Yep."

"Well, did you have something you wanted to talk about before? I'm sorry, I wanted to hear it, but Mrs. Jeffries needed to ask me something."

"It was nothing. Really. I was only going to see if it's okay if I go to Bethany's house sooner. Regan said she could drive me."

"Well, that's fine, but are you sure that was all you wanted?"

"Don't worry about it, Mom, it was no big deal." She started to push the earbud back into her ear, turning away.

Sondra persisted, "I'm sorry I couldn't talk right at that very moment, but I'm here now and am all ears. Can you please share with me whatever it was?"

Exasperated, CiCi turned to her. "It doesn't matter, okay? I'm used to taking a backseat around here."

"That's not fair, Cecilia. You don't take a backseat."

"Yes, Mom, I do. You don't want to admit it, but you're always busy. Either helping Mylah or one of your friends or busy with your writing or stuff Dad needs your help with. But it's okay. I'm used to it. I'll be out of here soon enough, and you won't have to worry about trying to fit me in."

Stung by the statements flung at her like piercing arrows from her daughter's mouth, Sondra protested, "That's not true, Cecilia. You know I will always make time for any of you children. You come before anything else I'm involved in."

"Fine. You're right. I'm wrong. You're always available. Is that what you want to hear?"

Sondra stubbornly persisted. "I'm not trying to make you say something you don't believe, Cecilia. But you're not being fair. I was on the phone for, like, ten minutes. Are you saying you can't wait for ten minutes for me to help someone else out? Because if that's the case, how about you think about how selfish that is instead of getting mad at me for trying to help people?"

"Right, I forgot. It is all my fault. That's fine."

"I'm not saying that." Fresh frustration swept over her.

Why is it so hard dealing with her sometimes? Why does she never want to take responsibility for her own actions?

Watching her daughter as she turned her attention back to her iPod, Sondra backed out of the door, hurt by the sudden wall CiCi had put up.

Once again, I'm a failure.

"Stop it Sondra," she muttered. Her horrible habit of negative self-talk wasn't going to help.

Things will smooth over. I just have to give it some time.

On her way back to the kitchen, she heard music coming from Tommy's room. She stood by the door, listening to her son playing his guitar and singing, the song somehow familiar.

"When people are succumbing to temptation all around, and Your name is being trampled on the ground, help me, Lord, to keep my eyes on You, Your infinite grace and love will carry me through, and at the eeend of the daaay, this whole world will melt awaaay, and the strength and the power and the glory of Your name will remain . . ." The music stopped with her knock on the door.

"Come in."

She walked in. "Tommy? What are you singing?" She sat on the edge of his bed, looking at the sheet before him.

He looked at her, blushing. "I hope you're not mad. I saw this sitting on your desk a couple of days ago, and I liked the words, and well, I thought I could put it to music."

"Mad? How could I be mad? I am surprised, that's all. When I wrote that, I had no tune in mind, but I really like what you have done with it!" She smiled at him, amazed at how God had gifted their boy.

Tommy grinned. "Well, don't get excited just yet. I'm sort of stuck on some parts. I was planning to surprise you when it was done."

"Oh, honey, I'm so pleased you think the lyrics are worth working with." She gave him a hug and left him to his task, heading back to the kitchen to finish prepping for dinner.

She set the Crock-Pot to cook and began praying quietly, "O God, please, won't You grab hold of Cecilia's heart? I don't know how to reach into the dark place she seems to be sometimes. I hate to admit it, but I worry if she's even a Christian. There are times she sure doesn't act like one. Please, won't You do what only You can and soften her heart for Yourself?"

CiCi came into the room. "Mom?" she said softly.

Sondra felt tears fill her eyes. "Yes, honey?"

"I'm sorry for what I said. That you don't make time for us kids. I know that isn't true. Will you forgive me?"

Sondra hugged her. "Oh, sweetheart, of course, I will. I'm sorry too. I don't want to fight with you, CiCi. I love you." She brushed the hair off her daughter's face, desperately wanting peace between them.

"I love you too, Mom."

Regan stepped into the kitchen. "You ready to go, Ceec?"

"Yeah."

The girls grabbed their bags and headed for the door.

"Drive carefully, girls. And please don't be late for dinner." She paced restlessly. The real heart of the issue with CiCi had not been addressed; a temporary bandage was put on it. She headed into her room and spent a few minutes trying to pray, but her mind wandered.

Should I read?

She picked up a book by one of her favorite authors but couldn't stay with the story. She closed the volume and saw her computer on the little desk.

Should I write a post in my blog?

It had been a long time since she'd posted anything, mostly because she felt like it was another area of failure in her life. She had started with such excitement, eager to see how God might use it to encourage others and create healthy dialogue about Christian living. Instead, she had garnered only a handful of readers who tuned in with any regularity.

Sondra clicked her computer on, pulled up the blog, and reviewed her last post, written the past winter. Rene had left the comment, "Love this! Thanks for sharing!" It had gotten four likes by others.

She sighed.

I need to call Rene. Boy, do I miss her.

When Rene and Patrick had moved to Texas, they found the help needed to overcome his disease. His surgery had been successful, and his healing, miraculous. The couple rejoiced in God's goodness as they found a wonderful church that offered them the support they needed in their time of trial. Their daughter, Mariah Jane, was a beautiful girl, with all of Rene's passion and exuberance for life and Patrick's good sense.

Still feeling agitated, Sondra shut down the computer.

I could write in my journal.

Sondra had kept a journal most of her life. She grabbed her current one. Flipping open to a random page, she began reading.

> March 22: I don't know how to help TJ. He is overwhelmed with school and all the demands. He has a couple of tough teachers this year, and it's frustrating. After all, they have the kids all day; do they have to dominate their evenings and weekends too? I would love to go in and ask these questions, but John told me to stop always trying to fix things for the kids. So I told Tommy, "Listen, honey, not everyone in life is kindhearted. You have to get used to that, and do your best to be respectful and obey. I don't know what else you want me to tell you." He got upset with *me* and stormed off, muttering, "Not that." I never know the right thing to say. It sure was easier when the kids were little, and I could control their world better.

Sondra lowered the journal to her lap, discouraged. She noticed a loose paper was sticking out of the bottom. Sondra pulled it out and unfolded it, reading:

> My heart is heavy as I see how much Cecilia is squandering the love and peace our home could have. Her sarcasm and quick anger are mystifying. I sometimes catch a fleeting glimpse of the sweet little girl she used to be hidden underneath the belligerent teenager that she's become, and I can't help but wonder: where has she gone?

Sondra felt weighed down by the unresolved problems going on with their daughter. Every time she and CiCi had an argument and dealt with it, Sondra hoped that would be the turning point, the one that ended the pattern of sin and repent, sin and repent. So far, though, even though Cecilia would come and apologize, there had always been a next time with the same broken cycle.

Do any other families have these struggles happening in their homes? It feels like we are the only ones. I feel like such a failure sometimes.

She pondered that thought.

That's not really fair. You're not the only ones suffering with rebellious teenagers. Don't forget about Theresa and Melissa.

Sondra shook her head, arguing out loud with herself, "Yeah, great. I'm supposed to meet with a woman whose daughter is giving her challenges. Talk about a pot calling the kettle black."

Or think of it as sharing with her the things God's trying to teach you through your trial.

She bent her head. "Okay, Lord. I will trust You through this. Help me handle these situations with my daughter in a way that honors You."

Sondra sighed and put her journal away, suddenly feeling too agitated to write. She opened the deep drawer filled with her writings, pulling out a huge stack of folders. Leafing through, she found an old poem she had written years earlier. She read it, noting with wry amusement the truth of the words her younger self had written, but couldn't possibly have fully understood.

When from messy handprints my windows are free
And a swing no longer hangs in the tree,
When peanut butter on sale does not bring delight
And I no longer read nursery rhymes each night—
What else shall I do?

When small hands reaching up for mine are grown
And my children have children of their own,
Will I care about the time I spent cleaning their messes?
Or will I MISS the stray toys, books, shoes and dresses?

O Lord, let the stains and the smears they leave
behind
Be reminders of happy years in a home where
kindness lived.

Help me see past the childish prank
And look in those eyes so wide and frank,
And help me to teach, not scold,
So that when my children are old
They'll tell stories of sweet times past
And have good memories that will last.

Torn pants, frogs in pockets, dirty, drippy faces
Are all things that time erases,
And the stories will take their places—
"Remember when?" will be all that is left
Of these precious moments and days,
Let's enjoy these tender young lives
God has given us to raise.
Lose yourself in their sweetness and charm,
Pray for them, that God keeps them from harm,
Laugh at their silliness; be sad with their sorrow
And you'll have less to regret on that distant
tomorrow.

She found more of her works, similar in their urging to
embrace the years before they were gone. Sondra sat on the edge
of her bed.

Have I even heeded this myself?

She loved being a mom and wife. It was her biggest blessing
and gift. But she had also spent many hours, wishing, dreaming, and
pursuing the other goal that had eluded her.

*I don't get it . . . library shelves are filled with the collective output
of millions of minds that have followed through on their personal goals
and accomplished them. Why can't I seem to? Worse, though, if I'm going*

to be honest with myself, did I let my pursuit of this consume me to the point of damaging my relationship with CiCi?

Sondra spotted a bright yellow envelope in the drawer. She fingered it, wondering.

"Wow. I'd forgotten all about this."

It was a letter from Jennifer Bianchi, now known as Jennifer Wright since remarrying several years after her husband's death.

Sondra thought back to those hard long months after they had learned the shocking truth of Carolyn and Nicholas's betrayal. To her credit, and Sondra's surprise, Carolyn had gone to see Jennifer the week following Nicholas's death. She had told Jennifer that she, at least, owed her some answers to the questions she certainly must have had.

Apparently, Carolyn and Nicholas had first met while at a local coffee shop. She'd arrived early for a meeting with a friend, and he had stopped in and seen her sitting alone. Carolyn divulged that initially, Nicholas's charming friendliness had drawn her in—something no one had any trouble believing. As she had opened up to the attractive Italian, they found some mutual interests. They exchanged contact information, and over the next several months, they met. The whole liaison had offered an air of excitement for the lonely housewife.

"He opened up a whole new world for me, one that was exciting and fresh and vibrant. I couldn't help myself, and although I feel badly that we hurt other people, I can't help that I don't feel sorry for the time we had together."

Jennifer had handled the whole discussion with extraordinary grace, something she later told Sondra and Charlene was "completely God's doing." Sondra remembered how she had looked, sitting in the Martins' hearth room, appearing so small and vulnerable, and sharing the suspicions she had had for years with the two women who'd become her friends.

"Nicholas was always charming to people. That was one of the first things that drew me to him too." Tears had formed in the beautiful Italian woman's eyes. "We weren't that far into our marriage when I started to notice that he was very attentive to other women.

I thought maybe having children would make him more loyal, and it seemed to at first." She had held a teacup in her hands but had yet to take a sip. "He was very proud of our children." Jennifer had looked at them imploringly. "He wouldn't have done anything to hurt them . . ."—the pain sliced into her voice—"so I can't understand how he couldn't see that his cheating on me would eventually hurt them."

Now, sitting in her room, Sondra opened Jennifer's letter and began to read the lines, with the gently looping letters, written by the hand of a woman who had gone through so much pain yet had chosen to let God work in her life through it all.

> Dear Sondra, I know you didn't know me that well before—well, before everything. You need to know how much I appreciate the many cards and letters you sent me as I was going through that extraordinary time. My whole world was falling apart, and having you there to walk through it with me, well, I can't fully express what that meant.
>
> Those were terribly dark days. I look back and wonder how I even made it through sometimes. But God is faithful, and He uses people willing to be used by Him to carry out His purposes. Please know that I will always hold you in such high regard for the way you carried my burden with me. Now that I'm further away from it all, I can clearly see God's hand in protecting both me and my children.
>
> Through most of my marriage, I had forgotten something my mother used to tell me—that I am "*amato, perdonato, e redento*"—loved, forgiven, and redeemed. It took me going through this hard thing to bring those words to mind again.

In one of the letters you sent me, you included a poem that you wrote. I hope you do something with it. It really is very good. I made a copy of it to share back with you. Since you sent me so many verses and poems, I didn't know how else to let you know how much this particular one ministered to my spirit.

Thank you, Sondra. Thank you for taking so much of your time all those months to walk beside me. I count myself blessed for having known you.

Jennifer

Jennifer had included the copy of Sondra's poem, and Sondra read it.

Tragic despair all around us
Hopelessness threaded through pain
Suffering, loss never-ending
Betrayal, corruption and shame

This is the cry of existence!
On our own, there is no good we bring ~
This is the place where He met us~
Paid the price, felt God's wrath, took sin's sting

Disappointment and sickness and sorrow
Trials, temptations and tears
Life overwhelming and daunting ~
Praise the Lord! He's erased all our fears!
Praise the Lord! He's erased all our fears!

This is the cry of existence!
On our own, there is no good we bring ~
This is the place where He met us~
Paid the price, felt God's wrath, took sin's sting

Now my future outshines all the darkness
This journey, though hard, is just brief
There's heaven awaiting the faithful ~
And a joy that's replacing my grief!
Yes, a joy that's replacing my grief!

Victorious over death He conquered!
Now to my Savior I cling!
Shout His praise! May His Name be uplifted!
My Jesus! My Savior! My King!
My Jesus! My Savior! My King!

How insensitive! What must I have been thinking? That song speaks of betrayal and pain.

She remembered back to some dark days she herself had gone through that had led her to pen the words.

Compared to what Jennifer went through, what do I know of suffering?

She was almost ashamed of the callousness she must have had in thinking that the words might somehow comfort Jennifer at a very dark time in her life.

And yet . . . Jennifer said that of all that I sent her, that was the one that spoke most deeply to her. So somehow God used it for good.

Sondra sighed, tucking the letter back into the drawer, where another folder caught her eye. It was full of dozens of songs, phrases, and stanzas that she had started and not completely finished. Glancing at one, she read it quickly:

Help me Lord, to keep my eyes on You,
To see the trying things that come my way,
As chances to rely upon Your grace—
That I might draw much closer to the very heart
that gave His life for mine . . .

Sondra wasn't really reading the actual words. Instead, she was comparing her life to other people's: all around her, she had seen successful people doing exactly what she had always dreamed of doing but had failed at repeatedly.

She fingered a thick stack of rejection notices for various submissions she had made over the years.

Why would God put this longing and gift in my heart but then deny me the chance to actually use it?

Slowly, the thought crossed her mind: what if it wasn't really a gift at all? What if she had just wanted it so badly that she had latched on to the few compliments she'd received over her life and hoped that she had what it took to be a writer?

That's sobering.

Sondra couldn't exactly pin down what she was feeling, seeing all those words that she had written through the years—so many attempts to share her thoughts with others.

Sondra knew she had a propensity toward self-pity. She needed to fight it all the more as only one word came to her mind to define how she saw herself: *loser.*

* * *

That night, John came home super late from work, changed into some comfortable clothes, and gathered her in his arms.

"Ah, this feels good. It's been a long week."

"John, it's only Monday."

He laughed. "Yeah, well, it feels like it's been a full week already."

Sympathy welled up in Sondra's heart for all her husband had to endure.

Lord, please give him Your strength as he goes through this hard stretch at work.

John stretched out on their bed, grabbing for Sondra. She curled up in the cove of his arms, loving to snuggle with him.

He kissed the top of her head. "Ahh," he sighed wearily. "This is fabulous. I could stay here like this with you forever."

She nestled in close and listened to him breathing. Had he fallen asleep? Her mind wandered. She started thinking about all John did for their family.

Lord, why did You give me such a wonderful husband? I don't deserve him.

Tears started to well up in her eyes. Why should John be proud of her? He worked with dozens of women who balanced a full career with motherhood.

Is he disappointed that I'm not doing enough with my life?

She sniffled, and John turned her head up to look into her eyes. "Honey? Why are you crying?"

Sondra wiped at her tears, upset that he had discovered her crying. "Oh, it's nothing."

John persisted. "Sondra, clearly, you are upset about something. I'm not leaving you alone until you tell me why."

Sondra looked at him. "Sometimes I wonder why you ever married me. I mean I know you love me, but I don't understand why. I haven't done anything very wonderful with my life and am starting to wonder if I ever will."

John shook his head in amazement. "Sondra, where did you ever get the idea that you aren't doing something wonderful with your life? You mean, because you don't earn a paycheck? Is that it? Because I'm here to tell you, that doesn't matter. That is nothing. I am so thankful for the wife and mom you are. You have this crazy idea that what you do doesn't matter to this family. You couldn't be more wrong."

She started to squirm. "I thought you were sleeping."

"Well, I wasn't. You need to hear me on this." He looked at her seriously. "Honey, what you do every day is so important. You pour out your energies making a haven for us to come home to. You cannot measure what that means to the kids and me. This is a hard, cold world. Every day I see people who have no hope, no joy, no tenderness, battering over anyone in their way." He shook his head. "The heartache out there—" He broke off, looking at Sondra, and began stroking her cheek tenderly. "You cannot understand how much I value you and your sweet gentleness. You are precious to me, and I thank God every day for giving me a wife like you. Have you forgotten our word?"

She ducked her head into his chest. "John, no."

"Come on. I want to hear you say it." He started to tickle her, and she laughed out loud.

"John, stop!"

He grabbed her wrist, grinning. "Not until you say it."

After she had shared her long-ago embarrassment about Gisele Waters's French phrase, he had turned the word into a private joke they shared. Whenever he felt she was going down the path toward self-pity or feeling like she was less valuable than others, he wanted her to remember their conversation and used that word to trigger her memory of how he viewed her.

Sondra was laughing hard now. "Okay, okay. *Lavi.*"

He released his hold on her, saying, "There it is. You said it. Good job."

"You're such a big goof."

"Yeah, but a lovable one."

He grabbed her again, pulling her close to him, and she snuggled into his arms. "I love you, Sondra, just the way you are."

She was so grateful for her husband. He always knew what to say to encourage her heart.

"I love you too, John."

"Honey," he continued, "you've got to start finding your identity not in what the world says, but in what Christ says about you."

Sondra nodded. "I know. You're right." She often mixed up the difference between feeling unworthy and worthless. They weren't the same. She wasn't worthy—no one was. She was a sinner in need of God's grace. But she wasn't worthless either. God saw her as highly esteemed and much loved—not because of anything she had done, but because He chose to put that value on her. She couldn't earn it and would never deserve it.

She snuggled closer to her husband's side, grateful that he was such a godly man who could remind her of these truths when she floundered, and fell asleep with a contented heart.

* * *

The next morning Loni Pearson came for the promised visit. The two women sat out on the patio, enjoying the sunshine and fresh air. Sondra wondered when her friend would bring up her real reason for their get-together. Loni nervously fingered her ring, twisting the sparkling diamond around and around on her finger. Sondra grew nervous watching her.

"I know that I said I was hoping we could talk. And I still want to, but well, it's kind of something I stumbled on that really isn't any of my business, regarding someone whom I understand is an old friend of yours—her daughter, actually."

Sondra quickly thought through her friends with daughters, not jumping to any particular one. "Okay. Who?"

"Kayla Carpenter."

Kayla Carpenter?

She had graduated the same time as Regan had a few weeks back, but they had no further involvement than a casual awareness of each other ever since the whole breakup so many years ago. She couldn't imagine anything Kayla might do or say that could have any impact on her or her family anymore.

"Oh. Well, what about her?"

Loni fidgeted a bit in her chair and then burst out, "I hate putting myself in the middle of something where I don't belong. Please trust me, ordinarily, I would never insert myself into something like this, but it affects you and your family, and I really respect you, Sondra. I think you and John have a really great thing going, and your kids are all so sweet. I hate having to—"

"Loni, for heaven's sake, would you just tell me?"

For crying out loud, how bad can it be?

Flustered, Loni nodded. "Kayla is going around, telling people that . . ." Loni closed her eyes a second and then pushed on, "That Regan had an abortion."

Sondra nearly dropped the glass in her hand. The color drained from her face.

"Please believe me, when I heard it from Kyle, I told him that it was absolutely untrue."

Sondra sat like a stone. She was afraid, if she moved, she might explode.

It's an outright lie! Oh my god, what must Kyle think? Or Loni? Please, God, help her know that this isn't true. Oh, my poor Regan! I . . . I can't believe Kayla would say such a thing!

"I know your daughter well enough to know that she hasn't done any such thing. I wrestled with whether to even come to you or not but felt that you deserved to know. If that was being said about my daughter, I would want to know."

How could anyone be so vile, so full of hate and vengeance?

"Oh, Sondra, I'm terribly sorry. I wish now that I hadn't said anything to you. To be honest, I'm sure that whoever has heard it knows your family well enough to know it couldn't be true." Loni was wringing her hands as if wishing she could undo the words spoken and go back to before when they were chatting about what fun the younger girls must be having at camp.

Sondra blinked back tears. "O Lord," she prayed quietly, "please help. This hurts."

* * *

Loni had the graciousness to see that their little party was over and discreetly left after hugging Sondra and assuring her that she would be praying for this to be resolved and the blemish on her daughter's name removed.

When will the ripple effects from Carolyn's poor choices stop flying outward and hurting the people around her?

Proverbs spoke of the foolish woman who "tore down her house with her own hands." Terrible choices led to tragic consequences, and Carolyn and the fallout around her were proof of that unavoidable truth.

Kayla, no doubt wounded by the whispers and malicious gossip, had had to grow up under a cloud of shame and an absentee mother, who had walked off the job of instilling godly values into her daughter. Lashing out at others was probably her only way to cope.

She probably didn't care if they were lies as long as someone else was hurt the same way she was hurting.

And really, it's two lies because for Regan to have had an abortion first means that . . . Sondra could not go there.

But what are we supposed to do about the rumor being spread around church and school?

If unaddressed, Regan's name could be completely and unfairly tarnished. What about the younger three kids? They had to live with the reputation of an older sister who was being falsely accused as well. It wasn't fair.

She moaned and prayed out loud, "Lord, you know this hurt and the entire mess. What do we do? I love my daughter. I don't want her life ruined by this terrible lie being spread about her. Part of me wants to march over there and punch Kayla or pray that You bring great punishment down on her for this." Sondra knew that temptation was not from God, but she struggled to say the next words and mean them. "Oh Lord, help her to see that what she has done is wrong, and help me to love her with Your love because right now, I can't."

When John came home, weariness was all over his face. Sondra hated to add one more thing to his burden but needed his wisdom and strength to help her carry this and know what to do.

He was as broken by it as she had been when Loni first shared it with her. But it really alarmed her when she saw him tearing up. She ran to him, putting her arms around him, wanting to console him, alarmed by the unfamiliar sight of him crying.

He brushed at his eyes, took a breath, and resignedly faced his wife. "Have you spoken with Regan yet?"

"No, I wanted to ask you if you thought she needs to know. Can't we spare her this hurt?"

Sondra looked pleadingly at him. He stared back at her, weighing out their options.

They both saw Regan in the doorway at the same time, taking in the scene before her.

"Mom? Dad? Is this an okay time to talk? I have something I need to tell you both."

An uneasy feeling started in the pit of Sondra's gut.

John was the first to speak. "Of course, honey, come in." He sat, patting the couch cushion between him and Sondra. Regan sat down, leaning against him. He stroked her hair and looked at Sondra over her head. "What's this about, sweetheart?" Concern clouded his eyes.

Regan cleared her throat and said, "Well, I've wanted to tell you for a while, but wasn't sure how to, that, well, that I've decided that . . . that I really want to go out of state for college."

Sondra was certain her relief was palpable by the huge breath she expelled.

Regan continued. "I know that MCC is a great college. But there's a small Christian college that I sent information for—Delaney Christian College in West Virginia. Jillian Cooper was telling me that they have amazing chapel times with really great guest speakers who bring convicting messages. The campus is so beautiful. Really, the only drawback is that it's ten hours away from here."

Encouraged that they were listening, Regan eagerly went on. "I think it would be amazing to be with other young people who really love God, where my faith can keep growing, and I can see what else God has for me in life."

Sondra's heart rejoiced to hear her daughter's words, and she leaned in to hug Regan. "Oh, honey, I am so glad to hear you say that."

"You are? I thought you'd be like, 'No way, it's too far away from home.'"

John laughed and said, "Yes, it is far, but we are willing to talk about it. And, darling, no matter which school you end up going to, Mom and I are so proud of your desire to follow Christ with your life. That's more important to us than anything else."

"Oh, thank you, Mom and Dad! I'm going to tell Jillian you didn't say no yet. I love you!"

She kissed each of them, then jumped off the couch and ran back to her room, blond ponytail flying out behind her.

John looked at Sondra. They both became sober again at the situation that hadn't been yet resolved, just pushed to a back burner for a few wonderful moments.

"You know we still have to talk with her about this, right?"

"But why? Why does she have to know about this? Hasn't she been through enough at the hands of Kayla Carpenter?"

John shook his head. "Honey, Regan is going to need to learn how to handle conflicts eventually. We cannot shield her from every last thing that comes her way. We must learn how to trust her to Jesus's care and let Him worry about her reputation. Now that we know this is out there, we need to let Regan know. You wouldn't want to have it come to her ears from someone who cares less about her than we do, would you?"

"No, that's true. I'd rather she hear it from us."

John nodded. "Let's wait till tomorrow though. Let her rest tonight and enjoy the idea of going to Delaney Christian College without her joy being marred."

Sondra nodded. She was thinking that, somehow, when things were put into proper perspective, things that might have frightened her, like the idea of Regan going so far away to college, seemed less important when weighed against more crucial things, like her daughter having a heart that was clean before God and who wanted to pursue Christ fervently with her life.

Thank You, God, for Regan's desire to grow in her faith. Now, I need Your peace about the idea of letting her go so far away from home and everything she has ever known.

* * *

The rest of the week sped by quickly. Home again, Mylah was full of excitement about all that summer camp had offered.

"On the first day, we all got tested to swim across the lake, and I got a blue tag. Blue is for the best swimmers. We could go anywhere we wanted and not have to stay close to shore. There was a girl there named Katrina who got stuck with red. Red means you can't even get in the water because you don't know how to swim. We felt bad for her, so Trixie and me spent some of our time in the pottery barn since Katrina couldn't do any of the water sports. I made this!"

Mylah proudly set a clay object on the kitchen table.

Tommy asked, "What is it?"

She indignantly replied, "A turtle, of course. Anyone can see that."

CiCi dryly remarked, "What turtle is bright pink? It looks like blob of bubble gum."

The talkative girl had had a marvelous time and wanted to share every last detail. Her chatter dominated nearly the entire dinner conversation.

Sondra noticed Regan barely picking at her food. She had been quiet ever since hearing the sobering news of the rumor. Regan had cried and denied that there was any truth in the wicked accusation, something Sondra had known already, but it was good to hear her precious girl confirm.

Through their tears, they had gone to God's Word together to see how to handle this in a way that honored the Lord. Sondra had opened to Romans 12: "Do not repay anyone evil for evil. Be careful to do what is right in the eyes of everybody. If it is possible, as much as it lies within you, be at peace with all men. Do not take revenge, my friends, but leave room for God's wrath, for it is written: It is mine to avenge; I will repay, says the Lord." Psalm 112:6–8 also brought comfort: "A righteous man will be remembered forever. He will have no fear of bad news; his heart is steadfast, trusting in the Lord. His heart is secure, he will have no fear; in the end he will look in triumph on his foes."

They decided to take the approach of waiting on God to see how He would work through the heartache and prayed for clarity and wisdom while they waited. Regan even prayed for Kayla, something that brought tears to Sondra's eyes when she heard the words—not of revenge, but of forgiveness—coming from her daughter's mouth.

She was so proud of Regan. Even in the middle of such a hurtful trial, her young daughter was standing tall, trusting that God would work out the details.

Oh please, God. Please work this somehow for good.

* * *

As hard as it would be, she and John had decided to allow Regan to attend the college in West Virginia. Sondra wasn't sure how they would make it through without their eldest child around. She found herself crying at random moments at the thought of her leaving.

What am I going to do when she is actually gone?

She was back to tucking each of the kids in at bedtime and praying with them, something that she had gotten away from over the years. To quit doing such a simple thing flew in the face of everything she urged other women to do and the message of purposeful engagement she often spoke about.

There's a word for that: hypocrite.

"Stop the negativity, Sondra." She was trying to curb her terrible habit by turning to prayer instead.

"Lord, I want to engage with my children and not just let them drift into adulthood. Sometimes I get so distracted with my own pursuits that I sacrifice the one role that has a limited time of being a hands-on mom. Please help me."

Starting with Mylah, she spent twenty minutes or so, sitting bedside with each of the kids, hearing about their days, praying with them, and listening to things that were on their minds.

Finishing up in CiCi's room, Sondra tried to ignore the mess. Piles of clothes were strewn everywhere, as if the closet had vomited up all its contents. But Sondra wanted this time to be positive, not filled with criticism. Cecilia already was the most shy about her mom coming to tuck her in.

Maybe if I hadn't let the practice die off, she wouldn't feel so awkward.

Sondra perched on the edge of CiCi's bed as her daughter gazed at her. "How are you doing, honey?"

"I'm fine."

Sondra longed for the days when things were easier between them. She smiled gently at Cecilia. "I'm glad to hear it." She plucked at the blanket. "How was your time with Bethany today?"

"Good. She's doing okay." Cecilia paused, then looked directly at her mother. "Her brother, Brad, was smoking pot when their mom was gone today."

Sondra sucked her breath in slightly but resisted the impulse to lecture her daughter, instead waiting to hear if she would share any further revelations.

"Bethany said he has been doing it for a month. He offered her some."

Sondra gulped, quietly waiting.

"But she said she didn't want to try it. We went through health class last year, and they talked about the effects of drugs on your body. It scared most of the kids to see what you're doing to yourself when you do drugs."

Sondra nodded, softly stroking her daughter's hair. "Oh, my girl. I'm glad that Bethany made a good choice." Sondra ached for the world her daughter had to grow up in, where drugs and sex and so many temptations were all around far too easily for the taking. "How Dad and I love you, Cecilia. We are proud of you." She sighed. "We don't want you to throw away your life, making stupid choices. I hope you know that if you ever feel tempted to try any of the things that are out there, you would stop and remember: the one you are hurting most is yourself. And God. And me and Dad."

CiCi nodded. "I know, Mom."

"Well, I'm going to be praying for Brad that God would reach his heart and that he would stop before he throws his whole life away in such waste."

"Mom?"

"Yes, honey?"

"You won't call their parents, will you?"

Sondra hated that question.

If it were one of my kids, I would want to know.

"I don't know, I guess I could wait a little while anyway. You said he's been doing it for a month. Maybe we can be praying that God lets his parents catch him at it so we won't have to become directly involved."

Cecilia nodded, relieved.

Sondra prayed then kissed her daughter good night and stood outside CiCi's bedroom door for a moment.

What other confidences have I missed out on?

227

She sighed and went to her bedroom, where John sat on their bed, working on his laptop as the nightly news played in the background.

Sondra slipped into her closet, shed her clothes, put on her lounging pants and soft pajama top, and headed to the bathroom to remove her makeup and brush her teeth. As she crawled into their bed, John turned to her, muting the television.

"Honey, I have some news. But I need your attention."

Sondra looked searchingly at him, concern etched on her face.

John laughed at her look. "Don't worry, it's nothing bad. In fact, it's a very good thing. We were finally able to track down the employees who have been posting all that hate speech."

"Oh, John, that's marvelous! Who was it?"

"Two women in Promotions and a guy from the loan department. They don't know yet that we are on to them. Once we talk to Legal about exactly how we should go about it, they'll all be confronted and fired. Tom is considering whether to bring charges of libel or just let it go since we were able to unearth them, and he wants to get this behind us."

Sondra was about to say how glad she was that the perpetrators had been caught and that she hoped the company would decide to pour its full wrath upon the individuals when she felt a still small voice speaking to her heart.

Suddenly, she was convicted about the reality that apart from God opening her eyes up to her need of Him, she too was a sinner capable of great ugliness and hate. She felt God putting His heart of tenderness and mercy in the place where her self-righteous anger had been only moments before.

Oh God, please open up their eyes to their need of You. I pray that all three would somehow come to know Your Son.

"But the big news is, because of how quickly we were able to bring this to a close, I'm being considered for a promotion. Rumor is that my name tops the list in a role for senior director."

Sondra gasped. "Oh, John! That's wonderful. Oh, honey, I'm so proud of you! All your extra effort—it's really paying off now. When will you know?"

"I don't exactly know. It could be a couple of weeks before I find out, but there's something else you need to know." He ran his hand through his hair and looked at Sondra. "For me to take this promotion, we would have to move to the corporate offices in New York."

Sondra sucked in her breath.

"Move?" she said dumbly.

And to New York City, of all places?

She sensed an undertone of desperation in John's voice. "If we pass on this opportunity, there might not be others down the road. I'm already forty-two." His voice turned pleading. "The thought of this job is exhilarating, Sondra. I know I can do it. I'm qualified, and I could bring a lot of experience and fresh vibrancy to the role. If I just could get a sense that our family would thrive, this decision would be a no-brainer." He took her hand. "There are so many things I've wanted to give you, honey. This promotion would make some of those things possible."

"John, I'm perfectly happy. I don't need anything." She moved to assure him. "All these years, you've given me and the kids everything we could hope for—I don't want you feeling like you have failed us in any way."

He shook his head. "I don't mean to say you haven't been grateful, Sondra. I'm just saying, a job like this could change our lives for the better. We could take nice vacations—it would open up new doors for us."

I want to encourage him, but a move?

She said carefully, "I'm not trying to burst your bubble, honey, but have you really thought about all the ramifications of this? What about my parents? And yours? As they get older, they could need our help more."

John nodded. "I know. Trust me. I've thought about all those things too. I didn't say it's an easy choice. But let's, at least, pray about it and see where God leads."

Sondra nodded. "Of course. That's exactly what we need to do." She squeezed his hand. "And either way, no matter what we decide, I want you to know how proud I am of you. There's no doubt that you could do that job magnificently, but you need to know—I am happy. I love you, and I love our life together. A job and move like this might give us a lot of different things, but the question we need to figure out is, at what cost?"

John drew in a deep breath and let it out again. "Precisely."

* * *

That week Sondra and Regan spent an entire day shopping for some of the things Regan would need for her dorm. Finishing up at the mall, Regan noticed Sondra wincing with pain.

"It's these shoes, honey. They're not good for walking a lot."

Her daughter pointed to a nearby bench. "Why don't you sit for a while while I pick up the last few things? It won't take me long."

Regan entered the nearby store while Sondra lowered herself onto the bench, which overlooked a beautiful waterfall. She watched water cascade over the rocks and splash into the basin below that glimmered full of pennies. Sondra was glad for the few moments of peace and the chance to rest her aching feet.

I still can't believe she's leaving.

Since John had shared his news a few nights earlier, Sondra's mind had been engaged with little else except the two biggest things sitting right in front of her: Regan going far away to college and their potential move to New York City. She was torn. She loved living near enough to her family to get together occasionally, and being part of a church they loved was not easily replaced. It wasn't going to be a simple decision, but she berated herself for the next thought that entered her mind before she could stop it.

Maybe John won't get the offer.

Quickly she admonished herself.

John deserves this chance. How can I wish anything less than good for him?

She knew it was sin to worry. God said again and again, "Fear not."

As Pastor Paul had recently preached, "To worry about the future is to go into God's territory and try to usurp His hand in your life."

But wouldn't it be downright irresponsible for me not to feel some of the weightiness of these decisions facing us?

The sound of the water rushing over the rocks and splashing against the boulders at the bottom was peaceful. Sondra closed her eyes, listening to the soothing sound for a few minutes.

"Hello, Sondra."

She opened her eyes to see Victoria Wilson staring at her. Though they attended the same church, Victoria ran in a far different circle from Sondra. She was known for being coarse and gossipy. Sondra wasn't sure why she even attended their Bible-believing church, since she disagreed fairly vocally with their church's position on quite a few matters. Sondra generally tried to avoid her—not a difficult task since her attendance was sporadic at best. Victoria's usual look of smugness was firmly in place.

Terrific.

"Oh, hi, Victoria. I wasn't really sleeping, just resting my eyes. I guess I was lulled by the sound of the water falling."

Why do I feel I owe her any explanation?

"Well, what are you doing here? Are you waiting for someone?" Victoria glanced around.

Sondra stretched. "Yes, Regan is buying a few last things. We've been out shopping all day, so my feet were tired."

A condescending look covered Victoria's face. "Ah, I see. That's one reason why I exercise. It keeps me from feeling fatigued by midafternoon."

Sondra knit her lips together, searching for a different response than the unkind one circling in her mind.

As they noticed a group of men walking toward them, Victoria fluffed her hair, moistened her lips, and struck a pose of regal beauty, even tilting her head like a model might. Sondra's eyebrows shot up at her overtly flirtatious moves. She knew Victoria was a single mom who had dated nearly all the eligible men in their congregation, but this was almost comical.

"So what brings you here?" Sondra didn't really care; she was just trying to make conversation.

Victoria indicated the bag hanging off her shoulder. "My fitness club is here. I work out every day."

Sondra could believe it. The other woman was shapely and attractive and fully aware of the admiring glances that most men cast her way.

"Ah, I see." She breathed deeply, suddenly weary of the effort to find something to discuss with Victoria. The silence between them grew to an uncomfortable level.

"Well, I'd better get going." Victoria made a move to leave. "I've got to pick up my kids from their sitter."

Sondra nodded, grateful to see her go. "You take care."

"Yeah. You too, Sondra."

She watched the woman as she walked away and started to feel badly for her rudeness.

God, I'm sorry for letting my dislike of Victoria get in the way of being kind to her anyway.

She felt convicted for her poor display of Christian love. It shouldn't matter what the other woman did; she still needed to do her part to get along as much as she was able.

She sighed and closed her eyes again.

Then again, if John does get the promotion, I wouldn't have to deal with Victoria ever again. Of course, probably every church has someone like her.

The thought brought the possibility of the move back into her mind, which caused her to wrestle again with worry. She thought of a quote she'd once heard: "Worry is a kind of insult to the Lord. It's like throwing His promises and assurances back into His face and saying they're no good and you don't trust Him."

That brought her up short. She opened her eyes and watched the glistening water streaming over the rocky edge.

"Okay, Lord," Sondra murmured, "even though it feels like we're on a really rocky road, help me trust You through it."

Thinking of rocky road made her think of ice cream, one of her favorite treats.

Regan returned, carrying bags. "I'm all done, Mom."

Sondra stood and looked at her daughter resolutely, taking one of the bags. "You know, Regan, life is too short to spend it worrying."

Regan cocked a questioning eyebrow at her. "Are you okay?"

Her mother laughed. "I'm great. Come on, let's go get some ice cream before we head home."

* * *

The day that Sondra was to meet with Charlene Jeffries and Theresa Johnson, she woke with a terrible headache. Hurrying to get dressed, she discovered that her favorite pair of jeans had sat in the washing machine the past two days. Opening the circular door, an odor arose.

"Yuck." She crinkled her nose. "Everything smells like mildew."

TJ came around the corner. "Mom, there's no milk for cereal."

She added fresh soap to the washing machine to run the load through again, turned knobs, and pushed the Start button before answering him, "Then have some toast."

"There's no more bread."

Aggravated, she sighed and rubbed her forehead. How had she let things get so out of control?

Keep it in perspective, Sondra. This doesn't make you a failure. It just makes you human.

"Okay, listen. There has to be something in this house to eat. Can you just have crackers and peanut butter? Or make a hard-boiled egg? I promise I will run to the store for food and milk on my way home from my meeting." Tommy sighed and went back into the kitchen. She finished getting ready and left.

Charlene's home was cozy. Sondra admired the room where they sat, grateful for the cup of tea to calm her jittery spirit. She knew Theresa faced some real hardships with her daughter. When she arrived, the three women opened up in prayer.

"Lord, we need You. Theresa is hurting and wants to follow You in raising her daughter to know You. Only You can change hearts. Help Melissa see the wrong path she is on, and give her a longing to turn to You. We pray for wisdom and words that would comfort and not condemn. In Jesus's name, we ask. Amen."

Sondra asked, "Charlene shared a little bit with me, but why don't you tell me what kinds of things you've been facing with Melissa?"

Theresa nodded and began tearfully, "She is openly defiant to me. When I confront her, she walks away from me and slams her door. She is such a poison in our home. Sometimes I'm actually afraid of her." She blew her nose and confessed, "This isn't how I pictured life would be. I'm ashamed to admit it, but to be honest, there are times I hate her, and then I feel guilty for feeling that way. It's gotten so bad I . . . I don't know what to do anymore." She held a tissue to her eyes, quietly crying.

Charlene looked imploringly at Sondra, who inwardly sighed.

Lord, I am so inadequate for this. Only You can give words that bring healing to her heart and offer her help.

Sondra put her hand on the other woman's hand. "I don't know if this helps, but you should know that you are not alone in this struggle." She swallowed her pride that wanted to hide the truth about their battle with CiCi. "John and I are also going through a season of some challenges with one of our kids. So trust me, I know it's hard. But I also know that God wants to teach us some things through it."

Theresa nodded and blew her nose, listening.

Sondra continued. "You are Melissa's mom. God has a job for you to do in her life to help shape her ideas about obedience to authority. Even though someday she'll no longer be under your authority, she will *always* be under God's, and she needs to learn how to submit to Him. You and Jack need to be on the same page, and Melissa needs a firm hand. After all, she is only eleven years old, and like it or not, there must be appropriate consequences for her behavior. It's important to make those clear to her and then stick to them." She looked seriously at the other woman. "Better to face the pain of consistent discipline while the consequences are smaller than to let it spiral out of control. Because if she doesn't learn these lessons soon, in a few more years, you'll find you're dealing with a monster, and the fallout could be much more severe."

Charlene added, "You and Jack should read Romans 13 together. It talks all about the importance of obeying authority."

Theresa nodded, making a note on a paper she pulled from her purse.

Sondra gently added, "I know it's hard to believe when we are in the thick of the battle, but we must remember: God can work *all* things for good—even hard, unfair trials. One of the best gifts we can give Jesus is our trust—the belief that we know He loves us and is at work for our good."

Charlene said, "I know one thing that has helped with our daughter is to have regular talks that let her know we are on her side." She paused. "Frankly, being a kid these days can be really hard. The world is even so different from when we were young. It's a lot to navigate—and I think most kids lack the maturity to handle it with much grace. It's important they know that their parents are a safe place to bring their worries and fears. If you're always fighting back with Melissa, she will have a harder time seeing you as an ally."

Sondra nodded and shifted in her chair, looking the hurting woman in the eye. "What we cannot see, what none of us can know, is what God might do in Melissa's heart through your obedience to Christ in dealing with her. By you choosing to respond in *love* and not give in to the temptation to lash back at her and instead show her firm boundaries paired up with gentleness, a fruit of the Holy Spirit at work in your life, God could use that in some powerful way to soften her heart."

Theresa cried and nodded. "I haven't been doing it God's way at all. I get so angry I scream right back at her, which enrages her more." She cried fresh tears as she implored them, "I hope it's not too late."

Sondra assured her. "It's never too late to start doing things the right way. Paul reminds us, 'But one thing I do: Forgetting what is behind and straining toward what is ahead, I press on toward the goal to win the prize for which God has called me heavenward in Christ Jesus.'" She gave Theresa's arm a squeeze and smiled. "Thankfully, God is in the business of offering fresh starts."

Theresa nodded, tears of hope filling her eyes. "Thank you so much. I needed to hear this today. I just have been at the end of my rope and didn't know what else to do. You've given me a lifeline."

"We all face trials, Theresa. God is the one who has given us a lifeline. I'm just glad we can encourage one another as we go through hard times together."

New optimism shone on Theresa's face as the ladies departed.

Sondra thought about the struggles she faced in her own life. Really, it was a miraculous truth: that He could make something good come from something bad.

"Who but You, God, could do such a thing?" she marveled out loud in her car and answered resoundingly, "No one else."

* * *

A few days later, John burst through the door in great excitement, calling through the house, looking for her.

"I'm in here," she called out from the pantry, where she was searching for what to make for dinner. His tall frame filled the doorway.

"Sondra. It's mine if I want it. Tom offered me the role of senior director." His eyes shone brightly.

Her heart plummeted as she turned to fully look at him.

"But you didn't tell him you'd take it yet, right?" She held her breath.

"No, I told him I needed to talk with you before accepting it."

Relief flooded her heart.

Over the next few days it became their only topic of discussion as they inspected the pros and cons from every angle—what they would be giving up; what they would be gaining; how it would affect the kids, their friends, their family, and their marriage. They left nothing unturned, analyzing it repeatedly till there was nothing left to say. But they were no closer to an answer. Many prayers for wisdom and guidance hadn't resulted in any great revelation. Heaven was being very silent about this one, and Sondra couldn't help but feel restless and forgotten by God as she begged Him to help them make this decision.

* * *

Besides the possible move, the other big topic on everyone's mind was Regan's approaching departure. Everyone was grieving in his or her own way. Regan brought such life and light to their home; the hole she left behind would feel like a chasm for a very long time.

Saturday morning Mylah piped up at the breakfast table, "Regan, will you ever live here again?"

"Oh, Mylah, of course, I will. I'll be home at Christmas and next summer—so don't even think about moving into my room." She squeezed the younger girl's shoulder in a hug, and Mylah eyed her adoringly.

CiCi stared down at her plate, moving food around on it but not really eating anything. Sondra looked at her with concern. "Honey, are you okay?"

"Oh, sure, Mom, I'm fine," she said unconvincingly.

John looked questioningly at her across the table. Sondra shrugged. "Well, what are everyone's plans for today?" she asked brightly.

Regan took a gulp of orange juice. "I need one of the cars 'cause I need to go over to Jillian's to pick up a book she said I could borrow, and I told Tommy I could take him to Drew's house on my way if he still needs me to."

"Yep, I sure do if that's okay, Mom?" Tommy asked.

Sondra nodded. "Oh—yes, certainly, honey, that's fine. What time will you be done at Drew's?"

"I don't know . . . maybe late this afternoon. We're going to practice in the studio that he and Mr. Phillips set up in their garage."

"Okay, so, John, what are you up to?"

He looked at the clock and grabbed another slice of bacon. "Actually, I have to head out soon myself. Denny and I are meeting with Jack."

Sondra knew that could end up being a few hours since Jack Johnson, Theresa's husband, was going through some tough situations not only at home with their daughter, Melissa, but also at work, and he valued both Denny and John's counsel.

Mylah swirled the juice in her glass, tilted her head, and said, "I was hoping I could go over to Trixie's house today. She said I could see her pig before they bring him to the food pantry. Can I?"

Since camp, the two girls had grown even closer and loved each other's company. Trixie was involved in a 4-H program, where she had raised a pig to show at the county fair. Everyone was amazed when it had taken first prize. Loni and Denny wanted to donate it to the local food pantry.

CiCi looked at her sister's eager expression and said slightly mockingly, "You do know what that means, right, Mylah?"

Mylah looked confused. "What do you mean?"

Sondra interjected, shooting a warning glance at CiCi. "Honey, what CiCi is saying is that, well, we have a feeling you think that her pig is about to become the food pantry's new pet, right?"

Mylah nodded. "Trixie has a pink leash she puts him on. I thought they would just walk him over and let him live there."

John snorted, and the older kids started laughing.

Sondra frowned at them and explained, "Well, darling, that's not quite it. You see, a food pantry gives food to people. Like fruits and canned goods . . . and meat."

The look on Mylah's face changed as she thought about that. "Do you mean they're going to kill Harvey?"

John dryly noted, "They usually prefer that their meat donations come in a little more processed than a two-hundred-pound pig on a pink leash, walking in through the front door."

Sondra couldn't help laughing.

She saw her daughter's crestfallen face and said, "Oh, Mylah, I'm sorry. That's what they raised him for though. I know you like Harvey."

TJ piped up teasingly, "Now there will be more people who can like Harvey," which made the others laugh and earned him a jab in the ribs from his mom.

CiCi looked at the plate of bacon on the table. "Maybe we just ate his cousin."

Sondra saw Mylah's sad face and tried to comfort her daughter. "I'm sure Trixie will really appreciate having you around because at first, it might be hard for her too. But yes, her pig will first be taken to a slaughterhouse, then they'll donate the meat to the food pantry." She held her daughter's hand.

Mylah's bubbliness returned quickly. "That must be why Trixie is getting a new little piglet—to take the place of Harvey. So she'll still get to have a pig on a leash." She smiled happily again.

John said, "Well, that's perfect. Since I am picking up Denny anyway, I can bring you over, honey." Chairs scraped as everyone got up and headed out, leaving Sondra alone with CiCi.

Sondra turned to her. "What about you, Ms. Magoo?" She used the term affectionately, hoping to see a smile on her daughter's face. That was not to be.

CiCi mumbled, "I'm not feeling really great. Thanks for the meal, Mom. May I be excused?"

"Of course, honey." She was perplexed. "Cecilia, is everything okay? Can I help you with anything, sweetheart?"

"No, Mom. I'm fine."

"Well, you don't seem fine. Are you sure you don't want to talk?"

"I'm sure. I'm going to my room for a while."

She turned and left the room.

What is better to do? Let her have some time alone, or pursue her and possibly hound her, which might make her shut me out completely?

She began cleaning up from the big breakfast, mulling over her daughter's behavior.

She hasn't really been in one of her bad moods lately, but she seems tired a lot.

Suddenly, it occurred to her.

What if she's sick with something like mono?

Sondra muttered to herself, "Of course. That would explain why she's so tired lately and why she is always wearing layers and bundled up in long sleeves. Sondra, what kind of mother are you?"

She berated herself for her lack of insight to diagnose the obvious fact that her girl was probably fighting some infection or illness. Promising herself to book a doctor's appointment for Cecilia, she rinsed and piled the dishes into the dishwasher, put away food, and decided to tackle some laundry.

Bringing a basket of folded linens and towels to Regan's room, she opened the door; the movement of wind caused a piece of paper to flutter from the bureau to the floor. Sondra bent to pick it up and curiously read it.

> People can look so differently
> From what others think they ought to be
> And often, far too easily
> We harshly judge accordingly.
>
> But God alone can see inside
> Both humility – and pride.
> He alone gets to decide
> The line where right and wrong reside.
>
> Our scars should remind us of our common thread:
> Born in sin, we all are dead.
> Some haven't yet come to the place
> Where sin is surrendered and forgiveness embraced.
>
> So as for sinners, broken all,
> We'd best give grace and heed the call
> To model mercy and offer care,
> Give compassion and salvation share.
> It would be better to just provide
> A place where hurt and love collide.

Sondra sat on the corner of Regan's bed, holding the paper. She couldn't stop the tears from falling as she cried with fresh grief over the upcoming loss in their home. Their precious daughter, so sensitive, with such a heart for God and others . . . when she left, she would take her life and light out of their home, and they would lose the joy of her cheerful heart and gentle, teachable spirit . . . how were they going to let her go?

"This is going to be an impossible year to get through," she whispered miserably.

Sondra adored each of their children and would lay down her life for any one of them. But she could not deny the simple fact that Regan was easy to be around. She had entirely skipped the phase that CiCi was going through and that Tommy was starting to show. Sondra wished she had the same relaxed friendship with each of her kids.

I don't know why I butt heads with some more than others.

As she sat on the bed, she felt a tug to pray for her kids and for herself. She dried her tears, gulping, and prayed, "Lord, please give me eyes to see my children how You see them. I know You love them and have good plans for each of them. Help me to be gentle and loving. I don't want these years to be filled with regret or unresolved conflicts. May they see You at work in my own life too."

* * *

The next day, after attending the early service at church, the family went to one of their favorite restaurants for brunch as a special treat.

"After all," John said, "with Regan leaving soon and the way things stand at work, we might not have very many chances left to do this." He was holding on to the hope that Sondra would be struck with a newfound excitement at the idea of a move to New York City, one that would allow him to accept the promotion guilt free.

Their waitress took their drink order. John ordered coffee, and she brought a pot of the hot beverage and left, giving them a few more minutes to decide.

Sitting there, Sondra wrestled with the idea of leaving everything familiar. A pang crossed her heart at the thought of giving up all they had known to leap into the unknown.

I am not going to mar this special morning, one of the last we'll have for a while with Regan, worrying about something that hasn't been decided yet.

Freshly resolved not to dwell on their looming decision, she reached for the pot sitting by her elbow. She flipped the mug by her placemat and poured half a mugful, taking a sip. "Ah, there's nothing quite like the first taste of coffee in the morning." She smiled contentedly.

CiCi pointed out, "You didn't order that, Mom."

"Well, no, you're right, I didn't. But since the waitress brought Dad a pot, I just figured I could have a small cup. I didn't want to pay $3 when I'm only drinking fifty cents' worth," she joked.

CiCi looked at her accusingly. "How is that any different?"

"Excuse me?" Sondra was confused. "Different from what?"

"You and Dad said that movie hopping was wrong because the management trusts that we will only watch one movie while we're in there. You told the waitress you didn't want coffee, but you are drinking from the pot she brought for Dad, who did order it. I don't think it's any different."

Flustered, Sondra put the offending cup down.

John spoke up, "Cecilia, that's enough, I don't like your tone. Your mother can have some of my coffee."

CiCi sat sullenly, and Tommy spoke up, "I agree with CiCi. I don't think it's any different."

Sondra looked at her children and felt the sudden conviction in her heart.

They're right. It is no different.

John started to defend Sondra, but she put her hand on his. "John, stop. The kids are right." She looked at them. "You're absolutely right." A tear escaped her eye as she felt the shame of her own hypocrisy.

John said, "It's not exactly the same, Sondra."

"It's close enough," she rejoined, "and really, how very different is it? I was taking something I didn't pay for, and that's wrong."

The waitress came back to take their order, and Sondra asked, "I've changed my mind. Could you please add another cup of coffee to our order as well? Thank you." The young lady took their food order, and the family sat back, waiting.

O God, please help me. What other blind spots do I have in my life? Am I really as transparent as I like to think? Lord, I know I prayed for You to let my kids see You at work in my life. But that's going to be a pretty painful unveiling. Please help me as You strip away the ugly in me. I really do want my life to honor You.

* * *

A few days later, sitting in Linda Peters's home, Sondra sipped her tea and noted what a sense of peace the older woman exuded. Lovely green plants brightened every corner of the room, bringing a welcome sense of life. Sondra breathed deep and exhaled, soaking in the moments of refreshment with Linda.

She shared some of what she was facing: the grief over Regan leaving, the difficult decision with John's job, dealing with hardships in the teenage years, and feeling pulled too many directions—things that were good endeavors but that were sapping her strength.

Linda was sympathetic. "Jesus said, 'Come to me all you who are weary and heavy burdened, and I will give you rest.'" She continued. "God doesn't want us stressed and exhausted. If you're feeling that way, it's not His doing."

"I know. I know He wants me to let go and let Him equip me, but how do I make choices between all the demands that face me? That's where I struggle sometimes."

She knew she sounded so defeated but couldn't help confessing, "We've had some battles with CiCi and a little with Tommy too. Then things are fine again. I know that it is probably normal teenage angst, but it's wearying. There are times I feel so guilty, like maybe I've let too many distractions in, too many ministries—good things, but things that have pulled me away from my first ministry—being a mom."

Linda nodded. "I understand. It can be so hard to balance everything in life."

"I also think about how hard this season is going to be, watching Regan go, wondering how it's going to affect our whole family. I will miss her terribly. God doesn't want me to idolize my daughter, and I don't want to. I recognize that He has wonderful plans for her life—plans that, if I get in the way with my selfish heart, won't be best for her. But it's hard. My head knows all these things, but my heart is resisting."

Linda pulled her Bible close and opened it to Psalms 62. She pushed her Bible toward her, gently resting her hand on Sondra's. "Read this, starting at verse five through verse eight."

Sondra read aloud haltingly, tears springing up as she read the words, "Find rest, Oh my soul, in God alone; my hope comes from Him. He alone is my rock and my salvation; He is my fortress, I will not be shaken. My salvation and my honor depend on God; He is my mighty rock, my refuge. Trust in Him at all times, Oh people; pour out your hearts to Him, for God is our refuge."

Sondra grabbed a tissue from her purse and blew her nose. God would be her refuge. He would take care of her, just like He would take care of Regan and CiCi and TJ and Mylah. His capacities were limitless.

"Thank you, my friend. It's precisely what I needed to hear."

Linda smiled. "Well, I'm sure there will be a day when I'll need to be reminded myself. We all do from time to time, you know."

Sondra finished her tea, grateful for the gift of a godly friendship.

* * *

That night John nervously paced the kitchen floor. "I told Tom today that we need a few more days to decide. He understands and is being very gracious in allowing us some more time, but we don't have forever."

"I understand." Sondra felt weak at the urgency of such a major decision. She watched her husband head to his office and sat down at the kitchen table, putting her head into her hands.

"Please, God, show us what we should do," she pleaded into the silence.

* * *

On Saturday the girls were helping their mom go through the attic while TJ and John were working in the backyard. The front doorbell rang.

"I'll get it," Regan called out, happy to get away from the dim and dust for a few minutes. She raced downstairs and opened the door and, to her shock, saw a nervous-looking Kayla Carpenter.

Regan was speechless. Until the agonizing turmoil she had gone through on the discovery of Kayla's lie about her, she hadn't thought of her practically at all these past years. Now, here she stood on their front porch. She didn't know what to say.

Kayla broke the ice. "Regan. I hope it's okay that I came over here." She fidgeted. "I know I'm probably the last person you want to see, and I wouldn't blame you a bit if you slammed the door in my face. That's what I deserve." She stopped as if Regan might take her up on the suggestion, but seeing her still listening, she pushed on. "I came to apologize to you for, well, for everything. I know that what I told Kyle Pearson was a lie. I'd heard that your mom had become a close friend with his mom. I thought it was a way I could hurt you and your family." She shuffled her feet, looking down, ashamed. "I was so messed up, Regan. I was jealous and angry and full of bitterness. I was messing with the wrong crowd and making terrible decisions. I guess the one good thing I can say is that Kyle is the only person I told that lie to. Not that it makes it okay or anything, but you don't have to worry that I passed it around."

Regan stood, amazed and listening as Kayla made her confessions to her.

"It was wrong of me, and I truly am sorry. I came over here hoping you might, well, even though I don't deserve it, if you would forgive me." Tears glimmered in her eyes. "You see, I got saved two days ago, and I want to make things right with people I've hurt. I knew you were one of the first ones I needed to come to . . ." She drifted off, shifting her feet, not sure what to say next.

Mylah came careening around the corner. "Regan, Mom says you need to come back and help—oh!" she exclaimed as she saw Kayla standing outside. She stammered, "Oh, um, I didn't know" and ran back toward the stairs to the attic.

Within minutes, Sondra descended and was quickly running to the door, concerned with what her daughter might be facing. She never expected to see the sight that beheld her eyes: Regan out on the front porch, embracing Kayla Carpenter.

What is going on?

Both girls laughed as they saw Sondra's confusion.

Regan said, "Mom, Kayla got saved!" She wiped at her eyes. "She came over to apologize."

Sondra broke out crying, "Oh my goodness, Kayla. That's amazing news!" She stepped out on the front porch, gathering Kayla into her arms. It felt like her own prodigal had returned, and she rejoiced in what God had done in Kayla's heart and life.

Your wonders never cease, God!

The rest of the afternoon was spent marveling over God's timing of interceding in Kayla's' life as she shared her story.

"I went downtown to meet up with someone for drugs. I came across this group of kids around my age who were handing out tracts. A boy gave me one, and I crumpled it and threw it into the gutter, but then I heard this girl with a microphone. I can't explain it, but I couldn't stop listening to her. I've seen other street evangelisms, but there was something about this girl . . . I don't know what it was. I just stood there, listening and suddenly realized that Jesus loves me and died for my sins." Kayla shook her head wonderingly. "I've been around church most of my life, but it was like that day, God lifted the blinders from my eyes, and I saw my sin and knew I needed a Savior."

The joy on her face and the lightness in her voice spoke of the new life in her heart. It was evident God had grabbed hold of her, and she was a new creation.

Sondra shook her head, still amazed at how changed Kayla was.

God, You are awesome.

Kayla shared her plans, "I want to work for a year or two to save up enough money to go to a good Bible school and learn as much as I can." She paused. "I still hope my parents will reconcile and come to know Jesus as their Savior too. My dad said he might consider coming back to church with me when I asked him, but either way, I am so grateful God turned my life around."

Sondra was so glad they had waited on God to resolve the matter with Kayla. She wondered what might have been different if she had taken matters into her own hands and gone over to defend her daughter.

Would I have messed things up? Would Kayla have retreated farther into her dark world, full of fresh vengeance?

It was a good lesson for her as she knew God wanted her to become slower to anger and quicker to trust in Him with her heartaches and hardships. Sondra was grateful they had sensed God telling them to wait on Him back when they'd first heard the terrible report. Now, it was over, and they could rejoice that God had done a miracle in Kayla's life: He had turned an enemy into a sister in Christ.

As they lay in bed that night, Sondra told John, "I'm so thankful." She propped herself up on her elbow to look at him. "How much better to be able to have this conflict resolved and this weight lifted from Regan's shoulders before she leaves home."

"Definitely." John yawned. "It really is amazing, honey, but I'm exhausted. Let's talk more tomorrow." He turned off his light and fell asleep.

But all the excitement of the day kept Sondra awake, flipping restlessly till she got up and went to the family room, where she wrote out a poem praising God for His greatness. After expressing her heart so fully, she was able to curl up next to her husband and sleep soundly.

You are the Almighty! The Matchless!
The Only! ~
God! You reign from above!

In power, in glory
You author the story,
Perfect in justice and love!

There are none beside You
Around You, above You—
Alone You eternally are!

Yet You care for the wounded
Give ear to the lonely
Bring near those who have wandered far

You lavish Your grace
On a guilt-ridden race
Who deserve condemnation and death

Yet Your blood paid the way—
What is there left to say?
But, "Thank You, for new life and breath!"

We're declaring: You're holy!
You're righteous! You're solely
The only One worthy of worship and glory!
We'll ever adore Thee!
For You Lord—Are—Above—ALL!

Sunday morning dawned bright. There was a fresh vibrancy in the air. Sondra was invigorated by Pastor Paul's message of the hope found in Christ alone. Walking out of the building with her family, she found herself humming the new song the worship team had rolled out that morning to align with the sermon:

"This life is short—it isn't all there really is
So much lies ahead, for those who are His
Don't hold on so tight to the dreams we have here ⁓
This world and its sorrows will one day disappear ⁓

Eternity is coming and it's full of hope! . . . Joy! . . .
Dreaming, doing, fulfilling and pursuing ⁓
Christ! No loss! No pain! All gain! We really can't imagine!
So don't! Lose! Hope!
Hold on! Just wait! We're nearly at the gate!"

She couldn't remember all the stanzas but just how it ended.

"A breath ~ A wisp ~ A vapor and it's gone . . .
It won't be long ~ hold on ~ Just cling to Jesus
and hold on . . ."

She determined that would be her new life motto: Just cling to Jesus and hold on. She truly did want to live that way. It was hard when life reared up with some ugly heartache to deal with.

But that's when I need to cling to Him most.

She marveled again at what God had worked in Kayla's heart and life, recognizing again that He alone could turn beauty from ashes.

"Lord, I know life isn't done throwing fastballs at me. Please help me cling to You through every trial You allow. Thank You that eternity *is* coming, and we have all hope in You."

After church, the family spent the afternoon hanging out and playing some of their favorite games together. The raucous laughter and hoots of false indignation were salves to the wound of knowing these days were fast dwindling. For a few carefree hours, they played and talked and laughed.

Mylah, in her sweet funny way, had kept them chuckling with her hilarious observations and comments. As they discussed an upcoming reunion Sondra and John were invited to, she lamented, "Aw! You get to go on a reunion soon? I've always wanted to go on a high school reunion!"

Regan retorted, "Mylah, I'm pretty sure you need to get through middle school first."

Gathered together with her loved ones surrounding her, the good-natured jibbing and laughter were like a balm to Sondra's spirit. She looked into the happy faces of her family. Even Cecilia seemed to be herself again.

Just let time stop now.

Later, after the last game was done and everyone had gone off to do their own activities, Sondra found herself drawn to CiCi's room. She knocked and opened the door.

"Hi, honey."

"Hi, Mom."

"Can I come in for a bit?"

"Sure."

Sondra noticed the room was super tidy. "Hey, thanks for cleaning things up." She grinned at CiCi, who gave her a small smile in return.

"Sure."

Sondra settled herself on the bed next to her daughter. "That was a really fun afternoon. It's been too long since we've played together like that."

"Yeah, it was a lot of fun," her daughter quietly replied.

Sondra shifted on the bed, staring up at the chandelier, wanting the lighthearted banter they'd shared all day to continue. Her daughter seemed to waver between participating in and retreating from life around her.

She tried again, gesturing to the light above their heads. "That really did turn out nice."

"Yeah, I like it."

Sondra looked around the lovely room. For her sixteenth birthday, they let her remake her room. CiCi had selected everything, from the elegant black-and-white drapes to the chandelier she had found at a secondhand store and painted black. Pillows and pictures, vases and knickknacks finished the space and were artfully arranged. Her tastes had changed dramatically through the years when she had stubbornly wanted the obnoxious shade of purple. She now had a wonderful sense for decorating, and everything had turned out so beautifully.

"How are things going?" Sondra tried to be casual.

"Fine."

"Good."

They sat in companionable silence for a bit.

CiCi was the one to break it as she lay next to her mom on her bed, arm under her head, staring up at the ceiling.

"Mom, can I tell you something?"

"Of course, my darling. What is it?"

Is it another confidence to share about Brad's struggle with drugs?

The bed creaked as CiCi sat up and faced her mother. Tears spilled down her daughter's cheeks, and an unknown dread filled Sondra's heart.

O God, help.

In a whisper, CiCi shared her awful secret: "I've been cutting myself."

"What!" Sondra was absolutely stunned. "What! Why?"

This can't be happening!

"I started a couple of months ago." She looked at her mother's appalled expression and admitted, "But now, even though I want to, I can't stop."

Sondra's heart plunged in her chest.

There must be some mistake—this kind of thing can't happen behind the doors in our home . . . can it?

"Show me," she demanded.

CiCi lifted her sleeves, and Sondra drew back, horror-struck. She tenderly held her daughter's outstretched arms, staring in sickened wonder: ugly red scars slashed from her shoulders to above her wrists.

Her mother wailed, "Why would you feel compelled to do such an awful thing to yourself?"

CiCi gulped, crying quietly, "I don't know. I don't have a good reason. I just don't like myself."

"Oh, Cecilia!" Sondra gathered her in her arms, desperate to somehow convey how precious she was to them. Her body shook with uncontrollable sobs as she struggled to take in the truth of her daughter's terrible secret.

All my work and worry and effort to give my children a shelter from the ugliness of this world . . . all for nothing!

The pride in her heart toppled over as she realized that despite her hopes and dreams for each of their treasured children, a fearful thing had invaded the sanctuary she called home.

Still holding her daughter tightly, she cried till she could cry no longer. Minutes passed as she clung to her, weeping. Emptied of tears, exhaustion replaced her shock. With a heavy heart, she pulled back and looked at CiCi, who had been crying too. Sondra brushed a strand of her hair from her daughter's smudged face and said, "We need to tell your dad."

Together they went to John's office. He absorbed her news with the same dismayed disbelief that Sondra had. The three of them held one another close, and Sondra poured out tears all over again.

New recriminations invaded Sondra's thoughts as she frantically tried to make sense of this awful truth: their daughter was hurting herself in ways that they had never begun to imagine.

What kind of a mother are you that you didn't see this?

Sondra leaped to action, demanding, "Cecilia, I want every tool you used."

They went back to CiCi's room to take away each razor and scissors she could find, asking her where she hid others, removing every tool of torture she had secreted away in her room.

Sondra looked around the room—the same lovely room they had spent so many fun hours planning, the colors, curtains, and furnishings all designed to give their girl a perfect retreat, where she could escape the cares of this world.

I never guessed the terrible irony! That all alone in this space that was supposed to be a haven, she carried such a private agony!

Fresh tears of grief blurred Sondra's eyes. She was overwhelmed.

I am an absolute failure as a mom! This explains her morose behavior and why she has been covering her arms all the time. How could I not have seen what was going on?

This was a heartache she had never dreamed she would have to cope with.

What's next? Who else knows this? Is it my fault?

CiCi allowed her mom to swathe her arms in triple antibiotic ointment in an attempt to heal the long bloody marks. As Sondra gently applied it, flashbacks of the innocent toddler peering at her with a twinkle in her eye and a smile on her face, bathed in chocolate and whipped cream, rapturously happy and secure in their love, crossed her mind.

What happened to bring her to this awful place?

That night, in the privacy of their room, she confided wearily to John, "I'm afraid to let her out of my sight. I mean, what's normal procedure for this sort of thing?"

He shook his head. He was just as devastated by their precious girl's unthinkable struggle with self-harm. "It scares me to think what might have come next if she hadn't confessed to you."

John looked soberly at Sondra, and she dully stepped into the security of his arms. "It scares me too."

* * *

Slowly the days ground past. Sondra tried to convince herself that it would be okay, wanting to say that the worst was behind them. After all, now they knew, so now they could be on guard.

Poor Regan felt the burden of responsibility. She confided to her mom, "Is any of this my fault? I'll be leaving soon. Maybe CiCi is dreading the changes that are coming."

Sondra quickly shot that down. "Honey, no. You can't take that upon yourself. CiCi needs to be responsible for her own actions. It's her choice to cope with hardships in life the world's way or God's way."

Nor should you be carrying guilt for this.

The thought invaded Sondra's mind, but she pushed it back. She knew God didn't want her squeezing every drop of pain she could from this trial, but she resisted the comfort He offered: she didn't deserve any reprieve from the guilt she carried, preferring to beat herself up for her ignorance.

I can't let myself off that easily.

But Regan's question did raise a new issue. Though she hadn't divulged her struggle to her sister, CiCi regularly relied on Regan for advice and sisterly chats. Whom would she share with when she was gone?

* * *

Desperate for someone to walk with her through this storm, Sondra went to Linda's. She needed the older woman's godly counsel and time to pray together for God's hand to touch CiCi's heart in the way that only He could.

When Sondra arrived, Linda was pruning her plants, snipping off leaves, tending the soil, and speaking Bible verses out loud over them.

Sondra laughed a little. "What are you doing?"

Linda smiled. "Well, you know, a budding plant needs a lot of care—the right soil conditions, the correct amount of light, and sometimes, a trimming to cut out dead weight and encourage new growth. In fact, I like to think that plants are much like us. We need to plant our feet firmly in God's word to withstand the assaults from the world, we need to stay in the light and not wander into the darkness, and sometimes, God uses trials to trim us, to encourage new growth in Him."

She brought a lovely potted plant over to the table, setting it in the middle, where Sondra could see the delicate leaves and colorful blossoms pushing up through the damp soil.

"My dear mother always spoke Bible verses to the plants in our home. She said that they needed the carbon dioxide we breathe out, and we needed to hear God's word, so it was a match made in heaven." Linda laughed. "Mom's garden always seemed to flourish, so it's something I adopted, too."

Sondra loved the analogy her friend used: clinging to God's word was her only hope, and trusting in Him was what He wanted from her. She gained a renewed sense that God would bring them through this season, maybe not without some scars, but certainly, with growth in wisdom and faith if she would be trained by it.

The two women spent a lot of time on their faces before the Lord, asking Him to intervene and help CiCi.

Sondra cried out, "O God, please give me wisdom to know how to navigate these new waters. I feel like I'm drowning and don't know what to do." She blew her nose, pleading, "And, please, won't You help my baby, Lord? How can she not know how cherished she is?"

Linda's gentle voice broke through her heartfelt cries, and Sondra felt her arm softly resting on her shoulder.

"Oh, our precious heavenly Father. Thank You for Your love and mercy. Please help my dear sister as You carry her and her family through this hard season. Help us trust You, Lord. You are able, and we are not. Draw CiCi, Sondra, and John closer to Yourself, and allow them growth through this pain."

Sondra found such comfort in prayer. When they rose, she sensed God's peace taking the place where the raw wound had been.

Linda placed the plant in Sondra's hands when she left, sheltering her hands with her own.

"When you think God isn't hearing you or moving fast enough, I want you to look at this plant and remember: growth takes time. Sometimes it hurts. God needs to trim away things in our lives that aren't right or good for us. We need to stay firmly planted in His word and keep the soil of our prayer life fertile and healthy."

The older woman looked her straight in the eyes. "Sondra, I believe God has you in this season for a reason. I don't claim to know it or understand it fully, but I do believe that He makes all things beautiful in His time. Our job is simply to trust Him."

Sondra accepted the gift with tears and a heart so overflowing with thanks for the needed comforting words. She would trust God even though it hurt so badly and there were times she wondered if He was paying attention to all the things going on in her world.

* * *

Through the heartache that came with the revelation about CiCi's cutting, Sondra recognized her own misplaced confidence. Reading her Bible she realized that she had wrongfully thought something like cutting couldn't happen in their home. Yes, they were faithful church attenders and serious about their walk with Christ, but that didn't mean they weren't ever going to have to deal with the heartache and pain of the world. She confessed her pride again and wrote down the words to a song that came to her one night while she was restless and unable to sleep.

On my own I'm a failure . . .
On my own I'm a fraud . . .
I need Jesus my Savior . . .
I need Jesus my God . . .

Lord I'm humbled and broken
Right where I need to be
Finding hope in my Savior
I am down on my knees

Help me cherish my brokenness, for through it
I can see
That you are the only answer Lord, to the failure
and sin of me

There's much grace for the humble . . .
There's much hope for the meek . . .
When I admit that I stumble . . .
When I confess that I'm weak . . .

Lord I'm humbled and broken
Do what You need to do . . .
Trusting only my Savior
I surrender to You ~

Help me cherish my brokenness
For through it I can see
That You are the only answer, Lord
Keep your mercy and love on me!

The lesson was a hard one, but Sondra was grateful God was teaching her how He wanted her to see herself: always a sinner in need of His mercy, only a victor because of His grace.

* * *

Despite the long to-do list and the short time they had left together, Sondra was determined that before Regan left, they would sit down one last time with her bulging baby book between them. They reminisced at the various entries recorded there through the years.

Thank God, I took the time to record things.

They chuckled over many of Regan's comments as a little girl like "Mom, when you were a child like us, was Jesus born yet?" and, in a moment of utter glee, "I love you people!"

They recollected about weeks spent at camp and pictures of her playing her flute in concerts. School articles chronicled her involvement in softball and drama and activities like school dances and other functions through the years. Much of it seemed like a whole other lifetime ago, but that's what made up the fabric of her life to this point.

It was a bittersweet afternoon, but one Sondra was glad they spent together as she recognized the brevity of the moments that lay before them.

Lord, our time with Regan is almost done. Please protect and guide her as she launches, and help her to soar, Lord. Keep her in Your care, and help her to soar.

* * *

That night John took her hand and led her into their bedroom. "Honey, I need to talk with you. I've given this a lot of thought, and I need you to listen to me."

Concerned, she sat on the edge of their bed and waited.

He looked resolutely at her. "This was the answer I needed God to give me. I have wrestled with God over all the reasons for me to go for this job. I've thought about what I am passing up in my career if I don't take it. But, Sondra, I won't mess with our kids' lives. All it takes is one child suffering and drifting, separated from the anchors here like good friends, a good church, family nearby, to make what gain there would be in moving seem paltry compared to possibly shipwrecking CiCi's spiritual growth."

He saw her tears threaten and kept going. "How can I claim that my title of Dad matters more to me than any that this world can give me, if I am willing to roll the dice with our daughter's stability at a rough time in her life like this?" He shook his head, tears glistening in his own eyes. "As hard as it was, this decision became very straightforward for me to make: I'm not taking the job. I told Tom today."

Tremendous relief flooded Sondra's heart, and she simply cried as he held her.

"Oh, John," she finally was able to squeak out, "I know this had to be so hard for you to decide. God has gifted you, and I know you don't feel you're using all your skills to full advantage."

He nodded slightly, and his voice sounded strained. "I can't help but grieve this a little. It was one of those opportunities that had the potential to lead to even better roles."

Sondra sighed. *Why does life have to be so difficult sometimes?*

As she realized the incredible sacrifice of John's news, she gulped back the desire to weep. There was something she needed to say. Sondra faced him and took his hand, looking him in the eye.

"John, I have loved you practically since the day we met, and there are many things that I am so proud of you for, but tonight . . ." She started to choke up, and John started to pull her close, but she pushed gently away.

"I need to say this, and you need to hear this." She looked at him determinedly.

She took a deep breath. "The fact that you would set aside your own dreams that sit right at your doorstep, yours for the taking, but you are willing to deny yourself for the good of our children. What greater love is there than a man laying down his life for another?"

She gulped and went on. "I truly believe, John Martin, that you have earned many crowns waiting for you in heaven for such sacrificial love. You are a man of tremendous character."

John didn't often cry, but the tears that sat in his eyes shared some of what his heart felt as he listened to his wife's praise.

They held each other for a long time. Sondra was so thankful that a decision had finally been reached. She knew it wasn't necessarily going to be smooth from here on out. He could easily come to regret this decision. She also worried that he might become bitter or feel he had missed out.

Rocking in the hollow of his arms, she pushed the thought away.

Those are troubles for tomorrow. For tonight, just be glad that things are settled.

* * *

All too soon, September was upon them, and their precious Regan left, excitedly venturing out to West Virginia, filled with trepidation mixed with anticipation at the new season before her.

Initially, after Regan's departure, Sondra was checking in on CiCi daily. One night Cecilia snapped at her, "Mom, I know you are worried about me. But you need to back off. I'm fine."

Sondra argued, "Well, you have to be patient with me too. I don't know what the right way is to act in this situation."

"I know. But I already said I will tell you if I feel the urge to cut again."

Sondra nodded, troubled as she watched her daughter walk out of the room.

Lord, please help me. I only seem to make it worse. Give me wisdom.

* * *

CiCi walked into John's home office and sat on the chair across from his. He was turned away from her as he focused on the computer console behind his desk, writing notes onto a pad.

She fiddled with a plaque that read, "No deep character was ever forged under the pampering sisters of Comfort and Ease. Rather, only the hammer of Trial can shape Perseverance. Only the knife of Difficulty can sharpen a man's inner strength. Only the miserable master called Pain can birth the desired traits of Tenacity and Grit."

She put the frame down and cleared her throat loudly. Startled, John swung around to her.

"Hey, honey. What's up?"

"Dad, can we talk?"

He put his pen down. "Of course. What's on your mind?"

"I don't want to keep going to my small group. Michelle doesn't like me, and I'm tired of all the pretenders."

Michelle was her youth leader at church.

John looked at her doubtfully. "Why wouldn't she like you out of all the girls in your group?"

"It actually isn't only me. She treats a few of us differently from the rest of the girls in our group."

"Give me some examples."

"She cuts me off when I try to talk and gets a certain look on her face when I sit down at our table. I'm not an idiot, Dad. She shows favoritism. She follows Mandy and Cora and Audrey on Instagram, but not me or Tiff or Bethany. She texts them during the week and sends everyone else Bible verses, but never the three of us."

He looked at her uncertainly.

Exasperated, she added, "It's not all concrete stuff, Dad. Sometimes, it's just a feeling. I mean, can't you tell when someone doesn't like you? Why can't you just admit that not everyone at your church always acts like a so-called Christian?"

He snorted. "Well, I sure don't remember ever saying that they do. Is that what you mean by the pretenders?"

She nodded. "Audrey Anderson comes every week, and Michelle loves her. But the truth is that she's a bully. She's a jerk to a lot of people, but acts all sweet and like she's some perfect Christian Goody Two-shoes whenever she's around adults."

John sighed, leaning back in his chair and folding his arms. "Well, honey, I would think that you, of all people, would realize how important it is to have grace for one another. I mean you have had your struggles too. You just acted on yours differently from how Audrey does hers. You've hid yours behind self-harm. Maybe she lashes out at others instead of self-inflicting."

CiCi looked unconvinced. "Well, at least I'm not pretending. What you see is what you get. I think it's pretty hypocritical to pretend to be a Christian, but act like she does. And Michelle holds her up as some model of perfection when she doesn't know the truth about how she really treats people."

John nodded. "I can see where that would be very discouraging. But we're all in process, aren't we? No one is perfect. We need forgiveness and patience with one another. And meanwhile, why don't you pray that God works in Audrey's heart?"

"Does this mean that you won't let me stop going to youth group?"

John ran a hand through his hair and sighed. "Sweetheart, I don't think that's the answer. I really don't. You're only hurting yourself then. Is there any way we can have you switch groups?"

She shook her head. "I told you. My friends are in that group."

John rubbed his eyes. "All right. Let me think about this for a while, okay?"

CiCi got up to leave. "When I have kids, I'm not making them go to church if they don't want to."

Her dad looked pained. "Cecilia, you need to understand. No church is perfect because they're all full of sinners." He added, "Just like you and me."

She shook her head. "I never said I was perfect. But I am also no hypocrite."

He ran his hand through his hair. "Listen, I'm glad you came to talk with me about this. Can we agree to give it some time so we can pray about what to do?"

She nodded and turned to go.

"I love you, Cecilia."

She turned her head as she walked out the door. "I love you too, Dad."

With a heavy heart, he watched her walk away, lowered his head, and prayed.

* * *

John came to bed late that night. "Where have you been?" his wife asked.

"Talking with CiCi."

Sondra was a little surprised. "Why wasn't I included?"

"She just wanted to talk a little, honey." He pulled the blanket back and crawled under the covers. "You know how sometimes you can't resist the urge to jump in and fix things when the kids tell you stuff they're dealing with?"

Sondra looked hurt. "I only do it because I want to help."

John grinned. "Yeah, I know. But sometimes the kids don't want help. Sometimes they just want to vent."

"So what did she want to talk about?"

He told her the gist of the problem. "I have less of a problem that the youth leader gives preferences to Mandy. She is a likable girl."

Sondra snorted. "It doesn't hurt that she's also Pastor Paul's daughter."

Cora was Mandy's best friend. CiCi actually liked both girls very much herself, but not the double standard their leader, Michelle, indulged in. Sondra agonized for her daughter. She knew it was a tough age to get through in life, and she had sympathy for the challenges their daughter faced.

"I am more concerned with how CiCi handles feeling rejected. She needs to learn how to deal with it in the right way." John shook his head. "I certainly don't like her new reference to our church as *yours*. It shows she is distancing herself, which is a slippery slope in the making."

Sondra knew CiCi had been skirting along some dark and lonely path. "I wonder if this sort of relational conflict accounts for why CiCi felt driven to cutting?"

"I'm sure it hasn't helped."

She grumbled, "Belonging to a church sure doesn't solve all your problems."

John snorted. "Of course, it doesn't."

"And the hypocrisy found in the walls of a church, of all places, can be like poison. Especially to a skeptical teenager's mind that is forming her ideas of the world."

John grunted, turning to her. "Sondra, exactly what are you trying to say?"

"I'm just saying that of all the places on the planet, the church ought to be the one place spilling over with love. No one should make anyone else feel unwanted, like Michelle is making CiCi feel."

John grimaced. "Honey, we don't know for a fact that Michelle is making CiCi feel unwanted. She might be playing favorites, and Cecilia could be reading into it further."

"Well, Michelle's double standard certainly won't nurture a love for the church in our daughter's heart." She ventured, "Maybe I should make a few phone calls tomorrow."

John grunted again. "Sondra, that's exactly why you weren't invited to start with. We need to let her work through some of these things herself. If we run to defend her every time something hard happens to her, first of all, she will stop confiding in us. Secondly, she won't learn how to handle conflict in a right way." He looked at her sternly. "Besides, you have to admit, CiCi isn't exactly walking rightly herself right now, so how sound is her judgment about someone else? No, I think we need to wait on this. Let's be praying God works in her heart to be less abrasive. Perhaps this leader is seeing the rough edges that we've seen and doesn't know how else to handle her." He turned off the light.

Sondra lay in the dark unable to sleep.

I don't want to be harsh, but the facts are the facts.

There ought to be ongoing kindness in the church, paired with euphoric joy over the fact that sinners had been forgiven and salvation had been granted to all who accepted it. But that was the rub: living out the Christian walk in reality was a lot harder than simply knowing the truth in your mind.

Sondra knew she was as guilty of this as anyone, wanting to do right, but missing the mark far too often. She gained comfort from Paul's words in Romans, "For what I do is not the good I want to do; no, the evil I do not want to do—this I keep on doing . . . oh what a wretched man I am! Who will rescue me from this body of death? Thanks be to God—through Christ Jesus our Lord!"

Thinking about those verses, she prayed, "Lord, help me to forgive Michelle and not to try to squeeze every last bit of pain from this trial. I keep wanting to soak in it and prevent the healing that will come from letting go and trusting You to sanctify me through whatever You allow in my life."

As she prayed, the words to a song she had penned came into her mind, and she quietly hummed them, wanting them to be true in her life.

> The anguish sometimes we are feeling
> And the loss that leaves us reeling
> Only God can do the healing that we need . . .
>
> May You be the balm to the hurting,
> May You be the peace to the yearning,
> May You comfort those in heartache and tragedy . . .
>
> May You help us find that we can say, Lord,
> "Go ahead and do what You may, Lord ~
> I will trust in You, no matter what comes my way . . ."

* * *

As Sondra had worried, John struggled with his decision and impossibility to change his mind about the prestigious role he had passed up.

Late one night he lamented to her, "What if that job opportunity was the vehicle God planned on using to take us to a place where there's better help for Cecilia? Maybe *that* was the doorway God wanted us to walk through to show we trust His provision. Now, are we going to miss out on His best for us and for Cecilia too?"

Did we make the wrong choice? What if we were supposed to move? What have we done?

She was agitated and tried to focus on verses of God's truth.

264

You will keep him in perfect peace whose mind is stayed on you because he trusts in you.

She made the drive to her parents' house for a visit one day, needing their advice. Her mom was out, counseling a woman who was in the middle of a desperate situation, but her dad urged her to come. "Mom's not here, but I'd love to help you, honey." Sitting in the comfort of her childhood home, Sondra shared the strain she and John were under.

"I mean, how can we know if we made the right decision?"

"Sondra, do you think, for a moment, that God, in His limitless love for His own children, would leave John to wither, not wanting His best for him?"

"Well, when you put it like that, no."

"Then you cannot second-guess decisions that were made following God's lead. You and John prayed about it, you sought godly counsel, and you left it in God's hands and asked for direction, right?"

She nodded.

Her dad continued. "So now you need to move beyond that and trust that God has better things for you. We have such finite vision, we can't see beyond this second, let alone down the pathway of life. We must trust that God, who knows what the future holds and loves us, is working out His best plan in our lives if we let Him. Do you see that, honey?"

Sondra nodded. "Yes, I do see. Thanks, Dad." She stood, giving him a hug. On her way home, she prayed in the quiet of her car, "Lord, please help us to walk the road You have set before us. We know that You work all things for good. We want to trust You. *Help* us trust You."

* * *

A couple of weeks later the young woman who was CiCi's table leader called Sondra. "Hi, Sondra. It's Michelle Stevenson. I'm hoping you can help."

Sondra was flustered. "Of course, Michelle, what can I help you with?"

"CiCi is just so negative all the time. I feel like no matter what we are talking about, she only looks at the bad side. I'm wondering if you would talk with her and see if she could at least try to be more upbeat and positive, like the other girls in our group."

Sondra bit her tongue to keep from responding with pent-up frustration.

"I am glad you called, Michelle. To be honest, CiCi isn't in a great place right now, and I would be grateful for your prayers for her."

Michelle said, "Certainly. And you'll encourage her to be less negative in group?"

"I'll do my best," Sondra said resignedly.

"Great," the younger woman continued, "and could I also mention that maybe you can ask her to be kinder to Audrey?"

Sondra paused, confused. "I'm sorry, has CiCi done something to her that is unkind?"

Michelle dropped her voice. "Well, since you ask, yes. Audrey shared with me that Cecilia hurt her feelings."

Sondra waited. When that appeared to be all Michelle was going to say, she asked, "Um, may I ask how?"

Michelle cleared her throat. "Well, CiCi just isn't very nice to her. Audrey told me that CiCi doesn't seem to like her."

Well, what am I supposed to say to that? The truth is, CiCi doesn't like her.

She stammered, "I-I'm sorry, Michelle. I think there is some issue between the girls. CiCi did mention that Audrey hasn't always been exactly kind herself."

On the other end of the line, Michelle drew in a deep breath. "Well, in my experience, it usually starts with one person. The other person is simply reacting to the first person's behavior."

Sondra wanted to be careful with her words. "That certainly can be true. But don't you think both sides of a story should be heard before making judgments?"

Michelle's voice became defensive. "Mrs. Martin, I've been a youth leader for a couple of years now. One thing I've noticed is that when someone is negative, it can affect the entire group. Audrey is a lovely girl with wonderful Christian values. But I think that Cecilia's negativity is affecting the entire group. I am simply calling to ask that you, as her mother, work with me in curbing it."

Frustration and embarrassment welled up in Sondra's heart.

She shook off the sudden desire to burst into tears. "Listen, Michelle, I will do my best. And I would appreciate it if you would pray for our daughter. She is struggling and could use patience and wisdom right now."

When they hung up, she ached from Michelle's criticism.

Talking with Susan the next day, Sondra shared the weight of the burden she was carrying.

"I feel like such a hypocrite. Here I've been telling moms of young children how to build a haven of protection and acceptance and love." Her voice quivered. "When all along, my own daughter, product of the very equation I tried so hard to adhere to, was struggling with this terrible activity and the pull of it on her heart."

Susan said quietly, "It sounds like Satan is having a heyday in the playground of your guilt."

Sondra sighed. "You could sure say that. I feel such a sense of failure. I don't know if heavyheartedness is an illness, but if so, that's what I have." Her voice cracked. "I mean, I knew she had her struggles. I just never dreamed she would—that she could, you know, hurt herself like that." She brushed away a tear.

Susan took a deep breath. "One thing I know, Sondra, is this: just because we *know* the truth doesn't mean it translates into some kind of perfect life. You shared truth with moms. To the best of your ability, you've tried to be a good mom. That doesn't mean you won't face struggles and heartaches sometimes. None of us are perfect, we can only try to do our best before God."

Sondra nodded. "You're right. I just never dreamed we would face this kind of trial."

"Those are the kinds that can hurt the most—the ones that catch us off guard. But don't make the mistake of thinking God can't use it for good still." Susan paused. "And I probably shouldn't be saying this, but you're my friend. Don't put too much stock in what Michelle said. She's not married and has no children, but she's got all kinds of opinions about raising them." Susan chuckled. "If she's lucky, life will teach her soon enough about the realities that come with the enormous task of parenting."

Sondra laughed lightly, grateful for a few minutes' escape from the crushing heaviness that seemed to hover over her since her discovery of CiCi's struggle. The counsel of her good friend was timely.

Susan is right. It will be okay. I just have to trust that God will carry us through this hard time.

* * *

At church the next evening, she ran into Victoria Wilson. The familiar look of superiority rested on the other woman's face as she walked directly over to Sondra.

Surprised, Sondra greeted her, "Hi, Victoria. How are you doing?" She tried to smile warmly, remembering their last uncomfortable encounter at the mall many weeks earlier.

"I am fine, Sondra. But I heard about your daughter Cecilia. Frankly, I'm not very surprised. She's exactly the type of girl who would do that sort of thing."

Sondra felt the blood drain from her face.

Victoria continued. "I think you should reconsider taking on any teaching roles in women's ministry or in any ministry, for that matter. After all, you do realize that this blemishes your and John's reputations as well, don't you?"

Sondra felt tears warming her eyes as the other woman's harsh words washed over her. She bit her lower lip to keep from crying.

Does the whole church know? Oh God, please help me!

She whispered, "Excuse me" and ran to her car. Once inside, the tears were let loose, and she wept. Crying bitterly, she poured out her heart again to God. The tears ebbed, and Sondra blew her nose. She sat reflectively in the silence a few more minutes and drove home, feeling defeated and alone.

* * *

During this time, Sondra turned even more to reading her Bible. She poured over scripture, letting God's truths minister to her broken spirit. While she wanted this for Cecilia too, she didn't want to force Bible study on her. She wanted it to be something she longed for and sought after with her own desire.

Sondra had taken it upon herself to write out dozens of Bible verses on slips of colorful paper and tape them all over CiCi's room— on her mirrors, bed, tabletops, and walls. She wanted her girl to see reminders of God's love for her wherever she turned her head. She had been greatly encouraged when CiCi had thanked her for hanging them and left them in place.

Whenever she thought too much about it, she anguished over what their treasured daughter had gone through, but was so grateful that it seemed to be past as normalcy slowly returned to their home.

One day while CiCi was at school, Sondra went to her room with some fresh towels, humming along with a song in her head, when she spotted them in the garbage can: snowy white tissues with ugly red smears on them. "No, no, no!" she whimpered. "Please, God, no!"

* * *

My Precious CiCi~

I am compelled to write you what is on my heart as I went into your room today. I was just bringing in fresh towels, it wasn't to pry . . . but I must tell you, my precious girl, how heavy my heart was when I saw what was in there.

Oh, Cecilia, how deep my anguish is for the pain you are carrying around inside of you! I could not help but weep as I pictured it . . . is it happening again, CiCi?

I must know. All morning my thoughts have clung to you—my prayers nearly nonstop as I have opened my heart and poured out to God this ache I have for you. The thought that you are suffering tears at me!

How did it come to this? Oh, my precious girl. I remember back to days when you were just a little girl—such a smiley one. Filled with such merriment and joy. You were mesmerizing to all who knew you. Such a delightful personality, bubbly and sweet . . . those were such happy years . . . and I can't help but wonder—when did you lose that joy? And why? And probably more importantly—will you ever get it back again?

I sat on your bed and cried fresh tears as I thought such horrible thoughts—the very idea of you hurting yourself—how could it be? What can cause a pain so deep that a mother can't see it coming?

All these thoughts jumbled in my head, colliding with one another—a sense of despair, of urgency, of being overwhelmed, of grief, of gratefulness that there is still *hope* . . . That is the one I want to settle on, to focus on, to cling to.

The idea that this does not have to be the way it is, that this awful hurting and vicious self-destruction can—I pray, Lord, please—be in your past.

Oh, Cecilia—you are precious and beloved. Your dad and I adore you, and more importantly, God loves you. You are of great value and worth!

For you to live in our family for all these years and not come to the conclusion that you are loved and valuable and treasured showed me something very important . . . it's not enough to love you.

You see, I thought that the natural result of an outpouring of affection and attention—coupled with assurances and displays of love like saying it often, doing tasks like meeting your physical needs—would simply be a certain confidence of feeling loved. Who could doubt it with continual daily deposits?

We thought we invested heavily into each of you precious kids every day—kisses and hugs, snuggles, reading together, playing games, making meals, doing devotions, attending church and church functions, praying together—with you and for you. Doing life together . . . how Dad and I have loved being parents to each of you kids—it has been God's greatest gift to us outside of our salvation and marriage.

I wouldn't trade places with anyone in the whole world. I love my life. I love you children, and I refuse to let this be how it *is* for you. This may be a chapter in the book of your life. So be it. We all have trials and difficulties, challenges and regrets, but it doesn't have to be a very long chapter or the final one.

I long for peace for you, Cecilia. Not the world's peace, which is really no peace at all. The world offers numbing solutions, vehicles to help you deaden the pain or forget for a while. Those are short-lived and empty, resulting in more despair and heartache.

No. True peace will *never* be found in the things the world offers: drugs, alcohol, sex, entertainment, cutting . . . the peace I long for you to experience is only found in Christ.

In John 14:22 Jesus said, "Peace I leave with you; My peace I give to you. I do not give to you as the world gives. Do not let your hearts be troubled and do not be afraid."

No . . . it's not enough to love you . . . I need to lead you. Forgive me, my precious CiCi, for not doing a better job at leading you.

As I've really pondered these things since you shared the truth with me, again and again I've berated myself for not recognizing any signs of your ordeal—or maybe that's not quite right. I recognized signs but didn't place proper importance on what they meant.

I've seen you morose. You are not the smiley girl you used to be. These are outward signs of an inner hurt, and it grieves me to know now that I passed it off as a phase you'd get over.

Oh, the tears of regret that these eyes have poured out, realizing my ignorance. CiCi, you must know I never meant to come across as indifferent to what you were feeling.

I truly did not imagine for a moment that what you were feeling would be so painful that you would act it out in the self-destructive way of cutting yourself.

I waver between self-recrimination over my lack of insight and a sense of guilt, and I realize that even that is not how God wants me to respond.

Enough! My hand-wringing, futile tears, and guilt are not of God. That is where Satan would have me park: in the endless cycle of regret, doubt, and lostness.

No!

I choose, instead, to trust.

I trust that even through the pain, God can and will bring good.

I trust that God can use this for the growth and good of others who struggle and suffer in a similar prison, and we can offer hope to people who long to break free from their self-destructive ways.

I trust that by fixing my eyes on Jesus, the author and perfector of my faith, He can and will do great and glorious things through my submitted life.

I trust the words of my Savior, who promised me, "I have come that you might have life and have it abundantly."

And I trust, my precious CiCi, that Jesus, the one who saves, is more than able to lead your heart from the dark place you've been into His life-giving light. He loves you! He died for you so you don't have to go through the same anguish the world goes through. Jesus said in John 10:27–30, "My sheep hear My voice; I know them and they follow Me. I give them eternal life, and they shall never perish; no one can snatch them out of My hand. My Father, who has given them to Me, is greater than all; no one can snatch them out of My Father's hand. I and the Father are one."

I believe that, Cecilia.

No one, not even Satan, can touch one hair on your head if you belong to Jesus, not without God allowing it. And if it doesn't serve some greater purpose of God, He won't allow it. So if He allows us to go through some trial or difficulty, it can only be for good.

CiCi, the question is, are you one of His?

I love you too much to assume the answer is yes. Only you can answer that. I want to believe you are, and you very well may be, but do not get upset for me asking. If you know you are, then we have tremendous hope that the world cannot fathom, because not only do those who trust in Jesus have eternal life, but we also can live victorious lives here on earth.

Not perfect lives and certainly not pain free, but victorious over sin. Christ-honoring, God-glorifying, soul-satisfying, joy-filled lives.

I love you, CiCi. I love you beyond your ability to grasp. Not until you have a child of your own will you be able to begin to fathom the depth of my and Dad's love for you.

We are walking this journey with you. This is not some lonely road you're on. In fact, it's rather crowded with Dad, Jesus, and me all here with you. You are never alone, CiCi. Do you understand what I'm saying? When you hurt, we hurt. When you bleed, we bleed. When you suffer, we suffer. When you have victory, we have victory.

Choose, Cecilia . . . it's your life, your journey. We're all here with you, praying you'll make the right choice—to trust Jesus, to run to Him when life is hard, to cling to Him, and to let us help you through, to make choices you won't regret, to stay in the light . . .

You are precious and beloved ~ Mom and Dad
I have loved you with an everlasting love ~ God

* * *

When she got home, CiCi found her mom's letter on her bed. Then she confirmed Sondra's fears: she had started cutting again. CiCi had masked her struggle well.

Defeat swept over Sondra as she realized how addictive this behavior was.

She again collected hidden tools that her girl had used. Praying with an anguished heart and crying as she went, she poured out all her grief. "O God, this hurts so much! I can't even express my sorrow. The mere fact that she feels compelled to do such a thing to herself is eating away at me. Please take us through this storm. Will this ever end? Is it my fault?"

She gathered scissors, placing them carefully in a bag, along with razor blades and a small paring knife. Her heart broke as she pictured what her precious girl had done to herself with the sharp instruments.

She was spending more time with her daughter and prayed often with her, but CiCi still wanted someone younger, whom she felt could relate to her better. She had stopped going to her youth group. It seemed easier to avoid Michelle than to confront her biased managing style. Sondra worried CiCi would slide further from wanting interaction with anyone from church soon and kept praying that they would find someone who could step into the role of mentor for their daughter.

One day, CiCi herself came up with a solution. She came into the kitchen, where her mom was cutting vegetables for dinner. "Mom, I've been thinking. Maybe I could meet with Annabelle."

Sondra grabbed on the idea with relief. "Oh, honey, she would be perfect! Why didn't we think of her before?"

Annabelle was a younger woman who had been on a serving team with CiCi a few years earlier and who had a fondness for their daughter. Though Sondra longed to be the someone her daughter wanted to turn to, she realized that she had to choose her own confidante. If not her, then she was very grateful for Annabelle, a godly young woman with wisdom and the appeal of youth, but with available time on her hands as a single gal who had a heart for teenage girls.

Sondra called Annabelle and shared the struggle their daughter was going through. "John and CiCi and I were hoping you might be willing to meet with her once a week or so and just talk through things with her. She holds you in such high regard."

The younger woman graciously answered, "I would be glad to meet with her, Sondra. I'm touched that you thought of me."

"Oh, thank you! You cannot know my relief. Seriously, you are an answer to prayer."

They worked out the details, with the understanding that Annabelle could disclose anything at any time with John and Sondra if she thought they should know.

Sondra was haunted by the tenacity of the compulsion of cutting and knew she needed to find solace in the only place worth finding it: at the feet of Jesus. She clung to her Bible, soaking in the words of truth like a balm to her aching soul, wanting desperately to rescue her beloved daughter from the prison she had made for herself, but completely unable to.

She needed to trust that God Himself would carry her, tend to her, and somehow use this horrible situation for good.

Imagine that! That anything good could come from this is unfathomable.

And yet, she truly did believe that He could.

Sondra thought back to the days of Regan and Cecilia's colic.

This is a thousand times worse than that was.

And yet God used that trial for good. Through the years He had brought Sondra in touch with women who were struggling with the very same trial of having a colicky baby and under the exhaustion and disillusionment that they wouldn't make it through. Sondra was able to offer them a better perspective and assurance that the ordeal, though hard, was temporary.

As she pondered this new burden and all the pain it brought, she realized that the only way for God to use it for good in other people's lives was if she were willing to share it.

That meant letting go of the pride and having to admit they didn't have it all together, because the fact was, they didn't.

"O Lord, then so be it," she prayed. "May I rather bear the judging thoughts of men and be found humble and needy as I am in Your eyes than try to cover the truth that I carry shameful burdens and miss out on Your gentle touch of grace and healing."

Only God could orchestrate such a symphony of the right people connecting at the right time to bring fresh hope to a hurting heart. "So in this too," she prayed, "in this struggle we are going through with our precious CiCi, my prayer is, please, Lord, if we must go through this, use it for good, somehow, in Your time and in Your way, and bring glory to Your name."

* * *

Feeling trapped in his choice, John was really struggling. One night, he came home late, and they had a loud discussion in their bedroom. Sondra was certain the kids could hear the whole exchange.

She implored him, "We can't second-guess this. You're going to drive yourself crazy."

He turned toward her. "Don't you think I know that? I am so frustrated. You're not the one who has to live with the consequences of this decision. It's my fault for making it so hastily. There's no way to go back and undo it. Trust me, I would choose differently now if I could do it again. I mean, why do I have to be the one to give up the reward? I worked hard, I earned that promotion—and for what? Just to turn it down? I've sabotaged my own career." He shook his head and let out a big breath. "What was I thinking? It's unbelievable."

Sondra entreated, "But, John, we don't know how it may have turned out for CiCi. Maybe the stability we have here is the thing that will help her heal. I know it's hard, and you have sacrificed the most."

John nodded bitterly. "Yeah. I sure did. And for a daughter who doesn't appear to appreciate it anyway." He ran his hand on his head, biting his lip.

Sondra tried again, softer. "We don't know that."

John turned to her. "Well, I do know one thing. My career is dead. I'm never going to get another opportunity like that one. We don't know if staying will help CiCi anyway. She may struggle with this for a long time to come." He threw her a resentful look.

I don't have all the answers. What if he's right? What if we should have gone?

She voiced, "John, I know it's hard. You have every right to feel disappointed. This was not an easy choice. But when you made it, do you remember what you said to me? You said that the title of dad was more important than whatever title work could give you, and you were right. Just because you're feeling the loss of that does not mean you made the wrong decision. It just means it was a hard decision."

She looked at him and stated firmly, "I believe that God wants us here. I think God is helping CiCi through Annabelle. His purposes are bigger than we can understand. There could be other reasons He wanted to keep us here. We have to trust Him through this."

He rubbed his eyes and nodded slowly. "You could be right, Sondra. I'm driving myself crazy because it's too late now anyway." He sighed bitterly. "I can't help it. I keep replaying the decision over and over again, and I just can't let go of the fact that as the sole breadwinner for this family, I think I made a huge mistake that can't be undone."

He shook his head. "I can't deny that being where CiCi has support may help her, and of course, that matters most to me." He sighed again, running his hand through his hair, and looked at Sondra. "But even if that's true, it doesn't mean it's going to be easy for me to forget what I have walked away from." He grabbed his coat and keys. "You need to let me have some time alone to think. I'm going for a drive."

She gulped as she watched her husband head back out into the night.

* * *

The next day Sondra called Rene.

"John is really agonizing about his decision not to take the promotion. I have to admit, there are times I've wondered if it would have been better for us. I just wish the answers were clearer."

Rene replied, "I understand. We never would have come down here if it hadn't been for Patrick's brain tumor. Now, sitting on this side of those decisions, I can more clearly see how God used all of it to bring about other changes in our lives that we would have missed out on if not for that."

Sondra argued back, "But it's too late for us now. What if that was the path we were supposed to take?"

Renee took a deep breath. "Listen, Sondra, I know it's hard. But God doesn't do e-mail. We have to do the best we can with what we know at the time of our decisions. You and John arrived at the conclusion—after much prayer, might I remind you—that staying was the better way. You can't question every decision you make, or you'll go crazy. There must be a reason God led your hearts to decide to stay."

"You're right. I know it, but it's hard sometimes. Oh gosh, Rene, I sure do wish God did send e-mails."

Her friend laughed. "Well, He does have some things to say on this subject already. How about *you* send John e-mails with those verses that might offer him some encouragement as he wrestles through this?"

"Oh, Rene, that's a wonderful idea."

"Other than that, how are things going? How is your writing coming along?"

"Well, I still write, but I've stopped pushing to get published. It just wasn't going anywhere, and with all that's going on with CiCi, I haven't had the time to give it. Maybe I'll pick it up again in a few years."

Rene innocently asked, "I wonder if you know this woman who recently had a book published? She goes to your church."

"Who?" Sondra held her breath.

"Her name is Michelle Stevenson." Rene continued. "She was a guest writer on a blog I get, and her bio mentioned her new book. Do you know her?"

The jolt of jealousy that surged through Sondra shocked her.

I can't believe that she, of all people, got something published.

She slowly responded, "Yeah, I know her. She was CiCi's table leader. I wonder what her book is about?"

Rene said, "If I remember right, I think it was something about doing youth ministry and what she has learned through it."

Sondra bit her tongue. She desperately wanted to tell her friend how CiCi had been hurt at the hands of the table leader but knew that wouldn't be right.

Perhaps Michelle would do well to first learn not to play favorites before telling the world how to carry out that role.

She choked out the lie, "Wow. I . . . I hope her book does well."

Rene knew her old friend well. "Sondra, are you okay?"

Sondra reluctantly admitted, "I can't help but be a little jealous. I have tried to get published for years. Then here comes this woman who is a lot younger than me and has success at what's probably her first attempt."

"You don't know that it was her first attempt. She may have been trying for a long time too. It sounded like God has really taught her some lessons about being a leader for young ladies."

Sondra felt chastened.

Rene went on. "Besides, it's not a competition. Just because she is published doesn't mean you can't be too. I love your writing, Sondra. It has ministered to me many times."

"Thank you, Rene. That means a lot to me. I really appreciate your belief in me."

I just don't know if I believe in myself anymore.

After the friends hung up, Sondra went to her room to read her Bible. She opened to First Corinthians 12: "Now the body is not made up of one part but of many." She pondered that and continued reading. "If the whole body were an eye, where would the sense of hearing be? If the whole body were an ear, where would the sense of smell be?" She grew sober, and a tear fell from her eye. "But in fact God has arranged the parts in the body, every one of them, just as He wanted them to be." Sondra felt the Holy Spirit convicting her as God's Word probed her heart. "Now you are the body of Christ and each one of you is a part of it." Her eyes dropped down to the next well-known chapter. "Love is patient, love is kind. It does not envy, it does not boast, it is not proud. It is not rude or self-seeking." Sondra was completely broken. It sobered her to think of the years spent longing for something that God hadn't allowed her for His own reasons, and she had persisted in her quest for it anyway. Through her tears she confessed, "Instead of rejoicing that others are spreading Your fame further, God, I've been wrapped up in envy. Please forgive me, and free me from my struggle with jealousy. Whatever You put in my heart to write from now on, it's for an audience of one: You."

Tears flowed as she relinquished hold on this area she had held tightly for so long.

"O God, I want to honor You. Whatever Your purpose, please make my life count as righteousness for Your name's sake. You alone deserve all glory."

* * *

To: JohnMartin@TrinityBank.com
From: Sondra

Whatever you do, work at it with all your heart, as working for the Lord, not for men, since you know that you will receive and inheritance from the Lord as a reward. It is the Lord Christ you are serving. ~ Colossians 3:23

* * *

A few days after her talk with Rene, Sondra had an opportunity to test her resolve when she bumped into Theresa at church. Her friend shared her newest endeavor. "After talking with you and Charlene, I really began doing the things you both told me to. I started to see a few positive changes in Melissa—and in myself. I decided to start this blog. Originally, I looked at it as a place where others could draw encouragement from what we're going through. But I can't believe what God has done with it," she shared with excitement. "Now almost two hundred people subscribe and participate in discussions about Christian parenting."

Sondra was able to celebrate with her friend. "Theresa, that's fantastic." She gave her a hug.

"Oh, Sondra, to think that I almost gave up and walked away from Jack and Melissa, it was just too hard. But God used you and Charlene to infuse new hope into my heart, and I've been growing like crazy. It actually stopped being so much about Melissa and became more about what God wants for me." She smiled. "Even if Melissa doesn't respond the way I pray she does, I see now that God wanted to get *my* attention." Her excitement spilled out. "I can't wait to be in His Word and find new truths about Him and His love for me. With this blog, I get to share with others. I know this sounds funny, but I feel like I'm just the typist taking dictation from God, and there are times I feel like He might take over that role too!"

The friends laughed, astonished at how God could work to bring good from bad. Sondra walked away from their meeting, encouraged.

Lord, thank You for letting me hear that. I know You have good plans for us. Please help John come to a place of peace. Please help Cecilia find her hope in You and not succumb to the temptation to self-harm anymore. Help us, Lord. This journey can be so hard.

* * *

To: JohnMartin@TrinityBank.com
From: Sondra

Galatians 6:9 ~ Let us not become weary in doing good, for at the proper time we will reap a harvest if we do not give up.

* * *

Kayla Carpenter called Sondra. "I'm wondering if you have a few minutes to talk?"

"Certainly," Sondra replied, curious.

"Well," the girl started shyly, "I have been trying to read my Bible, but there are lots of things that I just don't understand. I was wondering if you might be willing to help me. I . . . I know you're busy, but I thought maybe if you have some time . . ." Her voice drifted off doubtfully.

A pang of sympathy and chastisement shot through Sondra. "Oh, Kayla, I would be delighted. I'm so touched that you even thought of me, dear."

The relief in the younger woman's voice was evident. "Oh, thank you. You don't know what this means to me." She faltered. "I really don't have anyone else. I'm the only Christian in my family. It's been somewhat lonely trying to do this on my own."

How thoughtless I've been! That should have occurred to me.

She assured Kayla, "I'm so glad you called to ask me this. I would love to spend time with you in a Bible study. I can make time each week if you can?"

"That would be wonderful! I really appreciate it."

Sondra smiled.

Maybe I wasn't able to make an impact on Carolyn, but that doesn't mean I can't make one on her daughter.

The two made plans to meet a few days later, and Sondra hung up the phone, marveling at the way God orchestrated things.

* * *

To: JohnMartin@TrinityBank.com
From: Sondra

Matthew 19:30 ~

"But many who are first will be last, and many who are last will be first." ~ Jesus

* * *

That evening when John got home, he asked to talk with Sondra, and she settled in his office, unsure of what he was going to say.

He looked at his wife, his eyes weary. "I haven't mentioned getting the e-mails you've sent the past couple of weeks, Sondra, but I want you to know that I appreciate them."

He rubbed his hand across his face. "I'm grateful you were willing to give me some space and time to work through it all." He looked up at her. "This morning I was reading my Bible and felt like God was speaking to me about all this remorse I've been carrying around."

Tears started streaming out of Sondra's eyes as she heard her husband share what was on his heart.

"It's like my head was in a dark cloud for a while, and I didn't know how to get out of it. I'm not saying I don't still regret passing on the job, but I'm starting to see that maybe I've been living too much for the satisfactions of this world instead of recognizing that God wants me to be grateful for where He has me right now." He paused. "It will probably be a painful choice for a while yet, but I am thankful for the job I do have, the opportunities that are here around us. Especially as it seems CiCi is doing better now. Maybe having the stability will help her get off the path she's been on."

Sondra nodded, too choked up to reply.

He ran a hand through his graying hair and continued. "Who knows how long we are even here for? I don't want to waste another minute, regretting anything."

She recovered herself and ran to hug him. "Oh, John. You don't know how much I've been praying about this. I know it hasn't been easy for you. You've given up so much for the good of others. But I truly believe God has good things in store for us. We just have to trust Him."

He held her, stroking her hair. "When you told me that you were going to start meeting with Kayla Carpenter, it hit me—what if that was another reason God wanted to keep us here? You have a lot to share with her, and she doesn't have anyone pouring into her life in the ways that matter."

Tears flowed as Sondra rejoiced in her husband's God-honoring response to the disappointment he faced and his new outlook. His situation hadn't changed, but his attitude had, and it was going to make all the difference.

Ten Years Later

May 2017

Sondra stood in the kitchen, pulled a hot tray of cookies out of the oven, and set them to cool on the nearby rack. Mylah would be home soon, and she and her college friends always loved the treat of home-baked cookies. Sondra was glad to have something that she could do to bless her youngest daughter in what might be her final year of living at home.

Mylah had ended up going to the school that Regan had first looked at, Marina Community College, just thirty minutes from home. But despite how close it was, Sondra and John rarely saw her more than a few times a week. Her schedule was jammed with classes and work and activities with friends.

She squinted at the recipe card and reached for the reading glasses perched on the top of her head. Last month when she had turned fifty, she'd finally given in to the fact that she needed glasses. Without them she could barely read her mother's scrawling handwriting on the card for the next batch of cookies. She sighed. "Growing old isn't exactly wonderful, but I'd like to do it with as much grace and dignity as I can muster." She talked out loud to herself a lot more now too.

Seeing her mom's distinctive handwriting reminded her that she wanted to call her later to chat and check in on her and Dad.

Quickly, she assembled the ingredients, formed the dough into balls, and popped the trays into the oven, bending then stretching, trying to relieve her sore back and aching muscles.

"Ooh, that hurts." She stretched again, longing for the days when aches weren't the norm. She looked at a picture of the four kids taken together a few years earlier, and thoughts of CiCi crossed her mind. Cecilia was living on the East Coast for her job. It was just a short-term post, and she'd been gone about five months, but Sondra missed her. She wanted a good job for her daughter; she only wished it could have been closer to home.

The cell phone near her vibrated; the phone's speaker identified that the caller was Regan and asked her if she wanted to answer it. She waved her hand over the infrared beam to accept the connection.

"Hi, honey!" she greeted her eldest child.

"Hi, Mom," Regan replied. "Would it be okay if Gavin and I stopped by tonight to talk about something with you and Dad for a little while?"

"Oh, sweetheart, of course! We would love that! What time works for you? Would you like to come for dinner? I'm making one of your favorites—parmesan-crusted chicken and marinated rice."

Regan laughed. "Well, when you make that offer, how can I refuse? That sounds great. We can be there around six o'clock if that's okay?"

Sondra assured her that was perfect and hung up, excited for the unexpected treat of seeing her daughter and her husband of three years. Regan and Gavin lived thirty minutes away, but life was busy, and they didn't get to see them nearly as often as Sondra and John would have liked.

Regan loved her job as a kindergarten teacher. The school she worked at was where she had met Gavin as he taught there as well. They both were wonderful with kids, and Sondra and John couldn't be more proud of them. Regular phone calls kept them close, but face-to-face visits were the best. Sondra started humming with anticipation of the evening ahead.

She thought about Tommy, who was traveling with his band in Europe.

His parents had agreed: he should take a year or two to see if he could make a career with his music. He might never have another chance to follow that dream. Life was short, and the season for taking such a risk was now while he was young and single. He was enjoying his music with the adventure and travel and seeing where God led him. With the time difference and his busy schedule, they rarely heard from him. Soon after he'd gotten settled, he had told them about a young woman he'd met, Marguerite, who seemed to have captured his interest.

"She's beautiful. And she really loves the Lord. I met her at one of our concerts."

Sondra and John had been elated. What more could a parent hope for than God-loving spouses for their children?

Tommy had continued. "I've got a lot of competition though." He laughed. "She's always surrounded by guys trying to get her attention."

John had told him, "Son, if she's the girl for you, don't worry. God will work out those details. You just keep doing your part, and leave the rest up to Him." John grinned. "Though you may want to try attending her church and seeing if you can get an in with someone who knows her."

Tommy had laughed and nodded on the phone video. "I know, Dad. But I wonder if I'm aiming too high. I mean, she's really something else."

Sondra had smiled. "Well, Tommy, for what it's worth, I think you're a real catch yourself."

He had laughed. "Thanks, Mom. I'm grateful to have your vote."

The timer dinged, pulling Sondra's thoughts back to the present. She took the last batch of cookies from the oven, setting the sheet on the counter. Stopping to water the plant that sat nearby in the sunshine, she thought back to the day long ago that Linda Peters had given it to her. She smiled, seeing how the leafy green vine had flourished and grown over the years, spilling out of the pot and onto the counter.

You've grown me too, Lord. Linda was right. It took time, but You've deepened my trust in the fertile soil of Your love and faithfulness.

While the cookies cooled, she went to her room to take a few minutes to rest before she would have to start making dinner. Her back troubled her more these days, and being on her feet for long stretches wore her out more quickly than it used to.

In her room, she opened her drawer to fish around for a letter that Tommy had sent with his address. His birthday was coming up, and she wanted to send him a card.

She came across an envelope full of cards and letters she had written to John over the years. He usually read them and then gave them to her for safekeeping. She wasn't sure what she was saving them for, but if anyone ever wanted to follow the trail, it might make for interesting reading as they had progressed through life together.

The first card in the stack that she had written as a young bride made her blush with her candid messages to her new husband, written so long ago. The next was simple in its wording: "John ~ you are my best friend, and I thank God for bringing our lives together. I wish I had a way to show you the depth of my appreciation—oh, wait, I do! You are the most funny, wonderful person in the world, and I will love you forever!" She had signed it with a bubble heart. Others, farther down in the pile, reflected a deeper love that had been tested, but stood firm.

Sondra tucked the whole bunch back into the drawer and rummaged in the other corner. She found some of her old songs and recalled the memory of how she had asked the worship leader in their church if they could use any of her material.

Caleb had apologized, "I'm sorry, Sondra, we can't. In order to avoid making anyone feel badly, we have a blanket policy of never accepting work from anyone who isn't on the music team."

"Oh, okay. Well, how do you get on the music team?" she had asked.

"Invitation only. Sorry."

Sondra had had a hard time resisting the temptation to feel rejected again.

"They won't even look at them," she had lamented to her husband.

John had tried to comfort her. "Honey, think about it. Some people could get hurt feelings if their work was rejected."

"So they reject everyone so we can all feel the same?"

John had chuckled. "Well, if you want to go to college and get a degree in music, maybe then they'll take a look at your stuff." She hadn't found that humorous in the least.

Now, reading the verse of one song, she laughed. *Perhaps I should have been grateful God spared me the embarrassment of having this one sung out loud.* She chuckled and glanced at another song. *Oh, but this one—this one had held promise.*

She remembered back to the day so long ago when she had written it. It had felt like God was feeding her the very words to put on the paper:

> Jesus praying, "Your will, not mine"
> Trusting His Father's
> Full plan divine . . .
> Knowing this, would set sinners free
> And give us faith, when He said, "Follow me"
>
> If that's what it takes, to lead them to You, Lord,
> And to show that You are more, than they could
> ever dream
> Then help me on You lean,
> If that's what it needs, for them to find
> Why You are mine—and I am Yours,
> Then help me cling to You
> As You carry me through
> If that's what it needs . . .

Unfair trials, unjust hurt,
Hold me close, Lord
While You're at work
Using these, to show me more
Your deepest grace, Your endless love
If that's what it takes, to lead them to You, Lord,
And to show that You are more, than they could
ever dream
Then help me on You lean,
If that's what it needs, for them to find
Why You are mine—and I am Yours,
Then help me be meek
And turn the other cheek
If that's what it needs . . .

Grief and sorrow, pain and loss
Sometimes You ask us to carry a cross
But the strength is not my own
Cause You are on Your throne ~
And it's Your power alone!

If that's what it takes, to lead them to You, Lord,
And to show that You are more, than they could
ever dream
Then help me on You lean,
If that's what it needs, for them to find
Why You are mine—and I am Yours,
Then help me trust in You
As You carry me through
And help them believe . . .
In You too . . .

She had penned those words after going through a particularly
trying time with CiCi. While fighting her battle with cutting, Cecilia
accused her of being an absentee mom, something that wounded
Sondra to the depths of her heart.

Sondra knew she wasn't perfect. She was fully aware of the many areas God needed to grow her in. But to be told that her efforts hadn't been enough was a dagger to her, one that CiCi very quickly regretted when she saw the tears that had sprung to her mother's eyes.

She had meekly apologized, "That was stupid and wrong of me, Mom. Please forgive me."

Of course, Sondra had immediately forgiven her, but the accusation had left a raw wound that God had healed by the writing of this song.

Alone and sitting on her bed, Sondra held the paper and sang it out loud, her voice warbling a little.

"Mom?" The sound at her door startled Sondra.

She stood up. "CiCi? Good heavens! What on earth are you doing here?" Sondra ran to hug their twenty-six-year-old daughter. Gathering her close, she crooned in her ear, "Oh, sweetheart, what a wonderful surprise! You absolutely stunned me!"

Cecilia pulled back from her mom a bit, her green eyes showing hesitancy, and said, "I'm sorry. I let myself in with my key." She held the metal object in her hand to show her mom.

"Oh, honey, of course, you can come in anytime—this is your home. You just surprised me." She pulled her daughter in for another hug. "What are you doing here?"

"Well, the company said I could come home for a few days to gather the rest of my things."

Sondra pulled back to look into her daughter's eyes. "Your things?" she questioned.

"Yes. They've offered me the job permanently, and I've decided to accept."

CiCi looked steadily at her mom, knowing that the news would be hard to swallow. She hadn't given them any chance to really absorb her going out to the East Coast to begin with. She saw the hurt in her mother's face.

Sondra struggled to voice her thoughts. "Oh my goodness, wow, well, honey, congratulations. Dad and I are so proud of you, darling."

Sondra hugged her daughter again, pushing back the tears. "I can't believe you didn't let us know you were coming home. You could have texted me. I would have, oh, I don't know, done something wonderful for you if I'd known!"

CiCi laughed. "No worries. It's good just to be here." She looked around, already drawing comfort from the warm, familiar surroundings.

"How long can you stay?"

"Only through the weekend. I booked my flight back for Monday, and the moving truck will bring the rest of my things from my apartment next week."

When she had turned twenty-one, she had moved out of their home, something Sondra had resisted at the time, but John had said they needed to let her go. Thankfully, she had picked a small apartment that wasn't too far away. The last few years, they had still seen her frequently. But then, when this job opportunity had come last winter, she jumped at it, leaving most of her things in the apartment that she had sublet to a friend's friend.

"Will you be able to stay here?"

"That would be great. I already put my bag in my old room, figuring you and Dad would be okay with that."

"Of course, sweetheart. We're delighted you can stay here. Well, your timing is good. Regan and Gavin are coming for dinner tonight too, and Mylah will be home soon, so you'll get to see everyone except TJ, of course."

They walked into the kitchen together, and CiCi nibbled a cookie.

"So what were you singing when I walked in?"

"Oh, just a little song I wrote a very long time ago."

Embarrassed to have been heard, Sondra flushed. She pulled the glasses down off her head and began to follow the recipes on the cards for their dinner as they chatted.

"It sounded good, Mom. You should try to get it out there somehow; you could put it on YouTube," she teased.

"Ha! Yeah, no . . . those days are long past for me." She changed the subject. "Tell me about your new job."

They chatted about that and about her life in Boston.

"I love the city and exploring the amazing history and culture in my free time," her daughter shared.

Sondra asked, "Have you found a good church yet, dear?" She was conscious of the sudden tension.

"Well, not exactly. I mean, I have looked around, I just haven't found one that works for me yet."

Sondra could see CiCi hedging about this and prayed quickly for wisdom as she navigated the delicate water of urging her precious girl to keep after her own spiritual growth without coming across as bossy. "Well, honey, you know how important it is to find a good church. I hope you'll keep looking and asking God to help you. You don't want to let too much time pass. It really is important."

Her words died off as she saw Cecilia's face. "I know, Mom. These things take time. It's been really busy with work and now this new offer. Don't worry, I will find a church soon."

Nodding, Sondra eased away from the touchy topic by sharing about what her days had been busy with lately. "Did we tell you we had to transfer the power of attorney for Papa and Grammy to your dad's name?"

CiCi shook her head. "No, I didn't know that. Why?"

"Well, since she needs continual care in the nursing home now, Papa was so overwhelmed to meet all the deadlines and requirements. Your dad asked if I would take on the role as main administrator." She stirred the pot of soup on the stove. "Every six months I have to reapply for their benefits, filling out an endless trail of paperwork for housing, funding, and medications. It hasn't been easy, but I'm learning."

The two chatted about a variety of things, making dinner together and catching up on all the family news and happenings till John arrived, delighted by the surprise of Cecilia. Mylah soon came home, exclaiming at the unexpected sight of her sister; the girls laughed and teased each other like old times.

Soon, Regan and Gavin arrived. A pang in her heart made Sondra sad that Tommy wasn't here to complete the picture.

O Lord, be with him wherever he is tonight, and thank You for this chance to see our precious kids.

As she carried covered dishes to the table, Sondra enjoyed hearing the voices of her children talking and laughing over shared memories as they retold old favorites.

John's eyes twinkled at her, and she smiled at her beloved husband of thirty-two years. He was balding, and his eyes were a bit dimmer, but his laugh was as youthful as ever.

The phone rang, the speaker announcing, "Thomas J. Martin is calling."

A mixture of voices urged, "Quick! Answer—it's Tommy!"

John accepted the call and pushed the button that projected Tommy's face onto the screen on the wall, allowing them all to see him, and he them, as they spoke.

"Tommy!"

"Wow! What are you all doing home? I was expecting to see Mom and Dad but not the rest of you. Are you having a party without me?"

They all laughed, CiCi replying, "Well, we sure wish you were here. Where are you, anyway?"

"I'm in this amazing village in France called Mougins. It's close to the French Riviera. It's after midnight here, but I wanted to catch Mom and Dad home together. Someone very special is here with me that I want to introduce to everyone, so this is great since now you can all meet her." Joining TJ on the large screen, a striking girl stepped into view. Tommy hugged her close and said, "Everyone, this is Marguerite Dubois. Marguerite, this is my family. I wanted you all to hear the wonderful news: earlier tonight I asked this beautiful woman if she would marry me, and she said yes!"

They could feel Tommy's pride and joy across the ocean that separated them, and a scream of happiness went up from everyone seated around the table, looking at their brother and his lovely bride-to-be.

Sondra could barely contain her elation at his news. Marguerite shyly blushed at Tommy's pronouncement and his family's joy at hearing it.

"Mom, you'll be glad to hear that Marguerite's family attends the same church that your friend Charlene Jeffries goes to.

"Oh my goodness, Tommy, that's amazing."

Her son nodded. "Yeah, I don't know who was more surprised—me or Mr. and Mrs. Jeffries—when I first walked in. They were standing in the vestibule area, greeting people. I knew you had mentioned they'd moved to France several years ago, but I hadn't known where. Mrs. Jeffries was so excited to see me and told me to tell you hi, which I might have forgotten to do," he admitted sheepishly. "Then she introduced me to one of the good friends she's made since moving here, Marguerite's mom."

TJ clearly was elated at his prize of the lovely girl. She radiated a sweetness that Sondra knew her searching son had been drawn to, and she rejoiced in her heart for what God was working in his young life.

"Oh, Marguerite! Welcome to the family! We wish we could hug you both in person." Sondra choked up.

"When is the date?" Regan called out.

"Well, that's our next bit of news. We don't want to wait too long, so after talking it over with Marguerite's parents, we decided to get married in six months. Can you all fly to France?" He laughed, knowing that if they had to, they would fly to the moon to witness such a blessed event.

Tommy, ever her endearing one, said shyly, "Mom? We were hoping you might consider writing something we could include in our ceremony, like maybe a poem. You have such a way with words, and it would mean so much to us."

Sondra stood by the screen, seeing her precious son and her soon-to-be daughter-in-law looking back at her expectantly. She choked up and was touched beyond words. "Oh, Tommy. Of course, I will. What a lovely request, my darling."

Today, sitting here among her family, she felt this honor her own dear son was giving her was worth all the agony of what she'd learned in her quest to feel her writing was a blessing to others.

Lord, what an undeserved gift from Your loving hand.

She brushed at the tears, feeling John reach out and squeeze her arm.

The family called out their congratulations till, finally, it was time to say good-bye. Laughing with happiness, they saw Tommy give Marguerite a kiss, followed by a euphoric thumbs-up to his watching family.

As they disconnected, the screen changed back to a piece of artwork that adorned the wall.

Mylah marveled, "Can you believe Tommy is getting married?

John nodded. "I'm so glad we all were here to hear his news together."

Sondra happened to see Gavin and Regan look at each other, clearly wanting to share something too, but not wanting to steal any of the joy that belonged to Tommy with his announcement.

Sondra caught the look on her daughter's face and remembered back to their talk on the phone that afternoon. As it dawned on her, she looked wonderingly at Regan, who, seeing her mom's inquiring gaze, slowly nodded, smiling.

The expression on Regan's glowing face told her all she needed to know, and her heart began to rejoice again, freshly marveling at God's goodness.

"Oh, my darling girl!" Sondra couldn't help the tears and couldn't have cared less as she ran to gather her daughter in her arms.

Regan laughed, with Gavin at her side, and informed the rest of the astonished group why Mom was sobbing and hugging her.

"We're going to have a baby! I'm three months pregnant."

Another shout of celebration went up around the table.

Sondra didn't think her heart could stand much more of the momentous announcements. John looked at her with tears in his eyes. He too was feeling overwhelmed at the wave after wave of blessings pouring over them.

First, their dear CiCi home unexpectedly, then Tommy with his surprise call and amazing announcement, and now Regan and Gavin with their joyous news. Sondra marveled at the goodness of God and was so grateful for the husband with whom she shared this incredible journey.

Sondra thrilled in the moment, wishing time could come to a halt so they could just luxuriate in the joy. She was content knowing that God had good things in store for them all. They just had to keep living life one day at a time, walking faithfully forward, and trusting in Him.

* * *

The hustle and bustle of getting ready for two momentous occasions, both happening at approximately the same time, added chaos to Sondra's days, but she wouldn't complain. She was thrilled with the coming wedding and glad that the bride's family would be responsible for undertaking most of the planning. For this one, they could just go and enjoy the celebration.

She was focusing most of her attention on helping Regan get ready for the baby's arrival, doing whatever little tasks helped her daughter, and encouraging her to get as much rest as she could.

CiCi had gone back to Boston, feeling a little homesick at leaving her family with all the exciting planning and preparing going on.

Regan had assured her sister, "Trust me, I will keep you posted on all the details as long as you promise to come when he or she is born."

CiCi hugged her sister. "Are you kidding? You couldn't keep me away!" And they had parted, each to their own exciting life ventures.

Mylah was eager to "start living" like she put it to her mom one night and felt the angst of being last at home. "I'm the last to do things and the last to get to explore some of the excitement in life," she shared unhappily.

Sondra smiled. "Your season is college right now, my darling. There's so much out there for you too. Don't worry. Life isn't going anywhere. It will all be here waiting. God has some marvelous plans for you as well, I promise."

She covered Mylah's hand with her own. "Meanwhile, can you see that your season of being home lines up with your dad's and my season of having any of our children at home? When you go, not only does a new season start for you, but also a new season begins for us as well. I don't want to make you feel badly, but you can help ease us into that new phase too, my dear, by embracing where we are all at right now and not trying to prematurely rush through all that God has for you."

Mylah hugged her mom. "I do love these days too, Mom."

She saw the wisdom in her mother's words and agreed to wait quietly, patiently, for God to unfold the rest of His plan to her heart in His time and in His way.

* * *

The months passed in a blur. A few days after Tommy and Marguerite's wedding, Sondra spoke with Rene.

"Can you believe our Tommy is married?" she marveled.

Rene laughed. "How did that little boy grow up so fast? I remember the day he tried flushing your shoe down the toilet. Boy, were you hopping mad."

Her old friend chuckled at the memory, and Sondra laughed along with her.

"Tell me about Marguerite. Charlene's last e-mail said that she is a beautiful girl."

"Oh yes, she is stunning. Tommy is head over heels in love with her." She assured her friend, "I think they balance each other well. She comes from a solid Christian family. Her mother is a lovely woman, very down-to-earth and a really sweet lady." Sondra thought back to the few days she and John had spent with Marguerite's parents. She laughed. "Her dad was having a hard time letting his little girl go, but he is very kindhearted. They've grown to love Tommy too, so we are grateful for that."

Rene asked, "What was the ceremony like?"

"Magnificent. The whole thing was an absolute storybook wedding. You couldn't have found a more romantic setting, with old-world European charm, mixed in with lavish details. I've never seen more gorgeous flower arrangements. Marguerite's mother used to be a wedding planner, so she knows all the tricks of the trade. It certainly was the loveliest wedding I've ever been to."

Rene sighed. "I can't wait till Mariah Jane gets married. I think it will be fun to plan everything."

Sondra laughed. "Well, I can assure you, it is fun, but it's a lot of stress too."

Rene laughed, remembering the months that Sondra had been so frazzled when she'd helped plan Regan and Gavin's wedding.

"On second thought, maybe I'm not in such a hurry after all," Rene said jokingly.

"I'm so glad we had a chance to see Charlene and Tim while we were there. They're doing really well. It was amazing to see how their daughter, Christine, is all grown-up. Charlene said she met a family at their church who owns a successful import/export business. She loves working for them."

Rene said wistfully, "I wish I could have been there. I would have loved to see everyone. Was Regan able to make it?"

"Sadly, no. She could have that baby any day now. There was simply no way for her to travel so close to her due date."

"Oh, Sondra. Can you believe your little girl is having a *baby*? It's hard to imagine. You be sure to call me as soon as that little one arrives."

"Are you kidding? Of course, I will. How are Patrick and Mariah Jane?"

Rene laughed. "They're both doing really great. Mariah Jane auditioned at the community theater down here. They're performing *Les Misérables*, and she got the part of Fantine. She's been working so hard memorizing her parts."

Sondra marveled at the talent of her dearest friend's daughter. She had a natural gift for acting, and it was exciting to see how God was allowing her to develop her passion for it.

Rene continued. "Patrick is almost done earning his degree. I don't know where God might call us. We're praying we get to stay here, but it's pretty amazing when we think about how God has worked out the details in our lives. We never imagined we would leave the Midwest, now we can't imagine leaving Texas." Rene laughed. "Can you picture me as a pastor's wife? I don't quite fit the stereotype, you know."

Sondra chuckled. "You'll be perfect for wherever God plants you and Patrick. They'll be blessed to have you both."

The two women chatted some more before hanging up, promising to stay in touch.

Sondra felt a little restless. She texted her sister, Sophia, but got no response.

Maybe you have jet lag.

She went to lie down for a short nap but couldn't fall asleep.

Lord, is there something I am to be doing? Should I be praying for someone? Why do I feel so agitated? Nothing came to her mind, and she stifled the impulse to sigh. She grabbed her Bible and spent a couple of hours studying and in prayer.

Gavin's call, though not completely unexpected, still gave her a jolt. "She's ready! She's having the baby! We're heading over right now!" the frantic new father-to-be was beside himself.

"Oh my goodness. We'll be right there, Gavin. Don't worry. Tell her we love her and are on our way."

Sondra called John at work. "John. It's time, honey! We've got to go now."

Flustered, her husband agreed to meet her there. "Drive carefully, Sondra."

She brushed back the tears of excitement, grabbed her cell phone and the gift they had ready for the baby, and ran out the door. As she drove, she called Mylah, CiCi, and Tommy, alerting them that their sister was about to give birth. As she left messages on their voice mails, she wondered where Mylah was. Arriving at the hospital, she was surprised to see her youngest there already. Kyle Pearson was with her.

"Gavin texted me. I was studying with Trixie at her house, so Kyle drove me over."

"Oh, wonderful. Thank you, Kyle." Sondra hugged him and gave Mylah a kiss.

"It was my pleasure. And congratulations, Mrs. Martin."

Seeing the way Kyle looked at Mylah reminded Sondra of a recent conversation she'd had with his mother.

"I don't want to give away any confidences, but Kyle has mentioned your daughter to Denny and me several times, asking if we would approve of him seeing her. Of course, we told him we would be delighted."

Sondra had squealed with happiness, "Oh, Loni! Of course, John and I would be so pleased if they found that they have a mutual attraction for each other."

Right now, though, her mind was on her eldest as they went in search of the neonatal unit.

Finding Gavin's mother pacing the hallway, they embraced, asking who else had arrived. The woman was somewhat flustered; this was their first grandchild as well. "I've seen Gavin but only for a moment when he came out to tell me how things were progressing. We could have a long night in front of us."

Gavin ran up to them. "Oh, Sondra, thank God, you're here. Regan really wants to see you."

"Of course." She turned to Mylah and Kyle and said in a voice that sounded more confident than she felt, "Honey, Dad is on his way. Please let him know where I am."

Her youngest nodded, and Kyle moved closer to Mylah. "I'll stay here with her, Mrs. Martin." Reassured by the young man's calm presence, she nodded her thanks, allowing herself to be led away by Gavin.

O God, please help me. Give me strength. I want to be a help to my daughter.

When she saw Regan propped up in the bed, she shoved back an urge to cry as she saw her lying there, vulnerable. Unable to do anything to relieve her discomfort, she felt helpless.

"My darling girl! We are here and praying. You're going to do just fine." She firmly nodded, rubbing her dear girl's sweaty brow as she fought off a wave of pain and panic.

Regan swallowed, letting the wave pass. "Mom, I'm so glad you're here. I know it will be okay, but I'm just scared."

Gavin took her hand and leaned in to kiss her forehead. "I'm here too, honey. Let me help you. Would you like some ice to suck on?" Concern was on his face as he watched her suffering.

Regan nodded wearily. "Yes, that would help."

He hurried out the door.

Regan reached out for her mom's hand, pulling her close. "Mom, I don't know what to do. I'm scared. How did you do this? Gavin is making me more nervous, and—oh!" She broke off as a fresh wave of pain pummeled her body.

Sondra looked at the machine that measured the length and strength of the contractions. They seemed closer than everyone realized. She continued to hold Regan's hand, speaking encouragingly to her daughter till that wave passed, becoming manageable again. "Have you timed your contractions?" she asked.

Regan breathed out, exhausted. "Gavin said they were six minutes or so, but they feel a whole lot closer than that." She grimaced as she felt the beginnings of another wave coming. Sondra read the fear on her face, and her own determination set in.

All right, Sondra. This is it. Your daughter needs you.

She held her hand and spoke firmly, coaching her, "Regan, you can do this. You're doing great, sweetheart. Don't fight it. Keep breathing. Relax and let it come. Work *with* the contractions. Remember, every second of this is working your baby closer to being born. Focus on your breathing." Her daughter nodded, feeling the ebb and flow of the pains as they retreated again.

Gavin came in, followed closely by a nurse, who was coming to check on the patient.

Sondra informed her, "Her contractions are coming close together."

The nurse looked at the machine that recorded all movement and jumped to life. "Dr. Benson, come quickly!"

Sondra melted into the background as Gavin took her spot, holding his young wife's hand. Regan caught a glimpse of her mom moving toward the door and, through gritted teeth, called out, "Mom, please stay."

Sondra turned, marveling at the absolute joy of being present at such a sacred moment as this.

Oh, dear God. How can it be that our precious girl is about to give birth to her own child? Thank You for letting me be here to watch such a glorious event.

She didn't stop praying as she watched the team of professionals do their tasks to help her daughter. Time seemed to stop as the entire focus in the room turned to the young woman who was intently concentrating.

The doctor and two nurses surrounded the bed, allowing Gavin to stay by her side, helping her in her endeavor. Sondra marveled anew, wishing she could share this moment with John but knowing that it truly belonged to Regan and Gavin. She thought back to the moment she herself had given birth to Regan and all the excitement that had surrounded the event. She couldn't help the tears that welled up in her eyes as she prayed again, thanking God for the miracle of life and the joy of this moment.

As Regan cried out in great pain, the doctor called out encouragement, "That's it, Regan, one more push. You can do it—you're almost there. One more push. Keep breathing. That's it—I can see the head. One more good push—come on—make it a good one—that's it!"

With a final agonized cry, Regan pushed, and Sondra watched in amazed astonishment as her precious granddaughter was ushered into the world.

* * *

Gavin proudly stood by his wife as the entire family entered the room to meet their new daughter. Regan was weary, but happy as she watched their family holding her newborn baby. John and Sondra laughed when it was their turn, cooing in her tiny little ear, "Oh, Carissa Nicole, you are beloved by God and by us. How glad we are that you have finally arrived."

Little Carissa was finally passed back to her waiting mother, who held her close and couldn't stop staring at her, smiling. Everyone took pictures on their cell phones, sending them to Tommy and Marguerite and CiCi, who couldn't be present to celebrate the event.

The room was abuzz with activity and laughter when one of the nurses interrupted the party. "I'm sorry, folks, but mother and baby need to get some rest after all their efforts."

Sondra and John kissed their daughter and son-in-law and new granddaughter, promising to come see them once they were settled back home in a couple of days. In the hallway, they said their good-byes to Gavin's parents, congratulating them on the momentous occasion as well.

Mylah pulled her aside. "Mom, Kyle asked if I could go to dinner with him. I'd really like to," she shared excitedly.

Sondra smiled at her, giving her a quick hug. "Of course, darling. Have a good time."

On the way home, she called her parents. "Oh, Mom, it was an absolute miracle. I never imagined I would have the honor of getting the chance to watch our first grandbaby enter the world."

Julia celebrated with her over their joy. "What a beautiful name. I can't wait to meet her."

They chatted a few more minutes, excited over the blessed event, finally hanging up when she pulled into her driveway. "Well, I'm home now, Mom. I love you, and I'll talk with you again soon."

She put a quick call in to Rene, leaving a message on her voice mail about the arrival of Carissa Nicole. "Call me when you get a chance. It was amazing! Can't wait to share. Love you!"

She went inside, straightened a few things, and waited for John to arrive. When he walked in, he was restless too.

"Should we call Loni and Denny and see if they want to go out to dinner?" he asked.

She nodded, remembering the way Kyle had been so protective of Mylah at the hospital. "Yes, that's a great idea. I'd love to talk with them about the kids and see if they know anything further."

The two couples met at a local eatery and spent a wonderful evening contemplating the possibility of their children making them in-laws as well as friends.

* * *

A few weeks later, after helping in one of the childcare rooms at church, Sondra saw Victoria Wilson. They seldom interacted, a fact

Sondra was grateful for. Clearly still an avid exerciser, Victoria looked marvelous, but unhappy as she greeted her.

"Hello, Sondra. I'm glad I bumped into you. There's something I need to ask you."

Sondra tried to be gracious. "Certainly, what can I help you with?"

"It's come to my attention that your daughter Mylah is dating Kyle Pearson."

Sondra looked confused. "I don't see how that involves you, but yes, they are seeing each other."

The other woman lowered her voice to a hush. "Well, really, Sondra, I would think you would understand without me having to spell it out for you. He's black."

A slow burn started in Sondra's neck.

"Victoria, I can't begin to imagine how you think it is any of your business—"

Victoria interjected, "Oh, don't get me wrong. I'm not racist. I just don't think that the races should mix."

Sondra sighed and prayed for patience before answering. "I need to tell you that not only do I think you are meddling in something that doesn't concern you, but I also think you are dead wrong. Frankly, I don't believe there are different races."

Confusion came over Victoria's face. "What do you mean? Of course, there are."

Sondra shook her head lightly. "God only created one race—the human race, made in His own image. Any divisions between people come from world geography and ensuing cultural differences. There are varying ethnicities and nationalities, but only one race," she finished firmly. "Why do I think this is important? Because saying there are many races opens the door to saying that one is superior to another. And mostly, because I haven't seen any evidence that supports it."

Victoria scoffed. "Right. The entire world is wrong, and only you, Sondra Martin, knows better."

Sondra chuckled, but not with amusement. "Listen, Victoria, the reality is that every human being ultimately comes from Adam.

Any divisions are simply differences that Satan uses to try to divide us further. So to my way of thinking, there is only one race. We are all viewed equally in the eyes of God."

The other woman was unfazed. "Well, that may be, but I still wouldn't want my daughter to be seen with one of *them*."

Sondra began to turn away but then stopped. "You know, Victoria, for years now, I have tried to give you the benefit of the doubt. I have prayed for you that God would grab your heart, and you would grow in your understanding of His Word. But all I've seen you do is stick your nose where it doesn't belong and try to drive wedges between people. You have spent years working to make sure your outside looks good while doing nothing to let God change you on the inside. You are the worst kind of danger to a church, and I don't want you to come near me or my family anymore."

The shocked look on Victoria's face was little comfort as Sondra turned and walked away.

* * *

"So you finally built a backbone, hmm?" Susan chuckled. "Good. That woman needed to be put in her place."

Sondra shook her head. "I don't know what came over me. I have never done anything like that in all my life. But when she started attacking Mylah and Kyle's right to see each other, I got angry."

"Well, you realize that you're considered almost a hero at church now, right?"

"Oh, stop it, Susan."

"No, I'm serious. Linda, Dawn, Kelly—they are all glad you dug in your heels." She turned her phone toward Sondra. "Look. I texted Charlene, and she sent you three thumbs-up."

"You told Charlene?" Sondra shook her head.

"You should be delighted—she never scores anyone that high."

"How does everybody know about my conversation with Victoria anyway?"

"Because she's gone around telling half the church herself." Susan grinned mischievously. "And I've told the other half."

"Oh, Susan. You shouldn't joke around like this. You don't know how bad I'm feeling about the whole thing."

"Bad? Listen, Sondra, Victoria Wilson has caused more divisions than I think you realize. Plenty of people have tried to talk with her. She was even under church discipline for a while though you didn't hear that from me. Maybe this will be the final push that shoves her out the door."

"Oh, Susan, I hope not. Really, I mean, I know she has hurt a lot of people and is rude and divisive. But where else will she ever hear about Christ's love and forgiveness?" She protested, "I never meant for her to leave our church. Just to leave me and my family alone."

Susan took a deep breath. "You don't have anything to feel bad about. She's had years of hearing the truth. Christians have the right to question anyone who calls him- or herself a brother or sister in Christ, like she did. In fact, it's more than a right. It's a responsibility. Otherwise, we'd be overrun by wolves in sheep's clothing."

"Maybe you're right. I just feel badly for her kids. They're the ones who will suffer if she leaves and doesn't find a good church to grow in."

Susan nodded. "That is the hard part, I agree. Sin always hurts. In the end, sin always ends up hurting someone. And not always the person who deserves it the most."

Sondra nodded soberly. "Exactly what I was thinking."

* * *

"John, do you know where I put that blue bag full of stuff for Carissa?" Increasingly lately, she was misplacing things.

John came in, pointing to the front hall closet. "Did you check in there?"

"Yes, certainly." She looked again, seeing the stuffed bag. "Good grief. I would have sworn that it wasn't there a minute ago."

She shook her head, rifling through the items as her husband watched her with a look of concern. Sondra had been collecting some clothing the past several weeks for Carissa.

Regan had reported how rapidly she was growing: nearing ten months old, she had grown out of most of the clothes Regan had for her. Sondra loved looking for bargains and shopping for her granddaughter.

"You're sure you're okay going over alone? I could go in to work late if you want."

"No, don't be silly, honey. I'm fine. I will stop by my parents' for a while and then spend the rest of the day with Regan and Carissa." She smiled. "I'm good."

He gave her a hug. "Okay, then. I should be home by dinner-time. I can bring home Chinese food if you want?"

"That sounds wonderful, dear. Thank you." He left for work, and the silence of the house closed around her.

She grabbed her cell phone, keys, and bag and headed out the door. As she drove, her cell phone rang. Her sister's excited voice filled the space of Sondra's car through Bluetooth. "Guess what? Sadie and Frank got engaged last night. They want a fall wedding, so we have some time to plan."

"Oh, Sophia, that's wonderful news. I won't mention it to Mom and Dad. I'll let you tell them when you're visiting tomorrow."

"Thanks." Her sister was elated.

"And how is James doing?"

"Pretty much the same. He's not willing to talk about anything spiritual. He hangs out with a crowd who seem to only want to go out drinking." Her sister sighed. "The truth is, he's really struggling."

"I'm so sorry, Sophia."

"Adam is planning a fishing trip for just the two of them. I'm praying that God does a work in his heart as they spend a few days alone together."

"I will keep praying for him. Trust me, I know it's so hard. But remember, as long as there's breath, there's hope," Sondra quoted one of their parents' favorite sayings.

She arrived at her parents' house and pulled into the driveway. "I just got to Mom and Dad's. I'll be sure to let them know you'll be stopping by tomorrow."

"Okay, sounds good. Tell them I'll be there sometime in the afternoon."

"Will do. I love you. Bye."

"Love you too. Bye."

She turned off the car, ran to the front door, rang the bell, and stepped inside. "Hello? Dad? Mom? I'm here."

Her dad called out, "Hey, honey, come on in." He was seated in his favorite chair of the family room. "Hi, Dad. How are you?" He stood, and they hugged.

Julia entered the room, moving slowly. "Hi, sweetheart. Do you have time for a visit, or do you have to run off right away?"

"Hi, Mom." The two embraced. "No, I can stay for a bit. Are you okay?" Sondra was worried. "You're walking like you're in pain."

Her mom smiled. "Oh, I'm fine, dear. Just have a bit of arthritis. It comes and goes."

Sondra nodded slowly. She saw the signs of aging written on them—in their strength, their movements, and even in their voices. She knew they both dealt with more pain than they would admit to. Sondra's heart grieved the unstoppable process, knowing things were only going to get worse.

Seeing her concerned face, her dad joked, "I asked your mother what her new perfume was, BENGAY?"

Julia laughed. "I'm glad he admits that he said it. He followed that up with the encouraging words, 'Good golly, woman, hugging you is like snuggling up to a medicine cabinet.'" Her parents chuckled, looking at each other with great affection, and Sondra relaxed.

They're still my same old parents, teasing each other just like always . . . and besides, they're a lot healthier than most people their age.

The three of them sat down, enjoying the sunshine pouring in the windows while they sipped tea. Sondra showed them the most recent pictures of Carissa on her phone and shared news from various family and friends they knew.

"You're so busy, honey. Are you getting all the sleep you need?" Her mother frequently expressed worry over Sondra's schedule.

Sondra smiled. "Yes, Mom, I'm fine. Really. I'm doing just great." She appreciated her mom's concern, but sometimes it could be a bit annoying. "What are you guys up to today?" she asked to change the subject.

Julia sat up brightly. "Well, we have someone coming in a little while for counseling. Then Dad and I are going to run some errands and go to an early dinner with our old friends, the Cassidys. You remember them? They have a son around your age."

Sondra nodded. "Oh sure, I remember them. How are they doing?" She hadn't thought of the old family friends in many years. Her mother updated her on them, sharing bits and pieces of news of other various friends and acquaintances they'd known through their lives.

Julia asked, "Honey, do you remember Mrs. Harrison from church?"

Sondra responded darkly, "I sure do."

Julia chuckled. "Why do you say it like that?"

Sondra shook her head. "Oh, nothing. It's just that growing up, I remember how mean she could be. She was bossy and rude, and I never liked her."

Her mom looked pained. "Oh, sweetheart. I know she wasn't always easy to get along with. I guess we never told you kids, maybe we should have. It might have helped you to understand if you had known."

"Known what?"

Julia cast a questioning look at Sondra's dad, who explained, "Mrs. Harrison struggled with an alcoholic husband for years. She really suffered. And because of her husband's refusal to be the leader of their home, their sons were out of control."

Sondra remembered that about the Harrison boys. She said slowly, "She was the teacher for my Sunday school class from fifth through seventh grade. I always thought it was hypocritical how she let her own boys run wild while scolding the rest of us for the littlest things."

Sondra's mom replied, "Her life wasn't easy, so she probably tried to exert control in the few areas she could."

Sondra snorted. "Yeah, well, she sure was a piece of work. She was cold and unkind, and I couldn't wait to get out of her class."

Julia took a deep breath. "Well, if you think of it, please be praying for her. She doesn't have many personal friends. I think others saw the same things you did, and not knowing how tragic her life was, they kept their distance. For some reason, she has opened up a little bit to me this past year. Maybe because we have served at the same church together for so long."

Her mother shifted positions and sipped her tea before continuing, "Last week, she shared that she's just been diagnosed with bone cancer. She's bearing this all by herself. Her husband died quite a few years ago from liver disease, and her boys are a grief to her. One is in prison, and the other has been in and out of trouble with the law his whole life."

Sondra drew her breath in. She had never looked at Mrs. Harrison with the feeling she now felt: sympathy.

You never can tell about people, can you?

Her dad echoed her thoughts, "It's funny how your perspective can change when you realize the truth about people, isn't it? I understand how you kids wouldn't have much compassion for Mrs. Harrison based on how she treated you and others. But when you get just a glimpse of the heartache in her life, it becomes a little easier to show her grace and love."

Sondra nodded, feeling a little guilty for judging the woman who had masked her pain behind a wall of sorrow for so many years.

Julia poured more tea, and they caught up on the news of other friends and family. It was reassuring to see how involved her parents were, and Sondra expressed that to them, exclaiming, "I can't believe how many people you've stayed in touch with."

Julia shrugged. "Well, we've spent our whole lives in this community, building relationships. I guess that it does add up to quite a bunch of people when you spend almost seventy-five years in one place."

Sondra nodded. "Yes, I guess it does."

She glanced at her cell phone, noting the time, and stood. "Well, this has been so nice, but I'd better get going."

Her parents rose too. Julia handed a small bag of some toys and clothing to Sondra to give to Regan. "I hope these fit Carissa."

Sondra smiled. "Thanks, Mom."

"Oh, hang on a second, honey." Her dad walked from the room and came back, holding a small wooden rocking horse. "Can you give this to her also? Tell her it's from her great-grandpa James."

"Oh, Dad. It's beautiful."

She admired the wooden toy, made by her dad's own hands.

"Carissa will just love this. Thank you." Tears shimmered in her eyes as she realized the rarity of the gift she had in her parents.

"I'm glad you like it." Her dad looked pleased. "I hope Carissa does too."

She hugged him. "I know she will," she assured him.

She gathered the items, gave them each another quick hug and kiss, and told them she would stop by again in a few weeks. "I love you both. Thanks again. Be sure to say hi to the Cassidys for me, and have fun at your dinner tonight. I'll call you in a few days. Bye."

They waved to her as she backed out of their driveway, and she smiled as she recalled her mother peering at her through the same window the night she had met John so many years earlier.

"Who could have thought all those years ago that John and I would be married with four beautiful children—and now a lovely granddaughter?" she marveled aloud. "Thank you, Lord, for Your many blessings," she prayed as she sped on her way to Regan's.

* * *

Regan and Carissa both loved the gifts, especially the wooden horse. "How wonderful," Regan exclaimed. "This is so special. I'll have to call Grandpa and Grandma and tell them both thank you."

Sondra admired her daughter's ability to care for her baby. "Oh, honey. You're such a natural with her." Her heart nearly burst with pride and joy.

Carissa was a sweet baby, curious and smiley. More than once Sondra thought back to the years when her own kids had been so little. The day rushed by as they visited, eating lunch, talking, laughing, and enjoying their time together. She passed along news from other parts of the family, and Regan shared tidbits of things from mutual friends.

"Did you know that Kayla and Matthew are expecting?"

Sondra drew back in happy surprise. "No, I hadn't heard that! Oh, that's marvelous. I'm so happy for them." She thought a moment then asked, "I wonder if her mother knows?"

Regan shook her head. "I don't think so. She doesn't have much contact with her. I think the last she heard, her mom is living with another boyfriend. It's her fourth or fifth." She shook her head sadly. "I don't think Kayla really knows where she is."

Sondra thought back to her long-ago friend Carolyn Carpenter and what a wreck her life had become by her own tragic choices. "That's so sad."

Regan finished nursing Carissa and handed the baby over to her mom. "Would you mind watching her for me, Mom? I'm going to just go stir the soup I made for dinner, and then I'll put her down for her nap. I'll be right back."

Sondra replied, "Are you kidding? I don't mind a bit." She held her grandbaby, making faces at her and repeating what she had told her mother, "Grandma doesn't mind a bit, does she? Of course, I don't. I love holding you, you dear, sweet thing."

Carissa smiled back at her, gurgling and chortling happily.

Regan came back in the room, looking at a text on her phone. "Mom, it looks like Dad's been trying to reach you. He asked if you have your phone near you?"

Sondra shook her head, startled. "Oh dear. I left it in my purse, honey. Would you mind grabbing it for me?"

She set Carissa on her floor mat and stood up, stretching.

Regan retrieved her mom's phone, then kept reading the texts on her phone. Her face went ashen as she read earlier entries John had sent her.

Her voice turned panicky. "Mom. You need to go. Something has happened to Grandma and Grandpa."

Grabbing her phone, Sondra saw the long list of notifications on the screen—texts, phone calls, and ping alerts from John, Sophia, Stephen, and Grace. She frantically scanned her thumbprint and saw the cascade of urgent texts. All had the same horrific message: her mom and dad had been in a terrible car crash. "Come quickly!"

Sondra grabbed her bag. "Regan, call Dad. Let him know I'm on my way. And pray!" She dashed out the door and to her car, crying out in prayer.

"O God, help Mom and Dad. Oh please, let everyone be all right!"

The entire drive to the hospital had her desperately praying. When she arrived, she raced inside, begging someone to tell her where to find her parents. When she shared the names Julia and James Spencer with the nurse at the counter, the other woman's eyes looked stricken.

Just then, John came and reached for her, pulling her along to a room where her mother was lying, urging her to hurry. "Sondra. Everyone is here. We couldn't reach you. I'm so sorry, honey."

"Oh, Mom! Oh God, please. No!"

Tears streamed down her face as she looked down at her mother's body all bruised and bloody. Sophia and Grace were sobbing as was Sondra, who had arrived moments too late. The monitor flatlined as her mother's life ebbed away, leaving an awful stillness in its wake. She held her mom's hand, feeling it begin to turn cold.

She wailed frantically, "No! Oh, Mom! How can this be happening? Oh please, someone do something! Please, God, oh please!"

John stood helplessly by, wanting to comfort her but knowing there was no immediate comfort for this. Death was an ugly, awful thing, and painful grief followed closely in its shadow.

Sondra sobbed, holding on to John, then pulled away suddenly. "Where's Dad?"

John looked at her, shaking his head, tears spilling from his eyes. "I'm so sorry, honey. There was nothing anyone could do. Oh, Sondra, I'm so sorry."

Could her broken heart hold any more pain? "No! Don't tell me that! I was just with him. I just saw him—he gave me a wooden horse for Carissa. He can't be gone! Oh, Daddy! Oh God, please, no!" She wept inconsolably in her husband's arms. The siblings and their spouses embraced one another, seeking comfort from the devastating loss.

* * *

News of the tragedy that ultimately left three people dead spread quickly. Dad and the driver of the other car had been killed almost instantly. It gave Sondra the smallest degree of comfort, knowing he hadn't probably suffered: the grief she carried was heavier than she felt she could bear.

She spent a lot of time in silence and prayer, thinking how she had held her mom's hand as she passed away—the same hand that had cared for her when she was sick, the same hand that had hugged her and held her through some of her life's deepest sorrows and joys and a thousand other acts of love and kindness. The continual ache was inescapable except in the short snatches of sleep she found.

How will I make it in a world without my mom and dad?

In the days following their deaths, she, Stephan, and Sophia woodenly went through the motions of preparing for their parents' burials. They all felt the same numbness.

Tommy and Marguerite flew home as did Cecilia. For a few short days, Sondra was comforted by the presence of her whole family together. She clung even closer to reading her Bible as the words there offered her hope in these darkest of hours. She realized the sacred gift God had allowed her in seeing them on their final day of life when they were healthy, happy, and whole.

O Lord, thank You for giving me that last bit of time with them. I will cherish the memory of it always.

* * *

The day of the double funeral arrived. As eldest, Stephan had handled most of the details. As they gathered before other mourners would arrive, he dully asked, "Is there anything the rest of you would like to say either at the service or graveside?"

Sondra shook her head. "I don't think I can." Sophia agreed.

John said, "I'll share some thoughts on behalf of the family."

Stephen thanked him somberly, and the two embraced.

Much of the morning passed in a blur. The room was filled to capacity as many people poured through the doors, all wanting to share in the grief of the passing of James and Julia Spencer. The funeral director had to open up annex rooms to help contain the endless stream of mourners, who came to pay their respects.

As the family stood in line, greeting the flow of people, Sondra stayed close to John, needing the support and feel of him nearby. She caught a glimpse of surprise on her husband's face as a man and woman she didn't recognize approached them.

John stared in amazement, then in a stunned voice, introduced him to Sondra. "Honey, this is my old boss, Hal."

Sondra's mouth gaped open.

Hal stood with tears in his eyes. "I'm sure seeing me here is a great shock to you. Please allow me to explain. You see, my wife, Jackie, was about ready to leave me. We had some very bad issues in our marriage, pretty much all my fault, and I guess she'd had about enough of me." He brushed at his eyes, explaining, "My old man was mean, and I always said I wouldn't be like him." With a regretful shake of his head, he went on. "Not only was I like him, I was worse than him. Even though I had never wanted to be like that, I found myself lashing out at everyone around me, even Jackie, who didn't deserve it." Hal paused. "It nearly cost me everything."

He addressed John. "Then I got transferred to the branch where I met you." His face held remorse. "After I was fired by Tom, I hopped in and out of a couple more jobs over the next couple of years and continued to struggle with my anger. When I was let go from another company, Jackie gave me an ultimatum: either I go to counseling with her to a couple whose names she had gotten from a friend, or she was leaving me. She'd never stood up to me like that before. Let me tell you, it shook me to my core, so I agreed to go."

Jackie gave a little encouraging nod to her husband.

He continued. "I didn't make the connection that the couple we met with, James and Julia Spencer, were John here's in-laws until

I heard about their deaths and saw the obituary that detailed the names of their children and their spouses."

Hal looked into Sondra's eyes and gulped. "Your parents helped me to see all my sin and anger and how it was destroying my life and my family. They spent months pouring God's love into us, leading us both to Christ, and helping us get our marriage on a new track." Grief filled Hal's eyes. "I'm so sorry for their deaths and your loss."

Jackie stepped forward, sharing tearfully, "We wanted to come today to let you know what a privilege it was to know them and how God used them to bring us to Himself."

The torrent of emotion Sondra felt at that moment, realizing that God had such incredible mercy on unworthy sinners, including herself, shamed her for her thoughts of animosity all those years ago for Hal.

O God, forgive me!

She cried on the shoulder of the man she had once held such loathing for, the one John had told her she should put down the rocks to stone and pray for instead. Through their tears the four of them hugged, marveling at a God who could soften hearts and draw broken people to Himself and, through the common bond of Jesus, create a spring of love where there once was hate.

The rooms were filled with people who had stories to share of how God had used the beloved older couple to speak truth and love into their lives. The legacy they had left behind them was like a healing balm applied to an open wound in the hearts of all those who were grieving.

A few minutes before they were going to head over to the cemetery, Sondra caught a glimpse of Mrs. Harrison hobbling in through the double doors, clutching a cane.

She's not nearly as formidable as I remember her being.

Rather, she looked old and frail and broken.

Sondra remembered back to the last conversation she had had with her parents as they shared her pitiable story, and compassion welled up in Sondra's heart. She made her way toward the old woman.

"Mrs. Harrison? It's Sondra. Sondra Spencer. Well, Sondra Spencer Martin."

Mrs. Harrison blinked in surprise. "Oh my goodness, Sondra. Well, you've sure grown up. I don't know what I expected. Of course, you have. I still picture all of you kids as the same age when I last knew you. It has to be almost forty years since I saw you last."

Sondra gave a small smile. "I just wanted to tell you how much my mom enjoyed her time with you. She mentioned the health issue you've been facing and asked me to be praying for you. I wanted you to know that I have been and will keep on praying."

Tears formed in the old woman's eyes. "Your parents were some of the only friends I've ever really had." She briskly brushed the tears away with the back of her hand. "I'm going to miss them," she finished simply.

Sondra nodded, tearing up again. She gave the old woman a small hug. "Me too."

* * *

At the graveside, John spoke stirringly for the family. "Thank you all for coming to be here with us at our time of sorrow. Though we are heartbroken at our temporary loss of James and Julia, we rejoice that God used their lives in such a miraculous way. How grateful we are to have the calm assurance of their place in heaven because they put their trust in Jesus Christ."

Many heads nodded.

Sondra let the comfort of those words wash through her mind.

The calm assurance of their place in heaven. Oh, thank You, Lord, that we can know that for certain. There is such consolation in that.

She started to feel the first glimmer of cloud lifting from her heart over the tragic loss.

Surrounded by her children and husband, sister and brother, family and friends as they watched the caskets being lowered into the ground, Sondra wept.

I don't want to ever again take anyone for granted in my life, Lord. Please use this to remind me to fully squeeze out every drop of joy with those I love.

* * *

In the weeks afterward, Sondra, Stephan, and Sophia read through countless letters and cards, written by people their parents had walked through life with. Although it helped greatly in their comfort, the realization that she couldn't just call her mom up for an old favorite recipe or hear her parents' voices reminding her of God's promises hit Sondra hard.

Why did I get annoyed when Mom asked if I was eating well? She was simply trying to love me.

Sondra deeply mourned the loss even while rejoicing in the certainty that she knew where they were. She spent a lot of time in her parents' home, just walking around, sitting in their favorite chairs, touching the things they had handled, and drawing comfort from the lingering smells and memories.

John was a tower of strength for her during those difficult days. Somehow in her mind, she just had not anticipated what it would be like to be in a world without her parents. She lived with remorse that she hadn't made more of the opportunities when they'd had them.

I refuse to make the same mistake with any of my other loved ones.

The tragedy had driven the family to make more effort to stay in touch and had given her an even deeper longing for Christ's return when they would all be together again in glory.

* * *

"I'll be back in time for dinner," she told John. "I'm taking Mrs. Harrison to her doctor's appointment."

Eight months had passed since her parents' deaths, and though she was healing, the wound was still tender.

John came over and hugged her. "Your mom and dad would be so proud to see how you've stepped up to help Mrs. Harrison, honey."

Sondra gulped. It hadn't come easy, and at first she had resisted. It was one thing to forgive the woman for unkind treatment and her brash, controlling manner from years earlier. It was an entirely different thing to inconvenience herself for that same woman. Although she was older and less intimidating, she still had a sharp tongue and could be difficult to be around. When she had sensed the Holy Spirit telling her to step in and help her, Sondra had found herself arguing with God until she finally surrendered.

"All right, Lord, I will do it. I don't know why You are calling me to, but clearly, You are, so even though I'd rather not, I will." She sighed, being sure to add, "But feel free to send someone else, and I will gladly step aside."

Sondra grabbed her keys and purse and gave him a kiss. "Thank you, honey. I'll just be a couple of hours."

As she drove over to the old woman's house, Sondra thought about the amazing turns that life took.

I never dreamed that difficult Mrs. Harrison would be back in my life in any way, and yet, here she is. My own parents, who were loving and kind, are both gone, and somehow I'm supposed to see this as all part of Your plan? Sometimes, I just don't get it, Lord.

Arriving at the house, Sondra knocked on the door, hearing slow steps approach. Mrs. Harrison opened the creaking door, grunted, and backed into the house. "C'mon in."

Sondra gingerly crossed the threshold, unsure what she might find. Sometimes the main room of the little house was kept decently; other times it was a total wreck. Sondra resisted the urge to pinch her nose, instead placing a tissue she had dabbed with perfume near her nostrils to mask the acrid odors of the old woman's house.

Mrs. Harrison glanced at her. "I see you've still got that cold."

Sondra shook her head. "I think it's just allergies."

Mrs. Harrison, sharp-eyed, looked at her. "I know the difference between a cold and allergies. You aren't sneezing. I don't want you getting me sick," she complained in a huff.

Oh, if only I had the courage to tell her the truth. I don't have a cold or allergies. I'm trying to keep the stench of her house out of my nose.

Suddenly, she felt convicted by the Holy Spirit.

Short-term that might feel good, but long-term you'd regret it, Sondra.

Trying to change the subject, Sondra asked, "Are you ready to go?"

Mrs. Harrison hobbled to her tattered recliner, pulled on her old shawl, and nodded.

On the drive to the doctor's office, the two were mostly silent.

Is this really helping, Lord? Sondra prayed in her mind questioningly. *It's awkward and out of my comfort zone.*

She felt a calm certainty in her heart like God was assuring her that, indeed, she was doing what He wanted.

Arriving at the doctor's office, Mrs. Harrison turned to her. "You wait out here. I don't want you hovering around in my business."

Sondra nodded, trying to be gracious while she watched the old woman struggle from her seat. "Can I help you out, Mrs. Harrison?"

"I'm perfectly capable, young lady," she snapped.

Sondra didn't know what to do. Finally, the cantankerous old woman successfully got to her feet and, glaring at Sondra, slammed the car door, leaving her in the silence of the car alone.

"O Lord, help me love her the way You want me to, because right now I feel like hitting her over the head with that cane of hers," Sondra prayed aloud then sighed.

Again she marveled at the turn of events, wondering what God was up to.

* * *

Talking with Rene about it the next day, her friend sympathized with her.

"I'm sorry, Sondra. I wish I had some really great thing to encourage you with. I know that if you are following God's lead on this even if it isn't easy, there can only be good in it for you. We may not understand why, but we can trust that God has His plan."

Sondra let out a deep breath. "I do feel badly for her. I mean, her boys' lives are ruined, her husband died of alcoholism, and now she is suffering with cancer." She paused. "I keep wondering why God brought her along my path though. I'm not a counselor or a health-care expert. I really can't offer her anything but a ride." She added hastily, "Well, that and pray for her."

Rene mused for a moment and then asked, "Have I ever told you how we came to name Mariah Jane?"

"I don't think so. I guess I just thought you liked the sound of it," she replied.

Rene chuckled. "Well, yes, we did." Her voice sobered. "But when I was facing the probability that I was going to be raising our baby alone, I begged God to let Patrick live. I mean I wanted him to live, of course, because he is my husband. But I was terrified of being alone with a new baby to care for, and I pled with God not to take him." She continued. "One night, I was reading my Bible and came to the story of Naomi and Ruth. I read where Naomi tells the other women to call her Mara because her life had become bitter. That struck such a chord with me. I completely understood how she must have felt, and I decided that I was going to name my baby girl Mariah after the bitterness I was facing. But when I told Patrick, he said, 'That's fine, Rene. You can do that. But be sure to make her middle name something that declares your trust in God then, so our daughter's name doesn't reflect only despair.'"

Sondra quietly asked, "What does *Jane* mean?"

With a catch in her breath, Rene responded, "My God is gracious." She sniffled. "I began praying all the more that God would spare Patrick's life and that our daughter's very name would signify not only the hardship but also my belief that He would grant us His favor and grace." She paused. "When Patrick's doctors told me that they didn't understand his healing, it was a miracle they couldn't explain, but I knew what had happened. I'm grateful for the treatments, but it was God who saved my husband."

Sondra brushed away the tears that had formed in her eyes. "I knew how Patrick was healed, of course, but I never knew the story about Mariah Jane's name. It's beautiful, Rene."

Rene laughed. "Well, I didn't share it for that alone. I was thinking that sometimes, when we are facing things that are hard, it's easy to forget that God is on the other side of it, and He knows how it will all turn out. He just asks that we trust Him." Rene continued. "I seem to recall hearing you say that yourself a time or two. I think that with old Mrs. Harrison, you just needed a little reminder."

"You're right. I did. Thanks, Rene." She sighed. "I still don't like how her house smells, and if I weren't a Christian, I sure wouldn't be able to put up with her crankiness." She chuckled. "About the only upside is that she refers to me as young lady, which, I admit, sounds nice when you're fifty-two years old." She became serious again. "But you're right. God must want to teach me something through this, and even though I don't know what it is, I need to trust Him."

The friends finished saying their good-byes, and Sondra sat on the edge of her bed, thinking for a long time. She saw her mom's worn old Bible on the lower shelf of her bed table. Thumbing through it, she turned to the book of Ruth. Written at the top of the margin in her mother's lovely scrolling handwriting were the words, "If we don't get something we think we need or something happens that we don't want, it doesn't reflect God's lack of love or care for us, but simply our lack of understanding what His best is for us."

Sondra thought about that then prayed, "Lord, I want to trust You. I don't always understand the things You allow into my life. Lately, things have not been easy, but I know You have a plan. Please help me trust You."

* * *

The next weeks found Sondra driving the old woman more frequently as she had scheduled treatments. As she spent more time in her company, the old woman slowly began to open up to Sondra. In the beginning, she would ramble on about a myriad of topics, but over time, she was confiding her disappointments about life, particularly her husband and sons.

One day as they were driving to the hospital for her treatment, she bitterly expressed, "Once Harold took to drinking, everything went downhill. We almost lost our house. I went to work, so I was never home to raise our boys. And Harold sure didn't lift a finger to help, not with anything."

Sondra didn't know what to say, so she kept silent.

Mrs. Harrison picked up the thread of story. "Before that, times were good. So good." Her voice grew wistful. "Harold was a real looker when we were younger. All the girls thought so, but he only had eyes for me." Mrs. Harrison's eyes misted a bit, remembering. "We had our first son, and he was a good boy. Pretty soon after, we had our second son. Then I got pregnant again, and that time it was a girl."

Sondra didn't remember the Harrisons having a daughter and started to wonder if the old woman's mind was confused.

Mrs. Harrison's voice got really quiet, and Sondra strained to hear. "She got sick. There wasn't anything anyone could do. She was only five months old when she died." She took a breath, looked over at Sondra, and went on. "Harold was never the same after that. That's when he started drinking. Our boys were little and needed their daddy, but he just didn't have it in him."

Glancing at Sondra, she gulped, continuing, "I haven't told anyone this before, and I'm not sure why I'm telling you." She swiped at her tears and looked at Sondra, who kept her eyes on the road in front of her. "I guess I just want someone to know the truth so that when I'm gone . . ." She trailed off.

Sondra wasn't sure what to say. She didn't want to say anything trite, so she remained silent.

They sat quietly for a few minutes. Mrs. Harrison said, "After our baby girl died, I got more involved at the church. My homelife was a wreck. Church was one area I felt I had some control."

Sondra thought back to her parents' words, recalling them saying that exact thing.

The woman shifted in her seat. "I've always known what I thought about God." Her voice cracked as she finished, "I just never really knew what He thought about me."

Suddenly, Sondra felt moved to speak. She pulled into the parking space at the hospital and turned to the woman seated next to her, looking her in the eye. "He loves you, Mrs. Harrison. Pure and simply, He loves you."

Sondra wasn't sure what to do when sobs burst from the cantankerous old woman, whose heart had held its secret pain for so long.

O Lord, please help me. I don't know what to say.

Sondra knew that God was up to something when she put her hand on the shoulder of the hurting woman and heard the next words come out of her mouth. "Mrs. Harrison, would you like to accept Jesus as your Savior?"

She would not have imagined the next thing that happened as old Mrs. Harrison nodded, tears spilling from her eyes, and prayed haltingly along with Sondra for salvation.

Marveling at God's grace, Sondra was overwhelmed.

O God, You did have a plan all along. I can see that now.

As a newfound joy shone on old Mrs. Harrison's face, Sondra was fairly certain she could hear the angels rejoicing.

Ten Years Later

April 2029

Her short hair completely gray at sixty-two, Sondra suffered with arthritis pain and struggled with lapses of forgetfulness. She was unable to recall names as readily as in the past and even occasionally forgot things like what month they were in, but this was something she brought to God.

Thank You, Lord, that even when my body fails and my mind betrays me, You never will.

Sondra drew great comfort from the truth that He knew who belonged to Him and would never let her go.

One ministry she still participated in was the women's prayer circle that had met every week since the terrible discovery of Carolyn Carpenter and Nicholas Bianchi's affair so many years earlier.

Back during that difficult time as knowledge of the affair became public, people realized that they had grown complacent in their corporate approach to God's throne. They instituted a weekly gathering that allowed them to pray for God's protection over their church body, the families, marriages, and kids represented in their own church: the group was still going strong.

It's hard to believe that was over thirty years ago. I wonder where Carolyn is now? God, if You hadn't intervened, that could have been me.

She felt the pain of regret in her heart and immediately stopped herself.

Lord, thank You for Your forgiveness for my sins. I cannot change what I've done in the past, but I can choose to walk rightly in my future. I don't want to waste my life regretting.

Sondra sighed with a grateful heart to God, who had been so faithful through so many seasons of joy even when they were mingled with trials.

The circle of close-knit women was one of the tools God had used to minister to Sondra's broken spirit during the days of CiCi's cutting as well as after her parents' sudden deaths.

Sondra had read in Revelation about the "golden bowls full of incense that are the prayers of the saints."

What a wonderful picture that my prayers are a "lovely aroma" to God because through them, I can show my complete trust in Him.

For quite a while following CiCi's struggle, Sondra had stepped out of all teaching roles. She had slowed down her pace but was still involved in the women's ministry at church, which was now led by Mandy Monroe, Pastor Paul's daughter. Mandy had grown into a capable young woman with administrative gifts, which the role needed since Linda Peters's retirement a few years earlier.

Mandy had asked Sondra if she would consider teaching again. After praying about it, she agreed, wanting to be used by God however He wished.

One week before teaching a group of women, Sondra spotted Kayla Carpenter, now Frederickson, preparing at one of the tables behind the rows of chairs. Kayla had been a table leader the past four years. She did a marvelous job leading the women in her group and meeting with them outside of group to counsel, encourage, and pray for one another. She shared her testimony often and without hesitation, knowing that by God's grace, she was no longer the person she used to be.

O Lord, thank You for Kayla and all You've done in her life.

She and her husband, Matthew, had two daughters, Jane and Charlotte. Her friendship with Regan was healed better than ever, and Sondra found it a joy to play a part in her life as well.

She walked over to greet her with a hug before class, and Kayla handed her an envelope. "This is for you. You can read it later."

Sondra thanked her, curious what it might be, and then went up in front of the class, greeting the women. Many seasons of life were represented in those gathered. Sondra saw faces of friends she had known for decades mingled in with people she didn't yet know, young and old, single and married. Gratefulness welled up in her heart as she looked out over the group.

"Last week, several of you asked for a copy of the song that I shared, titled 'Captivated.' I have copies today for anyone who would like one."

She passed the stack of papers to her good friend Dawn Phillips, who was seated in the first row, and went back to the podium, where she gathered her notes.

After opening in prayer, she directed the women to passages in their Bibles that talked about faith.

Sondra handled her own beloved copy of God's Word with great tenderness. The pages were worn with use through the years, heavily marked and nearly in tatters. She was rarely without the treasured volume as she found almost daily opportunities to share with people around her the precious truths found within its pages.

"Ladies, this is such an important concept for us to grasp. In Genesis 15, we look at the life of Abraham. The Bible tells us he was old in years and that Sarah, his wife, was barren. And yet God told him, 'Look up at the heavens and count the stars—if indeed you can count them . . . So shall your offspring be.' And verse 6 says, 'Abraham believed the Lord, and He credited it to him as righteousness.'

"What we see here is that Abraham's *faith* was willing to look past the impossibility of the circumstances he was in. His faith wasn't rooted in the likelihood of the situation." Sondra paused, emphasizing the fact. "In fact, if he had to look at the odds, they were zero. But he believed that God could do anything, and that was where he put his faith. Not in the situation or the likelihood of God's promise itself, but in the likelihood of *God being able to fulfill His promise*—in the fact that God is God and can do absolutely anything. The question we need to be asking ourselves is, are we living with that kind of faith in our lives today?

"Ephesians 3:20 says, 'Now to him is able to do *immeasurably more than all we could ask or imagine*, according to his power that is at work within us, to him be glory in the church and in Christ Jesus throughout all generations, for ever and ever!'

"I believe in a big God, with a capital *G*. If I am willing to let Him, there isn't anything in my life that He can't handle, direct, change, or work good through. If we are living with that faith in our lives no matter what is thrown at us, we can live as Paul tells us in Romans 5, 'We rejoice in the hope of the glory of God. Not only so, but we also rejoice in our sufferings, because we know that suffering produces perseverance; perseverance, character and character, hope. And hope does not disappoint us.'"

Sondra continued. "I have shared this before with some of you, but it bears repeating. I want my life to be a beacon that God uses to draw others to Himself. What more can I hope for than that?"

She paused a moment, then continued. "I love this quote by Tom Wilson: 'Wisdom doesn't necessarily come with age. Sometimes age just shows up all by itself.'"

The ladies laughed, and Sondra smiled. "We are told in Proverbs that we need to pursue wisdom, it isn't just given to everyone automatically. But for those who can find her, she is worth more than jewels. Living with wisdom is the thing that lets me look at trials and heartaches in my life and trust God with them because I can see that through those very things that, in my flesh, I would try to escape, God is *using* them to shape me to become more like His Son."

Sondra leaned forward. "I have so many favorite verses in God's Word, but some of my life-goal verses are found in Malachi 2:5–6. Malachi was referring to the Old Testament priest Levi and to Jesus Christ, the true high priest, but we can take application from them in wanting to be used by God in the same way. Listen to these words that God said: 'My covenant was with him, a covenant of life and peace, and I gave them to him; this called for reverence and he revered me and stood in awe of My name. True instruction was in his mouth and nothing false was found on his lips. He walked with me in peace and uprightness and turned many from sin.'

"Oh, precious sisters, isn't that glorious?" Sondra's face shone with radiance. "It's only through God's power at work in my life that I can even surrender my wishes, my goals, my dreams, my hopes and put them at Jesus's feet, saying, 'Take my life, Lord, let it be used by You in whatever way You choose. Let true instruction be in my mouth, and help me to walk in peace and uprightness and bring others to the cross through Your power at work in me.'

"Some of us in this room are dealing with difficult challenges, but we all need to be reminded: if we are putting our faith solely and wholly in Christ Jesus, this cannot end badly for us. It doesn't really even matter what we are facing—illness, loss of income, a broken relationship—even death cannot break the grip that Christ has on us if we are His own. Sometimes, we lose our ability to see that this life is just a stepping-stone to the next. God wants the trials we face to help bring into sharper focus our understanding on what His purpose for this life is for: to offer hope to a dying world and show them what trust in Jesus looks like at work in impossible valleys."

She paused. "Any heartache we face should cause us to cling to our Savior all the more. Let's stop wasting our chances to use the pains of this world to point to Christ. No other name is given among men whereby we can be saved. Not medicine, not money, not fame, nor a high IQ. Not organic food, exercise, or longevity. Just Jesus. He alone can rescue us from this temporary trial we call life and bring us into His forever kingdom of light and everlasting life. Let's stop trying to find hope where it cannot be found and, instead, behold the joy that is ours because we can walk this life with an open hand, accepting all God brings our way because we know He loves us."

She smiled out at the women collected there, beseeching them, "Who will join me on this remarkable journey called faith? It is never too late. God has so many wonderful plans in store for those who love Him and are called according to His purposes. If you find any encouragement from this message, praise God. Because I'm just a broken vessel that He has chosen to use for some reason of His own. I'm still learning these truths myself, but we can help one another as we walk this path of growing in trust of our Savior together. Pray with me."

She bowed her gray head, grasping the podium for stability. "Our dear Heavenly Father, I can lay all my burdens down, cast away cares, let go of my sorrows, and dry all my tears—because You sent Hope into the world! I'm so grateful, God, that there is purpose in Your plan and power in Your name. There is no valley experience where You cannot uphold us and no mountain experience that outsoars the amazing gift of Your presence, Your grace, and Your love. Help us, Lord, we pray. We want to be women who love and adore You and follow You wholeheartedly. In the matchless name of Your Son, we pray, amen."

Amid the chatter afterward, led by their table leaders as the ladies answered application questions and shared in a time of prayer at their individual tables, Sondra pulled a sheet from the envelope Kayla had given her. Handwritten at the top, it was addressed to her:

To Sondra, my spiritual mom ～

For so long I have wanted to share this with you. I still marvel that God chose to save me. I didn't deserve His grace or His mercy, but I'm grateful He chose to give them to me anyway. I hope you are encouraged by the words here, written from my heart. I truly believe that because of the way you prayed during those years, God chose to honor your prayers for me. Only because of His grace can this be my story. I love you and am grateful He put you in my life. ～ Kayla

I used to walk . . . along the path of sin
Heartache and pain were my companions . . .
Ashamed yet proud, I dared to shake my fist
In the face of him whose blood was shed for me.
But no more! No more!
By grace God rescued me and took away my shame
Now I'm new, I am new
Washed in His blood, forever cleansed
He has redeemed me, and I'm new!

I used to mock, and run from truth
Abuse His grace, spit in His face and taunt His mercy.
I wandered far—but not too far
For Him to reach with His forgiveness and His love
Now I'm free! I am free!
He conquered sin, He conquered death, He conquered me
Now I'm free, I am free
To live in grace and truth and joy and victory
Yes I'm free!

Now I am His, and I delight in Him!
He is my joy and my salvation
No longer chained, I choose to worship Him
And give glory to my God and to my King:
Jesus Christ! Jesus Christ!
His Name alone has power to save and none beside—
He's my light! He is my life!
I forever will adore and praise His Name ~ Jesus Christ!

Tears spilled from Sondra's eyes as she read and reread the lovely tribute of what Christ had done in Kayla's life. God had poured out tremendous blessing by bringing salvation to her soul and healing to her heart. Sondra rejoiced in the ripple effect Kayla's testimony was having.

Watching his daughter and how miraculous her turnabout had been, Kayla's dad, Keith, had given his life to Christ and was attending a men's Bible study regularly. Kayla's younger brother, Benjamin, was entering the ministry full-time as a pastor.

Out of their family, only Kayla's mother, Sondra's long-ago friend Carolyn, had rejected the truth she'd been given and was wandering lost and alone, still seeking peace and happiness everywhere except where it could only be found: at the foot of the cross.

Sondra and Kayla prayed regularly for her as did Keith and Benjamin, knowing that only God could work miracles. After all, He had in each of their lives.

Sondra's dear friend Susan came up to her. Her hair was white and soft around her face, her merry eyes lined with wrinkles that spoke of her steadfast joy despite some difficult trials life had brought to her doorstep. The two women were very close, and Sondra counted her among her most treasured friends. "Oh, Sondra, I'm glad you're still here. I'm wondering—would you mind if I read your poem 'God Alone' to the group of women I lead on Tuesdays?"

Sondra had shared it at their ladies' small group when they had gone through the book of Isaiah together. She had been inspired to pen the words, and the ladies had found it a blessing. Sondra was delighted to share it. "Absolutely. I will send it to you as soon as I get home. Are you still up for our visit on Thursday?"

"Yep. Loni said she can't make it this week, but I'll pick up Dawn, and we'll be over about nine o'clock."

"Perfect."

The two friends hugged and parted ways.

* * *

On her drive home, Sondra reflected on what she had taught that morning and marveled at what God had done through her surrendered life. In so many areas, she could see His fingerprints on her life, evidence of His intimate watch and care over her.

She was thankful she had finally released one of her biggest dreams to Him: to be able to claim the coveted title of "writer."

She remembered well the wrestling—the torment of wanting something so badly for so long, but always feeling it was just out of reach with no real sense that God would ever let something good come from her pursuit. When she had finally accepted that even if she didn't get to ever use her writing in a public way that blessed the masses, she had found sweet peace. And who knew? Perhaps, someday, long after she was gone, someone might stumble on something that she had written that would bless him or her.

That would delight me from the hallways of heaven if I knew it!

Then God did open a pathway for her to use some of her writings—in small ways right within her church body. She was encouraged knowing that the work of her hands was a blessing to others.

Isn't that just like God? Once I let go of it as an idol, He used it how He wished to all along.

He was more than able to use whatever means He wanted to accomplish whatever He wanted to. *What freedom I finally found upon that realization.*

The final mile home found Sondra singing one of her favorite songs that she had penned after reading Isaiah 46:10–11; her voice warbled a bit, but she belted out the words as she gloried in her Savior:

> "Your purposes will stand—You can do what you
> please—
> Your purposes will stand and Your plans will
> succeed—
> For nothing, no nothing, can get in Your way—
> Creator! Oh God! Our Redeemer! Yahweh!
> You Alone deserve all our praise!—We will wor-
> ship You always!"

At home, tucked in her computer desk, she found her stash of memory sticks. In his free time, John had removed everything from her archaic system of three-inch floppy disks and saved everything to the flash drives with their massive memory storage capabilities.

He had teased her suspicions about the dependability of the flash drives and had held up two sticks. "I know you don't completely trust that one is enough for you. So I made a backup of your original." He had pulled a third flash drive from his pocket and said teasingly, "And a backup of your back up." Sondra had laughed delightedly.

Not only were all her writings on the memory sticks, but he had also included written family history and genealogy, old stories, passed-down lore, and testimonies of God's faithfulness and love.

They gave each of their kids a flash drive with the entire collection as well.

Sondra appreciated her husband's thoughtful gesture and was astonished at all that could fit in one tiny device she was able to hold in the palm of her hand—truly remarkable!

She still dutifully printed off copies of everything; it was a habit she couldn't quit. Her family teased her a lot about this penchant for hard copies.

Last time Regan had been over for a visit, she had helped run a basket of clean clothes to her parents' room. She had seen a couple of stacks of papers piled up on the floor near her mom's bed table. "Mom, do you realize how much paper you've got around here? And I know you've got more jammed in your drawer with all your writings."

Regan had been trying to convince her to burn the papers for a long time. "Just get rid of it. None of us kids are going to take it when you and Dad are gone, you know. They're a fire hazard. Besides, what do you need all that for? Dad put everything onto the flash drives."

Sondra stubbornly insisted on keeping her papers. "I know, Regan. But what if the power went out or my sticks got lost? I feel better having a paper trail of everything."

She knew her children didn't understand, but she was from a different era and felt comforted knowing she had a written copy of all her works. At home, she pulled up the poem requested by her friend:

> Your majesty overwhelms me
> Oh God who named each star!
> Who is Creator and Utmost High?
> Oh God of All—You are!
>
> Your strength and power are staggering:
> I can't truly grasp, but believe—
> Adoration! Glory! Praise! Are all yours!
> Our love You alone should receive!

Your Splendor surrounds us daily—
Stunning beauty in each natural sight
Who can behold and be told yet be bold and
deny You?
Your greatness and Might?

Alone You are and alone You stand
With no other counsel or guide
Yet compassion and love you extend to me?
The proof's on Your Son's hands and side!

Magnificent God! Our awesome Lord!
Heavenly Father—Most high and true!
Who alone deserves our worship?
Oh God of all—You do!

With the click of a button, the missive was sent, already in Susan's inbox—astonishing!

Sondra thought back to the clunky old typewriter that had belonged to her mother and her father before her. When Sondra had inherited it, she put it in her bedroom, near her bureau. It was comforting to have the machine that her mom had clinked out her writing on nearby.

Who could have imagined back then how simple and swift it would be to share thoughts and words these many years later?

Her own precious mother would have been delighted with such ease those many years ago when she was writing. Sondra's thoughts turned to the hours she spent as a young girl listening to her mom tapping out her writing on the old typewriter in their basement. She sighed. "So long ago . . . such precious memories. Thank you, God, for giving me those sweet years from Your good hand."

Tears sprang to her eyes. Sondra missed her mom and dad, and a pang crossed her heart. God had allowed healing to come to her heart over time. And she knew that her parents, even if given the chance, wouldn't leave the delights of heaven to return.

She wondered at the rejoicing that must be going on in heaven—her parents, her grandparents, old Mrs. Harrison—and all the other loved ones who had passed on already, all healed and dancing with Jesus. The thought took her breath away. "Thank You, Lord, for Your lavish love and grace."

* * *

The next day while on the phone with Rene, Sondra shared how John's parents were doing. "I can't believe how much Margaret's memory has failed. Timothy especially appreciates our visits since he is so homebound and lonely with a wife who has forgotten everything of the life they spent together. I'm just grateful they're in a good nursing home together. At least there are people to help care for her as her health has declined."

"I know. It's so hard. My mom is feeling the frailty of her age as well." Rene's dad had passed away several years earlier, and her mother had moved to Texas to be closer to her two daughters and their families. Rene continued. "There are times I feel so overwhelmed with the fact that I'm getting old, I want to resist it with every fiber of my being. But then I think of my grandmother, who would say to my sister and me, 'Don't fight aging, girls—it's unavoidable. Use your age to have fun: old people and young children can get away with all kinds of crazy things the rest of the world can't.'" Rene sighed. "That old gal sure knew how to have a good time."

Sondra chuckled. "I like that. That's how I want to be when I get old."

Rene snorted. "You're old now, you old coot."

Sondra laughed. "Not too many people could get away with saying that to me, you know." She delighted in their friendship and trusted Rene implicitly. She was counting on her friend to be honest with her as she brought up something that had been troubling her for some time.

"Rene, we talk a lot. I need you to tell me the truth." She grew sober. "Have you noticed any difference in me? Like, am I repeating myself, or do you find you are telling me things multiple times?"

The other end of the line grew quiet. Sondra wished she could see her friend's face. "Rene? Are you there? I'm going to push Eye Genie if you don't answer me."

Rene cleared her throat. "No, I'm here. Sorry. I was just thinking. I wanted to be sure I don't say this in a way that scares you or makes you worry, because I think that it's normal to some degree, but yeah, I guess I have noticed it more these past few months."

Sondra thought about that. *That lines up with what I thought.*

"Thank you," she answered simply.

Rene rushed to assure her, "I know what you're thinking. But that does not mean you have Alzheimer's, Sondra."

"No, I know. I just have had this feeling lately that I'm forgetting things more than ever before, and I can't seem to grab hold of thoughts before they fly right out of my mind." She grew quieter. "I guess there isn't much I can do about it anyway, but it's somewhat scary to think of stepping into the future without being able to remember the past. Like Margaret."

"You have a lot of years left before you would be like Margaret, Sondra. You said she isn't even communicating anymore."

"No, that's true. She hasn't spoken in months now. The only upside to that is that, at least, she stopped asking how my parents are doing. I would remind her, 'Remember Mom? My mom and dad passed away.' That would start her crying. She'd go through a fresh grief each time she forgot and was told." Sondra stopped for a second, remembering. "Finally, we all agreed that when she asked, we would say, 'They're doing very well,' since that is certainly the truth."

"I'm so sorry, Sondra." Rene knew the agony of caring for elderly parents. "How is Timothy doing?"

"Well, he's still really sharp and loves when we visit. Actually, we are going over there tomorrow."

"Be sure to tell him I say hello."

"I will."

The two women said their good-byes, promising to talk again soon.

Sondra walked along restlessly, praying out loud, "Lord, Rene confirmed what I suspected, and You already know. I love my family. I don't want to burden them, and it makes me sad to think that I might forget the wonderful life we've shared together. But I don't want to spend even a moment worrying about it, because that doesn't honor You. So help me accept whatever You choose to allow in my life, and help me be a beacon that points the way to You for as long as You give me breath."

She spent the rest of her afternoon sorting and taping pictures into her photo albums, with dates and names and as much detail as she could remember with a black pen and large script.

I might not always remember, but maybe making these notes will jog my memory someday when I can't remember them on my own.

* * *

On their visits to John's parents, Sondra and John shared pictures of their kids and grandkids as well as news about everyone, which Timothy really enjoyed hearing.

After sharing the updates of news about the family, Sondra and John talked with him about coming to live with them in their home, but Timothy shook his head. "Your mother can't leave here, and I can't leave her, so here is where I'll stay." He looked squarely at them. "I made a promise to love her and cherish her—till death do we part. Well, no one is going to take that away from me." He shook his head. "I've messed up enough in life. I want to get this one thing right and be able to stand in front of the good Lord on the day I got to answer to Him and be able to say, 'I kept my word, Lord. I didn't leave her before it was time!'" He nodded determinedly.

Sondra usually wept tears of sadness over the decline of her mother-in-law. Today, they were tears of joy for the strength of spirit her father-in-law displayed. There was a precious beauty in the gentle way he cared for his wife, feeding her and talking to her as if she shared the same thread of memory of their life together. Sondra recognized and valued Timothy's tenacity to do the hard thing and stay with his wife. It was the same trait she saw in his son. Sondra knew the day could come when she herself would benefit from such loyalty and felt bad for placing temptation in front of him.

John choked up. "You're right, Dad. You belong here with Mom."

Margaret sat quietly. Often, she would drift to sleep, unaware and unable to stay with the thread of conversation. Sondra would stroke her hand, trying to be a comfort to the old woman, who had aged so drastically.

Sondra longed all the more for Christ's return after these draining visits, hating to see the pain and heartache of the world, the breakdown and decay as a result of sin.

Lord, help us see Your grace in the midst of this pain.

John bent to kiss his mother's white head, deep in slumber. "Good-bye, Mom. I love you. I'll see you soon." He hugged and kissed his dad too, and Sondra did the same.

"I love you, kids. Thanks for coming by. It means so much to me." A tear squeezed out of the older man's eye, and he hastily brushed it away. Self-pity wasn't his style, but grief had grown to be a more frequent guest.

John gave his dad another hug, wishing he could strengthen him with his own strength, but knowing the resources God poured out on him would be sufficient. Timothy stood forlornly, watching them walk down the hallway away from the lonely apartment he shared with his wife, who could no longer remember who he was.

* * *

When they got home from the nursing home that afternoon, the home phone was ringing. John picked it up, answering, "Hello?" The voice coming through from the other end was loud enough for Sondra to hear though she couldn't make out who it might be. Her husband held the instrument out to her with a puzzled look on his face. "It's for you. Someone who says his wife goes to your Bible study." Sondra took the phone. "Hello?" she said pleasantly.

"Sondra Martin?" the brisk voice demanded.

"Yes, this is she." A pang of worry pierced her.

"This is Alex Peterson. My wife, Debra, attended the Bible study you held this past week."

340

Sondra listened, trying to place the woman as he continued. "Deb came home with some nonsense you fed her about looking at the trials in our lives with grateful hearts. Well, let me tell you, we don't need your platitudes. Who are you to preach to her like that? You don't know anything about us or the heartache we are facing. I wouldn't usually call someone like this, but she has been crying for two days, and it's all your fault."

Sondra felt like the wind had been knocked out of her. *Oh, dear Lord, please give me Your words. Help me have a gentle heart to answer him.*

John stood nearby, watching her with a curious look. Sondra turned her back, not wanting him to hear or intervene.

Alex was still talking, his voice rising. "You're telling us we're supposed to walk around joyfully when we got the news of our daughter's leukemia? You've got to be kidding me. What kind of a crazy woman are you? You know, it's hard enough to hear such a terrible diagnosis without having to be subjected to a holier-than-thou like you who has no sympathy for what others might be facing. Even if I believed in God, I wouldn't tell people to laugh their way through heartache. You want to be joyful in your trials? Go ahead—but leave us alone!" He slammed the phone down, causing Sondra to pull the instrument from her ear.

The blood drained from her face, and she sank weakly into a nearby chair. John looked at her uneasily. "Honey, what was that about?"

Tears filled her eyes, and she shook her head for a moment, trying to remember exactly what hateful words the caller had used even while wishing she could forget them. "He said he was Debra Peterson's husband. I'm not sure I even know who she is, but she must have misunderstood what I was trying to say the other day in class." Sondra felt mournful and unsure of herself.

"O God, please help me," she prayed aloud. "What have I done? Who else might I have unintentionally hurt?"

She lowered her head into her hands. John came over to her, rubbing her back, trying to soothe her. "Anyone who knows you knows your heart, Sondra. If she misunderstood you, well, maybe you can clarify next week."

She looked up, pain clouding her eyes. "Oh, John, I never meant to make it sound like we aren't going to cry through difficulty or that suffering isn't real and painful." She shook her head. "I wish I could go back and change how I phrased it. I feel terrible knowing that someone is suffering and thinks that I am callous to it."

John pulled her to her feet, wrapping his arms around her. "Well, first let's see if we can find out who this couple is. Maybe we can go over to their home in a few days when they've cooled down and try to explain things."

Sondra nodded, grateful to have John's calm steadiness to lean on.

* * *

The next day Susan and Dawn came for their visit. Sondra decided to tell them about the call she'd gotten the night before. She needed to hear their perspectives since they'd both been there.

The shocked look on their faces made Sondra think that, perhaps, this was an isolated case.

Dawn asked, "Are you kidding? What did he say exactly?"

Sondra related the one-sided conversation as best as she could remember it.

Susan shook her head. "No, Sondra. You didn't say you thought we should be laughing our way through our heartaches. I would remember that." Her old friend shook her head again, trying to encourage her. "I think this Debra was probably feeling the sting of her daughter's horrible news. I'm sure she's struggling to see it as a chance to trust God. I mean, let's face it, that doesn't come naturally to any of us."

Dawn agreed. "I agree. I was there the whole time. You didn't say anything like that at all. But it's a hard message to hear even as true as it is."

Sondra nodded. "I have to confess, I'm relieved. I was up most of last night worrying about how many others might have left confused and hurting. You both are making me feel a lot better. Thank you." The women smiled at her. Sondra continued. "I'll ask Linda Peters if she has this woman's contact info."

She breathed a sigh of relief, turning the conversation to other matters. "So, Dawn, I have orders from Tommy to ask you to pass along his greetings to Drew. When do you leave to go see them?"

"Next week and I can't wait." Her son, Drew, lived in California with his wife and three kids. "They love the West Coast." She sighed. "I can't blame them, but I wish they were closer by."

Susan nodded. "I understand. I miss Meghan too. I'm going to go see her and Brad at the end of the month. You know I love Brad, but he is such a glum fellow." She sighed. "Meghan is so upbeat and positive, maybe that's what they mean by opposites attracting."

"What has he done that makes you say that?" Sondra asked.

Susan squinted, thinking. "Well, for example, last summer he and I got in a little discussion. I had told Meghan that maybe her new doctor would have some advanced methods to help them conceive, and he didn't like that."

"But clearly, she *did* have some advanced methods," Sondra exclaimed with a laugh. "After all, Meghan *is* due next month."

"Right. I know. But when I said that, he told me I shouldn't get Meghan's hopes up. I said, 'Why not? What else is hope for if not to help lift our heads?'" She shook her head again. "I don't know. He's a nice-enough guy. I just would go crazy married to someone so cautious all the time."

Dawn ventured, "Maybe he was afraid she might shoot for things that are out of reach and get hurt?"

Susan smiled. "You are kinder than me, Dawn. You're right though. It could be that, I guess." She sighed. "Well, one thing I do know—David would have loved this season with a grandbaby coming." Her husband, David, had died after a vicious battle with cancer several years earlier. Sondra reached out to touch Susan's hand, wanting to comfort her friend. The pain had lessened over time, certainly, but there were some losses one didn't ever really completely heal from.

Susan asked, "When are you and John going to see Tommy and Marguerite?"

Sondra's eyes lit up. "Their boys will be coming to spend an entire month with us when the baby is born. Marguerite isn't due for five more months. But when we take Marcel and Pierre back to France, we'll spend a week with them."

Susan laughed. "You're going to have to sleep for a month after you get back."

Sondra chuckled. "Tell me about it, but I do love this season of having our grandchildren to love on." She continued, admitting, "I remember feeling when my children were home that all the ordinary, everyday things I did for them went unnoticed and unimportant. Only now after they're all gone have I come to the place where I see God's glory in the ministry of the mundane."

Dawn said, "Years ago I had an old aunt who taught me a poem: 'My tiny, little platform, as small as it may be, is plenty to do what You've called me to: live a life that glorifies Thee.'"

Sondra said, "I like that. I always wanted to reach a wider audience than what I felt God gave me. Now, I realize what a waste of time that was." She sighed. "I would love to go back and have another go at it, but it's too late for that."

The other two nodded understandingly. "Now I just wish I had the strength to watch our grandkids more. I feel like I've been tired my whole life. I thought that when I got older, I would finally have freedom to sleep all I wanted. But it hasn't worked out that way."

Susan said, "Isn't that the truth? My first grandchild isn't even here yet, and I'm already trying to figure out how I'll still get my afternoon nap in when he arrives. I can't seem to sleep all the night through, but Lord knows, I can't stay awake all day either."

Dawn asked, "Have you been using the lavender essential oil I gave you? I'm telling you, you will sleep like a baby." Dawn was their expert consultant on the myriad uses for essential oils.

"Oh, it's true," Sondra attested. "It's almost scary how effective it is."

Susan mused, "Well, maybe I'll try it. I need to try something, for crying out loud."

The morning drifted by as they laughed and shared, enjoying their sweet friendship.

* * *

While at church that evening to help with the seniors' ministry, Sondra bumped into Linda Peters, her old mentor and friend. Linda's husband, Charlie, beloved by all in their church, had died a year earlier, peacefully in his sleep. She bent down and gave the older woman a hug as she sat in her wheelchair, noting some weariness in her lined face.

"Linda, hello. It's wonderful to see you."

Linda gave her a smile, patting her hand. "Hi, Sondra. It's nice to see you too. How have you been?"

"Good. Good. Busy with the grandkids, but that's always good, right?"

Linda's white head bobbed in agreement. "Oh yes, there's nothing quite like those years spent with the grandkids, watching the next generation as they grow up. My own grandchildren are already young adults, off living their own lives." She shook her head wonderingly. "I must say, it happened a whole lot quicker than I expected."

Sondra sympathized.

How lonely she must be. I wonder what she does with her days? Does anyone spend any time with her, or has she just been forgotten?

She felt badly for the woman, who had always found good in everyone around her, remembering back to the time Linda had ministered to her so deeply as she walked with her through the pain of CiCi's cutting.

Sondra asked kindly, "Are you enjoying the free time you must have now?"

"Oh yes, I sure am. I've got more time than ever to hide God's Word away in my heart."

"That's wonderful, Linda. You're an inspiration to me." She beamed at the older woman.

Sondra hated to trouble her, but needed to find out if she knew Debra Peterson, the wife of the agitated caller from a few nights earlier. She briefly related the interaction. "He was so upset, and I felt terrible. Clearly, his wife walked away with a different take on my message than I meant to convey. I just really want a chance to clear the air if possible."

Linda's eyes closed for a moment as she adjusted the heavy glasses that covered them.

Maybe I shouldn't have brought this up to her. What if her heart can't take such stress? That was thoughtless of me!

As waves of doubt were going through Sondra's mind, Linda opened her eyes again. She fiddled with her glasses a moment more, and Sondra wondered if she was having trouble seeing. Suddenly, Linda stated, "Debra and Alex Peterson. 21 Continental Way. In the older section of town."

Sondra gaped at the old woman, who smiled at her mischievously. "Are you serious? How did you do that?"

Linda tapped her temple. "You wouldn't believe the information I've got stored up here."

Sondra's eyebrows shot up in disbelief. "I'm speechless and very impressed."

The older woman laughed appreciatively. "I'm just pulling your leg, dear. I've been trying out the newest invention at the company where my grandson works: eyewear that stores all the contacts from my cell phone right here on my lens. Lucas uploaded the data for me. It's taking me some time to learn how to access it, but that's one thing I've got plenty of these days. After all," she continued, "why should the young folks have all the fun?"

Her blue eyes danced merrily behind the thick lenses, and Sondra's mouth dropped open in amazement at the old woman's willingness to stay on top of the latest technical gadgets. "Besides," Linda added, "these glasses have opened up new worlds for me. With a touch, I can see names of people I want to pray for, and I can even call them right through these tiny microphones and a speaker located under the lens—it really is wonderful."

"Oh, Linda, that's marvelous." Sondra laughed. "Now I really am impressed." She copied the address into her own phone and patted the old woman's hand again. "Thank you for the information."

Linda turned a dimpled smile to her. "My Charlie always said that life is meant to be lived." She continued proudly, "He would be happy to know our grandchildren are helping me to stay engaged in life and not just sit on the sidelines."

Sondra felt tears come to her eyes. "You're right about that, I'm sure he would."

Linda sighed. "I miss him a great deal. But I'll be joining him soon enough. Until then, I want to make the most of the time I have. And frankly, some people lots younger than me have forgotten how to have a good time." She threw her shoulders back, straightening in her chair. "I plan on living with the joy of the Lord until the moment He calls me home."

Sondra nodded, greatly encouraged by the older woman's tenacity and grit. "Amen, my friend, amen."

* * *

The next morning, Sondra drove over to the home belonging to Alex and Debra Peterson. She wasn't exactly sure what she was going to say, but felt that she needed to try to make things right.

Lord, please give me clarity of speech, and Debra, ears of understanding.

A small-boned woman answered the door. Her puffy eyes were red, her face downcast, her shoulders slumped in defeat. She shuffled a few steps back when she opened the door as if Sondra were delivering yet another heartache that would break her completely. Sondra's heart broke in pity.

"Debra?" she inquired gently. The meek expression on the other side of the door changed little; the tiny nod was the only indicator that she was, indeed, Debra.

"I'm Sondra. Sondra Martin." Recognition lit her eyes, and Sondra continued. "Your husband called me the other day. When he told me what you thought I had said in class, I felt so badly."

Sondra hated having this conversation through a doorway, but the smaller woman hadn't made a move to invite her in, so she pled her case from the concrete stoop. "I wanted to come over here to apologize if there was something I said that you misunderstood and see if there is anything I can do or pray for you about?" She hesitated. "Would it be okay if I came in for a moment so we can talk?"

"No." The word rushed at her hotly.

Sondra was stunned. Till now, the smaller woman had stood meekly by, clearly crushed under some massive weight of pain. But energized by a torrent of unbearable anguish, she unleashed her dagger of words straight for Sondra's unsuspecting heart.

She flung the door open, and Sondra repelled from the onslaught of unbearable stench coming from the house: death resided there—maybe not in physical form yet, but in the promise of it.

Sondra's mouth dropped open as Debra raised her arm as if she held a club, threatening Sondra with the invisible weapon of pain. Astonished, she watched an avalanche of anger come tumbling out.

"How dare you come here and lie to me? I know what you said! You think you can try to make me believe God has a good plan for our daughter? Nina never did anything bad to anyone. She doesn't deserve this. I used to think that God cared about us, but no more. What kind of a God lets a good little girl suffer the way our little girl is suffering? I hate Him, and I hate you!"

Sondra stood, her mouth agape at the anger hurled at her.

Tears wracked Debra's small body. Worse was the wail that tore from her throat as she grieved her daughter's suffering. "My baby!" Sondra stood bearing witness to her indescribable pain, but unable to move. "My baby girl! I can't take this, please, no!" The torrent of emotion completely wore the exhausted woman out, and she stumbled, crumpling to the floor.

Sondra felt helpless, then she remembered that she held the only tool that could help any of them: the weapon of prayer. Tears streamed as she cried out loud, "O God, we are desperate. Please shower Your grace on Debra and her whole family. She needs You, Lord, she needs to know that You love her and her daughter."

As the words left her mouth, Sondra watched Debra, who lay still, listening. In the silence, Sondra prayed again, "It was never Your plan to have sin enter the world and so destroy Your beautiful creation. But it did, and it brought pain and disease and death. So You made the only way to break the certainty of death: life through Your perfect Son, Jesus Christ. Thank You for the truth that *anyone* who calls on His name has hope. Help us to trust You, God, even through the painful things in our lives. We have no other answers, Lord, no other place to run to except Your open arms."

Again, she stopped, watching and waiting.

Suddenly, the door opened all the way. A large man filled the space. He wore a workman's jumpsuit with the name *Alex* stitched across the top pocket. His barely restrained silence held more menace than Debra's rage had. Looking into his hate-filled eyes, Sondra felt very vulnerable. He stood for a moment and then bent over, easily picking his wife up where she lay quietly, holding her in his arms as if she were a doll.

Sondra gazed at him with tears in her eyes, wishing he could see her heart full of sympathy. "Mr. Peterson, please, I'm so sorry for your pain," she beseeched.

He looked squarely at her with intense loathing. Then he stepped back into the house, carrying his wife, and slammed the door shut with his foot. Sondra heard the finality of the bolt slam home on the other side.

* * *

Several weeks passed after the episode at the Petersons'. Sondra thought about them often, praying for them, knowing the only hope they had was the one they had so far rejected.

She carefully added the names Alex, Debra, and Nina Peterson to her pages for salvation. She scanned the many names listed there, her eyes lingering the longest on her own daughter's name: Cecilia.

Please, Lord, let me live to see the day my daughter gives her life to You completely. I know she prayed as a little girl, Lord, but there's been no fruit since. I don't know if she's one of Yours or not. Oh God, please don't let her leave this earth without coming to know You as Savior and Lord!

Sondra regularly prayed for every name listed on the sheets. The only way off her list was to either accept Christ as Savior or pass on from this life. Sadly, more than a few names were crossed off for that reason, with the date of their death written nearby. She hoped that at some point in their lives, these loved ones had accepted Christ that only God knew about.

She thought back to her dad's favorite saying: "As long as there's breath, there's hope."

Sondra grappled with the fact that life's pains could blind people to the very thing that could free them from pain for eternity. She did what she often did when she found herself wrestling through hard lessons: she wrote.

Across the top of a fresh page, she asked the question: What do you think when you see the plight of our fellow humans who suffer the blight of this earth and her troubles? Of pain and distress? Of disease and poverty, anguish and death?

She put her pen down, suddenly grateful to God for unblinding her eyes and helping her see, so many years ago, her need to come to Christ and accept His free gift.

O God, thank You for making a way. Please let these who still have not accepted Your salvation do so before it's too late.

She spent the next couple of hours praying fervently for each of those listed on her pages, trusting God for the outcome.

* * *

Sondra and John were heavily engaged in the lives of all their grandchildren and children except for Cecilia, who mystifyingly kept her distance.

Whenever they visited Regan and Gavin, which was as often as possible, John stocked his pockets with candy and spare change to hand out to their three children, just like his own father had. Sondra taught them songs and ditties from when she was a child that she remembered her own parents and grandparents teaching. She loved the idea that she could be linked to people she'd never known through the passing down of such traditions and didn't want to be the one to break the chain.

While visiting at Regan's one day, she heard her grandkids singing a familiar song in their sweet voices: "God says of Jesus, 'I am pleased with You, on You my fullest favor rests, You obey everything I ask of You . . . my Son, my Son, my Son."

Sondra laughed with delight. "Oh, honey, Grandma would have been so pleased that that song didn't die off."

"They've been singing that one a lot lately." Regan smiled. "They know all the verses."

After lunch, the younger kids played quietly nearby. Regan's oldest daughter, Carissa, strolled past with her nose in a book, completely absorbed. Her mom and grandma watched as she selected an apple from the wooden bowl on the counter, crunched into the juicy fruit, and then made her way back out of the room, all while her eyes stayed glued on the written pages in front of her.

Sondra laughed. "She reminds me of myself when I was her age."

Regan said, "She is such a reader. She already plowed through that whole series you gave her last Christmas."

"Well, there are a lot more up in our attic I can dig out. I'm so glad my mom saved all my old books." She smiled. "It's fun to pass them along to someone who will enjoy them as much as I did."

"She'd love that, Mom. Thanks."

"Of course. So how is Gavin's new job?"

"Oh, he really loves it. When he lost his job, I was so worried he might not find another one. We never dreamed it would take two years." She sighed. "It was rough, but good that I had the option to go back to teaching." She took a sip of her drink. "I missed being home with our kids, but I have to admit, looking back now, it taught me to appreciate so many things."

Sondra nodded sympathetically. "It can be so hard sometimes to understand what God is up to. He doesn't always explain. He just wants us to trust Him."

Regan confided, "You and Dad just always seem to know how to turn things over to God, Mom. I am grateful for your example, but I feel like sometimes I struggle more in letting go and letting God handle things than you guys do."

Sondra shook her head, marveling at her daughter's perspective. "Oh, trust me, sweetheart, that is not true. There have been plenty of times I've struggled with doubt." She gulped and went on. "I've questioned God about why He allows unfair situations. I mean, certainly, I've seen growth in my life, but there are times that I struggle with anger and frustration, self-pity and fear."

She took a sip of her tea. "For years, a big one for me was jealousy." She smiled at Regan. "You were pretty young, but one of the consuming things in my life was my desire to get published. It seemed that everyone around me was pursuing their dreams and getting chances to do big things except me." She admitted, "The part I too often missed was this: God just wants us to glorify Him with everything He gives us and let Him decide how He chooses to use the outcome of that obedience." She shook her head. "I know I didn't handle every situation with grace. I still don't. But I'm growing."

Regan was quiet for a minute. "Thanks, Mom. That helps." She stopped. "It's just so hard when I see hurtful things going on, like what's happening with Carissa right now."

A small tear formed in the corner of her eye as she explained, "She wants so badly to be part of this certain group of girls, but they leave her out, only letting her join when it fits their agenda."

Sondra squeezed her daughter's hand. "Hmm. I know that feeling. And so do you." She smiled gently.

Regan nodded and took a sip of her tea. "Gavin and I have told her to choose her friends carefully, we don't want to see her waste time chasing people and trying to get them to accept her. Especially since she has so many other girls she could choose from. There is one little girl named Jenny who is so sweet. Her parents separated a few months ago, and she seems a little lost. I have told Carissa that that might be a friendship she should cultivate. Jenny sure could use someone who can tell her about Jesus and give her some hope."

"Oh, honey, you are such a good mom. I think it's amazing to see how God let you go through experiences in your own life that you can turn around and share what you learned with others, including your children."

Regan nodded again, biting her lower lip. "Yes, I've thought about that too. And I did share the story about Kayla with her, hoping it encourages her to trust that God can bring the right friends into her life at the right time."

"Well, then now you just need to wait on His timing. One thing I've learned is this: God wants to use trials in our lives to show His power at work. If we never faced difficulties, He wouldn't be able to display His intimate care for us."

Regan nodded slowly. "Yeah. I can see that. But sometimes, it isn't easy."

Her mom snorted. "Tell me about it. Let me assure you, you are not alone in your struggle of always trusting God. It has taken me a lifetime to get to the place where I'm starting to see His purpose in allowing trials in our lives." She sighed. "I wish I had been a quicker learner. Who knows how much further I'd be ahead if it hadn't taken me so long to learn that one thing?"

Regan smiled, and the two spent a lovely rest of their afternoon sharing and being together.

* * *

Mylah had fallen in love with and was married to Kyle Pearson, son of their dear friends Loni and Denny. Last year the young couple had adopted a sweet little baby from China, whom they named Faith Joy. They were working on the process to go back for her older sister, whom they'd already named Emily Hope.

Sondra and Loni and John and Denny took tremendous joy in their friendship as well as the shared family bond of their children and granddaughters. While visiting together later that week, she and Loni planned how to divide up the time with Faith when Kyle and Mylah were overseas the following month.

Loni chuckled. "I may have to let you take extra shifts with her since Trixie and Brian are keeping Denny and me busy as grandparents."

Kyle's sister, Trixie, was still Mylah's best friend. She and her husband, Brian, had two sets of twins, with a fifth child on the way.

"Those four sure keep their household busy—and loud," Loni admitted, laughing heartily. "Thankfully, Brian's mother, Brenda, lives so close that she often pops over to help them."

"Did you ever think these years would be this much fun?" Sondra asked her dear friend.

Loni agreed. "Hmm. You said it, sister. Being grandparents is truly the best. You get to have all the fun without any of the stress and responsibility you had with your own kids."

They laughed, catching up on other news. "How are Regan and Gavin doing?" Loni asked.

"Much better now. Of course, when Gavin lost his job, it was a really tough stretch. But they trimmed back on their spending and knew God would supply their needs." She sipped some of her tea. "As much as she didn't want to have to take it, God provided a good job for Regan, and they were able to make it through." She chuckled. "Gavin, on the other hand, may be permanently damaged from handling the day-to-day operations of their home."

Loni smiled. "It sure is a lot harder than people think, isn't it?"

"Oh yes. Of course, he did fine overall." She chuckled. "I think the kids ate some unusual lunches and got away with a few things that Regan will never know, but all in all, they made it through even if the road was a bit bumpy here and there."

Loni nodded. "It's hard to watch people we love go through hard times."

"That's for sure," Sondra agreed. "I find myself wanting to spare our children the trials and heartaches that we went through, but that's just not possible. We all have our road to travel, and it's often pitted with difficulty." She paused. "The one I worry the most about is CiCi." She looked at her friend, who nodded sympathetically. "I just don't understand. She was raised in the same home by the same parents with the same teaching and love and acceptance, but it's like she's turned her back on all of us." Sondra blinked to keep back tears. "I've prayed so much for that girl my knees are worn-out. By now, all of heaven must be perfumed with the incense of my continual prayers for her."

Loni gave a small smile and reached out her hand, covering her friend's hand with her own, her beautiful dark skin a lovely contrast to Sondra's. Her eyes gazed gently at her friend. "There are some situations that are not going to make any sense to us, Sondra. You and John have done all you can. Now you need to wait on the good Lord. Just because we can't always see His purposes doesn't mean He doesn't have any."

Sondra gulped and nodded, grateful for the needed reminder.

* * *

One day the following week, Sondra was driving two of her grandkids home to give Regan some time alone with Carissa. She listened to the conversation they had in the backseat.

Six-year-old Macy informed her brother, "Look, Samuel. We're going to see the cows pretty soon." They passed the farm where cows usually stood but saw only an empty field. Macy called Sondra, "Grandma, what day is it?"

"Wednesday, darling."

Sweet little Macy turned to her brother, offering up the explanation, "Oh, I accileedent forgot, Samuel, cows can't go outside on Wednesdays."

Sondra chuckled the rest of the way home.

That night after dinner, John showed the kids an Eskimo kiss by gently rubbing his nose against theirs. Samuel giggled. "That's funny, Grandpa! Do Eskimos bite when you pet their heads?"

John threw his head back and howled with laughter. "You've got to record that one, honey." Sondra nodded, laughing and making a note of the funny exchanges for everyone else in the family to enjoy.

Regan had created an online column, like a shared journal, which she'd entitled, "Nuggets Crumbling from Our Gems." It was an easy space for the entire family to access, where any of the parents or grandparents could record observations and comments about any of the grandchildren to share funny stories and celebrate life's special moments. As the kids had grown a bit, some of the sections expanded, and a page was added where insights, stories, and even prayer requests could be shared.

After they got their grandkids tucked in for the night, John checked the site and came across the latest post by Regan. "Honey, listen to this."

He read aloud:

> Today, I was reminded of a time when my brother, Tommy, was just a little older than Carissa is now. He and his friend Drew had been playing near a creek near our home and came across a box of magazines. They hauled them home and were looking through them in the garage when Mom walked in. Seeing what it contained, she took the box and closed it, sat all of us kids down, including Drew, and told us, "I know you were just playing, and it wasn't your fault to stumble across that box. But what you boys found today was something that if you don't flee from, it will snare you. God says, 'Guard your heart.' This includes all the ugly things that Satan would love to have you trapped by. Pain is the only sure thing that will come from looking at material like what is in that box." Then Mom said something that I remember hearing her say throughout our years growing up:
>
> "Today is tomorrow's yesterday, let's live it in such a way that we won't regret the choices we made when tomorrow becomes today."
>
> Tommy made the suggestion, "Mom, maybe we should burn the whole box so no one else stumbles on it either." So she gave each of the boys a match, and together they burned the box in the backyard while we all stood watching with the hose ready nearby.

I had forgotten that little saying until today. I went into Carissa's room, where she and her friend Jenny were watching music videos. As I walked up from behind them, I could see the screen. One of the videos loaded on Jenny's device was really risqué. It led us to have a great discussion on the importance of guarding our eyes and hearts and minds from the junk in this world, and that little saying popped into my mind, and I shared it with the girls. We prayed together that God would help them recognize sin quickly, and they'd have the courage to run from it. Thanks, Mom—your godly wisdom is still rippling out to bless these future generations.

John turned to her, hugging her close. "I'm thankful for you, Sondra. You used your time well, building into our kids, teaching them the important things they needed to know to help them get through life." He kissed her. "I'm proud of you, honey."

"Oh, John, thank you for letting me stay home all those years to raise our children. God has been so good to us."

He raised her hand to his lips and kissed her fingers, which were wrinkled with the signs of aging, the thin skin stretched delicately over the bones of her fingers. "He has indeed."

Sondra gazed at him. "Do you ever think about what our lives might have been like if we had made that move to New York City?"

John took a deep breath and exhaled. "Well, not lately, but yeah, sure, I used to sometimes wonder about that road not taken." He paused. "Certainly, it would have allowed us to leave a better inheritance for our children. All they're going to really have now is this dilapidated old house that none of them will want." He laughed. "But then I think about all the people God has brought into our lives whom we've been able to minister to and be ministered by, and it becomes easier to see His hand and purpose in keeping us here." He looked around their familiar bedroom. "And I have to admit, I've grown content here. We've spent a lifetime making memories together, raising our children, and seeing them all launched out into the world and other wonderful moments. This old house has seen us through most of our life together." He kissed the top of her head, and Sondra bit her lip to keep from crying, nestling into her husband's arms.

"We may not have a lot of money to leave our children, John, but I feel certain we are leaving them a better thing"—she turned to look at his face—"and that's a legacy."

He nodded thoughtfully, and they sat like that for a while, cradled together, grateful for the grace God had given them, and reminiscing over old times. They laughed over new things the grandkids had recently said and done and rejoiced together in God's goodness and love.

* * *

A few days later while John was over at the church, helping with some handyman work, Sondra spent some time catching up with her sister, Sophia. Right after they hung up, the phone rang again. She snatched it up. "Did you forget something?" she asked teasingly.

"Excuse me?" a voice replied.

"Oh, I'm sorry." Sondra laughed lightly. "I thought you were my sister."

The woman on the other end of the line chuckled. "Well, in a way, I am."

Now it was Sondra's turn to be confused. "Excuse me? Who is this?"

A pleasant low-throated laugh came over the line. "Is this Sondra Martin?"

"Yes, this is she." She had no idea who was on the other end.

"Oh, Sondra, I'm so glad to reach you. This is Gisele. Gisele Waters."

She hesitated, struggling to remember where she knew that name from. "I'm sorry. Who is this?"

"It's been many years. I don't expect you to remember me. Our husbands worked together at the bank a very long time ago."

Recognition struck her, and Sondra cried out, "Oh, of course, I remember you, Gisele! My goodness, it's been such a long time. How are you doing?" She was delighted to have finally connected the dots.

The other woman laughed. "I've been fine—actually, really good."

"I'm so glad to hear that." Sondra was pleased though a little puzzled.

It must be more than thirty years since we last spoke. What on earth could she want with me?

The other woman was speaking. "I just wanted to let you know something that you played a part in bringing about."

Now Sondra was truly confused. "I can't imagine what that might be?" she offered honestly.

Gisele chuckled. "Well, let me first say that a lot has gone on in my life over the years. When my husband, Jonathon, and I knew you and John, I was pretty consumed with pursuing anything that kept me busy. My life was empty. The few times I met you, I felt like you had a rich and rewarding life that I could never achieve no matter how lavishly I tried to live."

Sondra marveled: she remembered feeling exactly the same way about the other woman's experiences and accomplishments.

"The day I called you to ask about a woman whom I suspected was having an affair with Jonathon, I was humiliated. I remember hanging up with you and regretting that I'd admitted my concerns to you." A small sigh came through the line as the woman relived the pain of the past. "I don't need to get into all that transpired with all that right now, but I couldn't get out of my head the things you told me about God loving me. Even though I turned you down when you invited me to your women's Bible study, just the fact that you invited me stuck with me for a long time."

Sondra gulped. She honestly couldn't remember doing so and wasn't sure where this was headed. She listened carefully, not wanting to interrupt.

Gisele went on. "For a long time I was angry. I thought that if God loved me, He had a strange way of showing it. He took my grandmother, whom I adored, and allowed me to be in a painful marriage." She paused and then said simply, "A few months ago I gave my life to Christ."

Sondra drew her breath in a small gasp.

Gisele continued. "I was tired of running from Him, and when someone gave me a Bible with all the verses of salvation highlighted, I decided to stop running and turn my life over to Him."

Sondra couldn't stop the tears from falling from her eyes. "Oh, Gisele, that's what you meant when you said you're my sister."

Gisele laughed, answering, "Yes, we are sisters in Christ. And I want to thank you for being bold, all those years ago, to share the truth with me. I know I could be hard to be around—I didn't like myself, how could anyone else? I've got a long way to go, but I'm grateful to know the truth now. I don't want to waste any more of my life. I'm in all the way and have no intention of looking back."

Sondra rejoiced with this newfound sister in salvation. "I'm so happy for you, Gisele. And what about Jonathon? Has he also accepted Christ as his Savior?"

Gisele let out a breath. "It's ironic, really, that through years of mutual betrayal and pain, Jonathon and I stayed together." She bitterly noted, "It took me giving my life to Christ to make him leave me for good."

Sondra sympathized with her. "I'm so sorry."

"Well, the truth is, he left me years ago, it's just that his body finally caught up. He said he could take other men in my life since he played around on the side too."

Sondra stayed silent.

"But having God enter into our home was too much for him. He said he would rather have the freedom that a wandering wife gave him than the constant conviction of a faithful one."

Sondra thought of Jesus's words that His coming would divide brother from brother and parent from child. Some would choose to follow Christ, but many others, even precious loved ones, would choose to remain in Satan's camp.

"Well, you mustn't lose hope. God can touch anyone's heart. John and I will be praying for him and for you as you keep walking forward, trusting Christ to provide all you need. And He will," she finished simply.

"Thank you, Sondra, for everything. I mean it. You were one in a line of people God brought across my path, but you didn't break the thread God was weaving. You did your part, and I'm grateful."

The two women talked for a few more minutes, exchanging numbers.

"Please, let's get together for coffee soon. I have so much I want to ask you and really would like to see you."

"I would like that too," Sondra said sincerely. They made a date that she put on her calendar. When she hung up the phone, she prayed, "O Lord, thank You for Your goodness that keeps on reaching the lost. Please continue to let me be used by You for Your glory for as long as You allow me breath. I love You, Lord."

* * *

Afterward, she called Rene, but it went right to voice mail.

"Hey, it's me. Give me a call when you have a chance. Love you."

She felt nostalgic and wanted to talk with her oldest friend, especially with Gisele's news.

Rene will remember her and remind me of any details I've forgotten.

Sondra walked around their home, looking at the picture frames that adorned nearly every room. Mixed in with the traditional framed pictures she had taken from her parents' home and put on display, they also had frames that contained changing images.

John stayed up to date on technological developments. Sondra marveled at the equipment that let them display thousands of pictures stored in a tiny memory pin within as well as short clips of their loved ones' voices. The last advancement they'd bought allowed the playing of thirty-second recordings their kids could send through the computer. John would download the posts into tiny receivers and insert the receivers into the port on the sides of the frames.

One of the frames showed Tommy with six-year-old Marcel and three-year-old Pierre, who looked so much like TJ had at that age it brought tears to her eyes.

She smiled as she tapped the screen, allowing for the message to move from mute to sound. She loved hearing his sweet young voice as he roamed about their home in Mougins, France, singing "Jesus Loves Me" to the recorder. She watched as the recording ended, slowly fading to another picture, one that CiCi had sent of herself in front of her home in Boston. Her daughter was as beautiful as ever, but a hunger in her eyes carried a lingering look of someone still searching for some elusive goal.

Though they talked infrequently, Sondra suspected that Cecilia had also met someone in Boston. She hadn't confided so; it was just a feeling Sondra had. She wasn't sure why Cecilia had such wanderlust, relinquishing her chance to play much of a part in the lives of her sisters and brothers and all her nieces and nephews. Certainly, most of her peers were married with children. While she seemed to be accepting of that, Sondra wasn't so certain that Cecilia was truly happy.

Sondra wondered again if there was a special someone she had found.

If so, whoever he is, my only prayer is that he is a man who loves You, Lord.

She waited patiently for their daughter to share more fully with them about her life, not wanting to pry, grateful for whatever glimpses she allowed them. Her prayers for her were simple. *Bring her to Yourself, Lord.*

Sondra and John desired that God would not only watch over their kids and grandchildren but also draw them to Himself and create a yearning and eagerness to follow Him fervently, with an urgency that recognized the days were short.

Sondra went to her computer, looking at her writing file, full of poems and stories, funny anecdotes, and family lore. She stumbled across a letter she had written to John three years earlier when she had gone through an uncertain period with her health. Her doctor had found a tumor in her breast, but then miraculously, it had vanished as unexpectedly as it had arrived, leaving her breathless with the abrupt curves life could bring and grateful that she was solid in her faith. There'd been no explanation, no certain diagnosis, just the fact that it had served its purpose in God's plan, and He must have removed it.

She read the letter, eyes crinkling at the memory of how John, usually steady and strong, had cried upon receiving it.

> If I go first, do not despair. I know you'll be tempted to. We've had such a wonderful life together despite the trials this world contains. There isn't anything left unsaid between us, and for that I am grateful. I have loved you increasingly as the years have passed. Who but you knows my wishes and hopes, dreams and fears, peeves and preferences? You are my best friend and soul mate. God has faithfully woven our hearts into one, and it cannot be undone—till death do us part. What a mystery! What a delight! And a rare treasure to find . . .
>
> If I go first, try not to dwell on whatever it was that took me. I would hate for you to grow bitter over what is simply inevitable for every person who walks this earth. Instead, think about all the joyous times we have shared, knitting our hearts together in the common love of Jesus. Cling to Him, won't you please? When you are lonely or sad or missing these days that we have right now before us . . . cling to Jesus and remember: Don't squander what time you have. Wring out every drop of promise and purpose and potential in every opportunity you face, because you never know when it will end. May that legacy of awareness intertwined with thankfulness be something that makes you smile with contentment that we didn't squander a moment, and I hope that it

spurs you on to take risks, climb hills, and jump in puddles, just for the fun of it, if I go first.

If I go first, don't resist falling in love again. It is too marvelous a gift to turn away from. I truly want for you what is good and lovely, precious and tender ~ and healing may come through the strength that love can give . . . so do not, please, do not feel like you are betraying our love, our life, or our legacy . . . this life is so rich with someone to love by your side. I would want you to embrace that treasure if it comes again, if I go first.

If I go first, you will need to be there for our children. It will be a difficult time in their lives as well. We have such hope with our faith in what Jesus did for us, so any time apart is just for a short while. Then we will be reunited again in a far better place beyond our wildest imagination and forever. So gather together and comfort one another with reminiscing and laughter even among the tears. Sorrow will come in this life, but our victory is secure in what Christ has already accomplished, so be quick to encourage one another with His promises, and don't let the pain of the loss trample on the memories of the marvelous times we have all shared, if I go first.

If I go first, finish our dreams for us. Don't let my leaving stop you from living life to the fullest. You are my precious and my beloved. You have shaped me into the person I am today with your love, patience, and faithfulness to me. If I don't have a chance to say it at the end of my life, may you know it now and find tremendous comfort in knowing: looking back over my life, I wouldn't change a thing. Outside of knowing Christ as my Savior, you are my heart's greatest treasure and pleasure, the one I think about, and the one my dreams contain . . . These days aren't over yet, and Lord willing, we may have more delightful decades together to share life's dreams and roam this world hand in hand, but I want you to know what I want for you, if I go first.

Lavi~and all my love,
Sondra

Forty Years Later

2069

The old door creaked loudly as it opened, turning back on hinges that hadn't been used in many years. Tonya and her daughter, Bethany, crossed the threshold, pinching their noses at the musty smell that greeted them. They stepped into the rickety old house, gingerly walking through the front room, stale with age. A couple of pieces of wobbly furniture lent evidence that human life once occupied the rooms. Mostly empty nail holes dotted the walls, but here and there, a few pictures, the kind people used to use to decorate their homes, hung covered in cobwebs. Faded smiling faces looked back at them, people they came from, even resembled, in their line of human history, but had never known.

They wanted to take their time roaming through this old dwelling, exploring the lives of the individuals who had called this place home so long ago. Surely, their laughter reverberated off these old walls, and dreams were conceived, realized, and sometimes crushed in the space of these rooms.

Tonya stopped at a doorway, blocked by a massive cobweb painstakingly built from the generations of spiders who had taken up residence. She pulled a stick of wood from the fireplace, using it to tear down the webby home, and continued on their exploration.

As they made their way through the rooms, Bethany was full of questions about the contents in the old dwelling. Bare of anything of value, much of what they saw reminded her of things she had seen in a museum back home. She marveled at the way people had lived half a century earlier.

The house itself was quite large by the day's standard. The tiny-house craze that had swept the nation hadn't really picked up momentum until 2040 or so. Then more recently, the government made such dwellings mandatory, and old homes like this one were being razed to make room for tiny-home communities since four to six homes could fit in the same space as one of these larger homes.

Inside one room, Bethany found some interesting materials. She held up a square package holding a round disk. "What's this?" she asked, her freckled nose crinkling with curiosity.

Tonya replied, "Those are called digital video disks, DVDs for short. They used to be used for recording and watching all kinds of media. They are obsolete now. You can't even find the electronic unit needed to play them on, so they're useless to us."

Bethany stopped at a wall shelf containing quite a few paper-books, titles written on their spines. "Why did people still use this method to read books? My instructor says electronic reading became widely available in the late 1990s."

Tonya smiled at her daughter. "Yes, it had, honey. But you have to remember, people get used to their habits. Not everyone embraced that new mode of reading right away. It took time to switch people from their old ways to the new ones." She picked up one of the dusty volumes, shaking the cobwebs from it, and fanned through the pages. "Now our government has tighter prohibitions. But back then, trees were plentiful and cheap, so paper was a widely used resource."

She opened the door to a closet and inspected a heavy leather case sitting on the floor. Time had worn and cracked the leather and eroded the inscription on a brass plate that she could barely read: Julia Spencer. Unlatching the buckle revealed an ancient typewriter, like the kind used over a hundred years earlier. The actual machine held no practical use for Tonya, yet something about it called to her, and she set the whole case aside to bring with them. The govern-ment-housing agent had said they could take as many of the few remaining contents and as much time as they wanted to go through the house as long as it was done within the three weeks before the bulldozing company was scheduled to come.

How the house had sat so long, abandoned and forgotten, Tonya didn't know. She only knew that the contents could be some of her last connections to the past.

For years her bitter father had stood in her way, preventing her from meeting her mother's people. Though she hadn't understood as a little girl, she knew now that her father had been the main reason for the estrangement between her mother and her mother's parents and siblings.

After her mother's death, he'd hired a long line of caregivers to raise Tonya, rarely spending time with her himself. But now, since his recent death, there was some potential for her to discover the truth. She had family—people who knew about and cared for her. Her aunts and uncles would all be quite old. Tonya wasn't certain if any of them were even alive anymore.

Her mother, Cecilia, had given birth to her later in life, at age forty, and had died far younger than was fair from a dreadful disease, amyotrophic lateral sclerosis. A devastating illness, it stole the victim's muscles, voice, and finally, her life. It was a bittersweet irony that a few short years after her death, a breakthrough discovery was made, allowing patients with this feared disease to survive much longer than they had before and with much better quality of life.

The only clue Tonya held that had brought her to this place had been found in her mother's bedside table back in Boston: tattered, creased, and barely legible anymore, the letter read, perhaps, many dozens of times as her mother must have found great consolation in seeing her own mother's lovely scrawling words across the sheet. Years after Cecilia's death, no longer in the grip of her tyrant father, while going through her mother's belongings after her father's passing, Tonya had found it, and it had led her here. She'd only wished she'd found it sooner. She had read it so many times that without even looking, she could still remember the carefully scribed words, tenderly written from the heart of a loving mother to her dying daughter:

My precious CiCi-

How I would love to be able to gather you into my arms one last time, this side of heaven, my darling girl, and assure you that God has such marvelous plans for you even in death, my CiCi, because if we have put our full faith in God's Son, Jesus Christ, death is not the separator, but the bridge to eternal life with our Lord.

How blessed your father and I were to receive your letter saying you had returned to following Jesus wholeheartedly. How grateful we are that we serve a God who gives us chance upon chance to turn to Him. He loves you, Cecilia.

That you might see the sweet face of Jesus before I do is something I never dreamed would happen. Do not fear, my precious girl. The life beyond this one is more vibrant and gloriously alive than a thousand lifetimes here!

Our one regret is over Tonya. She might never know how dearly we have loved her since the moment you brought her into the world. We pray she knows that she always has a home here. Dad and I and, of course, Regan and Gavin, Mylah and Kyle, Marguerite and Tommy and all the cousins would be thrilled beyond words to have a relationship with her, but we entrust her to God, who makes all things beautiful in His time . . .

Our prayer has continued to be that Edward would relent and allow her to come see us. We pray for his anger and rage every day that God would soften his heart.

I don't know how much time your father and I have left. My cancer has returned with full vengeance, and the stroke he suffered has left your dad without the use of his right arm and leg.

But we are rejoicing all the same, my dear girl, knowing how whole, healed, and new we will be when we pass from this life to the next.

We encourage each other with Bible verses. In fact, I taped all the ones from your bedroom all those many years ago onto our walls, where we can see them every day and draw comfort from His promises . . .

Psalms 91:1–2 "Whoever dwells in the shelter of the Most High will rest in the shadow of the Almighty. I will say of the Lord, 'He is my refuge and my fortress, my God, in whom I trust.'" If you say, "The Lord is my refuge" and you make the Most High your dwelling, no harm will overtake you, no disaster will come near your tent. For He will command His angels concerning you to guard you in all your ways; they will lift you up in their hands so that you will not strike your foot against a stone. You will tread on the lion and the cobra; you will trample the great lion and the serpent. "Because he loves me," says the Lord, "I will rescue him; I will protect him, for he acknowledges My name. He will call on Me and I will answer him; I will be with him in trouble, I will deliver him and honor him. With long life I will satisfy him and show him My salvation."

Farewell for now, beloved daughter. You are never far from our thoughts and constantly in our prayers. Your name is on my lips, and I treasure you, my Cecilia: a gift from the very hand of God Himself. If you get there first, kiss the hand of Jesus, and keep watch for us soon, my dear girl . . .

All our love,
Mom and Dad

Tonya had read the letter many times, marveling in the words of warmth and affection.

What made Mother walk away from such a wellspring of love?

Growing up without any such tenderness after her mother's death, Tonya couldn't understand why she had chosen to abandon it voluntarily and had decided to find out more about her mother's beginnings.

Armed with her grandmother's letter, she had traced the address on the envelope to this house. Granted time off work, she and Bethany had applied to make the trip westward. They had set out, finding the condemned property, long sitting empty, with the sign in the front yard, declaring it was to be destroyed by order of the county. With little hope, she had contacted the agency listed and explained her story, asking if she could get inside before it was taken down. She was amazed when an agent agreed to meet her and even gave her a key, since anything left inside before the house was demolished would also be destroyed.

Almost thirty-eight years old, Tonya hoped to find some of her mother's secrets and maybe even belongings buried from the past here in this old house, where she had spent the first years of her life. She wanted to learn more about these people, their beliefs, and what her mother had meant when she had urged Tonya to seek God.

She had been so young that the details had grown fuzzy, but Tonya could remember her mom dying from the debilitating disease, exhausted from the smallest exertion, almost unable to speak, but straining to tell her a crucial message, "God loves you, Tonya. Find Him." They turned out to be the final words her mother ever spoke as she died not long after.

Something tugged at Tonya's heart. She held the envelope bearing Sondra's name and address. Who was this woman whom she had never met? What dreams had her heart held? Her grandmother's letter to her mother was the only clue she had to the kind of mother she had tried to be.

Bethany gave a shout. "Mom!"

She was standing excitedly in a room, empty except for a few pieces of very old furniture: a four-poster bed with a musty old mattress and a large decrepit bureau with cumbersome drawers. It looked unlikely to yield up anything of value; surely, any contents had been removed long ago, but Tonya didn't want to discourage her daughter.

"Wow, honey, what did you find?"

Though she hadn't really expected anything different, she felt disappointment that each of the drawers they opened was empty, offering up only a slight odor of cedar. As they tugged the knobs of the final bottom one, they had to work hard to jar the drawer loose. Finally, the long unused wood creakily yielded up its contents, revealing a pile of folders and notebooks.

First appearances didn't give her much hope. It looked like a lot of jottings and random papers. But within the stack, they found several scrapbooks.

Bethany held one out to her. "Look, Mom, this is filled with old pictures. Someone wrote down names and details."

Tonya was elated. "Oh, Bethany, this is wonderful!"

She thumbed through the volume, delighting in finding the information someone had taken the time to record. Pictures of her mother and her family taken through their years of growing up stared back at her. She stopped at one photo, reading the words written underneath: "Tommy and Cecilia search for whales on the ocean waves." The two sat on the floor in a laundry basket, a wooden yardstick in her mother's hands and her uncle Tommy rowing with some kind of orange club. Tonya flipped pages, seeing pictures of music recitals, visits to pumpkin farms, birthday celebrations—here was one of her mother as a toddler, covered in what looked like whipping cream and cake, all neatly captioned.

What a find!

Bethany gave another small yelp. "Look! There's more."

They pulled the whole mass out, laying it on the dusty floor to better inspect the discovery, an act that revealed further treasures within. Deeper in the drawer, there were bundles of envelopes and stacks of papers—a quick glance revealed page after page of prayers written out for various people.

Tonya recognized the names of some of them: Cecilia and Edward. Even her own name was written on the top of a packet—

Tonya—followed by pages of written prayers: for her to come to salvation, for God's protection, for God to tenderize her heart—on and on the list went.

I had a grandmother who prayed for me?

"Mom!" With a start, her eleven-year-old daughter's exclamation pulled Tonya out of her reverie.

"What's this?" She held out another book, worn and old, stuffed with many dozens of letters and cards and yellowed brochures someone had tucked in long ago from the funerals of John Timothy Martin and Sondra Louise Spencer Martin. The two had died just weeks apart many years earlier—in fact, according to the dates shown, not long at all after their daughter Cecilia's death. Tonya remembered her mom telling her that theirs was a great love . . . it must have been.

"This is amazing." The chance of finding such a precious volume . . . words eluded her.

The book was simply stuffed with papers, mostly printed, but some handwritten. There seemed to be hundreds of poems and stories. Tonya held the top one, yellowed with age, and read out loud:

> What do you think when you see the plight
> Of our fellow humans who suffer the blight
> Of this earth and her troubles? Of pain and distress?
> Of disease and poverty, anguish and death?
>
> As they wander and ponder the meaning of life,
> Observe all the scandal, partake of the strife,
> They can glimpse of the beauty that lies all around
> But have no understanding, no footing, no ground.
>
> They persist in the cycle, but long to be free.
> What must they think of you and of me,
> When they see that true joy can exist in this place,
> Despite all the trials and chaos and waste?

Are we fragrant? Inviting? Attractive? Or no?
Do we carry the sorrow and reek of the woe
That they long to escape? I must ask this dear friend:
Does your life reflect hope for a better end?

Do we bask in God's goodness despite earthly pain?
Trust that our Savior has a perfect plan?
Keep our eyes trained on heaven where eternity dwells?
Are we offering hope while the world offers hell?

This world's pains *are* hard, prolonged and deep—
But for those without Christ, it's the *best* they will see.
Are we sharing our faith while there is still time?
Or getting bogged down in the muck and the grime?

Are we resting in Him when the storm swirls around?
Clinging to Him when our enemies hound?
Running to Him when lonely and scared?
Praying and soaking our mind in His word?

Storing His scriptures away in our hearts
When the enemy comes with his fiery darts?
Do we thank Him—yes, thank Him for allowing us pain
That would tether us to Him again and again?

This is difficult—no—an impossible task—
Except we have Jesus to whom we can ask
To carry our burden and fix our eyes,
So our load becomes his—he's our fortress and prize!

Rejoice in the gifts that his love has bought!
Oh friend—this is big—has your heart been caught?
We have the Answer, the Hope and the Key~
Are we sharing with prisoners that they can be free?

Bondage and heartache should *not* be the plight
For the child of Jesus who is offered delight—
Yes—delight that our troubles though hard and so deep,
Are *temporary* afflictions—they will not keep!

Our hope lies in a future place
Where pain does not live, where sorrows cease.
Where tests and tears do not abound,
Where heartache and death cannot be found,

Where His will is done and perfection reigns,
Where right does rule and joy remains—
This place *does* exist and it's free to the one
Who would come to the cross and believe in the Son
Who has paid *all* the debt we owe for our sin—
Impossible, yes—but not for Him!

He's building a mansion—working details out—
And soon He will come back with a shout!
And take us home to be with Him there—
Can you picture it friend? Are you fixing your stare?
Toward the place we'll reside forevermore?

No more death or mourning or crying or pain
Where glory goes on and on and on ~
Rejoice in this truth! And share it with men
Who need to hear it again and again!

So I ask once more time: What does your life say?
Are you trusting in Jesus or throwing it away?
Get your eyes off your troubles. Get your knees
on the floor—
Seek Jesus—you'll find Him . . . His grace ~ and
much more.

—Sondra Louise Martin

Tonya looked at her daughter's eager face, her lovely green eyes shining. She closed the cover and read the inscription written at the top of the heavy tome out loud:

Through the gift of writing, God allows us to close the gap of time and space to touch the soul, the very heart of people we may never meet. What a thrill! That the innermost part of the human spirit can connect with others in such a deep capacity. Therein lies a great mystery and yet a glorious truth. ~ Sondra Louise Martin

"Wow." Tonya shook her head. "I'm pretty sure that all these writings belonged to my grandmother, Sondra Martin. She was your great-grandmother—my mother Cecilia's mother."

Tonya could relate to some of the lines about suffering. She'd seen plenty of pain and distress and chaos and death. The last several years had brought unbelievable challenges closer—and even across the nation's borders. War was rampant, and food shortages spanned across parts of the entire globe; epidemic plagues were not limited to third-world countries anymore, and it seemed that almost all sense of human decency had been abandoned.

But what did she mean that joy can exist despite all the pain in life? How?

Tonya wanted to understand. This was what she thought her mother had tried to share. Was she close to discovering some important secret that had always been just out of her reach?

And how does one become a child of Jesus to be able to find this delight?

She reached for a thick notebook that sat to the side on the floor. The cover bore the same faded script as the other handwritten sheets and identified the contents as "My Favorite Bible Verses." Tonya opened it, and her mouth fell open: The book was absolutely jammed with verses. Nearly every page of the book was filled.

Something softened in her heart. Could she find some answers to questions that had been plaguing her for years? Did anyone care about her? Was she valued? Tonya wanted desperately to believe the words her mother had said to her when she was little—that God loved her and had a plan for her life. Could some healing come from going through these worn-out old remnants from the past? Perhaps so . . .

Unbidden, tears sprang to her eyes. "I know this can't be true, but it almost feels like, somehow, all this was left here just for us to discover. Just think, Bethany, we might be able to learn some really important things through all these writings—things I haven't understood before. Maybe we can learn about our history, our heritage, maybe even about the lives of people who have gone before us and what they believed. Clearly, they believed there is a God and that He cared about them . . . maybe He does. And maybe . . . maybe He cares about us too . . ."

Her daughter nodded, tears in her eyes. "It's so good to see you smile, Mama." Bethany had wondered if her mom would ever find peace. Here, in this place, she was starting to believe that they both might.

Tonya held the volumes closely, stroking the worn covers, wanting to dig deeply into the riches within. She looked at her precious daughter's expression, and together they laughed with joy at what they had discovered on this journey. She held the notebooks jammed with many pages of prayers and Bible verses and folders spilling over with poems about God and family stories just waiting to be devoured by her hurting and hungry heart that longed to know the secrets they contained.

Tonya smiled again, and fresh tears filled her eyes. "I feel like we've discovered buried treasure."

Bethany nodded happily, and Tonya continued. "I really don't know anything about my grandmother, but it looks like she was a gifted writer . . ."

They couldn't hear it, but the sound of delighted laughter filled the hallways of heaven.

THE END

Author's Note

Most of what's contained in this story and the characters are completely fictional; however, a few of the life happenings I used in the story have been drawn from experiences with our five treasured children, for which I asked permission to share.

One of the hardest we had to face was the addiction that CiCi faced: self-harm in the form of cutting. I'm thankful to be able to say that our daughter has healed from that horrible pull upon her and is walking with the Lord. As Third John 1:4 states, "I have no greater joy than to hear that my children are walking in the truth."

At first, I was hesitant to share anything about what she, along with our family, went through with that terrible addiction. The stigma that is attached to such an act is hard to bear. But if we are not willing to be transparent and truthful about the trials we are facing, how can God work through them and bring glory to Himself or use it to bring fresh hope to some other hurting heart?

As I had Sondra state, "I would rather bear the judging thoughts of men and be found humble and needy, as I am in the eyes of God, than try to cover the truth that I carry shameful burdens and miss out on His gentle touch of grace and healing."

Through the heartache of caring for someone with the level of anguish needed to engage in the awful act of cutting, I wrestled to come to a place of peace. One fruit of that hardship was writing songs to, about, and praising God as He faithfully carried us through the trial, bringing that terrible season to a close with His tremendous healing. Many of the songs I wrote while we were going through that storm are within the story. I'm including one more here, which I have titled "Cling to Him."

"There may be tears for a moment
There may be grief for a season
But we can know that God uses all things
And He has a reason ~
He allows us pain
So we'll cling to Him
More deeply than we would
If our lives were completely untested and good

There may be heartache and trial
There may be pain and deep sorrow
But we serve a God who gives all we need
And He's covered all our tomorrows!
He allows us pain
To display His power
More clearly than it would
He is all sufficient, merciful and good
We need to trust Him more fully
For we can't see what He's doing
What He is weaving for our ultimate good
If we'll just keep believing;
He allows us pain
So we'll cling to Him
More deeply as we go . . .
And one day we will see and know . . .
He loves us so . . ."

I pray that through this story, you may be blessed and encouraged to turn to Christ and bind yourself ever closer into His loving arms. He will never leave us. He is our constant comforter and the one in whom we have all hope. May He receive all glory due Him!

Praising Him for any work He chooses to do through the sharing of this story and trusting that His purposes *will* stand.

Sarah Depledge

About the Author

Sarah Depledge is wife to Mark and mom to their five children. You can learn more about her on her blog at www.LetsTalkBetweenFriends.com. Still She Speaks is her first published work.

CPSIA information can be obtained
at www.ICGtesting.com
Printed in the USA
LVHW03101028 0121
677610LV00001B/41